A JOURNEY FAR

AJ SAM

A JOURNEY FAR

IBERE
(BEGINNINGS)

A Journey Far: Ibere

For information about this title or to order other books and/or electronic media, contact the publisher:

Mincey Publishing LLC
www.theajsam.com
theajsam@gmail.com

ISBNs:
979-8-9869467-0-2 (softcover)
979-8-9869467-1-9 (eBook)

Printed in the United States of America

Interior Illustrations: Mary Osmun
Cover and Interior design: 1106 Design and AJ Sam

Acknowledgments

To God the Father, God the Son, and God the Holy Spirit—thank You for sending me on my journey, for watching over me during my journey, and for bringing me to this point in my journey. And for the journey yet to come.

To my wife, Linda (my spouse of 2+ years and the love of my life; the helpmate I'd sought for 25 years, now the completion of me God always intended), thank you for saying yes on December 29, 2019.

To my daughter, Ya'Shantaye (thank you for being the person I never imagined having and the person I can't imagine not having in my life).

To my son-in-law, Mike (thanks for giving my daughter a foundation to build a home on).

To my granddaughter, La'Tayjah (I thank God for you, and for the second opportunity to raise my child in the way she should go).

To my immediate biological family—

To my father, Arcilous, Sr. (may God have mercy on your soul; thank you for my life and your lessons that prepared me for the SOHK).

To my mother, Juanita (truly the rock and foundation of our family; thank you for your nurturing spirit, your sense of humor, and your way of putting people at ease).

To my brother, Calvin (the epitome of Godly masculinity; thank you for showing me the errors of my ways by your actions).

To my wombmate, Arnita (thank you for being my sounding board, listening ear, and the one who can sense my thoughts).

To my second sister, Sharon (thank you for your personality, which I've learned to appreciate and learn from).

To my baby sister, Geneva (thank you for showing me our generational divide, which offers me a glimpse of what was, what is, and what's to come).

To my sister-in-law, Peggy (thank you for your spirit of sacrifice you share with so many, which showed me how far I still need to grow).

To my brother-in-law, Bo (may God have mercy on your soul, thank you for your genuine masculinity, which makes you the most Christian non-Christian I ever met).

To my extended family, too numerous to mention and too important to forget—includes aunts, uncles, cousins, and in-laws: thank you to all of you, including special thanks to . . .

Uncle Sonnie T (may God have mercy on your soul; thank you for deftly bridging the gap between father and brother magnificently).

Aunt Estella (may God have mercy on your soul; thank you for being my 2nd mom).

Aunt Addie (thank you for your gift of giving and for sharing your journey of survival, which inspires so many).

Cousin David (may God have mercy on your soul; thank you for watching over me in so many ways. I lost count but fully acknowledge).

Cousin Janice (thank you for the pact we made, one that kept me on this journey, even when doubts swirled).

Cousin Maria (my "1983" cousin; thank you for improving my life in countless ways).

Cousin Maedean (my "city, country, city cousin." Thank you for keeping it real when real is exactly what I needed).

Cousin Sybil (thank you for bringing the wife God had for me, to me, at the precise time I was ready to receive her).

Personal Special Thanks

The Rev. Dr. Shawn E. E. Thomas (may God have mercy on your soul; thank you for your friendship, your insight, your wit, and your spiritual foundation you freely shared with me. This book has the impact of you throughout it).

Deacon Rob Williams (my twin from another kin; thank you for your friendship. I have and will always appreciate it)

Deaconess Bettye Jenkins (may God have mercy on your soul; thank you for your quiet strength, which exemplified the proverb that people will strain to hear a whisper).

Rev. James Butler (may God have mercy on your soul; thank you for your humility and sage advice you freely shared with me)

Mrs. Sadie Camon (My first editor; thank you for your insight and encouragement that propelled me from being a writer to becoming an author).

Thanks to the contributors of the "Soundtrack of my Journey" (Stevie Wonder, Earth, Wind & Fire, Parliament/Funkadelic, Prince, the King of Pop, the Queen of Soul, the Godfather of Soul, the Maestro, Gladys Knight, Maze, the Motown Sound, TSOP, and so many others). You infused into my writing its lyrical quality.

Professional Special Thanks

Mrs. Stacy Duncan (My writing Coach when I began teaching fifth-grade writing at Miles EL; thank you for helping me grow exponentially as a writer through the two years we worked together; you helped take this tale I penned and made it a story to be shared with the world).

Mr. Frank Kresen (My editor; thanks for honing my voice. Thanks for your insightful corrections. Thanks for your words of encouragement. They all mean the world to me.).

Ms. Mary Osmun (My interior illustrator; thanks for taking my ideas—and scenes from the text—and bringing them visually to life).

The Poynter Institute (Thank you for the lessons I received during the Writers Camps I taught at as well as the seminars I attended in the early 2000s, which helped shape my writer's voice)

The Writer's Digest Magazine staff & contributors—from 2000–2010. Thanks for the help you gave me—especially how effective dialogue can move the plot, how to create unique and well-developed characters, and various ways to show—not tell.

The staff of 1106 Design (Thank all of you for your professionalism in turning my story into this book).

The ALLI organization (Thank you for leading me in the direction of **IngramSpark**, which led me to **1106 Design**. Thank you for what you do for independent authors worldwide.)

And finally, thank you to all of you I interacted with, passed by, overheard in conversations, observed up close and at a distance; watched, read, and listened to. When you see yourself in this story, remember it is because you found your way into my mind, heart, and soul. Thank you.

History merely repeats itself. It has all been done before. Nothing under the sun is truly new. Sometimes people say, "Here is something new!" But actually it is old; nothing is ever truly new. We don't remember what happened in the past, and in future generations, no one will remember what we are doing now.

—Ecclesiastes 1:9-11, NLT

Now all glory to God, who is able, through His mighty power at work within us, to accomplish infinitely more than we might ask or think.

—Ephesians 3:20 NLT

The journey of a thousand miles begins with a single step.

—Lao Tzu

TABLE OF CONTENTS

Who Am I?

PROLOGUE

MaryBelle was crying again.

Way more than a wail. Decibels beyond screams. She was experiencing an up-all-night, inconsolable-mother, afraid-to-let-it-all-out, terrified-to-keep-any-of-it-in cry. Through the flow of her emotions and the lone window of their cabin, she stared in the direction she last saw her son, Ọba, three days earlier. The dawning sun reflected twinkles on dew-stained leaves outside and streaks on her tear-stained cheeks as, "M-M-My baby. My—my baby . . ." escaped through her quivering lips.

Standing next to MaryBelle, her husband Josephus' left arm lay helplessly on her shoulder, offering whatever comfort it could. His right arm was filled with their squirming baby, Iyin. He looked out the same window at the same scene with a stoic, lonely stare that masked his torment.

Nature was awakening, and one by one, animals began scurrying and cawing and crowing and flapping and running and dashing and cooing and darting about. MaryBelle's cries lessened.

Josephus cleared his throat and uttered, "Uh, honey. Uh, ol' man Tom be callin' d'rectly. You, uh, you want—uh, need—need anythin'?"

Acknowledging neither his touch nor his words, she continued staring toward the scene, as intermittent sighs slipped through her sobs. His inadequacy tore at him. He racked his brain for words of comfort for his wife, but a gentle squeeze of her shoulder was all that came to mind.

She blurted, "I want my baby! I need my baby. Cee, I need my baby. I—I need my . . ."

For a moment, her crying ceased as she searched her husband's face for hope. He embraced MaryBelle—one, to avoid looking into her eyes and two, to hug their angst away. Rocking her gently, he hummed their family tune.

Gradually, the rising sun illuminated their shanty, exposing its interior. The bare walls with the one window and door; the dirt and straw floor; the wash basin and a lone cooking pot; their bed and an empty crocheted mat that had comforted their son three days earlier filled the small abode. While Ọba hadn't been taken from that spot, Josephus sensed his cries emanating from there, the last spot of comfort for his family he could remember.

The clanging of the dawn bell interrupted the tune and his thoughts, and signaled the start of the workday. Josephus kissed his wife's forehead, walked to the bed, and laid Iyin down, his innocent coo giving him seconds of solace. A smile creased his countenance but rapidly disappeared as the current reality returned.

His mind raced back to that day, that terribly tragic day, when his firstborn was dragged off screaming to who knows where. His own crumpled form lying prostrate, his shoulders heaving up and down as tears flowed. His pain, deep and wrapped around that personal place where life begins, radiated out through his organs, skeleton, and skin, dwarfing the agony of the cracked ribs, bruised face, and assorted scratches—the remnants of his struggle to keep his son. And the realization that Iyin could be next.

A muffled sound broke his train of thought, bringing the stark reality back to light. He trudged to the door, paused, and pulled the rusted handle, allowing more of dawn's light to enter. He tried to speak, to say something—anything. But nothing came out. He opened his mouth again, but the words were washed away by his love's emotions.

A sigh finally escaped. Without turning around, he stammered, "Bye, Belle. I—I—I—"

His words choked off again. His face contorted in anguish. He fought back tears with hard swallows and deep breaths. He blinked his eyes rapidly, and a tear escaped and trickled down his cheek. He reluctantly turned in the direction of his wife and eyed her still staring out the window.

MaryBelle was crying again.

CHAPTER 1

"Massah J. got somethin' up, huh," said Smitty as he struggled to be heard above the clickety-clack of the wheels and the clops of the horses' hoofs along the gravel road.

"Whatcha' mean?" Bosco asked, as he held tight to the reins of the two-horse team.

"That boy back there. He usually get grown folks—and sell chillins," Smitty replied with a nod toward the rear of the wagon.

"Yeah, he sho' do. Hey, here come Mr. Boo and Riley. Maybe they know," Bosco replied as two riders came into view.

The eight slaves in the wagon—five adult males, two women, and a boy whose feet dangled out the back—were shackled to each other and to the wagon frame. Echoing screams and anguished faces were etched in the boy's traumatized mind as he rode in silence. He looked down and watched the gravel pass underneath, haunted by images of people and places and times, haunted by sounds of laughter and singing and crying and screaming. The screams were the strongest. Screams he couldn't ignore. Screams he could feel.

Smitty switched places with Mr. Boo as Bosco continued driving.

"That boy back there. Ya' know anythin'?" Smitty asked Riley, now riding side by side on their horses.

"Johnson must have somethin' special in mind fo' him, I guess," Riley shrugged.

"Yeah. I suppose."

❧

"But daddy, we never do nuthin'! You always work, work, work," Carlton Johnson complained as he alternated between looking up at his father and looking into his book satchel.

Hiram Johnson, the owner of the Penelope Farms Plantation and father of one son, was seated behind his desk. Cut from what he felt was the best tree on the plantation, his oak desk stood three feet high, six feet wide, and two feet deep, and was adorned with brass trim.

The four desk legs were carved into stallions raised on their hindquarters, their front legs running in the air, one higher than the other. The initials "BA" were carved into the front of the desk, with gold-leaf paint filling the indentation. The top was covered with stretched leather held in place with brass tacks. A matching chair, which fit under the main drawer and glided on four wheels, had a swivel that allowed him to lean back, forward, or spin around. Six drawers, three on either side and all finished with brass handles, completed the ensemble.

Never looking up, he went through papers on his desk and replied, "I'm a bitnessman, son. That's what I do. Shit, wheah the hell is that paper? I jest seent it!"

Finally getting the satchel latched, Carlton peered up and over the desk and was happy to catch a fleeting glimpse of his father's eyes.

He moved closer and replied, "Yeah, but I ain't got nobody to talk wit. Or—or play wit. Me and you, we don't do nuthin'. You always busy. And I—I—"

"Oh, yeah, it's down heah in the desk drawer. Let me see— wheah is it? Uh, guess what? Guess what, boy? I got you somethin'. Somethin' you been askin' fo'. Yeah, it should be in heah," Master Johnson rambled as he continued rummaging through the desk drawers. "A play—a—wait, this ain't it. Wheah is that paper?"

"Huh. What? What you say, daddy?"

"I got you—nah, this ain't it. Maybe this is—nah, uh, I got you a—a playmate. Maybe it's ovah heah."

"What you got me? A slave? A slave! You got me a slave, daddy?" Carlton exclaimed and moved closer to the desk. In his excitement, he disturbed several piles of papers on his father's desk.

"Shit, this ain't it neither! Yeah, I did. Now you asked fo' a little playmate, so he's yo'—uh, uh, yeah, he yo' responsibility, you heah? Maybe it's in this heah drawer."

"Okay, daddy, I will. When? When will he be here?"

"All the time, that's when, and—yes. I found it! Thought I'd lost it! Okay, so I got this ready. Let's see—what else I need? Uh—oh, yeah. He yo' 'sponsibility all the time. Okay, I got what I need for Joe and Keifer."

Master Johnson leaned back and realized Carlton was leaning on his desk.

"Don't you mess up any of them papers, boy! I had them right wheah I wanted them!"

"Huh, uh—okay, daddy. I'm sorry. I mean when will he be here, huh? When—huh?"

"He'll be here today or tomorra'. Now git ready fo' school. Stanley! Git in heah!"

Carlton carefully moved the papers back to their original position and asked, "You gone be home today? When I get out of school?"

"Maybe. Now—leave that alone! You gone mess stuff up, boy! Now go on, git on to school."

"Okay. Bye, daddy. I love you."

Master Johnson dove back into his work as Carlton stood there, subtly rocking side to side. He sighed and repeated, "Okay, daddy. Bye. I love you."

"Yeah—I luv ya'. Stanley! Stanley!" he yelled as he looked past his son and toward the open door. "STANLEY!"

Giving up hope for the attention he craved, Carlton dashed out of the study and into the gut of Stanley, the plantation's overseer. "Guess what? Mr. Stanley, guess what? My daddy got me a slave! He really did!"

"Oh, he did, huh. Well, I'm glad for ya', Carlton," replied the stocky man with a bushy moustache.

"Yeah. We gone have fun!" Carlton added as he ran down the hallway toward the stairs. "I'll wait fo' ya' in the wagon."

"Okay. I'll be there directly."

CHAPTER 2

A melody, the constant companion that resonated through the boy's mind, continued, as the third day began. Remaining silent as he had been throughout the journey, he blankly stared at the ground while miles passed. The group's route took them through terrain that changed from mountains of blue to green, rolling hills to flat countryside.

A myriad of mental images continued. Adults holding and comforting and yelling and crying. Sounds of humming and screaming and singing. Smells of humans and food and cloth and earth. Feelings of texture and love and belonging and terror. And this tune, a soothingly familiar melody, comforted his soul.

. . . I loves you, Cee . . . Help yo' mama, boy. . . . we a family . . .
The sounds from the dull drone of the horse riders talking, the wagon wheels creaking, and the horses' hoofs clopping dominated the scene. Then a new sound surfaced. A creaking sound of metal against metal came to the forefront.

. . . clang, creak . . . come here, baby. . . wash up fo' supper, boy . . . we be there soon . . . . clang, creak . . .

"Oh, yeah. It sho' gonna be real good to sleep in my own bed a'gin," Smitty replied as Penelope Farms came into view.

"Yeah. And not havin' to eat yo' cookin' no mo' gone be real good, too," Bosco chuckled.

Smitty and Riley, several yards ahead, opened the gate of the main entrance to the plantation. The heavy, wrought-iron structure slowly gave way, its hinges straining with the movements. A 3-foot hedge extended from the 6-foot-high gates in both directions, an Old English style "BA" inlaid on them. Once the wagon passed through, the gates met with a dull clang. Ten minutes later, four slaves, two horses, and $300 in cash were exchanged, and the riders, their horses, and the wagon were on their way, out of the gates.

. . . Watch yo' brother . . . Massah Tom callin' d'rectly . . .

"Listen here, boy. I'se Mr. Boo. You jest look down-like—don't look at 'em," the old Negro implored in a whisper.

He led the boy with a firm grip by the arm in a different direction than the other slaves. He walked with a gait that resembled part skip and part shuffle, the result of a broken leg that never healed properly. His short, coarse black hair was fighting a losing battle with gray, and his chocolate-colored eyes showed little emotion. He looked back at the boy with a wrinkled brow.

"And say *'yassuh'* and *'nosuh.'* His name *'Massah Johnson,'* you hear. You be jest fine. Jest—you be fine."

The boy, maintaining his silence, barely acknowledged him with a glance. They walked up to a stately structure, two stories tall, with a prominent porch framed by stone pillars. Cubic tops and bases on the pillars and ornate architectural designs carved in salmon-colored bricks completed the scene.

After taking the 5 steps up onto the porch, Mr. Boo stopped, turned, and grabbed the boy by the shoulders. He knelt and,

6 inches from his face, whispered, "Hey, boy. They say you never made a sound once you stopped cryin'. Can you talk?"

"Yeah," he replied with an emotionless stare.

"Good. You needs to answer Massah Johnson when he talk to you. Understand?"

"Yeah," he mumbled.

"Huh? What? Speak up!" Mr. Boo replied, his face contorted with frustration.

"Yeah."

"You gonna be livin' in the Big House here. Johnson Hall here. You behave—you hear? You hear?" Mr. Boo asked, his face now reflecting concern.

"Yeah—yassuh."

Mr. Boo opened one of the ornately designed double oak doors and exposed an enormous painting hanging on a wall overlooking a spiral staircase. Other paintings adorned other walls, and a silver-and-crystal chandelier, hanging from the ceiling, captured the boy's eye.

The entryway had a polished oak floor that led to an oak staircase, which was flared from 8 feet wide at the bottom to 4 feet wide at the top, all the while maintaining a subtle arc to the left. They slowly walked up the stairs, turned left, and continued walking down the hall, past a grandfather clock, and stopped in front of a closed door. Mr. Boo looked at the boy once again as an uneasy smile creased his demeanor.

"It be okay. Jest—jest 'member what I tolt ya'. Say, 'yassuh' and 'nosuh.' Oh, and don't look at 'em when you talk. Keep yo' head down. You be okay. C'mon."

He opened the door, and they entered the room.

"Uh, here he is, Massah Johnson, suh."

"Oh, good, Mr. Boo. You can go now," Master Johnson replied as he glanced up from his desk and then back down.

With a forced smile, Mr. Boo stole one last glance at the boy, turned, and walked out. The boy stood in silence among this imposing room of books and oak, with this desk in front of him and the top of a head in sight.

. . . Thank you fo' ya' help, Oba. . . . This some mighty fine cookin', Belle . . . Hold your brother fo' me . . . Time fo' work . . .

Five minutes later, Master Johnson finally looked over the desk and at the boy, whose gaze remained on the floor.

"Hey, boy. You know who I am?"

Not looking up, the boy mumbled, "Massah Johnson, suh."

"What?"

The boy stumbled, caught his balance, and answered in a more audible tone, "Massah Johnson, suh."

"Good. You at Penelope Farms Plantation now. You mine. Your name gone be 'James' from now on. I don't care what yo' momma called you, you heah!"

"Yassuh."

"That was Jesus Christ our Lord's brother's name. A good name. A good Christian name! Don't want no trouble out you neither," Master Johnson added as he stood up and walked from behind the desk.

His 6-foot, lanky frame caused James to slightly lose his balance again. He looked up and then quickly down again and responded, "Yassuh."

"Come with me."

They walked out of the study, turned right, and walked down the carpeted hallway and into a room on the left.

"This my boy room. You gone stay heah, too. Sit down heah on the flo'. Don't move 'til my boy git heah. His name Massah Carlton."

"Yassuh."

Master Johnson left the room and closed the door, the thud echoing through both the room and James' soul. He looked around the room. A dresser with an attached mirror which faced the door. An oil lamp positioned on the dresser. A footstool next to a bed covered with a flower-pattern comforter.

A blue, green, and brown striped throw rug he was sitting on covered part of the floor, pine boards laid side by side and nailed. The walls painted a robin-egg blue. The room's lone window looked out to the tops of a stand of trees. And a door on the right wall.

He sat there with his legs crossed and head bowed as a tear trickled down his cheek, the first tear he'd shed in two days from a well that had been drained. The silence in the room allowed his thoughts, his companions during the journey he had just completed, to return. The images, sounds, smells, and feelings were playing a symphony in his mind.

. . . Get ready fo' supper boy . . . Mama! Mama! . . . Massah Tom wants ya' . . .

. . . No! Not my baby! Please! . . . Wash yo' hands good . . . Two hunnerd, three hunnerd . . .

I loves ya' son. . . . No! Please God, no! . . . Mama! Mama! . . . We's a family . . .

James sat on the rug with a slow, deliberate rock, deep in his memories. Suddenly, the grandfather clock he and Mr. Boo had passed in the hallway chimed: *Dong! Dong! Dong!* which startled him to tears.

"Mama, mama . . ." he muttered between sobs as his thoughts continued.

. . . time fo' me. A man needs his rest. . . . Two hunnerd, three hunnerd . . . I loves ya,' Belle . . .

. . . Nooo! Not my baby—please! . . . Watch yo' brother . . . I loves you, mama. . . .

. . . We family, Ọba. Me, you, daddy, and yo' brother. . . No, you can't—you can't . . .

Dong! Dong! Dong! Dong!

The memories maintained their grip on him. This man holding him on his lap as he laughed, hummed, and talked. Walking with him, going nowhere and everywhere. A lady's smile that exuded love and joy warmed his spirit. Her laugh, almost a cackle, her hugs, her rocking him in her arms. Her smell—a "mama" smell. Yeah, a smell of mama. Their screams, cries, and horrifically anguished faces. This man grabbing his arm so hard it hurt. That still hurt—in his memories.

♣

Drifting in and out of consciousness, faint sounds awoke James. Still at the place Master Johnson had him sit, he listened as the sounds of rushed footfalls grew louder. Seconds later, the door flung open and a boy rushed into the room and tripped over him. A white, gray, and black medium-sized mongrel followed and immediately began to snarl and growl.

Laughing as he rose from the floor, the boy said, "Hey. I'm Carlton."

After sitting back up, James looked at him at first and then lowered his gaze, as Mr. Boo had instructed him.

"Massah Johnson says I James, and, uh—you Massah Carlton."

"Nah, jest call me 'Carlton.' This heah 'Deeohgee,'" he replied as he patted his pet that had calmed to snorts and whimpers.

"Calm down, boy. This heah my daddy's plantation. All this. Named after my momma 'cause she died. This heah's where we gone sleep. You sleep over theah on the rug. We gone sleep on the bed. C'mon, let me show you the rest of the house," Carlton rambled as he grabbed James by the hand, yanked him to his feet, and roughly led him out of the room, as Deeohgee followed with barks and yelps.

Carlton ran down the hallway, past the study, and approached the gold inlaid grandfather clock that had startled James earlier. The pendulum was fashioned into the shape of a horse in full gallop, which swung back and forth on a golden rod, its polished features glistening.

Continuing past it, they stood at the landing of the stairs. A recessed sitting area, with a u-shaped settee with a flowered pattern, was below a painting. Carlton pointed down the hallway toward two other doors, the nearest one first.

"That wheah I used to stay when my momma was heah. It was my nursery. The other one my daddy room. Used to be my momma, too. He—my daddy—had me move when my—uh, my momma—she died. . . ."

James remained silent but kept a watchful eye on Deeohgee, whose barks had lessened as Carlton rambled on. ". . . We don't need to go down theah. I like it wheah I'm at now. I was scared at first, but daddy—he say 'be a man'. So I be. We don't need to go down theah. C'mon, follow me."

"That's me, my daddy, and my momma," Carlton said as he pointed his thumb back to the large painting hanging over the landing of the staircase as they went downstairs. "That's when I was five. I miss her. I still miss her."

Releasing James' hand, Carlton ran several steps and jumped, landing on one of the throw rugs partially covering the wood floors. He slid several feet.

With child-like giggles, he said, "C'mon! It's fun. Try it, James!"

James walked hesitantly step by step toward him without emotion.

"Don't you even laugh?" Carlton asked as they walked down a hall. James' stoic countenance remained as they passed several doors.

"Stanley, the overseer, stay heah. Since my momma die, he live theah," Carlton added as they passed the first door to the right upon entering Johnson Hall. Eventually, they entered the majestic dining room with its finely polished walls of mahogany panels. In the center was a solid oak table, set with embroidered linen, bone china with black trim, silver flatware, and lead crystal goblets in a setting for twenty.

Along the back wall was an 8-foot-tall armoire. Animals in landscape scenes were carved into its side and base. There were 4 glass panes on its double-door front, revealing china and crystal. Three drawers, the full width of the structure, contained the silverware and serving utensils, and made up the bottom third. The brass fixtures glistened in the candlelight as the cavernous room carried their footfalls to an echo.

"This is wheah we eat. Me and my daddy," Carlton said in a hushed tone as they walked toward swinging double doors on the opposite side of the room. Walking through them and into the kitchen, James was startled by the bustle of activity.

"This is Ruth. This is James, Ruth," Carlton said as they rushed past several people there. The clatter of pots and pans, orders being given, and the aromas of different foods filled the room. James didn't speak, and the two people, a Negro man and woman, didn't either, although the woman stole a quick glance. He and Carlton rushed through and exited through another door, which led to the outside.

"Let's go back to my room. I gotta git somethin'," Carlton said, and they went around, re-entered the front of Johnson Hall, and walked up the spiral staircase.

"Oh, yeah. Never, ever go in theah, James. That's the one room you can't go in," Carlton insisted as they passed the room James had met Master Johnson in. "That's wheah my daddy do his bitness."

❧

The kaleidoscope of spring-green foliage framed the streets and harbors of Boston as Bobby Harris and his mother walked up the sidewalk toward their white- and black-trimmed house.

"I don't even see why I gotta help you today," Bobby complained as he struggled to hold the bundles of purchases in his arms.

A brisk breeze ruffled his mother's hair as they arrived at the door. "It's *have to*—or *must*. But not *gotta*. And you're the oldest, Bobby. You're a big boy now. You're almost how old now?" she asked as she fumbled for the door keys.

"Six. I gonna—uh, I will be six in uh, two—yeah, two days!"

"That's right, sweetheart! Me and your father need help with your brother and sisters. You're becoming a big boy. A man someday."

"I know, I know. But I wanted to play today. And I gotta—"

"*Have to!*"

"I have to go to school on my birthday," he replied as his mother opened the door to the silent house. She went in before him as he continued, "See! Nobody's here. They all having fun. And I got—I have to help you. Tomorrow is church day, then school, then—"

"*Surprise!*" screamed twenty-three children and twelve adults.

Bobby turned toward his mother and then back toward the people. His father, brother, and two sisters; the children of neighbors and friends; Free Negroes, and supporters of them, all beamed. With eyes wide and mouth agape, Bobby looked back at his beaming mother.

"*Ma!*"

"Happy birthday, baby," she said as she embraced him.

Turning around to the pile of gifts on the table, he asked, "Uh, are all—are these for me?"

His father, entering the room carrying a 2-layer cake with chocolate icing and six glowing candles, replied, "Yes, they are. But you must make a wish and blow out the candles first, son,"

"A wish?"

"Yeah, a secret wish. Only you will know it."

Pausing for a few moments, Bobby said, "Okay" and then blew out the candles, ushering in cheers, hollers, and the beginning of the party.

$\clubsuit$

Carlton and James were outside Johnson Hall now. After circling it once, they headed away from the mansion and toward the orchards. James noticed the pathway he'd arrived on that led away from the mansion in a serpentine manner. Large, tall, stout, and skinny oak trees dotted the plantation. But near Johnson Hall, a stand of mostly slender oaks was prominent. Their staggered placement and assorted underbrush obscured the view of buildings on the other side.

Carlton continued his tour. He pointed ahead and said, "There's the orchards over theah. We may go theah sometimes—maybe. And my daddy's forest right theah. We won't go anywheah else jest now. C'mon. I'll race ya' to the room."

He dashed off and, being three years younger and six inches shorter, James struggled to keep up as they completed the circuitous tour, with Deeohgee bridging the gap between them.

$\clubsuit$

The silence at dinner was interrupted by Deeohgee's whines and the clatter of silverware on plates as Master Johnson and Carlton ate. They sat across from each other in the dining room at one end of the oak table. Two place settings were moved off to one side, and they ate off regular plates.

"Anythin' else, suh?" Ruth asked as she stood quietly, her right arm bent at the elbow and close to her side, with a white towel draped over her extended forearm. Her sturdy build strained the material in her dress; her legs—seemingly too skinny to hold her up—reached out from her skirt and down to the floor.

"Nah. You can go," Master Johnson replied between bites.

"Daddy, thank you agin fo'—uh, fo' James heah," Carlton said as he turned and looked down at James, sitting on the floor several feet away, his head lowered and stomach growling.

"Uh, huh—yeah," he replied, his face buried in a newspaper. "Goddamn Nawthanuhs. What the hell these heah boys thinkin'. . . ."

Carlton turned back to the table and continued eating as Deeohgee panted at his feet, hoping for a mistake.

"Uh, daddy. Bill in school, he say theah some good fishin' cricks not far from heah. Maybe we could go sometimes," Carlton said as he dropped Deeohgee a chicken bone. The cracking bone became the dominant sound, as Master Johnson never replied.

Dong! Dong! Dong! Dong! Dong! Dong! Dong!

Carlton sighed and added, "I miss momma."

"Eat your food, son," Master Johnson replied as he peeked far enough from behind the newspaper to take a gaze at his son's plate. "You finished?"

"Yeah, daddy. I'm done," he replied as he pushed the plate of partially eaten food away. He looked over at his father, his eyes revealing his emotions of loneliness and distance.

His father's face turned toward James, though, and bellowed, "James. Take this stuff off the plates and finish 'em."

"Yassuh, Massah Johnson, suh," James answered.

He jumped up, grabbed the plates, and sat back down. For the next five minutes, he quickly filled his hunger—as a growling Deeohgee glared a few feet away.

"I gone go to my room, now," Carlton forlornly said.

"Uh, huh," Master Johnson replied as he disappeared behind the newspaper again, the smoky-sweet aroma of a just-lit cigar filling the room.

❧

". . . and we can race and stuff. And rassle, well—when you git bigger. And play and stuff, and—"

Dong! Dong! Dong! Dong! Dong! Dong! Dong! Dong! Dong! Dong! Dong!

"Oh, man! It's eleven o'clock, already. We best git to bed. I ain't supposed to be up this late!"

Carlton hopped off his bed, scampered over to the door to his room, and closed it. He turned, looked at James, and smiled.

"We gone have fun! Yeah, we is," Carlton added with all the enthusiasm he could muster, but it wasn't contagious. James maintained his stoic demeanor and kept watch on the one apparent threat in the room. Carlton sighed deeply, softly biting his lip as James' stare alternated between him and his growling pet.

"Ooo! Let me say my prayers," Carlton exclaimed as he knelt and continued, "Dear God. Bless daddy and bless me. And keep my momma happy. And thank You for my slave—for James. Amen."

He got up off his knees, walked around near and past James, who was standing near the dresser, and began playing with Deeohgee on the floor, whose growls lessened.

"You glad, too. Ain'tcha' boy! Yeah, you glad, too. He gone be heah wit us now," Carlton said. Roughly rubbing his fur, he looked up at James and said, "He ain't used to nobody else in heah. When

I close the door, it's just me and him. He okay, though. Ain'tcha boy! Huh—ain'tcha!"

Carlton got into bed, whistled for Deeohgee to hop on, and then said, "Okay, James. Just like I showed ya'. Blow out the lantern."

James got up on the footstool, lifted the glass covering the glowing wick, and, with a puff, blew in the darkness. He got down and lay on the rug where he'd spent the day. Looking up, he saw Deeohgee curiously looking down on him from the bed with a soft whimper. With the soothing melody in his mind, James silently cried himself to sleep.

CHAPTER 3

"Okay, how do I look?"

Carlton prepared for school as James shrugged his shoulders.

"Okay—uh, shoot! You need some clothes to wear, huh?"

Carlton walked over to his closet. James' clothes—a pair of pants a size too small and a shirt a size too big—were worn and dirty. His bare feet carried evidence of the type of road his journey had taken.

"Let's see—what I don't want? Yeah, uh, yeah. I want this. Okay. This is fine fo' him."

Carlton handed a pair of pants and a shirt to James.

"Heah, put this on. I'll git ya' some mo' when I go through this later. And some shoes. You ever wear shoes?"

James shook his head "No."

"Well, okay. You will," Carlton chuckled. "Okay now, stay in the house. And stay out of that room, you heah?"

"Yassuh, Massah Carlton."

"No, no, no. Jest 'Carlton.' Call me 'Carlton'!" he pleaded as James stared back at him. He sighed. "Jest try, okay?"

With Deeohgee tagging after him, Carlton rushed out of the room. James sat back down on the rug on the floor in the same spot as before.

Dong! Dong! Dong! Dong! Dong! Dong! Dong! Dong!

⚜

"Oh, chile!" a surprised Ruth said as she nearly tripped over James later that day. The only other slave to sleep in Johnson Hall, she served as cook, maid, and Carlton's nanny. One of her weekly duties was to clean up Johnson Hall, including the rooms upstairs.

"How long you been sittin' here? All the mornin'? My, my. What your name? 'James,' ain't it?"

"Yes, Ma—Massah Ruth," he replied as he kept his head lowered.

She let out a hearty laugh and proclaimed, "Whoo, chile! I ain't no *massah*. I'se Ruth, that's all. Ruth. You hear me?"

"Uh, yeah. Uh—Ruth."

"Ooo, chile. I think you be needin' me, huh. And a hug. C'meer—"

Dong!

"C'meer, darlin' . . ." After giving James his first hug in a week, she took him into the kitchen, fed him, and then watched him until Carlton got home.

♣

"I thank daddy for him. All the time. We been havin' fun, too," Carlton joyfully shared with Stanley.

Taking Carlton to school, Stanley was also transporting two slaves to a plantation on the other side of the county. Having been the overseer of the plantation for ten years, he had seen it grow both in the number of slaves and assistants required to watch them, now numbering seven. Never riding more than a week's ride out, he was the only one of the staff to sleep in Johnson Hall. A soft-spoken man, he stared straight ahead while Carlton chattered.

"We gone spend all our time together—when I ain't in school. We talk about stuff—well, I do. He jest listen, mostly. He talk some, now. Maybe more later, huh? You ever had a slave, Stanley?"

"Nah, ain't never had one. But that's good, Carlton. Glad you got somebody to play witcha'." He looked over at the happy Carlton, and a smile escaped his stone face, though it was hidden beneath his bushy moustache.

"Yeah, me, too. We been havin' fun. I take him most places. You know. The orchards, and—and—"

"You got that smile again, Carlton. Your momma's smile."

"Yeah, hee, hee," Carlton said as he grinned broadly. He sighed, though, as it disappeared.

"I—I wish my daddy could get it. You think he'll ever git it, Stanley? My momma smile."

"I dunno, Carlton. Hey—wanna go fishin'?"

"Nah—nah, that's okay. My daddy—he say he gone take me fishin' and huntin' and campin'! We gone have fun! We gone have lotsa fun! I'll wait fo' him. Stanley, you think he, my daddy, will ever get my momma smile? Huh . . ."

Chapter 4

The huffing and puffing of strained breaths echoed through the countryside. A desperate pair, their chests heaving mightily, determinedly raced through the forest. The sounds of hounds, chains, and horses' hoofs were in the distance, but getting closer. Josephus, with his wife's arm firmly grasped in his hand, galloped over underbrush, under hanging vines, and past nature's wildlife.

"C'mon, Belle! Keep movin', baby. Don't stop!"

She stumbled and struggled to keep pace. Eight hours into their jaunt, they were beyond exhaustion and approaching hopelessness. Her dress, tattered and grass stained, indicated how many times he'd dragged her until she regained her feet. His face, framed with angst and terror, indicated a realization that crept over him. A year after their son, Ọba, was sold, and two months after their son, Iyin was sold, they were on the run, fueled by the thought of being separated themselves.

"Cee—Cee. I, I can't—I can't go no mo'. Go on, baby. Leaves me here," she struggled to get out between deep, gasping breaths.

"Shaddup! Keep movin'," he yelled as he forcibly tugged at her raw wrist. "I ain't lettin' you go! We both make it—or, or . . . anyway, we both make it!"

"Cee—I—I—"

They came to a clearing and gazed out on a serene lake.

"Cee! What—what we gonna do? I can't swim!"

He looked dejectedly at his wife and then back, toward the sounds of barks and thrashing of the animals through the forest, which grew louder. Tears welled up in his eyes.

"Uh—Belle. It's—this the only way we be together forever. C'mon."

"Cee? What you doin'? What you talkin' about? You know I can't swim!"

"C'mon!" he exclaimed while dragging her through the marshes and into ankle-deep water. "This the only way we gonna be together. Massah Tom gonna sell us directly. Maybe to different folks. I can't—I won't live like that! I won't live without you, Belle!"

"Cee—I, I, I'm scared."

"I ain't. No more scared! We gonna be together, forever!"

The water, past their knees now, soaked her flower-print dress and his tan pants as they sloshed on. Looking back over her shoulder, MaryBelle saw the slave catchers emerging from the forest and motioning for them to come back. As she turned back, she saw wetness on Josephus' face. Unsure if it was water or tears but recognizing the anguish, she grabbed a tighter grip on his soaked shirt, the water now passing their waists. The sounds of horses splashing into the marshes behind them urged them on.

"Hold on, Belle. Hold on, baby. Don't let go," Josephus urged as he began splashing with his arms and heading for the middle of the lake. " . . .

. . ." he began to hum, and MaryBelle followed along as the water got deeper and the sounds from the slave catchers diminished.

Breathing heavily, Josephus turned on his back and looked at his wife's face, dripping with water, sweat, tears, and terror; then he looked past her toward the slave catchers, who began to circle the lake.

"We here, Belle. We here. This where it ends. No. This where it begins. We together forever," he said as he held her close to him.

"I loves you, Cee. I loves you," she uttered, coughing and gagging from swallowing water.

"I—I loves you, too, Belle. I sorry. I couldn't save us. I sorry, Belle."

Cough. "No! No, Cee. You did save us. We together. Forever, we together. They took our babies. But not us. Uh, we together. Forever."

"I loves you, Belle."

They continued bobbing up and down in the lake until they bobbed no more.

♣

James didn't go out into the fields like the other slaves who arrived with him did. In the time James had been at Penelope Farms, Carlton had kept him isolated in Johnson Hall. He did some dusting and watching cooking pots in the kitchen, while helping Ruth during the day.

"So, how ya' like it here, James?" Ruth asked as she deftly went from stove to oven to sink to cooking and baking and cleaning. James, following her with his eyes, shrugged his shoulders.

"You miss yo' momma?"

He nodded his head as he stirred a pot.

"You got children, Miss, uh, Miss Ruth?"

She looked at the little boy and then turned away, her heart breaking because she didn't know where her children were. She put a lid on a simmering pot, wiped her hands on her apron, and then looked back at James.

"Uh, yeah, I did. I mean, I do. Yeah, I do got children. They, uh, they were sold, too. I mean, I reckon. I was sold. Massah Johnson bought me here."

"'Sold'? What's that?"

"Well, being taken from somebody. Like you wuz from yo' momma, darlin'. Like I wuz from my chillins. Somebody gets some money. Other folks gets us."

"Why they do that?"

"I don't know. I guess 'cause they can, darlin'."

25

"That don't . . . seem . . . *right,* Ruth."

Her eyes filled with tears as she replied, "Yeah, it don't. Yeah, darlin'. It sho' don't."

He continued stirring the pot as his mind struggled with her answers. Answers that begged more questions. Other questions he wanted to ask. And questions he didn't know how to ask—yet.

♣

Master Johnson was unusual in the sense that few slave owners wanted their slaves to read, let alone be literate. Laws were in place in many states making the teaching of slaves to read a criminal offense, but Master Johnson was economically powerful enough in Montgomery County to survive his controversial decision.

And Carlton, taught repeatedly by his father and the Southern society the inferiority of slaves, never considered them capable of being educated. Lessons from the Bible were given to placate them—to teach them and help them accept their place in life. Additionally, the fact that he was 4 years older than James, the thought of James understanding his books never occurred to him. While Carlton was home at night, or on the weekend, he inadvertently gave James an education—a partial insight into slavery and a sliver into the world of knowledge.

Because James did understand. And he got much more than just basic reading lessons. In between the playing they did, Carlton showed James all his books and did his homework in front of him. All the education Carlton was exposed to was passed unintentionally to James. Not only did Carlton give James an old Bible, but he read in front of him. Never considering James could understand, it was just for play, or so Carlton thought.

♣

"The Bible supports the institution of slav'ry. How the Jews supposed to treat theyah slaves. That's what God wants me to do. I try to do it," Master Johnson said to Stanley in one of their weekly meetings in the study. Along with the two men was Rev. Hannibal Jackson Lee, who served as Pastor of Penelope Farms. With Master Johnson seated behind his desk, Stanley seated on a table to Master Johnson's right, and the Reverend reclining comfortably in an easy chair, they bantered back and forth the issues of the day.

"They don't like being slaves, Mr. Johnson. That's why they try to escape. I don't think they believe what you're saying. What right do we—" Stanley replied before being cut off in mid-sentence by a scornful glare from Master Johnson and a slamming hand to the arm of the easy chair by Rev. Lee.

"Cotton Mather's Rules gives me all the rights I need!" exclaimed Rev. Lee. "They should considuh whites like mothers and fathers. Folks to be honored. 'Do not covet' mean for them slaves to not try to escape or covet freedom. God is punishing slaves for they sin. They reward's in Heaven. That's what it say—and I believes it."

"So you're saying they're *supposed* to be slaves?"

"Damn right! I got—we got God-given right to own slaves!" Master Johnson bellowed as he sat up in his chair, scooted it toward the desk, and glared intensely at Stanley.

"We got superiority ovah niggers. Shit, that's why they slaves. If these 'people' would just read the Bible, they'd know this and accept it. Well, the few that *might* be able to understand it!"

An explosion of silence followed Master Johnson's tirade. He slowly exhaled while keeping a scornful eye toward Stanley, who sat there wishing he hadn't tried to make his point. Master Johnson finally released Stanley from his glare and turned toward Rev. Lee. "How many come fo' readin', Pastor?"

"'Bout twenty."

"Listen Stanley. You might not agree wit this heah. Hell, I know you don't. But I'm talkin' 'bout my goddamn money heah! Niggers runnin'—shit! Seems like every week. I got no time fo' this shit!"

"I know, Mr. Johnson. I'm working on it."

"Well, work on it, goddammit! Do somethin' 'bout it! *Work on it*, my ass. Sorry, Pastor."

"I understand, Mr. Johnson. Niggers need to know they place."

"I'll get it under control, Mr. Johnson."

"Uh, huh. You best get it under control!"

On the way to the bedroom after helping Ruth, James approached the grandfather clock, as Master Johnson, Rev. Lee, and Stanley exited the study.

". . . Yeah, I'll be gone fo' day tommora, and be back the end of the week."

"Yes, sir, Mr. Johnson. We got three new men, so we'll be okay."

"And make sho' you keep an eye on them young bucks. Pastor, repeat that message I like 'bout they's calling is to be slaves."

"One of my favorites."

"And Stanley. Willie Joe may come 'round here 'fo I get back and—hey, boy. You ain't causin' no trouble, is ya'?"

Master Johnson stopped in his tracks and towered over James.

"No suh, Massah Johnson," James said as he slowed his gait but continued toward the bedroom.

"Don't git my boy mad. He git mad, I git mad!"

"Yassuh, Massah Johnson, suh."

"He been teachin' you the Bible, ain't he?"

Dong! Dong!

"Yassuh."

Dong!

"What?"

"Yassuh!"

"Praise the Lawd."

"Good. Long as ya' know yo' place! Good. Now go on, git!"

"Yassuh, Massah Johnson, suh."

"Stanley, Willie Joe may come by here. Give 'im that $100 due him. And I want all that tabbaky tied up. I got some folks coming by Sat'day and . . ."

James arrived at the bedroom, grabbed his Bible off the floor, hopped up on the bed, found his place, and began to read.

"But Job answered and said, 'Oh that my grief were tho-ro-ugh-ly weighed and my c-ca-lamity laid in the balance together! For now it would be heavier than the sands of the sea; the-re-fore my words are swallowed up.

"For the arrows of the Almighty are within me, the po-i-son whereof drinketh up my spirit; the terrors of God do set themselves in array against me.

"Boy, he sure sound sad. Carlton say his children died. He lost what he owned. Arrows are like pointed sticks. Almighty is another name for God. Why is God sticking him with arrows? And these words . . . grief, po-i-son, terror—do they mean sad? Like me. Grief. Terror. Yeah, like me. I need to know those words.

"Doth the wild ass bray when he hath grass? Or loweth the ox over his fodder? Can that which is un-sa-vou-ry be eaten without salt? Or is there any taste in the white of an egg?'"

James read while periodically recalling rapidly fading memories of faces, places, sounds, and aromas. Portions of the Bible sounded familiar to him, and the succulent aroma of Ruth's cooking was also becoming familiar. But the images were slipping away. And James knew it. The one thing hanging on was the melody that had accompanied him on the journey to Penelope Farms. He leaned his head ever so slightly back, closed his eyes, and allowed the rhythm to comfort him.

Dong! Dong! Dong! Dong!
Ooo. Carlton be home soon. Better fix the bed.

He hopped down as his heart sped up. He smoothed over the bedspread, recalling the time he had leaned on it and incurred Carlton's wrath.

"It only fo' Deeohgee and me!" Carlton had screamed that day.
Don't git my boy mad!

James completed his housekeeping and sat down on the mat.

CHAPTER 5

" James! Put that down, darlin'!" Ruth exclaimed, her exasperation rising to a level of screaming. James was helpful around the house. And he did keep her company. But his social skills strained her patience. Her heart broke when she looked into his dark-brown eyes. She was reminded of her own loss as she imagined his mother's devastation. But many times, that was not enough.

"You can't go 'round pickin' up stuff. You gotta ask first!"

"Why?"

"Why? 'Cause—'cause it ain't polite. That's why!"

"'Polite'?"

"Yeah. Show ya' got manners. Like sayin' stuff like *please* and *thank you*. Callin' grown womens *ma'am*—grown mens *suh*."

"Like Massuh?"

"Nah. Like other mens—Negroes."

"'Negroes'?" he questioned, a puzzled look etched on his face.

"Yeah—grown folks."

"I say *thank you* and *please*. I guess that's not enough, huh—ma'am."

"Oh, you'll live. Unless you keep on sassin' like that. How's your knuckle?"

"It hurts! You hit me hard with that spoon!"

"I told you to stop. C'meer, let me see it, darlin'," she replied. She looked closely at the struck spot. "It'll be all right."

"Yeah, but it hurts," he whined.

"I'll give you a secret to stop it from hurtin'. Don't do that no mo.'"

♣

The wind howled as the first snow of the season blustered, causing the boys to spend their time inside. The deciduous trees were bare, and a fresh, thin blanket of white dusted the landscape. The fireplaces in Johnson Hall, including the small one in Carlton's bedroom, crackled while offering warmth and light as James and Carlton huddled over an assignment. Deeohgee, several feet away, curled up on the floor, moved only when the fire crackled.

"You see, James, this is how you do it. Five plus seven, you write down the three here, then the one here. See?" Carlton said while keeping his eye on the paper.

Subtly tapping his fingers, James shook his head and replied, "Uh, I don't know, Carlton. You so smart. I would have put down a two there first."

Laughing, Carlton answered, "It's not yo' fault. Y'all jest can't do stuff like this. I must be crazy thinkin' you would know. If you was White, we could have more fun. I could sho' you mo' stuff. Do mo' stuff. But, if you was White, you wouldn't be a slave."

He continued his assignments as James sat near and watched. James was enthralled at the way Carlton made marks on the paper, and they became words. An hour later, Carlton noticed James' stare and paused his scribbling.

James looked at Carlton and asked, "What's wrong, Carlton? Did—did I do something wrong?"

"Nah. You know what I was doing?"

"Uh, yeah. You told me it was uh, writing. Yeah, writing words. Am I right?"

"Yeah. Wow, you remembered. Boy, if you could write, huh. I mean, if I could teach you to write. Huh—anyways, well, you could see wheah you be wrong. I must be crazy. Deeohgee got a better chance at learning this heah."

"Can—can you show me my name? In writin' words?"

With an animated sigh, Carlton grabbed a piece of paper and pencil and wrote as he recited, "J-a-m-e-s," across the top. "See? 'James.' That say 'James.'"

James, tracing the formation of the letters, mumbled what Carlton had said.

"J-a-m-e-s. James. James. J-a-m-e-s. Huh, James. That's me."

"Yeah. But that's jest the furst part," Carlton added. Then he spoke and wrote underneath, "T-h-e S-l-a-v-e o-f C-a-r-l-t-o-n. Theah. That's yo' name. James, the slave of Carlton."

James took the paper and looked intently. He had seen his name in print in the Bible, but this was the first time he had seen it written.

"James. The slave of Carlton," he read and then turned toward Carlton and smiled. "That's me. James. The slave of Carlton."

"Yeah. That's yo' name. That's who you is."

CHAPTER 6

"I sho' hope that boy—uh, James. I sho' hope he keep Carlton busy. He been under my feet too much," Master Johnson said to Stanley as they approached Johnson Hall. Twice a month they took a tour of Penelope Farms, usually going over the orchards and forest, then to the slave-quarters area, which was beyond the view of Johnson Hall and near the tobacco-curing barns. As the overseer, Stanley spent most of his time in this area. Or transporting recently purchased or sold slaves to and from Penelope Farms.

They continued through the forest of slender oak trees that separated the slave quarters from Johnson Hall's view, and on to the cherry orchards to the northwest. And as always, they ended back at Johnson Hall.

"Mr. Johnson, sir. The boy needs his daddy. Wit his momma gone and all."

"That jest ain't me. Miss Penelope was so good at that kinda stuff. She and that boy—God, I sho' miss her."

"We all do, sir," Stanley replied as they arrived and started up the stairs to Johnson Hall's porch. An uneasy silence came as they opened the oak doors and continued toward the spiral staircase.

"You talk to him, don'tcha?" Master Johnson finally uttered as they reached the staircase. His voice trailed off, and he resisted making eye contact with Stanley as he stopped going up the stairs.

"Uh—yes, sir. Some. But, but he really needs you."

After no response, Stanley realized Master Johnson was no longer next to him. He turned and saw him stopped on the third step of the stairs. Stanley then looked in the direction of his gaze, and at the painting overlooking the entrance.

"Shit. That boy look more and more like his momma every day. Huh—I don't even like to look at him. Reminds me too goddamn much of Pea—of, uh, her."

"Yeah, he do, Mr. Johnson."

"I may get that painting taken down."

"That would hurt him something fierce, sir."

"Yeah, but seeing it every day hurts me! Anyhow, talk to him for me, will ya'. I'd 'preciate it."

"But he needs you. His dad—"

"Nah. Not me! I ain't the one. Shit, that's why I had a wife. This daddy shit! It ain't me. Anyways, I'd 'preciate it if'n you keep talkin' to him."

"I don't mind, sir. You don't have to ask me to. Just spend some time wit him, Mr. Johnson. Take him huntin', fishin', travelin'— anythin'. Long as it's wit you. He'll like that."

"Nah, I tolt ya'! That ain't me. Good ideas, though. You can do it if'n you want to. You can take him anytime—on me. I won't make it part of yo' job. But if you do it, I'll pay ya' like it's yo' job. Anyways, how's ev'rythin' goin' in Cupid's . . ."

♣

The slaves were already out in the fields by the time James began his workday with Ruth. There were two other slaves who worked in the Big House at times, though they never spoke to him with words—only glances and glares. As he moved through his days, he could see slaves walking around and several buildings beyond the stand of slender oaks. A million thoughts and questions of his existence began to swirl.

Who am I? Who is this little boy I see in Carlton's looking glass? And who are those people out there? I look like them, like the other slaves. Nothing like Carlton. What is different about me? We the same, ain't we? But these looks—they make me feel—they scare me.

They all had their chance in here, didn't they? Why they mad at me? I want to know them, to get to know them—like I, I'm learning about Ruth. They look like me. I look like them. We the same, ain't we? I want to know more. But how do I do it? Get to know them? I've only talked with Ruth and Carlton since I been here. Nobody else say anything to me. Who am I? I know I'm James—the Slave of Carlton. But is that it? Who am I? . . .

♣

The days spent in Ruth's nurturing companionship helped acclimate James to his situation. This particular day began with cleaning the rooms downstairs, dusting the dining room, cleaning up leaves and branches from around Johnson Hall, and now back to the kitchen to prepare the evening meal.

"Ruth, how long you been here?" James asked while washing dishes.

"Oh, 'round ten—'leven years, I suppose," Ruth replied as she alternated between several simmering pots on the stove.

"You like it here?"

"Where? Here—at Johnson Hall? It's all right, I reckon. Better'n where I could be, I suppose."

"Nah, I mean here at Penelope Farms."

"Like it! Well darlin', I can't answer that one. You can never like being a slave. No matter where you be."

"What that mean? 'Being a slave'?" James asked as he stopped what he was doing and took several steps toward her.

She turned and looked into those big, brown eyes. Eyes that searched hers for answers to life's most profound questions. Knots filled her stomach, lumps filled her throat, and sorrow filled her heart as she struggled to hold in her emotions.

"James darlin', don't—don't you worry 'bout that. Boy, you sho' was quiet-like when you first got here. Now, questions, questions, questions."

"I'm sorry. I ask too many questions. I'll stop," he replied as he went back to his dishwashing.

"No darlin'. It—it's okay. Yo' questions—uh, you, you got the right to ask 'em. It's jest—I—I don't got no answers fo' 'em. That's all," she squeaked out as emotions overwhelmed other words she wanted to say.

She looked at James with dry eyes while a torrent of tears flooded her heart. Memories of her children asking similar questions fueled her sorrow as the little boy sought life's answers. Answers that she didn't have back then. Answers that she did not have now. Answers that she would never have.

Clearing her throat, she finally said, "C'mon. I'm goin' to the orchards fo' some fresh air."

"Uh, nah. I'll go back and wait on Carlton. I could use a hug, though."

"Okay," she replied as her secret wails continued. She walked out of Johnson Hall for her solitary lament as James started up the staircase.

Dong! Dong!

Hmm, Massah Johnson say he be gone all day.

James walked down the hall and approached the study. Looking ahead and behind him, he dashed in and softly closed the door behind him. His heart pounded, his ears strained for noises outside, and his eyes scanned the room, with quick darts to the left and then to the right.

"All these books!" he mumbled in exclamation, as he walked around the room he hadn't been in for a score of months.

During the first meeting with Master Johnson, his focus was completely on that giant of a man and his barking orders. Now, his attention and eyes scanned the forbidden area, which seemed larger than before. Beginning at the floor and going up to the ceiling, James' head went up and down and back and forth and side to side as he gazed at the volumes of books covering the entire right wall.

"Wow! He even got a ladder," he marveled as his eyes caught glimpse of the wooden steps with rollers at the top and bottom.

He continued walking in awe while he gawked up and down the wall of books. He walked between the bookshelf and the desk, and approached a thick, opened book on a stand. He glanced at it as he passed and mumbled, "'Lone'—'long'—a lot of 'l' words. Oh, yeah, that's right. Carlton called it a—uh, dik—uh, yeah, a dictionary. Yeah, that's it! A dictionary."

Continuing his journey, he looked out at a different view of Penelope Farms than Carlton's room offered as he walked past the double window. Against the left wall, there were tables filled with newspapers and magazines. He peeked at several headlines without pausing his stride. Closer to the door were several four-foot-high cabinets. He peeked in and saw various documents, including maps, but James was overwhelmed at the number of books. As he walked back over to them, he changed his course, sat down, and was swallowed up in Master Johnson's chair. He spun it toward the bookshelf, his feet dangling a half-foot off the ground as they lazily swung.

I'm gonna spend all my time in here!

He hopped out the chair and walked up to the bookshelf. Peering up and down the wall of literature, James scanned the titles as he mumbled, "Uh, *Pride and Pre-ju-dice. Pride and Prejudice. Wu-the-ring Heights. The Rime of the An-ci-ent Mariner. Nature.*

Boy, there's a lot of books by this man. Uh—Shakespeare, I guess that's how to say it. Huh, Julius Caesar—*I seen Caesar in the Bible.*

James continued his tour through literary history while he slowly rubbed his fingers over the intricate designs on the bindings. Some had twine and leather coverings, while others included magnificent etchings with gold leaf. He slowly shook his head in amazement as he continued his stroll.

"*The Scarlet Letter. Rip Van Winkle. Moby Dick. Ru—Ru-bai-yat, Rubaiyat.* Huh, there's a lot by this man, too. Edgar Allan

Poe—I guess he writes poetry, huh. Uh, *The Pur-loin-ed Letter.
Ivanhoe. Fran-ken-stein. The Charge of the Light Brigade.* Massah
Johnson got lots of books in here," James exclaimed with a whisper
of wonderment. He took a step back and looked to his right, where
he had been, and then to his left, where he hadn't, and slowly
shook his head.

Grabbing a book off the shelf, James sat back down in Master
Johnson's chair, opened it to a random page and began reading.

"'*Silence!' then ex-claim-ed another stern voice which Mi-lady
re-cog-nis-ed as that of Felton.*

"'*What are you meddling with, stupid? Did anyone order you to
prevent that woman from singing? No. You were told to guard her—to
fire at her if she attempted to fly. Guard her! If she flies, kill her; but
don't exceed your orders.'*"

"*An ex-pres-i-on of unspeakable joy lighten-ed the coun-te-nance
of Mi-lady; but this ex-press-i-on was fleeting as the re-flec-ti-on of
lightning.*"

Dong! Dong! Dong!

Startled, James dropped the book. Only then did he realize how
long he'd been in the study. He wondered if he had been missed.
He scrambled out of the chair and carefully placed the book back
in its proper place.

"I got to be careful not to change anything," he said as he
looked around the room.

"The chair! How was it?" he asked himself as he slid it under
the desk. "I got to pay closer attention next time," he mumbled as
he headed out the door and down the hall to the bedroom to wait
for Carlton, his body tingling with exhilaration.

CHAPTER 7

James and Carlton were huddled on the floor, a panting Deeohgee near as Carlton reviewed his lessons in preparation for his classes resuming. He went to school only during certain months out of the year. The winter's freeze dictated when he stopped going, and spring's thaw when he returned—and the time was rapidly approaching. The active spring weather, the green of spring sprouting out of winter's frigid grip, the animals emerging from their warm hideaway—all indicated the time was at hand.

As Carlton reviewed the lessons, James sat near, watched, and learned. All the lessons unknowingly revealed by Carlton had begun to coalesce in James' mind. Carlton's discriminatory limitations shielded him from realizing the scope or depth of James' understanding. Coupled with his journey through the contemporary literature and the detailed dictionary in the study, James' understanding of Carlton's and Master Johnson's books were evolving. Mere letters, words, and sentences were becoming thoughts, emotions, and ideas, bringing to life robust characters, wonderful places, and insightful perceptions.

This evening's assignment was for Carlton to draw a picture of Penelope Farms. As James watched, Carlton looked at the drawing—Johnson Hall, with his father on the porch in the straw hat he usually wore, and Deeohgee at the foot of the stairs leading up to it.

"What's that over there?" James asked as he pointed to a far corner of the page. The spot corresponded to an area of Penelope Farms far away from Johnson Hall, somewhere James had never been.

"That's my momma. That's where she buried," Carlton replied, his voice trailing off into sadness.

"Oh," James responded.

He thought about the people in his dreams. The melody in his mind. And how both had faded out of his consciousness. "I guess you miss her a lot, huh?"

"Yeah. I sho' do."

"What about yo' daddy?"

"My daddy is—" Carlton answered with half a laugh—"he's a bitnessman."

"Oh," James responded again as he contemplated the term 'bitnessman.'

I don't remember seeing that word. I have to look for it next time.

"I miss my momma, too," was all James could think of saying as Carlton went back to his drawing.

Carlton laughed out loud and said, "James, slaves don't know nuthin' 'bout family stuff. 'Bout bein' nice and stuff."

"Yeah, maybe you're right. Sometimes they ain't nice."

"Uh, huh," Carlton said as he continued drawing.

"Yeah, I just say 'Hey' to them that time. That's all and—"

"'Hey' to who?"

"Some boys—they come by here sometimes during the day. Or when I was out front one day. I don't know. I see them. I just say 'Hey,' that's all. They wasn't nice, pushing me down and stuff."

"What? When?"

Carlton's reaction frightened James. Carlton dropped his pencil on the floor and glared at James, waiting for a response. James scanned his mind for the right words, sensing he may have already said the wrong ones.

"Uh—uh, last week. I mean, two—no, three—days ago," he replied, unsure of what would happen next as he remembered Carlton's earlier wrath.

"So that's how your—no, that's how *my*—clothes got so dirty and torn! Well, I'll git 'em!"

"I never knew why they would do that. I just say 'Hey' to them. That's all."

"They jealous. You got a White friend. They jest got nigger ones."

"What's wrong with having nigger friends?"

"They can't be trusted, for one. My daddy know. My daddy say they lie—they cheat. They lazy. They can't be taught to read, neither. You don't need no nigger friends, James."

As Carlton continued his assignment, James cautiously leaned near, and watched him complete the drawing. But "nigger friends" echoed in James' mind.

I wonder if that's in there—"Nigger"? Huh, I got to look for it. Did—do Carlton think I'm different? If so, why? And who am I? I look like them, like them niggers. What if I decided not to be Carlton's friend? Could I even decide not to be his friend?

"How does this look?" Carlton asked, which broke James' train of thought.

"Uh, it look good. Why, uh, why do you have a nigger friend, then?"

Shaking his head, Carlton laughed. "You're not my friend! I sure am yours, though. If it wutn't for me, you be out in the fields. I wouldn't let you play with my books, neither. My daddy bought you for me 'cause I wanted somebody to play with. You mine, you heah."

"But that—that don't seem right."

"What! You questioning me?" Carlton responded. He jumped up with fists balled and towered over James. "You questioning my Daddy?"

"No, I ain't, Carlton," James replied, sensing that was the correct answer to give. He continued looking down at Carlton drawing. Pointing at a random spot, he added, "So, what you gonna put on there? . . ." and was relieved when Carlton sat back down.

. . . Nigger. Taken to be offensive. "Okay—'offensive.' That mean we don't like it. I'll ask Ruth. . . ." James mumbled as he thumbed

through the pages of the dictionary. He changed his pattern of going through the lexicon alphabetically after the conversation with Carlton. Alternating between the books in Master Johnson's study and the dictionary, he felt the best way to understand the stories was to understand the words. Now, however, his search had a different purpose.

". . . let's see, uh, yeah—*'Slave. A person held in ser-vi-tude as the chattel of another.'*

"Huh, person, ser-vi-tude, ch-ch, uh, chat-tel, huh. . . ."

The conversation with Carlton had disturbed James. This was the first time he had come into the study since the incident. He was beginning to understand his surroundings, his environment, and his station in life. He was looking for answers to the questions life posed.

Who am I? Who am I? A slave on a plantation? Carlton say I am "James, the Slave of Carlton." A nigger. Most of the other slaves, as far as I can tell, don't like me. I don't understand why. Carlton views me as a—a pet, a toy, I guess. Who am I? Who am I? Who am I?

". . . **Person.** *Human being. Individual.* Hmm, that's me. . . ."

Who am I? Who am I? Who am I?

". . . Uh, yeah. Here it is. **Servitude.** *A condition where one lacks li-ber-ty, especially to determine one's course of action or way of life.* Carlton say I can't choose. I wonder—can any slave choose?"

Who am I? Who am I? Who am I?

". . . **Chattel.** *An item of tang-i-ble, movable, or immovable property, except real estate.* Huh? What does that mean? Anyway, one more."

Dong! Dong! Dong! Dong!

Uh, oh. Carlton will be home soon. It's past four o'clock. I got to hurry! Who am I?

"Just a coupla' more," he whispered as he thumbed ever faster.

". . . **li-ber-ty.** *The quality or state of being free.* What's *free?* . . ."

Who am I? Who is James? Who am I?

"*. . . **Tan-gi-ble**. Capable of being per-cei-ved, especially by touch or sight. . . .*"

. . . Who am I? Who is James? Who am I?

"*. . . **Property**. Something owned or possessed.* 'Chattel' means property owned by someone. He—Carlton—owns me. He even wrote it. James. *The Slave of Carlton. . . .*"

Is that who I am? James, the Slave of Carlton? Who am I?

"Uh, let's try one more. Hurry up, James! Uh, ***Free***. *Having legal and po-li-ti-cal rights of a ci-ti-zen*. What's a *citizen*? Uh—shoot! I better go!" he exclaimed in a whisper.

He turned the dictionary back to the "l" pages, looked around the room to ensure all was in order, and then left, exhilarated—but with more questions swirling in his head than when he entered.

♣

"How often you do this?" James asked as he and Ruth cleaned the dining room. Sweat beaded on her brow as she focused on her task—dusting a delicate piece of china. Once that was complete, she responded, "Ev'ry Tuesday afternoon. Come in here and dust and—"

"Why Tuesday? Why not Monday?"

"I duz the wash on Monday."

"How about Wednesday?"

"Jest don't you worry 'bout what I do on Wednesday, okay? Jest you keep on dustin'."

She looked over at James standing across the room. He was busy dusting the table settings and carefully placing them back in a pile. Ruth had taken the remainder of the place settings for twenty out of the armoire to dust its shelves.

"Okay. Ruth—is there slaves everywhere?"

The lump in her throat grew as she struggled to find the right words. "I—I don't know, darlin'. I don't think so. Now, James, make sure you dust them glasses good, you hear!"

"Like this?" he asked as he held a goblet up, the candlelight sparkling through it.

"Uh, huh."

"Yes ma'am. I will. Ruth—why is there slaves?"

"James. James. You keep askin' me questions I don't know the answer to. Ask me somethin' like—uh, like, 'How long you been here?'"

"Over two years."

"What! How—how you know that?"

"It's in Carlton's books. Calendars, months, and days. This is pretty. See how it sparkles?" he said, peering at a lantern through a crystal goblet.

"Chile, you readin'? You readin' Carlton's books?" she exclaimed.

Ruth nearly dropped a crystal pitcher. The lump in her throat now competed with an ache in her heart and the knot in her stomach. James, startled by the tone in her voice, stared at her.

"Yeah—uh, he let me, Ruth. He do. I read it with him."

"My Lord! Be careful, James, darlin'. Don't let him know that, okay?"

"Okay, but he let me, Ruth. He let me!"

She put the pitcher down and breathed in deeply; then she replied, "Yeah, I know darlin'. I believes ya'. But he think you don't know. Believe me, chile. He don't know you can read! He just thinkin' you be copyin' him. Don't let him know! Please, James."

"Okay, Ruth. I won't. But, but why? If he show me—"

"James! Please! Do this fo' me, okay? Don't use no words he don't use first, okay?!"

"Okay, Ruth. I don't anyway."

I better not tell her about Webster and the study.

"Please do this. Please, please . . ." Ruth replied as she hugged him for her.

♣

45

That evening, James' conversation with Ruth had him restless. Turning right, then left, over and over again, made sleep elusive. Initially, he read the Bible as he did one of the novels in the study, enjoying the tales of adventure, victory, and defeat. But he recognized that Master Johnson used names from the Bible for his slaves. He heard Carlton praying each night to God. And most of all, he heard Ruth calling out several names from the Bible—Jesus, Lord, Holy Ghost, and God—when she was troubled. It made him realize there was more to this book than the stories.

There were promises. There was hope. There was power.

Massah Johnson and Carlton both say it got all the answers. Ruth says so, too. It says God love us—all of us. Slaves and White people. It says He won't leave any of us—Slaves or White people. Maybe, maybe He will help me.

He whispered, "God? God. It's me. James. The Slave of Carlton. I want to tell you something, God. I—I don't know what to do. I'm sad. I—I'm scared. I feel . . . alone. . . ."

After a moment's thought, he wiped his tear-stained face and continued.

". . . Yeah, I feel alone. Help me, God. Please. Help me. Tell me what to do. What to say. How to be. Tell me who I am, God. . . ."

CHAPTER 8

"*V*iolence. **Caldron.** "Uh, *cal-e-fac-to-ry. A mo-nas-tery room warmed and used as a sitting room.* **Calendar.** *A system for fixing the beginning, length, and divisions of the civil year and arranging days and longer divisions of time.* Yeah, to tell the days, weeks, and months. Oh—and years, too. How I know how long I've been here. **Cal-lends.** *The first day of the ancient Roman month from which the days were counted backwards to the ides.* Huh, whatever that means."

"**Calf.** *The young of the domestic cow. A baby cow.* **Calf.** *The fleshy hinder part of the leg below the knee.* A word with more than one meaning." **Caliban.** *A savage and deformed slave in Shakespeare's* The Tempest.

"Huh, I got to read that one next. Something about a slave like me."

Returning the lexicon to the correct page, he left the study to find Ruth as he pondered his life. He considered the study, the knowledge acquired, the journeys taken there. He considered the words Carlton brought to light—words that Webster defined. He considered the faces of his parents, long faded into the past. He considered his new parent, Ruth, and all the things she meant to him. And he considered himself, this boy, "James," and who he was. And who he was becoming.

For James, days spent with Ruth was therapeutic. Her nurturing demeanor filled a void in his being that he couldn't explain, struggled to express, but fully realized. His first smile and reason to laugh at Penelope Farms were because of her.

She was brought to Penelope Farms when Carlton was born to be his nanny and remained after Mrs. Johnson's demise. She comforted James by assuring him the other slaves didn't hate him. But she also taught him that sometimes people could be cruel, especially when they didn't understand.

Walking back from the orchards later that day, Ruth and James stopped under an oak tree, for a respite from the summer sun. James had become comfortable leaving Johnson Hall as long as it remained in view, and Ruth was with him. Today, he was troubled as he helped Ruth slowly sit down with grunts and groans.

"Whoo, darlin'. These ol' bones. Gittin' harder to sit down day by day. And don't talk 'bout gittin' back up."

"Ruth, Massah Johnson ain't got no other slaves my age?"

As she rubbed her knee, she chuckled at her joke until what James said registered.

"Yo' age? Why you ask that?"

"I just see old people and women in the orchard. When we go there. I remember when I came, there was grown men and women in the wagon."

Ruth heard the tone in James' voice and understood the direction it was going. Attempting to dodge the question, she suggested, "How 'bout we make some biscuits today."

"But—oh, yeah! Biscuits! Can I poke the hole in them?"

"Yeah, you can. As long as you wash them ol' grubby hands of yours. 'Member when I caught you that time," she said and let out a hearty laugh as James joined in.

"Yeah. You was maaad! I thought I had fooled you, but I had biscuit stuff in my fingernails," he replied between chuckles.

"Yeah, darlin'. Can't fool ol' Ruth here."

"Yeah. Yeah, you right. But yeah, I only seen a couple of boys—"

"James, can't we talk 'bout somethin' else?"

"But, Ruth. I don't feel right. I want to talk about that! I mean this," he replied, and then he repositioned himself so that he was face to face with Ruth.

"Nobody here like me. Carlton, I don't know. I mean—"

"Them boys that roughed you up that time, they don't know what you goin' through. They think you livin' easy-like."

"Yeah, why they do that? I don't understand. I jest say, 'Hey'—that's all."

"They don't know, darlin'. Nobody here do but me. They see dem fine clothes you wear. James—you wear shoes! Shoes! You sleep in the Big House. They think you sleep in a big 'ol bed. They think you eat good, too."

"But—I sleep on the floor, Ruth. I eat what they don't finish."

"I know, darlin'. I know. They don't know. They don't see the clothes you wear is Carlton's old ones. The ones he don't want no mo'. They don't see you sleepin' on the floor in Carlton's room. They don't see you waitin' for Carlton to finish eatin', and you gittin' whatever left. That sometimes you even gotta wait on they dog. They don't see how you sufferin'. They have theirs, too. They's different ones. Yeah—different ones. But the same ones, too. What they don't see is you, me, them, all us—we all slaves, darlin'."

"I was so mad at them boys. I didn't know why they did that. When I told Carlton, he—"

"What! You told Carlton?" Ruth asked as she stopped massaging her left knee.

Frightened by the look on her face, James replied, "Uh—y-yeah. We was talking about something, I don't know. He asked why my—I mean *his*—clothes was dirty that day. So, I told him. He said he'll get them. What that mean? What's wrong, Ruth?"

"Oh, Lord! Lord, my Lord. Uh—nothin', nothin' James. Don't worry 'bout it. Jest, jest don't ever do that a'gin! Okay?"

"Okay. Ruth? You okay?" James answered. He tried to look into her face, but she turned away. Her deep sigh made him wonder but didn't stop him from blurting out his overriding question.

"Who am I? Where do I fit in? Huh, Ruth? Who am I? I feel different from you and the other people. Everybody! I hate that feeling. I hate it!"

"C'mon, get up. And help me up," Ruth said as she grunted and groaned again and rose to her feet. They continued back to Johnson Hall in silence until James recommenced with his prodding. "Huh, Ruth. Who am—"

"James, darlin'! Uh—accept yo' life, huh! Accept where you is! James. You read the papers that come with the packages to me. I know how smart you is. How much you is learnin' from Carlton's books. Use Carlton as much as you can."

"Use him? But—how?"

"They use us up and then get mo', James. They think of us as animals. Even less than animals. You can use them, take what they know. And teach it to us someday, maybe. I hear Master Johnson talkin' 'bout deals he gets 'cause people can't read dem—dem, uh, papers. I hear him tell his friends 'bout education. How readin' so important. He spends lots of money sendin' Carlton to that school. Not many children go to those schools Carlton goes to. Mostly grown men and rich folks' kids!"

"I been learning lots of stuff, Ruth. I'm getting good, too."

"Yeah, you is, darlin'."

They walked along in silence until they approached the steps to Johnson Hall. She stopped and grabbed James by the shoulders. For a hundred moments, she stood face to face with him, close enough to feel his breath.

Help me with the words, Holy Ghost, she silently prayed.

She looked past James, and behind her, and then directly at him and whispered intensely, "You see James, readin'—that's the key, darlin'! When we become free, we gonna to need book-smart Negroes like you to help us. To lead us. To teach us, huh! You smart. I see that. I know that! I want you to promise me that you'll learn all you can."

"I promise, Ruth, I promise. I'll use him. Yeah, I'll use him, huh."

"Be careful, though. Don't let them know. Don't let anybody know. This will be our little secret. Okay?"

"Yes, ma'am."

She gave James one of her everything's-going-to-be-okay hugs, and they went inside as she thought, *Lotta time a smart slave end up a dead one. God. Please protect this child.*

Dong! Dong! Dong!

♣

The ominous sound, an incessant tapping, was getting louder in the pitch-black surroundings. And it was getting closer. It began to drown out James' labored breathing, and his chest strained to contain his pounding heart as he eked out, "Who—who's there?"

The darkness gave no clues as he sat rigidly in a solitary chair, his knuckles growing pale, while his terrified grip threatened to snap the chair's arm.

"I—I s-s-say, 'Who there?'" he repeated in a cracking voice as tears began to trickle.

The tapping became louder and faster and louder and faster and louder and faster until, suddenly, an explosion of silence engulfed the room. Breathing slow and hard, James' eyes blinked fully and intermittently as he strained to pierce the enveloping darkness.

"Who—who? . . ." was all that escaped his lips while his pounding heart slowed. He kept his eyes shut for a time as his stammering continued, ". . . who—who...is...it? Who—who out th-th-there? Who out—"

He stopped speaking immediately when he heard it. A lone footfall. Then another. Then another. Then pairs, then groups with shuffles and scuffing as they got closer and louder. James opened his eyes and discerned moving shadows in the darkness coming toward him as the footfalls now vibrated the floor beneath him.

"Who is there!" James screamed, waking himself, Carlton, and Deeohgee up.

"Calm down, boy!" Carlton ordered the barking Deeohgee as he peered over the side of his bed at the trembling James. "What's wrong wit you?"

Struggling to understand exactly where he was, it slowly came to James that he was on the floor in Carlton's bedroom, as he had been every night since his arrival. "Uh, I—I uh, I had a dream. I had a dream."

"You mean a nightmare. You had a nightmare," Carlton replied as he fought off the sleepiness with a big yawn.

James rose up and looked around the moonlit room. He saw his sleeping mat under and around him in disarray, and his brown skin was glistening with sweat. He swallowed hard, placed his hand on his chest and uttered, "Huh! Is that what you call it? Nightmare. It makes my heart beat real fast."

Laughing, Carlton said, "Yeah. You'll be okay. It's only if it gits ya'—then you in trouble. Go back to sleep."

James straightened out the rug and lay back down, his heart still thumping.

I ain't reading no more of that Poe man, uh. Nevermore—huh, never no more!

Dong! Dong! Dong!

♣

Class was in session at Jericho's Wall Baptist Church. Fifteen males—from eight to sixteen years of age—were sitting behind six pine tables and several desks, all facing a bespectacled giant of a man. Behind him, a wall of slate covered with scholarly writings and academic muses completed the scene.

Sounds of scribbling on individual slate boards permeated the classroom, interrupted only by the snickers and whispers of the schoolboys.

"Frank. Whatcha' got fo' number three?" Carlton whispered to the boy seated next to him.

"That's a easy one, Carlton," Frank responded loud enough for everyone to hear. The snickers increased in intensity and volume.

"Mr. Johnson! Turn around," Headmaster Taylor demanded. "If you paid more attention in class, you would do better. You're barely passing Arithmetic."

The class roared in laughter as another one of his classmates said, "Hey, Carlton—maybe them niggers yo' daddy teachin' to read can help ya'."

The increased laughter of his classmates caused Carlton to stew.

"My daddy say so they know they place! That's why—" he attempted to retort through his fully flushed face.

"A strong whip on the back show dem their place!" Headmaster Taylor forcibly interjected.

"But—but he say it fo' they own good. He say—"

"I don't give a shit what your daddy say! If'n he wutn't so doggone rich, we woulda strung him up, and some of them uppity niggers long time ago! Now shaddup and get to work!"

"Yes, sir. Mr. Taylor," Carlton replied.

"Duh, 1 + 1 is 3, ain't it?" Frank teased.

"Nah. 1 + 1 is 11, I suppose," taunted Jerry as the class snickered.

♣

"*. . . or action. **Manage.** To handle or direct with a degree of skill or address. To treat with care. **Manage.** The actions and paces of a trained riding horse.* Huh, these words are spelled the same, sound different and have different meanings. How do you know which one is which?

"***Mañana.** At an indefinite time in the future. **Manasseh.*** Yeah, I remember that one. From the Bible. *A son of Joseph, and the tra-di-tio-nal e-po-ny-mous ancestor of one of the tribes of Israel.* There were, uh—twelve, yeah, twelve tribes. Huh, *eponymous.* I got to go back and find out what that means.

"*Manchet. A loaf or roll of fine wheat bread,*" James read as he continued his trek through the dictionary, affectionately referring to his tutor as "Webster."

Fifteen months into his study of the study, he had read several books, but stopped at the second of Edgar Allan Poe's novels. Webster helped his understanding of the stories and the Bible, and he was several weeks into his second time through it.

He turned the page of the dictionary back to its proper position, moved over to the shelf, and pulled down the book he had been reading. "Okay, now for today's story, I'll try to finish it, but I don't know," James mumbled as he sat in Master Johnson's chair, his toes barely above the floor.

"Let's see. Where was I? Ah, yeah. Here it is. *Welcome, dear Ro-sen-crantz and Guil-den-stern. Moreover that we much did long to see you, the need we have to use you did provoke our hasty sending. Something have you heard of Hamlet's trans-for-ma-tion. So call it, sith nor th' exterior nor the inward man resembles that it was. What should it be, more than his father's death.* Huh, what is *he*—what are they talking about? I have no—well, little—idea what they're talking about. Maybe after more Webster, I'll understand this Shakespeare man better. . . ."

Dong! Dong! Dong! Dong!

"Ruth, I'm going to go to the room, now," James said as he put the final dish away, completing the dishwashing portion of his duties. Ruth, busy stirring a pot and watching a pan that boiled near her, never turned around.

"You got dem dishes washed good?"

"Yes, ma'am. And the pots," he replied, as he stood there motionless, waiting for her permission to leave. The clatter of lids being placed, utensils clanging against metal pots and pans, and an occasional grunt and groan from Ruth was all he heard.

"I'm done, Ruth," he repeated, this time a little louder to rise above the din of the kitchen.

"Okay, darlin'," she replied, still not pausing from her duties.

Arriving in the bedroom, James hopped up on the bed and settled in with his Bible. "Let's see—where was I at? Uh, yeah," he mumbled as he thumbed through the pages of the Bible until he found his spot and began reading.

"Who shall separate us from the love of Christ? Shall tri-bu-la-tion or distress or per-se-cu-tion or famine or nakedness or peril or sword? As it is written, for thy sake we are killed all the daylong. We are accounted as sheep for the slaughter," James read and then paused to muse aloud.

"I wonder—is he talking about us—about the slaves? If we ain't citizens, if we're property. Ruth say like the animals. Like sheep, huh. I wonder if we get slaughtered, too. Anyway.

"Nay, in all these things we are more than con-que-rors through Him that loved us. For I am persuaded that neither death nor life, nor angels, nor prin-ci-pa-li-ties, nor powers, nor things present nor things to come, nor height nor depth, nor any other creature shall be able to separate us from the love of God, which is in Christ Jesus, our Lord."

James snapped the book shut and grumbled, "Oh, yeah? Huh, if God love us so much, how come we slaves? I don't understand that one. Why can't we be free? Have liberty? Be a citizen? Why we like the animals? And who am I? Who are we? What are we? You say You love everybody, God. So why don't You treat every-body the same?"

James sighed heavily and gazed at his familiar surroundings. Having Carlton's viewpoint helped him see the insignificance Carlton and those like him placed on himself and those like him. That first night remained with him, and that sorrowful stare Deeohgee gave him. Another sigh escaped, and then James began reading again.

"I say that truth in Christ—"

"James! James!" Carlton hollered as he arrived home. James hopped off the bed, straightened it out, and sat on the rug on the floor.

Chapter 9

Over the next several years, James made good on his promise to Ruth. No matter what Carlton said, James secretly learned. No matter what he did, James secretly learned. No matter the situation, James secretly learned. No matter how James felt, he secretly learned. But it evolved into more than just a promise to Ruth. It became the essence of his being. It fused itself into his psyche. His love of learning fueled his dreams, whetted his imagination, helped him tolerate Carlton's racism, and led him back to the study every chance he got.

When Carlton studied, James paid close attention, particularly in Arithmetic. When Carlton went to school, James would read all he could find in Johnson Hall. Packages in the kitchen. The Bible—thrice. But it was in Master Johnson's study that the hours and months became knowledge and understanding. He walked around the room this morning, visually ingesting the volumes of literature while virtually digesting the places and times. He was musing about his life when he eyed several maps and other documents on a table to the left of the study.

I feel so comfortable here. These books—my friends. This dictionary—my tutor. These times I spend here—my joy. I feel in control of my life. The only time I feel in control. I have a purpose here, huh, Ruth. To learn all I can.

There's a reason for putting up with Carlton. I'm getting something from him. Knowledge, something the Bible—and Ruth—says I should seek. I'm going to use him—and his daddy. Just like my people are being used. Huh, my people. Slaves—chattel—servitude. Not free. Not citizens. Property.

He looked more closely at the documents and maps on the table on the left side of the study.

I don't come over here often enough. To see these uh, these maps. But—I love the books! The stories! I love it all. I'll come over here more later. Anyway, the stories are better since I've learned more words. Reading Webster was a good idea. All the words fascinate me. So many ways to say so many things.

He walked toward the wall of books but stopped in his tracks as a newspaper on Master Johnson's desk caught his attention. When Master Johnson intended to keep a newspaper, he placed it on the table to the left of the room. This copy, however, remained on his prized possession, folded several times so that only a specific article showed. James picked it up and read aloud.

"What Now? by G. T. Rowe.

"'The South lost a valuable ally in the White House when President Zachary Taylor died recently. The Northerners will never elect another Southerner to lead this country. We're outnumbered unless we find ways to get more states and territories. I shudder at a world where the Northerners say who leads us. What now, Southerners?

"'Legislation and the courts remain possibilities, and we must insist that at least some Cabinet members, if not the vice-presidency itself, be representative of Southern—of our—interests. When President Taylor—a Virginian and native son of the South—died this summer, hope for a civil solution to this impasse we have may have died with him. What now, United States citizens?

"'Millard Fillmore, this Yankee, from New York of all places, surely will lead us down the path of conflict and dissension. I also note here, now, and forever more of my trepidation that the truth may be conveniently lost—or never revealed as those in power are prone to do. I have never been one to trust Northerners anyway, with their Abolitionists and Free Democrats scurrying about like the rats they are.

"'It is not beyond them—at least some of them, to do something as dastardly as this—assassinate the President of the United States.

Not in an honorable duel of pistols at some agreed upon distance—as gentlemen are prone to do. Not even with something as clever as a creative explosive device. No, with something as despicably evil as a disease their scientists may have created. What now, Northerners?

"'What I hope and pray for now is that the circumstances of this tragedy of the country be thoroughly investigated, and the entire truth be revealed and brought to the light, and that my suspicions are proven wrong. What now, President Fillmore?—Grantland Tobias Rowe, Editor. Montgomery County Monitor—September 3, 1850.'"

James carefully returned the article to the place it had been in and wondered what it was all about. Parts he understood, but the significance of the events—to him and to Master Johnson—eluded him.

"Boy, I wish I knew some more of what he was talking about. The President dead? I know that's the leader of the country. Legislation? Cabinet members? Impasse? Dissension? Abolitionists? Free Democrats? I got to read Webster some more to figure this out what's happening. It must mean a lot to Massah Johnson. Anyway, back to my friends . . ."

♣

Dong! Dong! Dong! Dong! Dong! Dong! Dong! Dong! Dong! Dong! Dong!

James was an hour into his study of Webster that morning. Having been with Ruth in the orchards, he'd seen Master Johnson leaving in his buggy and rushed back to continue his third journey through Webster. The supple pages had gotten familiar to his touch, as had the rough, leather-bound cover with the embossed, gold-lettered words "Webster Dictionary" that he periodically rubbed his fingers over. Never taking it off the stand, his growth over the years had him now leaning over the lexicon to read.

". . . let's see, **honeymoon.** Yeah, after a marriage. **Honeysuckle**, honeysuckle, uh—oh yeah, a kind of flower. **Honk**, what a goose

59

say. *Honor*, the word with many meanings, all good. One of the Bible words where—" James mumbled to himself until he noticed sounds. He blinked his eyes once, held his breath, and strained to listen as his forehead scrunched up. Johnson Hall was usually silent that time of the day. But the voices were unmistakable, and the footfalls could be felt. And both were getting closer.

Oh, no! He was supposed to be gone all day! That's what he said this morning to Stanley!

James dashed behind the drapes that covered the right end of the window just as the door opened. Master Johnson and another man walked in.

". . . So, you want three slaves? Two males and a female?" Master Johnson asked as he walked around to his desk.

"Yeah, I do, Hiram," the small, slender man replied.

"We say fo' five thousand dollars, right?"

"Yep—$5,000. That's what I said to," the man replied.

He stood on the opposite side of the desk. As Master Johnson took some papers out of one of the drawers, the man leaned over and glanced at what Master Johnson was reading.

"Good thing you caught me on the road. You woulda missed me. Just sign here, Albert," Master Johnson said as he slid a piece of paper and a quill toward the man.

"Okay. I'll jest put my mark here. I hope you ain't cheatin' me, Hiram," he chuckled.

"I been knowin' you how long now, Al? Ten—fifteen years? We always done good bitness, right?"

"Yeah, Hiram. I was jest funnin' witcha'," Albert replied with a laugh. Then he refocused on the sheet and slowly drew an "X" on it.

Master Johnson picked up a sheet of paper, thrust it toward Albert, and said, "Nah. Now c'mon over heah and see right heah. It says 'Negro male, 25 years old, two-thousand dollars. For a woman—nine hunnerd dollars.'"

Oh, God. Please don't let him catch me in here!

"Yeah, I sees it Hiram. I trust ya'."

"Nah. Now, c'mon. You sho'? Nah. I'll show ya'! See—it say right theah!" he proclaimed as he repeatedly tapped his finger on a spot on the paper.

"Yeah, I'se sho'," Albert responded as his eyes darted between the paper and Master Johnson.

"I sho' hope so. I'm a bitnessman, but fo' you, I barely made a hunnerd dollars. I usually make mo'."

"I'se 'preciate that, Hiram," he replied as he began peeling off hundred-dollar bills and placing them on the desk.

"I tell ya'. Tryin' to do bitness wit friends. They ain't never happy. . . ."

James, less than five feet away from Master Johnson, was terrified. His eyes began to water as he thought about the ramifications of getting caught.

God, don't let him catch me in here. I—I'm not supposed to be in here. He'll be real mad if he catch me. . . .

The men continued talking, drinking brandy, and smoking cigars after the deal was done. Mostly slave talk and the problems with having them and trying to control them. The smoke began tickling James' throat and irritated his eyes, which watered even more.

. . . God, please don't let me cough. Please, God. Don't...let...me... cough....

The men's conversation turned to family, and Albert asked how Carlton had adjusted to his mother's death, which sent a chilling shudder through James. He hadn't turned the page of the dictionary back before he hid.

Master Johnson and Carlton always kept the dictionary open to the last page Mrs. Johnson was reading before she died, and James had been doing the same. That page included the word "longevity" on it. "Long duration of individual life" was the definition James heard repeatedly from Carlton, as well as the story behind it.

Mrs. Johnson's genteel upbringing in the high society of Richmond had always been the main lure for Master Johnson. Cultured and educated, she was determined to raise the level of her husband's standing and motivate her son to the social class she had been accustomed to. She had a word of the day for them during breakfast, one way of civilizing them. On that fateful morning, "longevity" was it.

Dong! Dong! Dong! Dong! Dong! Dong! Dong! Dong! Dong! Dong! Dong! Dong!

Those torturous moments behind the drapes dragged on, as James prayed they wouldn't look at the dictionary. Several times, he nearly coughed from the smoke as his mind raced with thoughts of what Master Johnson might do to him if he were caught.

He might make me sit in the dark closet all night! Or, or not let me eat for two—even three whole days! He—He might take my clothes. Or my shoes. Oh, no—he might hit me! Or have them boys do it, again!

His eyes welled up with tears from the smoke and the fear, and they trickled down his face as he struggled to keep from crying out loud.

Dong!

Finally, Master Johnson and Albert finished and left, but James stayed motionless for several minutes, his heart still pounding. Peeking out from behind the drapes at first, he came out, turned Webster back to its proper place, and walked toward the door. But he noticed papers on Master Johnson's desk and stopped.

Must be the paper he was reading to Albert.

James snuck, at first, a quick peek, and then he took a longer look. It read "NEGROES AT PENELOPE FARMS" and had a list of numbers.

"Negro male $1,500. Negro female $700. But, wait—he say, 'a man was $2,000 and a woman'—oooh! Massah Johnson's cheatin' Albert!" James whispered an exclamation. This shocked him back into realizing where he was. He scurried out of the study before Master Johnson returned, passing him on the stairs.

"You ain't gittin' in no trouble, is ya?"

"Nah, suh, Massah Johnson, suh," James replied as he raced down the stairs and headed out to the orchards to see Ruth.

Thank You, God. Thank You!

♣

New England's annual morphing of green to multi-colored foliage was in full bloom as father and son strolled down Boston's cobblestone streets. Papa Harris strode, and Junior skipped past people and neighbors who exchanged pleasantries as they headed home. Papa Harris' concern was always highest for his firstborn. One, because of him being the only Negro in his classes. And two, his knowledge of people and the attitudes they possessed. Instead of scaring Bobby with questions, he chose to listen intently for revelations.

". . . and Mr. Carmichael said Mr. Jones is a nasty son-of-a-bitch, and—"

"Bobby! I don't wanna hear talk out your mouth like that ever again, you hear?" Papa Harris retorted as he stopped in his tracks.

"Yes, daddy. I'm sorry. What was wrong with what I said?"

"Just never you mind. Just don't do it. Where you gettin' that kinda language from?"

Bobby looked up into his father's angry eyes and felt fear. Rarely did his father raise his voice in anger at any of his children. Bobby had never seen the look that now glared back at him.

He stammered and finally got out, "I—I, uh, daddy. I don't know. I just—I just hear stuff. The boys in school say stuff. And—and—"

"Watch what you *just pick up*, you hear! Bobby, you can't be like—" he yelled until he noticed fear on his son's face. He paused, took a deep breath, exhaled a slight sigh, and then calmly pleaded, "Bobby—son. You, you can't be doin' that. You got to be careful.

Pick up the good stuff, son. You're not like the other boys, son. You gotta be different. You are different."

"Yes, sir. Okay, daddy, I will. Can—can I say 'a crook and a cheat'?" Bobby sheepishly asked as they began walking again.

"Uh, yeah. I guess—if it's true," Papa Harris replied with a chuckle and smile.

"Why would someone vote for a man like that, daddy?"

"I don't know, son. Sometimes you just don't know folks. Sometimes you find out later. You just never know."

"Who did you vote for, daddy?" Bobby asked, causing his father's spirit to sink as he swallowed hard and measured his response.

"Uh—the other guy. So, tell me what else you've been learning in school."

"Oh, math and stuff. And we write a lot of stuff."

"'Stuff'?"

"Uh, huh. Uh—nouns and verbs. Stuff like that."

"Well then say 'nouns and verbs.' Stop sayin' 'stuff'!"

"Yes, sir."

James and Ruth became closer through the years, as dreams about his family faded out of reach of his consciousness. Faces would appear—and then fade away. Sounds sounded familiar—and then foreign. And the melody that had kept him company those first, lonely days and weeks had dissipated, just out of his memory's reach. When he tried humming it to Ruth, he couldn't quite get it. They talked for hours over the years, though, with James confiding his innermost secrets, hopes, and dreams.

". . . I call it 'Webster' because that's the name on it. It got all the words, too! I'm gonna learn all them, too. And, and it got marks over the letters that tell you how to say the words. So, the words I already know—I look at those marks. That's how I learn the new words, Ruth. Like the word, uh, 'action.' I was saying 'ak-tie-on.'

But then those letters showed me the '-tion' says 'shun.' So, you say the word—ak-shun. . . ." James proclaimed as he told of his journeys through the pages of the study.

Ruth's legs gave way as she plopped down in a chair she barely made it to. She hoped her face didn't reveal the utter terror she felt as she silently prayed,

"Oh, God—what have I done? Help him, Jesus. Please, please look out fo' this boy. Oh Lord, my Lord—please! Help him, please!"

". . . I'm gonna keep on reading until I know everything, Ruth, just like you told me. I'm gonna use them like they use us, huh, Ruth? Just like you told me to. Reading. Arithmetic. Everything. I'm gonna get everything from them. And I—"

Blinking her eyes rapidly to clear them of tears, she finally looked into James' eyes and ruefully muttered, "James, darlin'. My Lord! Uh—James—don't, uh—don't you ever let the massah catch you up in there! He—he whup you somethin' fierce! And don't use those words unless Carlton uses them first, darlin'! Be sho' 'bout that, you hear!"

"Okay, Ruth. I won't. You say to use him, Ruth."

"I—I know, darlin'. I know. Jest be special careful, huh?"

"Okay. I will. But what's, uh, *whup*? What that mean?"

"Don't worry 'bout that right now. Just keep this 'tween you and me—you hear me, darlin?! Long as you a slave, James, don't let nobody know. Nobody!"

"Okay. We gonna make some cakes today?" James replied as he eyed the sugar, flour, and eggs on the counter.

"James, listen! I mean it! Listen!" she implored as she grabbed him by the shoulders with her hands, powered from grabbing large pots and pans and kneading dough. She pulled him into a smothering, maternal hug while she slowly rocked back and forth.

James barely turned his head to the side and let out a muffled, "I can't breathe, Ruth."

She released him some, and he huffed to replenish his lungs with air. Still maintaining a tight grip on his shoulders though, she said, "James, baby, this might scare you some, but you needs to hear this. Darlin', sometimes, uh—sometimes a smart slave can end up a—a dead slave. Don't ever let no one know you readin' like you do! Okay?"

"Uh, okay, Ruth. I don't understand, though."

His hands trembled slightly, and a hint of fear wrinkled his forehead.

"I don't understand, neither. But please, darlin', please! Promise me—okay?"

"Okay, I promise," James replied and then looked down at the shoes he was wearing.

The trepidation enveloping him worked its way through his being. As he looked back up at Ruth, a trembling whine escaped.

"Ruth—I'm scared."

"So am I, baby. My God, so am I."

She held him close for minutes as they thought about the ramifications, he not really knowing and she fully understanding. She released the embrace but kept the grip, as she tried to give him a reassuring smile that didn't match her feelings. She noticed questions etched on his face that he struggled with, even more than their recent conversation. She peered into his brown eyes.

"James, darlin'. What is it? What's wrong? I mean, what else is wrong?"

"Uh—nothing. I mean, well—I—uh, nothing."

"What darlin'? C'mon. Out wit it!"

"Uh—well, uh—what about—uh, what about writing?"

"What! You—you can write?! Oh, Lord Jesus!" she exclaimed as she jumped in the seat with amazement; then, she leaned back and buried her face in her hands.

James stood there for a moment as she shook her head and mumbled indistinguishable sounds.

"James—uh, h—h—how?" she finally uttered.

"I'll show you," he proclaimed and dashed to Carlton's room. He returned with several sheets of paper.

"See, here is the one where Carlton wrote my name for me. See, it say *James*. The other stuff say *The Slave of Carlton*, but I don't write that. Just *James*, over and over, see?" Full of pride, he turned the worn piece of paper over and over again, showing her his handiwork.

"Uh, yeah, darlin'," she said as she sighed. "I see you wrote it a lot."

"Even on the back—see?"

"Yeah, darlin', I see," she replied, as she took it into her trembling hands and admired the work.

"First, I traced it over and over; then I started writing it myself. On the floor, at first, with my finger. Then with old pencils Carlton give me to pretend-write. I just make lines when I'm around him. Like you told me about reading. But when I'm by myself, I write."

Ruth, her eyes full of tears by now, grabbed and hugged James again with her trembling arms, while she slowly rocked from side to side. Sighing, she asked, "Uh, James—can you breathe?"

"Yes, ma'am."

"James, darlin'. Be careful. Darlin', please! Be careful!"

"Yes, ma'am. I will. What's wrong?"

"What else you got there?" she said, as she noticed another piece of paper in his hands. This one was from thicker stock.

"Oh, this one got all the letters in the alphabet. Twenty-six of them. And the numbers. Zero, one, two, three, four, five, six, seven, eight, and nine. See—all of them. He tell me to throw it away because he got a new one. But I keep it. I don't write these on paper yet. Just with my fingers on the ground."

"Why not on paper?"

"Carlton keeps all his. All his paper."

"Oh, okay," she said. Slowly she got up and walked toward the cupboard.

"I write in the dirt sometimes. But only when I'm by myself, Ruth. Like you say. You know—like reading. I'm using him good, huh?"

"Yeah, good. Good, darlin'. Good. I'm gonna git you some paper—but you don't keep it! You just write and give it back to me. I'll throw it away. Okay?"

"Yes, ma'am. Thank you. Ruth, why are you crying?"

"'Cause—'cause I'm scared. That's why!" she exploded, causing James to jump back. "James, darlin'. I'm sorry. But, James—I—I—I'm scared. You a smart Negro. I'm glad, but I'm scared, too. Come over here," she said as she stopped at the kitchen table and motioned for him to come over.

"Why are you scared?"

"Uh, don't worry 'bout that right now. Uh, James. I never seent—I, uh—I never seent nobody write my name. Ruth. My name. Write it for me, darlin'—will you?"

"Okay, Ruth," he replied as he picked up the pencil and began forming letters. "You know—I know some stuff Carlton don't. Words he say wrong. Arithmetic stuff. He be getting it wrong, but I don't say nothing."

"James," she replied with a warning tone, but he didn't look up.

"Really, Ruth. I don't say nothing. But I could help him."

"James! Darlin', that's the last thing he want. A Negro man—huh, a *slave*—tellin' him he wrong. Don't you ever say anythin' like that!"

"Huh—okay. See, you start with a 'R' like that—but capital. Because that's what your name starts with. Then you write the 'u,' 't,' and 'h'—" James continued.

"That's nice, James. Thank you."

"But that's not all. You need a last name. If I could give you one, it would be 'L-o-v-e,' love. Because I love you, Ruth."

Attempting to hold back the torrent of tears that she knew wouldn't stop if they started, Ruth rued the day he would come to realize the danger of being someone like him. In between her wails of appreciation and trepidation, she uttered, "I love you, too, darlin'. I sho' do."

♣

"... *Whorl. A drum-shaped section on the lower part of a spindle in weaving or spinning machinery. **Whose**. Of or relating to whom or which. Possessor*. I guess for me the answer is Carlton. ***Whump**. A bang or thump. **Why**. For what cause, reason, or purpose. **Wick**. Bundle of fibers used in candles and lamps for burning. **Wicked**. Morally very bad*. Huh, I don't see no *whup*! What is she talking about, *whup*? I don't see no *whup*! Maybe she said it wrong. Anyway . . ." James mumbled as he turned Webster back to the page, grabbed a book off the shelf, and plopped himself down in Master Johnson's chair, with his legs swinging and the balls of his feet sliding across the floor.

"Okay, let's see. Where was I? . . ." he asked as he thumbed through several pages to find his spot. "Okay, here it is.

"*After this, I had been telling him how the devil was God's enemy in the hearts of men, and used all his malice and skill to defeat the good designs of Providence, and to ruin the Kingdom of Christ in the world; and the like.*

"'*Well,' says Friday, "but you say, 'God is so strong, so great.' Is He not much strong, much might as the devil?"*

"'*Yes, yes,' says I. "Friday, God is stronger than the devil, God is above the devil, and therefore we pray to God to tread him down under our feet and enable us to resist his temptations and quench his fiery darts."'*

69

But, say he again, 'If God much strong, much might as the devil, why God no kill the devil, so make him no more do wicked?"

"Yeah!" James screamed so loud his voice echoed. "Oops—yeah. I want to know that, too, Friday. What you gonna say about that, Mr. Crusoe? Why don't God strike down the Devil? And—and slavery, too. And let me and Ruth be free."

"'I was strangely . . .'"

CHAPTER 10

"Okay, James. We gonna let that stew fo' a while. I'm goin' to the orchards. Wanna come?" Ruth asked as she took off her apron. Another day, another meal, and she was out for one of her walks.

"Nah. I'll, uh, go back to the, uh—room," James replied, and they parted company.

Dong! Dong!

Two hours, huh. I can finish The Count of Monte Cristo. And still have time for some words with Webster.

". . . *Forte. One's strong point.* Huh, I wonder what my strong point is? *Forth. Onward in time, place, or order. Forthcoming.* Uh—yeah. Being about to appear," James mumbled.

Completely immersed in his acquisition of knowledge, he crouched over the lexicon's stand. As he gleaned the pages, he would recall stories where its definitions helped complete the picture of the tale and clarify the emotional environment. He turned the page of the book and continued.

"*Forthright. Directly forth or ahead. Without hesitation. Forthwith. Immediately.* Yeah, one of the Shakespeare words— 'Come here forthwith.' *Fortification. An act or process of fortifying. Fortify.* Yeah, to make strong. That's it, to make—" James mumbled and then stopped as a faint sound entered his consciousness. Growing louder with each passing moment, it soon became horrifically unmistakable in tone and horribly evident in ownership.

"James! James! . . ." screamed Carlton repeatedly. "Wheah you at, James? James! . . ."

Oh, my God! What—what time is it? Carlton home early! Uh, the book—uh, the dictionary. Put it back to, uh—oh, my God! Why he here so early? Uh—what time is it? . . .

James frantically flipped through the pages of Webster while his mind raced with plans and options. He calmed down somewhat as the l's came into view.

". . . James! James! Wheah you at, boy? . . ." Carlton screamed as he walked past the study, his footfalls shaking James to the core and bringing the pounding in his chest to pain.

*. . . Uh, okay, okay—here! Yeah—**longevity**. Here it is! Okay, how to get out? Oh, my God! How to get out? . . .*

James tiptoed to the door, remaining as quiet as possible. His rushing blood coursed through his veins, crashing into and exploding out of his pounding heart. He took in labored breaths, none of which ever gave his lungs enough air. He put his back to the door, closed his eyes, and listened intently.

". . . James! James! James! Wheah you at? If you with Ruth a'gin . . ." Carlton railed as he approached the study again after leaving the bedroom. When James opened his eyes, he saw the chair out of position.

Oh, God—please! Please let him walk past! Please don't let him come in here and catch me. Please, God!

James, his face wet with perspiration, pushed against the door.

Carlton's footfalls grew louder and closer as he screamed, ". . . *James!* Wheah the hell you at, boy? . . ." eight inches away on the opposite side of the 6-inch-thick door.

James flinched as his prayers became whispers sprinkled with whines.

". . . James! James . . ." Carlton angrily yelled as his voice cracked with emotion; then it became fainter as he went farther past the study and down the hall.

Thank You, God. Thank You. Thank You!

Slowing inhaling and exhaling again, James rushed to return the chair to its position. Then he slowly cracked open the door, took a cautious step out, and froze. To his left was a man kneeling in front of the clock, its pieces strewn all around him.

". . . James! James! . . ." James could still hear Carlton yelling as he went outside, the sound fading in the increasing distance. James quietly took the steps back in and closed the door almost shut.

That's what happened to the time. Oh, God. I can't stay here. Sooner or later, Carlton's gonna look for me in here! I can't stay here!

Ten minutes passed before the man left, and James rushed out of the study, ran outside, and finally found Carlton halfway back from the orchards.

"Carlton, Carlton! Hey!" James shouted, filled with feigned smiles and laughter.

"Huh? Hey, wheah the hell you been, boy?"

"I was hiding under the bed. You didn't see me?"

"See you. Hell, naw! I been callin' you. You best answer me, you heah!" he said—and then punched James in the face, knocking him to the ground.

"Ow! Oh, my nose! It's—it's bleeding!" James screamed as he lay on the ground, clutching his face.

"When I call you—you come heah! Understand? Huh! Understand!" Carlton ordered as he towered over the sprawled James. "You heah me, boy!?"

"Yeah. Okay, Carlton. I—I thought you was playing wit me, too. I touched your shoe and everything."

"What? You did?"

"Yeah. Yeah, I touched it. I thought you would feel it and look under the bed. Then we were gonna laugh. I'm sorry," James said as he cautiously began to get up.

"Okay—it's all right. Heah, let me see—hold yo' head back like this," Carlton replied as he helped James to his feet.

"You mine! Jest like I kick Deeohgee in the ass if'n he don't come when I'se call 'im. You heah?"

"Yeah, Carlton. I hear," James replied, thankful all he got was a bloodied nose.

♣

"So, Bobby. Is this how you do it? Eight plus six is fourteen. I write the four here and carry—uh, yeah, carry the one here," Martha asked.

"Good. Then what do you do?"

"Uh, add the one I carried, the six, and the two. I get nine. The answer is ninety-four."

"Yep. Sixty-eight plus twenty-six equals ninety-four. Keep practicing. William, you're going to read to me in a minute. Eve, you are doing great with your letter writing."

Every Saturday morning, Bobby led classes for his siblings. All were willing, but Martha was the most eager. Papa Harris tended the store with Hannah, a trusted staff member. Mama Harris began the weekly cleaning and prepared for Sunday dinner.

"Okay, Eve. Keep writing your letters and numbers. We will practice the letter sounds maybe today. William, you're on the 2nd chapter of *Tom Brown's School Days*, right?"

"Yeah. I just want to do Arithmetic, though."

"You got to learn to read first—or also. Read first; then we will do some Arithmetic."

"Okay."

"Martha, will you read me some more from your poetry book when you are finished?"

"Sure, Eve. I'm glad you want to learn to read better, unlike some people."

"I want to read—I just want to do Arithmetic more."

"Let's read, William."

"Okay, here goes—"

"Anyone hungry?" Mama Harris asked as she entered the study with fresh fruit, hot sandwiches, and cool lemonade.

"Yeah!"

"William, say grace."

"Ok, mama.

"Oh Lord, I pray You make us able

"to eat everything on the table.

"And if there's anything left in the pot,

"let us get it while it's hot. Amen."

As the children devoured the lunch, Mama Harris beamed with pride. Her children working together, helping each other filled her spiritually. Especially when she thought about the times they kidded each other, sometimes going too far. Tears of joy flowed in her mind as the love of learning grew in each of her children. Starting with Bobby, her oldest, all the way down to Eve, the baby.

As the children devoured the lunch, Mama Harris beamed with pride. Her children working together, helping each other filled her spiritually. Especially when she thought about the times they kidded each other, sometimes going too far. Tears of joy flowed in her mind as the love of learning grew in each of her children. Starting with Bobby, her oldest, all the way down to Eve, the baby.

She silently prayed, *Lord, please keep the love of learning, the respect of education in all my children. Thank You for putting in Bobby the want to teach his siblings what he is learning. Especially his sisters. Thank You, Lord. . . .*

"Mama, Bobby trying to eat all the sandwiches."

"No, I'm not. I'm eating my part because I'm the oldest and the biggest. I need more food."

"You're just greedy. That's what it is."

. . . Your grace and mercy is forever. Your love for us knows no end. . . .

"And I need more food because I'm the smartest."

"Says who?"

"Anyway. All the food you eat goes to your head."

. . . Thank You for sacrificing Your Son for us. Thank You for the blessings You've given Bob and me. . . .

"You just eat too slow. You need to learn to eat with a purpose!"

"I eat like a lady."

"You need to slow down and swallow your food. If you choke on something, I might help you. After I finish your plate."

"You're not a lady—you're a girl. If you want to become a lady, you need to eat, girl!"

. . . For our children. For our home. For our life.

Fifteen minutes later, lunch was completed, and the study continued.

"Great work, Eve. I can see all your letters and numbers clearly. Now, I'm going to say a letter or number, and I want you to write it on this paper."

"Okay. Can I keep the stock?"

"No. I want you to try writing them from memory. Once we're done, you can go back and check. I'll write the letters and numbers I call on this sheet, so you will know which ones."

"Okay. Thanks for helping me, Martha."

"Sure. First letter 'E.' 'M.' 'H.' '3.' '9.' 'T.'. . . ."

"Tom's nurse was one who took into her instruction very slowly— she seemed to have two left hands and no head; and so Mrs. Brown kept her longer than usual, that she might expend her awkwardness and forgetfulness upon those who would not judge and punish her too strictly for them."

"What does that mean?"

"Remember, Daddy always say, 'Begin with what you do understand.'"

"I understand I got a left and a right hand. It says she have two left hands—and no head?"

"Okay. Which hand are you best with?"

"My left."

"Okay. But most people are right-handed."

"Yeah, and they are best with their right hand."

"Go on."

"Okay. Uh, she was uh, clumsy. Dropped things because she didn't have a right hand, a strong one. Just two left ones, two clumsy ones."

"It's more than that, though."

"Hmm, she didn't have a head. You use your head to think, so she did not think good. She wasn't smart, and she was clumsy."

"Good, William. You got a head—and a left *and* right hand. But there's more. The word 'awkward' means clumsy, and somebody who is 'forgetful' is not smart. See?"

"I think so. So, Mrs. Brown kept her there to teach her more instead of sending her out to work. That's why it said she '*took into her instruction very slowly.*' She wasn't very smart."

"Nice, William."

"Thanks."

". . . Eve, you're getting them all right. Way to go! 'S.' '5.' 'B.' 'A.' '6.'. 'V.'—"

"Is Eve still getting them right?"

"Yeah!"

"She's taking after her big brother."

"No, her second brother."

"Eve, tell these *boys* who you are taking after."

"My big sister."

"Good girl!"

"You gonna read that poem to me when we finish this? About us joining the angel train."

"*Remember Christians, Negroes, black as Cain. May be refined and join the angelic train!*" the boys said in unison.

"*Choo, choo . . . Chooooo. Halle-loooo-jah!*" they all chimed.

"You like Phyliss Wheatly, don't you?"

"Yeah. I can't wait 'til I can read her poems, myself."

"Okay. Then let's continue with letters and numbers. 'P.' 'U.' 'L.' '7.' . . ."

"Charity Lamb was her name. It had been the immemorial habit of the village, to christen children either by Bible names, or by those of cardinal and other virtues; so that one was for ever heard in the village streets, or on the green, shrill sounds of, 'Prudence! Prudence! Thee cum' out o' the gutter' or 'Mercy, drat the girl, what bist thee a doin' wi' little Faith?' And there were Ruths, Rachels, Keziahs, in every corner.

"The same for the boys; they were Benjamins, Jacobs, Noahs, Enochs. I suppose the custom has come down from Puritan times—there it is, at any rate, very strong still in the Vale."

"I understand the names from the Bible have other meanings. *Charity* means . . . means *love*. Yeah, love! So, the place they lived at named their children after people in the Bible. Maybe to make people think they are nice and love God. I wonder if any other places still do that?"

James, playing with Deeohgee while Carlton was doing school-work after supper that evening, looked back and forth between what Carlton was doing and Deeohgee. It took months before James could extend his hand toward Deeohgee without him growling, and nearly a year before he could pet him, and then, only with Carlton around. When Carlton was at school, James never saw Deeohgee. His days were spent roaming Penelope Farms chasing things that flew, crawled, and hopped.

Minutes before lights out, Carlton was in the bedroom studying, and James was there watching—and secretly learning. These were the only times Carlton allowed James to sit on the bed. During a multiplication problem, Carlton added 4 and 2, and James noticed Carlton wrote a 5.

He casually looked over at Carlton's answer and mouthed, "I would've put '6' there." Deeohgee hopped off the bed and James slid off and continued playing with him on the floor.

"What . . . did . . . you . . . say?" questioned Carlton in a tone that chilled James. He didn't turn toward Carlton, but his brain was spinning.

Uh, oh. What now? What did I do? What did I say? Oh, my God. Maybe I shouldn't have—uh, uh, think, James! Think!

"I said it should be 6—or 7, or, uh, 23, or zero. How do I know, huh?" he replied, shrugged his shoulders, and tried to laugh. "Watch this, Carlton. Roll over, boy. Roll over."

"Shut up! I'm the White one heah. You the slave," Carlton screamed as he checked for the correct answer on a separate sheet and seethed at the "6" staring back at him. He jumped off the bed, towered over James and shouted, "A nigger will never be able to tell a White man anything! I'll have my daddy sell yo' ass!"

He went on a 10-minute tirade, his face flushing into an emotional crimson and his voice cracking under the strain of his screams and yells.

James was scared, confused, and thinking hard.

Carlton has gotten upset before. But this, this is different. Why would anyone not want to know the truth? Why is he so mad? What's wrong with what I did? What's wrong with what I said? Ruth told me. She told me. Be careful—that's what she said! Be careful, James! I messed up. How did I let that slip?

"Carlton, I—I was just playing with you. That's all. I don't understand what was wrong with—" James said, as he started to stand up.

"*Shut up, you nigger!* White people are better than y'all!" Carlton screamed as he pushed James down. "Hell, y'all ain't even real people! I don't want to hear shit like that out yo' mouth again, you heah!"

James, looking up from his prostrate position, nodded in fear without uttering a word, sensing saying anything would be the wrong thing to say.

♣

". . . James, darlin'. That's what I was tellin' you 'bout watchin' what you say! I don't know, darlin'—just keep doin' whatcha' doin', I reckon. I don't know, James," Ruth said the following morning, after Carlton had gone to school.

"I'm sorry, Ruth. I should've listened. I'm sorry, Ruth."

"It's okay, darlin'."

"N—No, it ain't. He mad, Ruth. He real mad!" And, and Master Johnson told me, he say 'don't get my boy mad."

"It gonna be okay. Just be sho' you where he want you. And act good!"

"I'm scared, Ruth. What are they going to do to me, Ruth? Huh? They going to let them boys beat me up again? Huh, Ruth? They not going to let me eat for days, huh? Is Carlton going to beat me up, again?" James asked as he moved around the table to get a glance at Ruth's face, who kept turning it away from him.

"I—I, uh, James, darlin'—I don't know. Don't worry 'bout that now. Jest be careful. And watch what you *say*!"

"What you mean, Ruth? You know something. Why won't you tell me? Huh, Ruth. Why won't you look at me? Ruth? . . ."

♣

Dong! Dong! Dong! Dong!

"Please, God. Don't let Carlton be mad at me. Don't let him beat me up again," James prayed. He sat on the carpet, not daring to even touch the bed anymore.

The Arithmetic incident a week earlier had become a turning point in their relationship. Carlton, more abusive toward James, stopped using his name. "Boy," "stupid," and "nigger" became

80

his preferred terms of revilement. Any demeaning thing he could think of doing, like cleaning his boots with James' clothes before he was to put them on, he did.

". . . When he ask me a question, I gotta answer wrong enough times to make him think I'm guessing. He got to think I don't know the answer, not that I'm lying. That would really get him mad—"

James froze in mid-sentence as he noticed Carlton's footfalls and Deeohgee's huffing as they came up the stairs. James inhaled fully and exhaled slowly.

Please, God. Please don't let him be mad at me no more. And no more hitting me. It hurts! Please, God, don't let—

"Hey, Carlton," James cheerfully replied as Carlton entered, followed by his dog.

"Hey, boy."

♣

A month after the incident, James' desire to read, coupled with his passion to learn, led him back to the study. He'd become enthralled with the adventures and journeys the stories took him on, relieving a lonely boy of a monotonous and mundane existence. He developed daily plans and was comfortable returning to the schedule.

See Carlton off. Watch Deeohgee run out of sight chasing Carlton's wagon. Listen to Master Johnson's plans. Eat with Ruth. Complete the chores she gave him. Then head off for his own travels to places and times. And with his invaluable translator and tutor, Webster, the adventures opened up even more. This led him back to the study like a moth to a flame.

". . . *Ordinance. A decree or direction, or an order.* **Ordinary.** *Regular or customary condition of things.* **Ordinate.** *Measuring the y-axis.* Arithmetic and Algebra stuff—I like that. **Ordination.** *To be ordained. To be a preacher.* **Ordnance.** *Military supplies, including weapons.* Don't confuse it with "ordinance." **Ordonnance.**

Uh, uh—disposition of the parts with regard to one another and the *whole*—whatever that means. Anyway, back to 'longevity,' then grab my new book," he mumbled as he returned the dictionary to the proper page.

Grasping a thick book from the shelf, he settled into Master Johnson's chair and slowly rocked back and forth in it, the heels of his feet on the floor serving as the pivot point. He read:

"I Am Born. Whether I shall turn out to be the hero of my own life, or whether that station will be held by anybody else, these pages must show. To begin my life with the beginning of my life, I record that I was born (as I have been informed and believe) on a Friday, at twelve o'clock at night. It was remarked that the clock began to strike, and I began to cry, simultaneously.

"In consideration of the day and hour of my birth, it was declared by the nurse, and by some sage women in the neighbourhood who had taken a lively interest in me several months before there was any possibility of our becoming personally acquainted, first, that I was destined to be unlucky in life; and secondly, that I was privileged to see ghosts and spirits; both these gifts inevitably attaching, as they believed, to all unlucky infants of either gender, born towards the small hours on a Friday night.

"I wonder what day I was born? He was destined to be unlucky in life? Are we—slaves—destined to be slaves? Nah, the only ghost I believe in is the Holy Ghost. Yeah. Anyway . . ."

"I need say nothing here, on the first head, because nothing can show better than my history whether that prediction was verified or falsified by the result. . . ."

CHAPTER 11

"I think it's time I show you a special part of Penelope Farms. C'mon, boy. I'll race ya'," Carlton said one Saturday morning, and James compliantly followed.

Unlike when he first arrived, James easily kept up with Carlton now. He always allowed Carlton to win, though. They regularly raced to the orchards and back, and all through the house. This time, they were going in a new direction.

Usually, they would scamper out of Johnson Hall, leap off the porch, take two quick lefts, and dash to the orchards. This morning they kept straight after jumping off the porch, crossed the dirt road that had initially brought James to Johnson Hall and which Carlton followed out each morning, and approached the stand of slender oaks and associated underbrush. Having to zigzag through the forest of leaning oak trees and calf-high shrubs that were spaced so you couldn't take more than five steps without changing directions, James tripped several times over protruding roots. He would lay sprawled on the ground, only to be helped up by a grinning Carlton.

Good. At least he is happy today. I'm glad of that.

They finally emerged on the other side of the forest, and a new world for James came into view.

"Okay, we heah. Watch this," Carlton said, still huffing, puffing—and grinning.

James caught his breath as he looked around the fields of Penelope Farms that were usually blocked from his vision by the stand of slender oaks. The first thing he noticed was the emotions of the twenty people there as he and Carlton slowly walked through the crowd of sobbing slaves. The second thing he noticed was a massive oak tree with multiple far-reaching limbs that created a 100-foot canopy. The limbs were 10 feet off the ground and more than five feet in diameter. The ground immediately surrounding the 30-foot trunk with its knobby bark gradually rose up several feet to the tree's base. Moss hung from many of the limbs.

The final thing James noticed was two straps hanging from a pair of limbs. And an adult male, *sans* shirt, shackled to one.

What—what's going on? I don't under—who—what is happening? Why is he tied like that? Who is he? Why—but, who, why . . .

In a cold tone, Carlton whispered, "This boy name is Jacob. He tried to run away. This what we do to niggers who try to run."

As one of Stanley's men uncoiled a 15-foot-long leather whip, minutes slowed to moments in James' mind. He gazed at the macabre scene. He listened to the cries coming from those who looked like him. He observed the caustic casualness of those who didn't look like him. He felt the evil in the smirk on the face of Carlton as their eyes met.

Stanley said something about not running and working hard, but James' focus, once he broke free of Carlton's glare, was on the man with the leather whip.

What, what is he going to do with . . .

Stanley stopped talking and motioned to the man. He uncoiled the whip and reared back, his right arm fully extended. Then, as a grunt escaped, he came forward with the whip *whooshing* in the air. Finally, it crashed into Jacob's back with a sickening *pow*. His screams drowned out the crowd's screams but increased their anguish as James' body twitched once and then went numb.

Wh-wh-whup? Th-th-that's—whup. Whip. Wh-wh-whup. Oh, my God. Wh-wh-whup! Oh, my God! Why, God!? Why!? . . .

James thought Jacob would die right where he hung. He never imagined a human being would be treated like this. He shuddered at the sheer inhumanity of it—whipping a human like a beast. This seared an indelible mark into James' psyche.

The sounds of the leather whip crashing onto Jacob. The looks on the faces of the slaves, who were forced to watch. The cries of pain from Jacob. The pungent aroma of tobacco plants. They all became part of James' memories, soon to reside in his dreams—and nightmares.

Especially the sounds. The *"grunt"* of Ellis as he drew back. The *"whoosh"* as the whip cut through the air. The *"pow"* as it exploded on Jacob's back. And his screams, those terrible screams. All this, amid a background of wails, sobs, and cries, would keep him up late at night and wake him up many mornings before dawn for months to come.

"This how slaves git treated. They git whupped. And *you* my slave, you heah. I can have you whupped any time I feel like it. You heah?"

James, saying nothing, turned and saw a sobbing Jacob cut down and carried off—ten lashes later.

Wait. . . . But—but there's two! Two straps. Oh, my God—no. Not me. Carlton, please—no! Not me!

"Anytime I'se feels like it. That can happen to you."

Carlton, please no. Not me. Don't—don't whup me, please. Please don't whip me. Please . . .

"Whatcha' thank of that? Huh? You mine. As long as you do what I say, that won't happen to you. C'mon. I'll race ya'."

. . . Wh-wh-whup. Th-th-that's—whup. Whip. Wh-wh-whup. Oh, my God. Please, God. I don't wanna get wh-wh-whupped! Oh, my God! . . .

James kept up with, but didn't overtake, Carlton. The knowledge of that vile word reverberated with each stride. For the first time, James understood just how precarious this "relationship" with Carlton was. How one misstep—or overstep—could be disastrous. For the first time, he had the fullness of Webster's definition of slavery.

. . . Wh-wh-whup. Th-th-that's—whup. Whip. Wh-wh-whup. Oh—my—God. Wh-wh-whup! Oh—my God! . . .

❧

85

. . . whup . . . slavery . . . whup . . . chattel . . . whup . . . servitude . . . whup . . . property . . . whup . . . citizen . . . whup . . . grunt . . . whoosh . . . pow . . .

Scores of sleepless moments later, James still struggled with the assault on his well-being. Going into the study, the place that had been his refuge from his miserable existence, now terrified him. The memory of that day—those sights and sounds sickened him and made his situation worse than he ever imagined.

. . . whup . . . slavery . . . whup . . . chattel . . . whup . . . servitude . . . whup . . . property . . . whup . . . citizen . . . whup . . . grunt . . . whoosh . . . pow . . .

"Watch that pot, James! You gotta stir it, darlin'. You gonna burn that food," Ruth warned as she was alerted with the smell of scorched broth.

. . . whup . . . slavery . . . whup . . . chattel . . . whup . . . servitude . . . whup . . . property . . . whup . . . citizen . . . whup . . . grunt . . . whoosh . . . pow . . .

"Okay. I'm sorry."

"Boy, where yo' mind at today?"

"Uh—right here, Ruth," James replied as he pointed to his head without emotion.

. . . whup . . . slavery . . . whup . . . chattel . . . whup . . . servitude . . . whup . . . property . . . whup . . . citizen . . . whup . . . grunt . . . whoosh . . . pow . . .

Laughing, she said, "Boy, sometimes you say the funniest thangs. No, darlin'. I mean, what's wrong, James? What's wrong with you?"

"Uh—Ruth, I, uh, I—"

Dong! Dong! Dong!

"Uh, Ruth—I, I—" he stammered.

The words choked off as he rocked back and forth with his head bowed. Ruth looked over when he didn't answer. He tried to speak again, but only wails came out.

Concern flushed across her face, and she rushed over to him. Grabbing the ladle he'd been using to stir the broth, she pulled him into the comfort of her bosom, muffling his sobs. She looked down upon him with a confused stare as she rocked him gently and stirred the pot slowly.

"James, darlin', what is it? It gonna be okay. Whatever it is, it's gonna be okay, darlin'," she said, offering him comfort he never accepted. "Listen, darlin'. Let 'ol Ruth get this here pot off the stove, and then we can sit down and talk 'bout what ails ya'."

James remained motionless; his head remained bowed as she released him and moved the large, black kettle away from the open flame. She grabbed his hand and led him to a chair, sat down, and placed him on her lap.

"Oh, darlin', you gettin' a lil' too big for 'ol Ruth here, but that's okay. Now, what's ailin' you, darlin'?"

James, still struggling with his emotions, opened his mouth and uttered, "Ruth—uh, I saw a man get—uh, *whupped* today, uh, I mean yesterday, I mean. I mean whipped, uh, I mean. Is that what happened to them—them boys?"

The day Ruth knew would come—but prayed would never come—had arrived. And her powerlessness to ease James' pain shattered her heart into enough pieces to give every African who had ever been a slave, three.

"Oh, Lord, no! Oh, no!" she screamed, her voice rife with pain and terror and sympathy and compassion and remorse. For 30 minutes, rocking back and forth in the creaking chair, they cried together.

"James. Darlin'—he didn't—he didn't, uh—whup you, did he?" she hesitantly asked, fearful of the answer.

James shook his head "No."

Ruth exhaled in relief. Her next inhale alerted her that James was losing control of his bodily functions.

"Darlin', you didn't know. Darlin'—you didn't. But, yeah, I reckon that's what happened to them boys," Ruth reluctantly answered as she tried to console a disconsolate James. Even her mighty, magical hugs didn't help.

"Baby, we gone git through this here. We all is. You got to be strong. We got to be strong, darlin'! We got to be—"

Dong! Dong! Dong! Dong!

"Uh, I got to go, Ruth. C-C-Carlton be home soon."

"I know, darlin', I know. Clean up yo'self. That'll be jest one mo' thing fo' Carlton to get mad at."

"I been doing that—this—a lot lately. He thinks it's funny. He laugh at it—and me."

"It will get better, darlin'. We will get it better."

James wiped his face with his sleeves, but the tears only spread. Ruth handed him a towel, and the stains and wetness disappeared, but the anguish remained. She hugged him once more, released him, and watched him trudge out of the kitchen and out of her sight. Then she exploded into a torrent of tears and wails.

♣

"Ha, ha, James. I gits to whup yo' ass, now, boy!" screamed Carlton. A 10-foot-long whip dangled from his hands; a wickedly, sinister smile curled his lips.

"Carlton—no! *Why?* I was good, Carlton. I did what you told me to do. Why you doing this? Why, Carlton? Why?" James yelled as he twisted and turned, his hands extending upward and shackled to a strap hanging from the whipping tree. The cuts in his wrists deepened each time he tried to run away, only to be snatched back.

Snapping the whip, Carlton continued sneering at the squirming James and replied, "Why? 'Cause I can! Ha, ha, ha, ha, ha. "'Cause I can! I'm yo' massah. . . ."

"No, Carlton. Please—no! . . ."

James turned over, mumbling, in the darkness of the early morning hours, soaked with sweat and tears.

A dream—it—it was, uh, it was a dream. A nightmare.

As he caught his breath, he rolled over, looked up, and noticed Deeohgee looking down at him.

I wonder if he'll ever whip Deeohgee. I wonder. And—and—oh, my God. What about me? Who am I? What can I do? I—I don't want to get—oh, my God! . . .

Dong! Dong!

❧

In the study again, James prepared to continue his journey through Webster as he attempted to make sense of his nonsensical reality. James tried his best to manage this situation he was a prisoner to. An insane system, giving authority to profane people, who perpetrated inhumane acts on God's creation. His growth over the past weeks had stripped him of his innocence, crushed his comfort, and brought him knowledge of terrible life lessons.

He pondered the words of King Solomon, *"To know wisdom and instruction; . . . to have the fear of the Lord is the beginning of knowledge."*

Yeah, Solomon—but you were a king. You were never a slave. Getting knowledge hurts. It hurts so much . . . so much . . .

The knowledge of living in another reality apart from the others who looked like him. The knowledge of another part of Penelope Farms that existed mere yards away from Johnson Hall, but miles away in evil savagery. The knowledge that his owner, Carlton Johnson, at any time and for any reason, could subject him to this barbaric cruelty. The knowledge that he may have caused someone to suffer this indignation. The knowledge that all knowledge isn't pleasant—or sought—but is necessary for growth.

The certainty of physical violations and the severe consequences of getting caught were clear. His escapes through the literature and the worlds they created were lessened. His joy from the learning was subdued.

But the seed to seek knowledge that Ruth had deposited—though latent—remained. Like a siren's song, it sang a tune of hope, of possibilities, of adventure, of a future far away from his present. Despite his fear, the seed summoned him back to the study time and time again. James' passion for learning remained steadfast, unmovable, and always abounding just below the surface.

In an existence where he had no control, escaping for moments through literature gave him fleeting solace. He accepted the risk, willingly took the journeys, and reveled in the modicum of relief they offered where nothing else existed.

"... *Whisper*. Talk softly. *Whistle*. Make a sound by blowing air out your mouth. *Whistler*. Uh—one that whistles, like many birds. *Whistle-stop*. A small train station. *Whit*. Uh, uh—the smallest part or particle imaginable. *White*. Huh—people! It should say mean, evil, hurtful, hateful, nasty . . ."

☘

Dong! Dong! Dong! Dong! Dong! Dong! Dong! Dong! Dong! Dong!
"Time for bed I guess, huh, Carlton," James said.

He closed the door and walked across the room to the flickering lamp. Carlton quietly lay on his back in the bed as he had been since supper. He stared at the ceiling as slight, intermittent movements of his body, barely audible sighs, and the slow rise and fall of his chest offered the only proof he was alive.

Carlton still wants me around. We still play, and I still don't go out into the fields. Or get—get uh, whipped. God, please—I hope I don't. Please, God—I hope. I guess we both are lonely. And now we're both alone.

As long as I do what Carlton wants, all is good, I guess. Okay, so I'll be with Carlton until he goes to school. If the Massah stays home, I'll stay with Ruth for the day. If he left—and make sure he's gone, James!—then I'll be in the study. No matter what I do, I got to make sure to be waiting for Carlton when he gets home. I got to be waiting for him. Before he gets home.

James bent slightly at his waist and blew in the darkness; then he walked to the rug on the floor. He stood there for a moment while his eyes adjusted to the darkness. Slowly, Carlton came back into view, in the same position he had been in all night. James struggled with what to say next.

"Goodnight, Carlton," he hesitantly uttered.

"Night," Carlton replied through the shadows with a sigh.

"I'm—I'm sorry about Deeohgee."

"Yeah. Thanks. He was with me forever. Forever!"

"Ruth say we all got to go sometime."

"Yeah. I—I 'member when momma and daddy got him fo' me. He was mostly black then. He got black and white later. When he got older and stuff. He was wit me forever. Forever!" Carlton muttered with a sniffle and began crying again. James lay down on the rug without saying another word.

God. Bless me and Ruth. And slaves everywhere. And God, bless Carlton, because his dog died. Amen.

Ruth's room was bordered by the kitchen and the dining room. Closed in with no windows, it was the same size as Carlton's bedroom, but appeared larger because of a lack of furniture. There was a small bed, barely large enough for her, and a lamp on the floor next to it. A door along the back wall opened into a closet, where she kept her clothes. While most of Ruth's days were filled with work to do, there were occasional days, like this day, that offered time for relaxation.

"It's been good, Ruth. He don't seem to be mad anymore—at least not *as* mad," James said as he walked around the room, gawking from floor to ceiling and back.

"I'm sho' glad, darlin'. I wuz sho' 'nuff worried 'bout you."

"Yeah, me, too. Ruth, if Carlton let me, I'd like to stay in your room some nights."

Ruth sat on the edge of her bed as James approached the lantern. He stooped down, admired it for an instant, and then picked it up.

"Want me to light this for you?" he jokingly asked.

"Nah, darlin'. Why would I want it lit so soon?" she asked before she noticed his grin. "What's so funny 'bout that?"

"It's just Carlton been making me do it since I been here. I got experience," he replied with another giggle as he sat the lantern down.

Ruth shrugged her shoulders and began rubbing her legs.

"So, Ruth. You gonna let me stay here with you sometimes?"

"Nah, you wouldn't want to sleep here."

"Uh, huh. I could go get a snack fast—hee, hee. Ruth, what's this door for?" he asked as he peered into the closet and noticed a door inside.

"Get outta there!" she exclaimed as she leaned forward and gave him a stern look.

"Yes, ma'am. But yeah, if Carlton let me. Why don't you—"

Dong! Dong! Dong!

"Why don't you want me to?"

"I'm going to the kitchen. Help me up, darlin'."

"Yes, ma'am."

Rustling paper, rants, and retorts were the sounds prevalent as Master Johnson, behind his desk, was engrossed in the business of Penelope Farms. Physically 5 feet in front of his father, Carlton might as well have been 50 miles away. He paced back and forth as he ranted and pleaded from the other side of the desk.

"I don't know why I gotta go so far. There's a good school right on the coast, daddy. Three of the boys from school are goin' theah."

Barely looking up, Master Johnson replied, with an accompanying hand gesture, "This a fine school. A good bitness school I'm sending you to. So, you can come back and run all this heah."

"But it's so far. I won't be able to git home much. I don't know nobody theah. Shoot—it's—it's too far! And, and it's in the nawth, of all places! They make me sick!"

"Son, you nevah met no Nawtherners in yo' life."

"No, but you tolt me enough 'bout them for me to know I hate them. And, and—"

"Well—yeah. I 'member what I tolt you 'bout them. But sometimes you gotta get to know yo' enemies. I read somewhere some Chinaman said that. I still don't know what they be thinkin', these Nawtherners. Maybe you can find out fo' me, huh. Another good reason fo' me to send you."

"But it's so far. I won't see you fo' a long time."

"Yeah. It's a little bit from heah. In the summer maybe. You can come home then. Jest git the education, son. Like I said, it a good bitness school. One of the best in the country. That mean it's good fo' you *and* me."

"But I can get that here. And I won't have to go so far."

"College ain't jest for the schooling, son. You'll meet folks. Maybe even a wife, huh. Make contacts. That's how I got wheah I'm at today. Sheffield, ovah in Fredrick County. A commissioner in B'more. Even yo' mama—met 'em all in college. She the reason I'm here. Had planned on goin' back to Alabama after graduation. Yo' mama didn't want to. I picked heah 'cause this area is called 'Montgomery County,' like the Alabama town. I found the right one fo' me. You can find the right one, too," he replied as he finally glanced at Carlton.

"So, you will be okay if I find a Nawtherner gal to marry—to bring back to all this heah?"

"Iff'n you can get her thinkin' right. School her on the right way, the only way—our way. Then, yeah. Jest make sho' she know what's right."

"But dad—" Carlton began, his eyes filled with disappointment and apprehension.

Dong! Dong! Dong! Dong! Dong! Dong!

"But daddy, I don't wanna go. I gone—I gone miss you."

The face on the opposite of the desk stared at him with growing consternation.

"Uh—uh—okay, daddy."

Master Johnson grunted, nodded, and continued his paperwork.

"Daddy, did you heah me? I said—"

"Yeah, I heard ya'. I'll miss you, too. I'm gone send James over to the Barksdales. As a houseboy."

"Huh? Why?"

"Why? Why not? He been yo' buddy. He ain't caused you no trouble. He been good for you and—"

"Well—uh, daddy. I didn't wanna say nothin' 'cause I—I ain't got nobody else heah. But, uh, James, he been readin', well, *tryin'* to read my books."

Master Johnson stopped what he was doing and looked into his son's eyes. Carlton finally had his full attention, and the look of concern he'd craved. The genuine care and acknowledgment from his father for the first time in years warmed his spirit.

"Take a breath in, Carlton. Relax, son. This important. Now then, tell me, why you say that?"

"Uh—he, he said some words that are only in my books. And he been saying some Arithmetic stuff."

"*James! Stanley!*" yelled Master Johnson toward the door. Then he turned back to his son and asked, "Why didn't you say something befo' now?"

"I'm sorry, daddy. I—I didn't have nobody else. Don't be mad at me."

"I'm not mad at you, but you should've told me. *Stanley! James!*"

"When I caught 'im—I know, daddy. But I—I didn't have no one else, and—"

"It's okay, son. *James! Stanley!* Jest don't keep stuff like this from me a'gin."

♣

James, sitting in Carlton's room reading the Bible, jumped up. As he headed for the door, he tripped on the rug and tumbled. He rose and noticed his reflection in the mirror, and he giggled. He waved at the reflection, straightened out his clothes, and ran out toward the study.

♣

Stanley, who had been relaxing from a long day, was finally dressed. He headed up the stairwell, his halted breaths growing deeper with each step.

♣

James eyed Stanley arriving at the landing, huffing mightily, waved at him, and then entered the study.

"Yassuh, Massah Johnson, suh."

Master Johnson snapped his attention away from Carlton to James—and stared with intense anger.

"I'm really disappointed in you, boy. What the hell was you thinkin'?"

James cut his eyes slightly over at Carlton, who was standing near the newspaper table with an evil grin. Then he cautiously looked back toward Master Johnson with his head bowed.

What? What is he talking about? Oh, no—Webster! He knows about Webster! Oh, God—how did he find out?

"I—I—What you mean, Massah Johnson, suh?"

"Don't you try that 'suh' shit! *Stanley!*"

"You think you some smart-ass nigger, huh?" Carlton exploded with feigned anger. "You ain't foolin' nobody!"

Suddenly, Master Johnson stood and slammed his fist on the desk, causing the glass decanter set to shake and tingle against each other. He then deliberately walked around the desk and toward James, slowly inhaling deeply and exhaling slowly.

"Reading the Bible. That's what I let y'all do. *Stanley—get yo' ass in heah!* Jest read the goddamn Bible! But no, you wanted mo'. Didn't ya', huh? Didn't ya'! *Stanley—wheah the hell you at?*"

Now right up and towering over a trembling James, Master Johnson forcibly grabbed him by the arm, shook him and screamed, "Huh! Didn't ya?"

"I told you not to read my books, but you did anyhow. You ain't so smart now, is ya'?" Carlton added as he strode toward James from the opposite side.

"*Stanley!* Well say somethin', goddammit!" Master Johnson screamed as he continued shaking James.

Confused at first, James quickly realized he didn't have all the answers—or many of the questions.

What? Carlton's books? He lets me. Webster? What do they know? At least they don't know about me reading Webster those times—I think? Help me, God. What to say? Huh, what not to say! Help me, God. Help me, please.

"Massah Johnson, I don't understand, suh—"

"*Shut up!*" Master Johnson barked as he knocked James down with a backhand. "I was gonna sell you to a family as a houseboy. So you could stay out the fields. Not now, though. Yo' ass goin' to the fields, fo' sho'. You gone work—and make me some money. *Stanley!*"

"Whup 'im, daddy. Whup 'im, too," chided Carlton as he kicked the sprawled James. "You ain't so smart now, is ya'?"

Finally making it to the study, Stanley said between huffs and puffs, "Yes—sir, Mr.—Mr. Johnson, sir?"

"Take this boy out to the shacks! He don't stay heah no mo'. Give 'im a hello whuppin', too," commanded Master Johnson.

"*Huh? Nooooo!*" screamed James as he tried to crawl away from Stanley.

"Yes, sir, Mr. Johnson. C'mon, boy," Stanley replied, grabbing James at first by the leg and then by the shirt.

"*Noooooo! Noooooo!*"

Why is Carlton doing this? Wake up, James! Wake up! Oh, please God, let me wake up! Quick!

The stout Stanley picked up the kicking and screaming James and put him on his shoulders, like he did the sacks of flour that were routinely delivered to Johnson Hall. Carlton rushed to the door, opened it, and kicked at James as Stanley carried him out.

"Let me go—please! No—no! Ruth! Ruth, help me!"

Stanley carried James down the spiral stairs and toward the door. A giggling Carlton ran past them and opened that door as well.

"I gone enjoy this heah, James."

"Ruth! Ruth, help me!"

"I'll go get Ruth for ya', like uh, nevah!"

Stanley struggled maintaining his balance with the squirming James in constant motion. As they began going through the slender oaks, James grabbed one of the oak tree branches, slid off Stanley's shoulders, and hit the ground face first with a thud. Immediately, he crawled to the nearest tree and hugged it with all his might.

"No, Mr. Stanley, suh. I'll be good, I will! I'll be good. I'll be good!" I—won't do—I won't do whatever I did. I promise. I'll be good."

Stanley turned around with a look of frustration. He grabbed James by the feet and snatched him away from the tree trunk. James began to violently kick, one of them striking Stanley below his belt, which caused him to release James and crumple to his knees.

James quickly got to his feet and ran away from Stanley as fast as his fear would allow him. Alternating looking behind him to see if Stanley was closing in and ahead to dodge the slender oaks, James was feeling some relief until he crashed into Mitch, who backhanded James and sent him sprawling to the ground. He looked up and was met with Mitch's boot to his face—and several more to his torso—until Stanley caught up.

"Mitch! Stop!"

Stanley pulled Mitch back and shoved him to the ground. "Don't do that boy like that! I don't ever wanna see anything like that again!"

Stanley looked over at James, who was trying desperately to catch his breath and make it to his feet.

"C'mon, boy. Let's go," he said, and, with a mighty yank, he was again dragging James toward his destiny.

Please, God. Please help me. Tell Ruth—tell her to come get me. Please, God . . .

They emerged from the forest, and Mitch, standing by the whipping tree, lowered one of the straps. The catcalls and laughter of Carlton and the grins, grimaces, and glances of some of the slaves as James was dragged, heightened his terror.

"Oh, God, no! Please don't! Please! Mi—Mi—Mister Stanley. P—P—Please don't! Mr. Stanley, please—please don't! God, wake me up—please!"

"Hah. You is awake, James! You *wide* awake!"

"Mi—Mister Stanley. Please don't. Please!"

"How ya' like being a slave, boy? You no mo' my slave. You my daddy slave, now!"

James struggled and pleaded as the shackles were clamped around his scraped wrists and arms.

". . . P—P—Please don't! Mr. Stanley, please—please don't!"

Once secured, Stanley released James from the neck hold. He walked several yards behind him and took a ten-foot whip from Smitty. Carlton walked around to face James. The wicked joy in his eyes heightened James' torment.

"James, James, James! You gone get it now, boy. We gone have fun, now! I gone like this heah! You gone get whupped, good."

"No—no! God, please—no," James whimpered.

His voice became lower and weaker. As he spun around, Carlton matched his moves step for step to remain in his field of vision. His flood of tears blurred the scenery.

Stanley hesitated delivering the first lash as James spun and faced him head on. "I'm gonna hurt that boy. Smit—Mitch. Untie him and put him up against the tree. And hold him there."

"No—no! Please, God—no! I didn't—I didn't do nothing! Please—uh, Mister, Mister Stanley—uh, suh. Please, I didn't . . ."

Mitch grabbed hold of the squirming James, and Smitty unshackled him. Together, they pulled him, hands flailing and feet kicking, into the massive tree trunk. Another pair of shackles attached to rope was connected to the trunk through a metal ring. They pulled the rope tighter so James was pressed against the tree trunk. He squirmed and turned his head to the left and right, which scratched his face and chest.

"No—oh, God, no! Please—suh, no! No, you can't—you can't do this! Carlton, stop him! Carlton! I'll be good. Talk—tell him to stop, Carlton! Please!"

"You want me to stop this, James! Ha! You must be dreamin'! Oh, I forgot. You *wide* awake."

The tingling pain emanating from his cheeks was overwhelmed by the audibly horrific memories of Jacob that attacked his senses, senses he began to question the reality of.

This can't be real. I must be dreaming. Yeah, I am dreaming. I didn't do anything to—to get whipped. I'm gonna wake up. Yeah, pretty soon, I'll wake up on the floor in the bedroom. Yeah, this can't be real. Yeah, like Carlton said before. A—a nightmare. Uh, huh, as long as it don't get you. Yeah, that's what this is. . . .

Then he heard the *"grunt"* of Stanley as he reared back with the whip.

James, you're dreaming. This won't hurt. You will just wake up screaming again. That's all.

The *"whoosh"* of the leather as it cut through the air reached his ears.

Yeah, you just remembering Jacob. You're having a dream about Jacob. Yeah, that's it. You gonna wake up soo—

The diabolical reality exploded upon him as the *"pow"* of the whip crashing into his back took everything but the life out of him.

"Aaaarrrrrgggghhh!!!"

The scream scared him, until he realized it was his scream. Those terrible sounds were coming out of his mouth, and then he was awash with sadness. His screams, the screams of a 13-year-old boy in searing, unfathomable-unless-you've-been-there pain, filled the area as Carlton continued his torment. Then the vile sounds repeated.

Grunt—whoosh—pow!
"Aaaarrrrrgggghhh!!!"
Grunt—whoosh—pow!
"Aaaarrrrrgggghhh!!!"
Please, God. Tell Ruth. Please.
Grunt—whoosh—pow!
"Aaaarrrrrgggghhh!!!"

Glimpsing a smiling Carlton, who was still in position to maintain eye contact, James writhed and moaned in pain as Smitty and Mitch held him up, his legs having given up the battle two lashes before.

Pressed up against the knobby oak trunk, James whispered a prayer, "God, help me. Get Ruth. Please, tell her to come get me. Plee—"

Grunt—whoosh—pow!

"Aaaarrrrrggghhh!!!"

♣

The crowd dispersed while Carlton skipped back through the slender oaks and on to Johnson Hall. Mitch, with an angry grip on his arm, led a crying and limping James off in the opposite direction to be cleaned and bandaged. The Hospital Shack, a depressingly gray building used to be, like most of the buildings on this side of Penelope Farms, a horse stable. They entered, and the bustle of the workers, the moaning of the injured, and the crying of several babies filled the room.

I—ugh, I wonder if Ruth even know—uh, yet? Somebody gonna tell—ugh, uh, tell her. I—I know it. They got—ugh—they got to!

Mitch sat him on a bench and stared at him for a moment. He got face to face and uttered, "Don't you get no fool idea to run, boy. Stanley won't be there next time to save yo' ass." Then he thrust a finger into James' forehead and walked away.

He screamed in agony as a woman peeled the shirt off his welted back. The sting of the medicine she administered paled in comparison to the whips, which were creating scars in a deep, permanent place.

"I think he be okay, Miss Netty," she said as she glanced over her shoulder. "Ain't no skin broke."

"Okay, then," came a voice from across the room, "bandage him up fo' me. I'll be back d'rectly."

101

Miss Netty? Miss—ugh, uh—Netty! I remember Ruth talking about her. Maybe she—ugh—she can tell Ruth to come—uh, ugh—to come and get—get me. That's probably where she is going now. Yeah, I know she will. She'll come.

He turned in time to see several women leaving but couldn't determine which one was Netty.

Yeah. When—when I see Miss Netty, she'll tell Ruth to come— ugh—to come get me. Yeah. She'll tell her. . . .

It was night before James left for his new home. Carlton's soft, comfortable cotton shirt had been replaced with a rough-textured pullover without sleeves, which irritated his skin as well as the lacerations.

"Master Carlton wants his pants back, too. I'll be by in the mornin' to get 'em," Mitch said as they walked in the dusk. James, now barefoot, stepped carefully and never replied. They passed several gray buildings as James began to feel he was in another place, or another country, if not another time altogether.

They entered one of the buildings; Mitch pointed at a cot and said, "This 'un yours, boy," and then he left.

James heard conversation as they approached the building, but silence now filled the room. He limped over to his cot and stood by it, looking out at a dusk-filled room full of young men avoiding eye contact.

As the moonless night approached, James couldn't tell the color of the walls. The pungent smell was nauseating, and James had trouble breathing or swallowing. It was the deafening silence that worried him, though, and James felt it was because of him.

I—I wonder—if, if them boys in here? God, please don't let them—please tell Ruth to come and get me. Send her here!

Slowly, conversations returned, though no one spoke to or looked at James. As his eyes adjusted to the surroundings, he noticed all were boys his age or slightly older. Their sizes were varied, though, from less than 5 feet to nearly 6 feet tall and 200 or more pounds. James sat down on the cot and was immediately reminded of the whipping. His back ached, so he lay down on his stomach, thought about Ruth, and dozed off.

CHAPTER 13

James awoke to heavy breathing and a pounding heart. He jumped to his feet, blinked several times, and looked around, trying desperately to orient himself. He eyed the single bed, with its flowered spread, the dresser with its lantern that he blew out nightly, the robin's-egg-blue walls, and then he looked down toward the mat he slept on, balled up in a haphazard heap.

"A—a dream. It *was* a dream! Thank You, God!" he exclaimed as he clapped his palms together and raised his face heavenward.

The giddy little boy shot out of the room, rushed down the hall, bounded the stairs in two strides, and landed on one of the throw rugs. He slid for a moment but lost his balance and landed on his back. Laughing even harder, he got up and ran into the kitchen to see Ruth.

"Ruth! Ruth! I had the craziest dream ever!" he exclaimed as he eyed her standing over the stove with her back to him. "I had a dream I got—" he added; then he paused, looked around, and whispered, "whupped!"

"Huh—oh, yeah," she replied without turning around. He giggled as he walked over to a pot near her. "Yeah, Ruth. That was one crazy dream I had last night," James said as he slowly stirred the pot of stew beef, its aroma assuaging his soul.

"Uh, huh. Musta been some kinda dream, darlin'," she replied as she kneaded dough with her powerful hands.

"Yeah—when, when Massah Johnson said, 'Give him a hello whuppin',' I cried—no I *screamed* NO! Just like that—I screamed *loud*! NO!" James said and then giggled again. "I'm surprised you didn't hear me, I screamed so loud and—ow!"

"What wrong, darlin'?"

"I don't know," James replied. My—my back kinda hurt. I fell on it when I came downstairs and slipped on the rug."

"I'll take a look at it when I'm done here. Anyways, I musta been in the orchards, not to hear ya' screamin' like that, darlin'."

"Yeah. Uh, Ruth. You ever been whupped?"

She stopped kneading the dough and stared straight ahead. She slowly rocked from side to side until she finally uttered, "James, darlin'. You—uh, you never forgets somethin' like that. Yeah. I been whupped. Fo' diff'rent reasons."

"Huh? Why—*ow*! Uh, why, uh—what reason can they have for whupping anybody? *Ow*, my back!" James replied as a sharp pain streaked down his back. He dropped the spoon, grabbed Ruth's arm for balance, and spun her toward him. The pain shot through him again. Only then did he notice Ruth's brown skin tinged in red, her face glistening with tears.

"Why you—*ow*! Uh, why you crying, Ruth?"

She stood there trying to catch her breath as the wails became audible, and fluids flowed from her eyes, nose, and mouth. "J—J— James, darlin'. I—I'm so sorry, darlin'. I'm so . . ."

"Ruth? What? Why are you crying? *Ow!*" James asked as the pain shot through his body again. He shut his eyes tight to control the pain and then opened his eyes to the dark and dusky shack.

It was then he realized he was sprawled out on the ground, his cot turned over on top of him, with several boys towering over him with angry glares. As he tried to get up, Luke, the biggest of the boys, kicked him in the face and knocked him back down.

"Ow!" James screamed from the blow on his cheek and the sharp pain in his back. Feeling the wetness of blood oozing from his earlier oak scratches, he grabbed his face, but he was afraid to look up at his attackers.

"Quit that sorry ass cryin', boy! You ain't sleepin' on no bed in here," Luke proclaimed as he stood over the sprawled James.

James cautiously looked around the shack as he spat out straw, dirt, and blood. The room was silent, except for their snickers and his sobs, and all eyes were trained on him.

"That's where you belong. On the ground. In the dirt!" Luke added, as others laughed in agreement.

What? Why? Who am I that they do this to me? Why are they doing this? Why are they treating me like this? Is he one of them boys? God. Please tell Ruth to come get me. Hurry. Please!

Little by little, the commotion died out until James was awake and alone in the dirt and straw, totally exhausted but terrified of sleep. Various mumbles, snores, and smacks continued to startle him throughout the night until sleep forced its way in.

❧

The bustle of the shack woke James. Then he realized someone was screaming, "Git yo' asses out o' bed, now! C'mon, git out heah."

James got up in the darkness and followed everyone outside, having no idea who was speaking, what was going on, or what he should be doing.

"How ya' doin' this mornin', boy?" Luke asked with a smirk as they approached the door. He laughed loudly, viciously elbowed James in the ribs, which sent him to the ground, and then exited the door in stoic silence. James struggled to his feet and continued heading out the door with halted breaths.

The line curved around the building, joined with lines of men and boys from the other shacks and approached ladies handing out square chunks of bread. Taking it and a bowl, which was later filled with broth, James continued the march. Stanley and his 10 armed men stood watch as the line traveled toward the fields.

James had never seen the fields this close or smelled the aroma of tobacco this thick, which made him nauseous. After several bites of the loaf and a couple of sips of the broth, they came to a point in this journey where the bowls were to be placed in a barrel.

"But—but I'm not finished yet," James mistakenly said to Bosch.

He had been looking down at the barrel where the slaves were dropping their bowls in silence. Now, he looked up with sheer incredulity and blinked his eyes twice to verify his vision. A slight grin creased his time-hardened face, and, in the next instant, he hit James in the face with a blow from the butt of his rifle, sending him staggering backwards and falling on his sore back. His bowl flew off to the right, the remaining piece of bread high into the air, finally landing several feet behind him.

"Boy! I don't ever wanna heah anything' like that outta yo' mouth a'gin, you heah?" Bosch screamed as the other slaves around them stood in submissive silence. He stood up and placed his hand on the revolver stuck halfway down the waist of his pants and ordered, "Now! Pick up that goddamn bowl and put it heah in this heah barrel rat now!"

James got up, picked up the bowl, and cautiously walked toward the barrel. Looking up, he replied, "Yassuh, massah, suh."

"What the hell you lookin' at, boy?" he screamed, and he punched James in the face again.

Huh? What—what did I do? I said "suh." I—I—Help me, God. Please. Tell—tell Ruth!

James continued wondering while he rose, a little slower this time. He snuck a peek at the other slaves and noticed they all kept their stares downward toward the ground. He copied them as he made it to his feet again and placed his bowl in the barrel.

"You best learn the way to talk to me, boy!"

The way I talk to him? What is he talking about? I better watch— and listen to the others. Until Ruth come and get me.

The line snaked around until it forked off. They would, what seemed like randomly to James, pull boys and men out of the line and take them elsewhere. The women who weren't serving were in their own lines, along with the elderly, headed off in another direction.

Approaching the fields, the tobacco plants towered over James and most others. He knew Penelope Farms had them from the aroma that permeated the plantation, especially over the last 24 hours, but he'd never seen them up close. The pungent aroma reminded him of when he'd first arrived. He was nauseous for a week until he got used to it. His stomach quivered now from the concentrated odor, the situation, and Luke's latest punch.

Boys grabbed sacks and began pulling leaves off the stalks. James watched and mimicked them for the rest of the morning. He also listened intently to the way they spoke and decided that was what "Bosch" meant.

Though no one spoke to James, conversation went on until one of Stanley's men rode by on a horse. James noticed that, whenever anyone responded to one of Stanley's men, none of the slaves initiated any dialogue; they kept their heads bowed and their tone subdued. Even the attitude, the jocularity, and the comfort disappeared upon their arrival.

I—I'm not like these people. Either of these people. The, uh—slaves, the people in servitude. The chattel. The property. Or the other people, these White people, the overseers, these citizens. Where do I fit in? How do I fit in? Who am I?

After a lunch of the same bread and soup, they continued until dusk. Returning that night, every part of his body ached. His palms were raw, his fingers were bloodied, his shoulders throbbed, his muscles ached, the soles of his feet burned, and every inch of his skin itched.

They were led into a building which James soon found out was the cafeteria for the slaves. He got his food and slowly sat down on a bare wooden bench at the first available table. Sounds escaped from his mouth as he recalled the noises Ruth made when she sat down or got up. He picked up a roll and gave it a squeeze, but it resisted, and he reminisced.

Carlton's breakfast yesterday morning was fresh. His biscuits were—squeezable. Eggs—bacon. Not, uh—this, whatever it is. The nice dining room with comfortable chairs I sat in—when Carlton left. The china—the silver, the glass. And—

The crash of his plate landing on the dirt floor startled him. He looked to the left—at his food on the ground—and then to the right—and directly into Luke's grinning face.

"Whatcha' gonna do, boy?" he bellowed as he sat down on the same bench with several giggling boys in tow. James looked back down at the spot on the table where his plate had been. Then out into the sea of disapproving stares—not daring to look in Luke's direction. He bit into the stale bread.

Lying in the dirt that night, he prayed in a hush, "Are you listening, God? I need you. Please, tell Ruth what happened. Tell her to come get me. Please God, help me. Please . . ."

CHAPTER 14

"Heavenly Father. Heavenly Father. We come here this morning to ask for protection for our son, Bobby. Going away to prep school is a big step for him—and for our family. He's our first child, Lord. Please keep him safe from harm. Help him to learn all he can, and keep him within Your hedge of protection," Papa Harris prayed that Monday morning.

The Harris family was less than two hours away from seeing the eldest child off to a new school in a new city. Bobby's parents, their apprehension building with each inhale and accompanying exhale, tried to project their best face. His three siblings, oblivious to the potential danger or the gnashing emotions of their parents, began attacking the meal.

"Now, baby, remember 'bout them slave catchers! Always keep your papers with you. And, and don't talk to anybody you don't know. Even if they Negroes, don't trust them!" Mama Harris warned in a soft scream as she struggled to be heard above the din of the clattering eatery and conversations.

"Daddy say I can move into your room and you moving downstairs—or out back," Martha said to William.

"No, you ain't! I got the room to myself—right, Daddy?"

"Mama, I'm gonna be all right. I'm just goin' to Cambridge. Ain't nobody gonna bother me there. I mean—I'm free, right? I ain't no slave!" Bobby replied as he fought his brother for control of a stack of pancakes.

"Martha, can I wear your blue sweater today?" asked Eve.

"As long as you Negro man, you in danger, son. Always be careful," Papa Harris replied.

"Man, this food is good!" William declared as he stuffed his mouth.

My baby just don't understand, thought Mama Harris. *Lord, help him understand. Just, please—don't make the lesson too hard.*

"Daddy, when can I start school? I want to learn, too," asked Martha.

"Mama, I can keep the room, can't I?"

God, keep the ugly of the world from Bobby, please, Papa Harris silently prayed.

"Bobby, baby. Just be careful. Okay?"

"I will, Ma."

"Martha," Eve said. "Can I—"

"Okay. You can wear it. Don't get it dirty. And thank you for asking—*this time.*"

"Listen—*really listen* to your Mama, son. Really—just please listen."

"William, pass me the syrup. Okay, Daddy. I'm listening."

"Martha, you gonna eat that sausage?"

"Ooo, Mama. William said, 'gonna.'"

"Daddy. Did you hear me?"

"Mommie. The food is great."

"Me and your mama will talk with you about that later."

The Harris parents struggled with how much of the ways of the world to share with their children. Enjoying a sense of normalcy most Negroes didn't have, they were torn. Should they allow their children's innocence to remain longer? Or should they rip the veil off and reveal the ugly reality of how this nation—founded on democracy—viewed them?

"I'm gonna—*going*—to miss all y'all. Even you, William."

"I'll miss you, too. This much."

"Huh? What—you didn't do anything!"

"Exactly. Can I have some more pancakes?"

⚘

At Penelope Farms, tobacco was king. Master Johnson was one of the largest producers in the state. Being the owner of the most slaves in Montgomery County, he was heavily involved in the slave trade as well.

He bought girls of childbearing age, many male and female field hands, and a few house workers. He sold children born there, as well as most of the people too old to work in the fields or to bear children. He named or renamed his slaves after characters and places from the Bible.

Originally "Bridle Acres," Master Johnson had renamed it "Penelope Farms" in honor of his wife after her death. When she was killed in the riding accident, Master Johnson killed that steed and stretched its hide across his beloved desk. He soon sold the rest of the horses he'd been breeding, which had been the major business there, and the slave trade filled the void.

Penelope Farms spanned more than 5,000 acres, and Master Johnson maintained more than 200 slaves on the plantation at any one time. The tobacco fields took up 2,000 acres, and most of the male slaves worked there. There was an 800-acre cherry orchard, and many women, children, and the elderly worked there. In the middle stood stately Johnson Hall, separated from the slave quarters by the stand of slender oaks, which bordered one side of the tobacco fields.

The plantation also had nearly 500 acres of hickory forest that guarded the front entrance, and, once a year, the trees were harvested. The rest of the plantation was made up of buildings to clean, cut, and cure the tobacco.

The days on the plantation were long, the work hard, and the punishment certain. The duties transferred from the fields and the orchards in the spring and summer to the forest and the curing barns in the fall and winter, and then back again. Months into James' exile, he was still isolated and shunned by the other slaves.

No one helped James learn his job in the tobacco fields. He still slept on the ground in the shack; he was beaten up regularly until he gave up his food and was ignored. Those evenings when the slaves would get together to sing and congregate, James would stay on the fringe in fear. Singers, dancers, and storytellers would entertain the slaves for hours until Stanley and his men rushed them off.

"I gonna tell a story tonight 'bout courage. 'Bout faith, uh huh," Mr. Boo, the Negro man who'd escorted James to Master Johnson those many years ago, began. A master storyteller, he would spin a yarn every night they got together. He was the only one who could stop the music, dancing, and singing with one word from his mouth.

Sitting on a porch of the only building in the area that wasn't formerly a horse stable, he would rock slowly in an old, creaking chair and spin yarn after yarn. The crowd of 60 quieted down as he continued.

"This here story deal wit these three boys—not much older than some of y'all out there. These boys brave. They leader brave. They didn't much care 'bout what wuz happenin' to 'em. That what brave is. Not carin' what might happen—jest doin' what's right! Them boys names wuz Shadrach. And Meshach. And Abednego. And their leader wuz Daniel, uh, huh . . ."

♣

"James. Here a b-b-biscuit," whispered a voice from the dark.

A crescent moon, periodically obscured by passing clouds, gave James glimpses of his benefactor. Turning toward the shadowy figure, he eagerly took the roll from the first person to be nice to him in all the time he'd been there.

"Thanks," James said between bites, chews, and swallows, as he satisfied his growling stomach. The clothes he had been given didn't fit snuggly any more—instead sagging noticeably on his slimming frame.

"Shh. Don't say nuthin'. Jest eat."

"What's your—" James began to ask, unable to tell who he was talking to.

"Shh! B-B-Be quiet, J-J-James! Jest eat," the silhouette said and then faded into the darkness.

"Thank you," James murmured before he took his final swallow. "Thank you."

♣

There was constant change in who James worked next to in the fields. Arranged in groups of four, they ate lunch and received water breaks together. Rare was the week they worked with the same group more than once. Many days, the groups changed twice.

This day it was three other young males, two from his shack, though James didn't know any of their names. Pulling leaves off, he overheard one of the boys talking with a stutter. Looking over at him, the boy never acknowledged James or returned his stare.

Is this him? Someone has been giving me food in the middle of the night for weeks now, and I still don't know who it is. It could be him. I mean, how many people could stutter around here? Maybe a lot. I wonder. Better be careful, though.

At the water break, James and the boy stood next to each other while drinking out of metal cups. The other boys had already gotten their water, and Bosch was impatiently waiting on them to finish.

I—I got to say something. What, though? What to say?

James pondered his next move until Bosch snatched the cups from their hands and rode off, screaming racial epithets.

James and the boy walked back toward the spot where their bags were, and James finally whispered, "Uh, thanks—thank you for the food."

The boy said nothing, and he never broke stride; he picked up his bag and began picking the leaves.

Hmm, maybe he didn't hear me. I better say it a little louder next chance I get. Ruth said I mumble and—

"You w-w-welcome," the boy replied, without turning his head or pausing from his duties.

Throughout the next several hours, they worked in silence. James' hand, having become conditioned over the weeks, powerfully snapped off leaves from the stalks and shoved them in his ever-filling bag. All the while, his mind raced with a plethora of possibilities.

I should say something. I'm going to say something. Uh—hey, my name James. Nah, uh, you been here long? Nah, I, uh—uh, maybe I should just let it go. Everybody mad at me. He don't want to get in trouble with them. He's already doing me a favor. I should be happy. I'll just stay quiet, and—

"D-D-Don't turn 'round. Don't say nuthin', neither," the boy finally said.

He continued to look away from James. Working side by side, they moved down a row of stalks to an opening. The boy walked through and continued down the row but now faced James. His eyes darted back and forth and all around—first into James' eyes, then past his head, then to his left and right, and then back into James' eyes again.

"M-M-My name Isaac," he finally said, as tension strained his voice.

"Thanks again, Isaac. For the food, I mean."

"D-D-Don't say nuthin' to nobody."

"Okay. I won't, and thanks."

After a few more silent minutes, Isaac asked, "Did you—d-d-did you really git dem b-b-boys whupped?"

James tried explaining to Isaac how it happened and that he hadn't realized what could happen. He was just answering Carlton's question. That he had no idea that would happen. He would've never said anything if he knew. That he didn't even know what "whup" meant.

"... we was just talking, I swear. I didn't know he was mad until I looked up and saw his face. I swear, Isaac. I swear! We—he was doing Arithmetic. Adding stuff, and he just asked. So, I answered him. About why his clothes was dirty. And how they got torn. I just said some boys pushed me down. I didn't know why they did that. I asked him that, too. They kicked me and stuff, and—"

"How old was you when the Massah g-g-got you?"

"I don't know. It's been seven or eight years ago."

"Damn, that make you 'b-b-bout six, maybe seven then," he replied, darting his eyes past James and toward a faint sound that was coming from down the row of tobacco stalks.

James, his eyes full of tears now, continued, "I would've never said anything. I had nightmares—still do. I didn't even know what 'whup' *meant*. I swear. When Ruth told me, I cried and cried."

"I b-b-believe ya'. Hmm—Shhh! Quick—Riley comin'. Git b-b-back to work and hush," Isaac warned as a man rode up on horseback.

❦

The shacks where the young males lived were former horse stables, but the stalls had been removed. The floor was a mixture of dirt and straw, and several windows had been cut out of the whitewashed walls for ventilation, adding to the flow of air from between the well-worn planks.

The boys slept on cots arranged side by side, with just enough room for someone to slide and shuffle between them. James still slept on the ground and was isolated. Isaac slept five cots down from him.

"Miss ya' nice, warm bed in the Big House, huh, boy," someone said as they passed James two nights later.

"I never slept in a bed," James replied with a puzzled expression on his face, though he never looked up.

"What you say, boy?"

"Huh? I say—I said I never slept on no bed. Why you saying that?"

Amid the laughter and catcalls, the boys declared, "Boy, quit your lyin'! . . . You wuz Carlton's boy! . . . Goddamn house nigger! . . . You had it easy! . . . We oughtta make yo' ass sleep outside! . . ." as a crowd began to gather around him.

"I—I slept on the floor in Carlton's room!"

James sat up, snorting in anger as the crowd moved closer. Then he cried out, "He said—Carlton say—uh, he say niggers don't sleep on no beds. They were, uh, just for White folks. Beds were for White folks. And—and—and Deeohgee, his dog. Ruth say we all—slaves—uh, we all slaves, too! No matter where we at! I think God says we, uh, are all slaves, too."

"What 'bout you g-g-gittin' dem b-b-boys whupped, huh?"

"Hell, yeah! . . . Huh, boy—what 'bout that? . . . That's right! We oughta stomp yo' ass! . . . Hell, yeah! . . ." retorted the crowd, who now surrounded James' cot. Someone pushed James, he tumbled over and landed on the ground.

"I didn't—I didn't know those boys got whupped—I swear. I swear I didn't know that would happen. I would have *never* said anything if I did. When I found out, when Ruth told me, I cried at night for weeks. I—I cried. I still cry inside. I was a baby when I got here. Nobody told me what could happen. I didn't even know what 'whup' meant! He—uh Carlton—he just asked me how—uh, why his clothes was dirty. I just answered his, uh, his question. That's all. I swear before God. I didn't know, I didn't know, I didn't know. I swear, I didn't know. Nobody told me. I didn't—"

"Quit that tired-ass cryin', boy!" Luke demanded as he emerged from the crowd. "How old wuz you when Massah got you?"

"S-S-Six, I guess. Six years old. I didn't know. Nobody told me. All I had was a song—and, and I don't even have that no mo'. I swear. Please don't hit me. I—I didn't know."

The room was now silent, except for James' cries, as everyone there looked at one another and then, finally, at Luke. He was standing over a sobbing James; he looked around the shack at the slowly dispersing crowd as they returned to the darkness.

Extending his hand, Luke helped James to his feet.

"I guess you know what 'whup' mean now, huh. And you right, li'l man. You right. We all slaves. No matter where we be."

James made eye contact with Isaac, who was smiling and nodding. James never slept on the ground again.

CHAPTER 15

As the weeks flowed into months, James listened, talked, watched, and listened some more to learn from and about his people, and gain slivers of insight into himself. He was introduced to a world, to an existence he'd never imagined. The boy in the bubble came out to interact with his world. James experienced the humor, the sounds, the aromas, the attitudes, the dreams, the desires, and the fears of his people. And of himself.

The sounds—spoken, sung, and played—constantly rang out. The music and songs about their struggles, including religious ones, and those of hope were always present. They included work songs, gospel songs, and songs of celebration. *Micah, Row Your Boat Ashore* became one of his favorites as he remembered reading the Book of Micah in the Bible.

The music was made with anything—pots and pans, buckets, jugs, sticks, handclapping, knee slapping, foot stomping, whistling, banjos, and harmonicas. Conversations, along with arguments and debates—melodic in their own right—emphasized feelings and perspectives. And the storytellers, especially Mr. Boo, wove tales of adventure and suspense and hope and justice, which buoyed his spirit.

The smells of food, the dinners cooked, and the tastes. Collard greens, sweet potato pie, fried chicken, and more than 100 ways to serve parts of a pig! Master Johnson's type of food tasted okay until this. The slave food tasted different—much better, and with *oomph*! And the smells of 40 men cramped into a shack barely large enough for 25 after being in a tobacco field all day created their own, unique memories.

Their attitudes were of a people determined not to give up. Willing to risk whippings or death for a chance at freedom. Not to be broken. Surviving with graceful guile and deft aplomb. Daring to dream, to hope. Believing their day would come.

The dreams, desires, and fears they coveted and faced were incorporated into the humor, sounds, smells, and attitudes of his people and soon became part of him. He grew more in that year there than in his previous 13 years combined. The *Who am I?* question became a dynamic declaration.

They were who he was. *This* was who he is. James, a slave on Penelope Farms.

When weather allowed, the slaves would get together and sing songs or have church. Stanley stood in the background, enjoying the music and happy to see the slaves enjoying themselves. He convinced Master Johnson to allow it as a way of keeping them in check. Master Johnson, seeing the Bible as supporting his point of view, wanted them to read it. James, accepted now, usually sat closest to the storytellers and always near Isaac. They arrived in front of Mr. Boo's cabin and were disheartened at the crowd already assembled there. They found a place as close as they could and settled in.

"Hey, James, what's the quickest way to freedom for a slave?" Luke riddled James that starry night as the singing was at a pause.

"I—I don't know," James replied with a shrug as he glanced over at Isaac.

"Death," Luke responded, as others howled in laughter. James crunched his forehead as Isaac chuckled.

That's not funny. How can they think that's funny? How can they laugh in the face of this despair? Laughing at themselves—at us, this situation, and even laughing silently at our oppressors? This somehow gives them comfort? I don't get it! I just don't get it. I don't think I ever will.

Singing flowed through the night as James realized the stand of slender oaks not only kept him at a distance visually but also blocked off this joyful noise of celebration and hope. His year of growth included learning to appreciate this, although the situation could've been considered worse. At times, he wondered what Carlton or Ruth were doing at that moment. Who blew out the lantern for him? Who helped her up after one of her walks to the orchard or after she sat down under a shade tree?

And whenever Mr. Boo came out to hold court, his mind raced to that forbidden room, the place that had taken him so far so many times. But this oral storytelling had its own magic that he quickly learned to appreciate.

". . . and so, whenever ya' hears that howl at night, git on up under yo' covers and don't peek out or—he'll gitcha'!" Mr. Boo said with a twitch, causing all to jump, startled.

"That sounded great, huh, Isaac?"

"Yeah, James. Mr. B-B-Boo sho' nuff good. I heard th-th-that one befo', and it still gits me."

"Yeah, I'm sorry I missed that one."

"Don't worry. He gonna tell it a'gin," Isaac replied as several of the singers rose and walked up in front of the crowd.

James thought about the stories he'd read in the study and longed to compare and share them with his friend, but a memory of Ruth guided him.

A smart slave is a dead slave. I can't let anyone know. Not even Isaac. Huh, if Master Johnson or Carlton or Stanley knew—whew! I know now why Ruth was so scared for me. She knew I would get whipped and—if I lived—sold off. Or I could've been killed. They might have killed me! A smart slave—a dead slave—a smart slave—a dead slave—a smart slave . . .

One of the young bucks, Shadrach, the most popular slave, began leading the choir in his deep baritone voice, *"Amazing Grace, how sweet the sound. That saved a wretch like me. I once was lost, but now I'm found . . ."*

"So, James. What you did when you was in the B-B-Big House?" Isaac asked.

"Mostly played with Carlton, waited for him to come home from school. And helped Ruth clean up and stuff. Do you know Ruth?"

"Uh—I think I seent her one time. M-M-Me and some boys had to take some stuff t-t-to the Big House one, uh, time."

"*. . . was blind, but now I see. 'Twas grace that taught my heart to fear and grace my fears relieved. How precious . . .*"

"Yeah, I sure do miss her. She taught me so much. She was like a mama to me. We used to have so much fun. And yeah, every now and then, some boys would bring stuff there. Huh, yeah, like them boys who—uh—"

James paused, looked over his shoulder toward Shadrach, and listened closer. The song Shadrach was singing caught his attention. Its lyrics—familiar. Its melody—comforting. A memory slowly entered his consciousness.

"Yeah, I know. They wuz solt off, quick-like, too."

"Huh—yeah. Ruth did so much for me," James replied.

"*. . . did that grace appear the hour I first believed. Through many dangers, toils, and snares I have already come. . . .*"

"So, j-j-jest in the Big House, huh. Outta the sun and stuff. Musta been nice, huh?"

"Yeah—I miss her. We used to—" James mumbled but stopped in mid-sentence.

Huh? What? That song. There's something about that song. What—is—it?

"*. . . 'Tis grace hath brought me safe this far and grace will lead me home. When we've been there ten-thousand years bright shining as the sun. . . .*"

"Yeah, long as I can 'member, I worked in the fields. First cotton. Then tobaccky. Had to get used to the smell and—"

James rose to his feet and took a step toward Shadrach.

That song—nah. I thought I knew it. It sounded like—I don't know . . .

"*. . . and n-n-not throwin' up. Even the food tasted different. What you doin' James? You goin' up there to sing?*"

James sat back down and grinned at Isaac. "I thought I remembered that song—never mind. Anyway, what were you saying about cotton and 'bacca?"

"We've no less days to sing God's praise than when we first began . . ."

"I started with cotton. The tobaccky—it made my food taste different."

"I went from the Johnson Hall smell to 'bacca. It is different."

"Yeah. How was it in the orchards? D-D-Did it have a smell?"

"Amazing grace, how sweet the sound that saved a wretch like me."

"That's funny. I can't remem—"

What is—wait. Wait—wait a minute! I—know—that—song! I do know that song! Oh, my God!

"James. J-J-James! What—what is it, James?"

Not acknowledging Isaac, James stood up and walked toward Shadrach. Isaac got up and cautiously followed his friend. Shadrach, seeing both of them approaching, stopped singing.

"No, no! Don't stop. Please, don't stop!" James shouted, bringing all pairs of eyes on him.

Shadrach, unsure of what to expect, continued, *"I once was lost, but now I'm found. Was blind, but now I see."*

Is that it? Is—is that it? That's it! The words—yeah. The melody, definitely. That's it. Yeah, that's it!

"James, what is it? What's wrong, uh, J-J-James?"

"Amazing grace, how sweet the sound that saved a wretch like me."

"*That's it! That's the song!* THAT'S IT! THAT'S IT! THAT IS IT" James screamed.

The melody that echoed in his head those first months. The lone possession remaining from his family. The tune that had faded from his memory had now been revived from its dormancy.

"Mama!" he cried out as he crumpled to his knees. "My mama, my mama used to sing me that song. She—she used to sing and hum me that song all the time. Mama!"

Isaac and others surrounded and comforted him.

"Please keep singing, Shadrach. Don't stop singing. Please! Please! . . ."

"Amazing grace, how sweet the sound that saved a wretch like me."

". . . I—I can see her. I can see her in my mind. Mama. I love you. Mama. I love you. . . ."

"I once was lost, but now I'm found. Was blind, but now I see,"

". . . Don't stop. Please, don't stop singing. Please," James whined.

His plea wasn't heard by Shadrach though. Instead it faded into the sea of humming of the "Amazing Grace" melody from everyone there—including Stanley.

❧

Shadrach was one of the oldest "young bucks," as Master Johnson called the teenage boys. They were the best workers and had the most value—for a variety of reasons—but were the highest escape risk. And Shadrach was Master Johnson's most prized slave. Since James' epiphany about "Amazing Grace," Shadrach listened intently to whatever he had to say, trying to find out where he was. His mother had been sold a month earlier, and he wanted to escape to find her.

I should know that. There were maps and stuff on the tables—but I kept reading the stories only. I should have been studying those maps!

"I know how to find north, Shadrach. The sun rises in the east, so if you keep the sun on your right shoulder in the morning and on your left shoulder during the afternoon, you're headed north," James whispered to him. But that didn't help Shadrach.

Before dawn one morning, he was gone, the third runner in a month. All young bucks. Stanley and three of his men took off after him as the morning line snaked toward the fields and orchards. Screams ruefully announced their return later that day, dragging a body. It was Shadrach, who had drowned in a river.

A livid Master Johnson gathered all the slaves who were around the whipping tree and went into a tirade about anyone running would be sold, or wish they were dead. It had been nearly a score of months since James had seen Master Johnson, but that sickness in his stomach was as fresh and strong as that terrible day.

"... I'm tired of this shit! God commands me to treat you people good! I'm good to y'all! You need to learn to 'preciate that! I give ya' a home! I let ya' read! I let ya' sing and dance! Things gonna change! I'm bringing someone in to get you people straight. I . . ."

Shadrach's worth as a worker and a breeder was enormous. Master Johnson had received offers from as far away as Georgia for him. He used to take him to auctions just to hear the accolades and bids. Now, he was dead, and someone was going to pay. He selected 5 from the group of 50 slaves there and ordered them each to receive 5 lashes—a woman, a man, and 3 young bucks, including Luke and James.

The Uglies

Chapter 1

Days like this were rare at the Lady Luck Saloon, a hole-in-the-wall watering hole in this whistle-stop of a town, catering exclusively to the riffraff of the region. One of three recognizable buildings in town, the jail and the funeral parlor being the other two, it was situated along the main drag. A trough of murky water that wasn't fit for man nor beast sat in front, inviting anyone or thing that dared. Inside was teeming with bad music, whiskey gulpers, loose women, and other assorted bad elements.

The main focus, however, was on the flamboyantly adorned poker table. A green-felt-cloth top was held tightly to heavily varnished mahogany with brass tacks. Similarly, green tassels hung down the four corners, fine leather bordered the tabletop edge, and intricate designs were carved into its wood frame. The 7 men—6 who seemed to emanate from the surrounding environment and the seventh, totally foreign to the area, were sitting around it.

The game was 7-card stud poker, and the game had started with 7 players. Plopping down $100 apiece—just for the privilege of playing—took its toll. That was a year's salary for most people. Now, there were just 2 players left. Attrition by ante. Tense moments passed as the previous players, along with most of the saloon patrons, wondered who would get the cash.

"I'll call yo' 10, son," Mr. Rathbone said as he sat there, with a grin that was easy to despise and as out of place as his tailored 3-piece suit. He threw several chips on the rising pile and leaned back in his chair—with one gloved hand slowly twirling his pencil-thin moustache and the other one palm down on his face-down cards.

Through his unbuttoned jacket, the plaid-coordinated vest was visible; it rose and fell ever so slightly with each breath. Rathbone carefully eyed his lone opponent, a scraggly-blond mane sticking haphazardly from beneath a dingy gray cap, and a pair of blue eyes that periodically peered from behind the 3 cards that he held high to hide his face.

"Well, son. Let's see whatcha' got. Or you gonna sit there all night?" Rathbone added and bellowed a laugh that no one else shared. Most of the noise, including the tune from the off-key piano, ceased as the suspense continued to build.

"Three ladies lookin' atcha, sweet and purty," Rogers finally replied as he slammed the cards down so hard that many of the poker chips tumbled off their stacks. A regular to this location, he was gruff and worn, just like everything else in the saloon except the poker table and Mr. Rathbone. A murmur trickled through the crowd.

"Lovely ladies they are, too, exceptin' I got pairs of 7s and 10s, my friend," Mr. Rathbone replied as he exposed 24 of his teeth and the winning hand—his fourth in 7 games. He made an aggravating, teeth-sucking noise as he began gathering up the winnings.

"Either you lucky as all git out—or yo' ass cheatin'," Rogers challenged as he slowly stood up from his chair, his eyes squarely trained on Mr. Rathbone. A hush came over the room, as the spectators took several steps back, and the other card players scattered.

"N-N-Now wait a minute, there, partner. Don't be—don't go being a sore loser," Mr. Rathbone stammered as he anxiously looked around for a pair of agreeing eyes.

The 5 men who regularly rode with Rogers grabbed and searched Rathbone, finding 3 extra cards. Rogers unholstered his revolver and deliberately strode around the table while his men pulled the shark out of his chair and away from the table.

"I—I hate cheaters wors'n anythin'—'ceptin' niggers," Rogers calmly said. Then he kneed Mr. Rathbone in the stomach, causing him to bend over. Rogers raised his gun and slammed the butt of it down on the back of the shark's head, sending him crashing to the floor.

Looking upon him with ultimate scorn, Rogers pulled back the hammer and fired once as he uttered, "This is fo' yo' cheatin' ass," hitting him in his right hand. Mr. Rathbone yelled out in agony as he grabbed the wound.

Pulling the hammer back again, Rogers muttered, "This 'un 'cause you cost me games I coulda' won. You no good piece of shit!"

The slug tore into Mr. Rathbone's left shoulder, who, by now, was pleading for his life and confessing to cheating throughout the southland. But it was falling on deaf ears.

"Shaddup!" Rogers screamed as he and his men viciously stomped the card shark until he stopped moving. "This 'un—is fo' being no better than a nigger, you damn cheater!" Rogers then shot the shark in the left foot.

As he sat back down and collected his winnings, Mr. Rathbone writhed in pain while Rogers' men rifled through the shark's pockets.

"Oh, ow, ugh, oh—somebody—somebody help me—*please*. Call the sheriff. Call, call the marshal. Call somebody, anybody . . ."

"Anybody wanna play some mo'?" Rogers asked.

He slowly counted the money as the crowd gravitated back to the table.

"Nah, we gotta go anyhow," replied Hamilton, one of the card players. "Y'all still ridin' with us to catch that nigger wench, Rogers?"

"Nah. We got us jobs over in The Gomp as overseers. Me and my boys gonna raise some hell there."

"I'm sho' y'all will. I didn't know there was money in overseein'. He got—uh, 10 from me, uh—Rogers," Hamilton said as he took several cautious steps closer.

"Only on big plantations like this 'un. There's more'n 200 niggers there. We gonna make us some money. Git us some honey. Right, boys?" Rogers proclaimed as his men laughed and cheered.

"Yeah, yeah. I sho' y'all will."

"Barkeep! Rustle up some grub and liquor fo' me and my men here. Here yo' 10, Ham."

Hours later, as Rogers and his men prepared to leave, one man's lamentations continued.

". . . ugh, ugh, oh, oh—help me—some, ugh, oh, some *ugh* body, help me . . ."

"Shit! You still alive?" Rogers incredulously asked as he walked past Mr. Rathbone, lying curled on the floor. "I thought you be dead by now."

"Please, ugh. Please Mister. I—I'm sorry. I learned ugh, ow, uh, I learned—my lesson, Mister. Oh—I swear. Please, sir—ow, it hurts. It hurts! Please, get a doc, a doctor. Please—"

"I shoulda put a bullet in yo' head from the git, wastin' my goddamn ammo," Rogers growled.

"I—I swear, I learned—"

"You sho' has, you sorry piece of shit," Rogers replied—and then shot him between the eyebrows. "Goddamn cheata'!"

⚜

Walking toward the curing barns, arms filled with bundles of twine, James passed other slaves hurrying back and forth to and from their duties. Tall and short, male and female, slim and stout, all passed before, behind, and around him. And they all passed the occasional armed White male.

Throughout the months of his banishment from Johnson Hall, James had seen most of the slaves—many came and went. One out of 4 slaves were bought from somewhere else, and all had at least one family member sold. Everyone knew someone who had been sold. At any moment, anyone could be sold. So, the time it took to build trust, to build a friendship, wasn't there. James' mind mused as he continued his daily journey.

I'm amazed at this world I now exist in. Just 100 yards east of the slender oaks stands Johnson Hall—stately and pristine. One hundred yards west, the slave quarters—dilapidated and weathered. Huh, Johnson Hall—comfortable and secure—was never my home. The slave quarters—raggedy and exposed—will never be my home. And between them is nature—separating the comfortable from the wretched, the sheltered from the vulnerable, the aroma of clean from the odor of labor. A natural divide that bridges the chasm between my 2 realities. Both maintain residence in my mind and serve to epitomize my bondage.

He was also amazed at the wide variety of personalities of his people. He observed the storytellers, the singers, the dancers, the musicians, the jokesters, the subdued. And he began to recognize those filled with impatient rage—usually the young and male—like he was becoming. He met them all in the shack, at the biweekly get-togethers, at church services, and at the Bible study. The commonality was a shared bondage, inextricably linked together like the twine he now carried to the barn. The echoes of Webster, its cold, factual definitions, continued to be his constant companion.

. . . nigger . . . slave . . . servitude . . . chattel . . . liberty . . . free . . . citizen . . . nigger . . . slave . . . servitude . . . chattel . . . liberty . . . free . . . citizen . . .

The giggling of approaching girls brought James back to the present and reminded him why the racing of his heart was wonderful. Why the quiver in his stomach was winsome. And why the disconcerting buckle of his knees was welcomed.

. . . Chloe's coming this way! I'll say 'hi' this time, maybe. Nah—I will this time. Yeah—uh, yeah! What you scared of, boy? Just say 'hi' to her . . .

James' mind raced as his thoughts bumped into and tripped over each other. This girl, Chloe, made his world spin and his head swirl whenever she neared him. Nearly 2,000 ounces of loveliness proportionately placed on a 5-foot, 4-inch frame, her pleasant face and mature persona belied her age and drew many young bucks to her.

As their paths neared, James barely cut his eye toward her as she walked by with a group of girls. They continued going their separate ways as James mentally kicked himself for not speaking.

"Why didn't you say something, fool? She was right there! You're scared, aren't you? Huh, aren't you?" James mumbled to himself as he shifted the bale of twine he was carrying.

"T-T-Talkin' to yo'self ag'in, huh?" interrupted Isaac. Hauling tied-up bundles of golden-brown tobacco, he was headed for a wagon being loaded.

"I seed ya' walk past C-C-Chloe. Whatcha' say?"

"Nothing, I said nothing—again."

They stopped walking but performed a slow pirouette as their eyes looked over each other's shoulder, keeping watch for Stanley's men.

"Whatcha waitin' fo'? You st-st-still a-scared, ain't 'cha?"

"No. Yes. No. I—I don't know! Every time I get near her—"

"She too good lookin' fo' you, anyhow. Yeah, she is. J-J-Jacob, maybe Caleb or Andrew, or—"

"Too good looking for? And Jacob? Caleb? Isaac, you supposed to be my friend! What you doing? What you saying—" James replied until he noticed the laughter.

"Just k-k-kidding you, James. You better make yo' move 'fo they do. That's all I'm sayin'."

"Yeah, you're—let's go," James warned as Mitch came around the corner on his steed.

☘

"Mr. Johnson, you're acting in haste, sir. I'll hire some mo' men to stop the runners. I'll get tougher. I will. We can board the windows or shackle the young bucks together. Maybe in pairs—or, or threes. They'se the only ones runnin'. But you don't need to bring no one else in," Stanley argued as he leaned on Master Johnson's desk.

Master Johnson leaned back in his swivel chair with his hand supporting his chin and in full contemplation. Heaving a deep sigh, he finally said, "Ovah the last year, we had at least 10 niggers that got away. Ovah fifty goddamn thousand dollahs of my money—gone! The ones we got back—we sold. I lost money on them, too. Them that die—shit, another twenty thousand dollahs—at least!"

"But sir, let me continue to try. I feel it's—"

"It's already done, Stanley. I'm cracking down on they asses! Your way worked when we had only 30 or 40 niggers. Now, with ovah 200—I need to keep fear in 'em. I tried the fear of the Lord our Savior. Now, I gotta bring in the devil his self. I can keep 'em mixed up by selling 'em off, but I need somebody mean to keep them scared. This heah Rogers man, he supposed to be one of the meanest sons-of-bitches 'round these heah parts."

"He crazy, Mr. Johnson. I heard of him. He gonna hurt yo' slaves. Hurt 'em bad. I know losing Shadrach upset you. And how much you spent on him and all. 'Member, I was there when you got 'im. But this ain't right. He gonna hurt some bad."

"Just as long as he don't hurt none of the good ones. The moneymakers all I care about. That damn Shadrach was worth more than $10,000! That's 10 goddamn thousand dollahs I ain't got no goddamn mo'! I can't be losing that kind of money! In the past 2 years, we had—what, 25 try to run off? And what—you caught 10, and 5 died? And I guess 10 mo' escaped to the goddamn Nawth!

"If this heah Rogers kill a $200 slave to scare the shit outta the rest of 'em, that's okay. You ain't gone never do that. You thinks of these niggers as people."

"Well, I uh—you don't, sir?"

"Hell, naw! They ain't peoples. They's property. My goddamn property," he shouted as he sat up in his chair and slammed his fist onto the desk.

Stanley subtly took two steps back from the agitated owner of Penelope Farms and slightly shrugged. Master Johnson stood up but remained behind his desk. He stared at Stanley for several moments; then he proposed, "You. Yo' men. Y'all ain't gotta go nowhere though, Stanley. Y'all can still work heah if y'all want to."

"Some of them is. But, nah—not me. I can't work with no one like Rogers."

"You mean with a mean son-of-a-bitch! Yeah! Yeah. Uh, listen heah, Stanley. If I can offah you some advice. You a good man. Hard worker. Honest. Likes that aboutcha'. Likes that I can leave ya' heah while I do my bitness. Let ya' manage my money—pay folks when I ain't around. Nevah gonna let this heah Rogers do that.

"But Stanley, ya' needs to lose that nigger-lovin' attitude you got theah. Ya' next boss might not be as nice and understandin' as me. Might even git yo' ass strung up somewheres. Heah's two month's severance pay. Good luck finding mo' work."

"Thanks, Mr. Johnson. Sir—just give me another month. I'll—"

"Ya' startin' to ruffle my feathers theah, Stanley! You need to git on board or get the hell outta heah!"

CHAPTER 2

" . . . And so there we was left, with nothing but our shirts— and smiles," Mr. Pierce said, and the camp erupted with laughter. The Harris males, along with 30 other men and boys, were on a weekend hunting trip in the wilderness north and west of Boston.

"That Clem can tell 'em, can't he?" Papa Harris remarked to his tent mate, Joe Sharp. Around one of the 4 campfires, flickering flames and floating embers illuminated the campsite as the Harris males sat huddled together, while tales and good times were shared.

"Oh, yeah. He do a mighty fine job telling them stories. Speaking of mighty fine, that boy ya' got there doin' some mighty fine shootin', Bob."

"Thanks, Joe. Both my boys getting better and better. But you're right, that Bobby's something else. Ain'tcha' son?" Papa Harris replied, his prideful glow eclipsing the campfire's.

"Yeah, Dad. I guess so," replied Bobby as he continued to stoke the fire with a branch of hickory.

"You guess so!" exclaimed Steve, an 18-year-old who was sitting nearby. "That shot on that rabbit you got musta been 50 or 60 yards! And a headshot, too."

Bobby shrugged and said, "What? My daddy say take headshots on rabbits. I don't know. I just aim and shoot."

Many of the men shook their heads in reverence and chuckled. Papa Harris beamed with paternal pride. William took aim with his imaginary rifle and pulled the trigger while making shooting noises.

♣

James had just made it to the field. This time of year, the tobacco towered over all but the tallest men. For James, this was the place where his talents shone first. He did the work of a 20-year-old and carried the stature of one even though he was 5 years younger.

Initially, the pickers carried their sacks over one shoulder and placed leaves in them once their hands got full. They normally took off and put back on their sacks more than 20 times a day.

James carried his bag so that it hung in front of him and pulled his shirt up across his mouth and nose. He loaded his sack this way, taking his bag on and off only once in a day. Not rushing, he paced himself so that neither Stanley nor his men would notice him getting 12 hours' worth of work done in 10.

Others began copying his style, but because of the ever-changing work groups, it wasn't apparent who was the source. Since the slaves rarely worked with the same person during the same week, his methods spread throughout the plantation. Isaac knew who he could trust and showed them James' methods whenever it was safe.

"Anybody seen Isaac?" James asked a group as he approached them, knowing this should've been one of the days he worked with him.

James had left the shack ahead of Isaac and assumed he was behind him. He and James were close friends now, as much as you could have any kind of relationship in their situation. Friendship at Penelope Farms was relative—born out of mutual oppression.

"Nah," someone responded as he walked past them.

He continued to his spot and began picking leaves. Isaac arrived several hours later.

"Where you been?" James asked Isaac as he continued stripping the tobacco stalk. "My bag is almost full. I better slow down so you don't look so bad, huh?"

Isaac was on the other side of the row of plants, shucking and stripping them. James was able to catch only glimpses of him through the greenery.

"Yeah, you th-th-the b-b-best 'round here. Yeah—the b-b-best."

James kept on talking and tried to peer through the stalks to see his friend's face but remained unsuccessful.

"I saw Chloe, again, today. She looked good, too. She had her hair like I like it, you know?"

"Y-Y-Yeah. Up off she n-n-neck."

"And no, I didn't say anything to her," James said as he stepped down the row and continued picking. "Huh? You got nothing to say about that? I'm surprised."

"Yeah—that's g-g-good. She h-h-hair, yeah,"

"Huh? What? Isaac. Are you listening to me?"

James waited for a response; getting none, he poked his head between the stalks, looked into Isaac's eyes, and got the answer.

Isaac had been to The Uglies.

That was one name of the buildings on Penelope Farms where slaves were forced to copulate. Tobacco brought 30 percent of Master Johnson's income but was susceptible to the changing climate and the environment. A cold snap, severe flood or drought, or a swarm of insects could devastate his crop.

Big, strong, young male slaves were invaluable as workers and breeders to Master Johnson. But they were the most likely to try to escape or turn violent. Extra costs were associated with them, because of security issues.

Young girls and children, however, were, by far, the safest and most stable business for Master Johnson. The Uglies was at the core of his empire and the source of his wealth. Keeping the girls pregnant or nursing, the children young, and the babies coming was his goal.

Master Johnson was a commodity broker. His commodities being human beings of African descent. He bought, sold, and bred slaves like he'd done earlier, with horses. Only the most athletic of slaves were chosen, some being mated in pairs while others had multiple partners. None had a choice. The only way to ensure staying at Penelope Farms was getting pregnant or impregnating someone, usually within a year.

Called "Cupid's Cabin" by Master Johnson and "The Place" by the adult slaves, the younger children called it "The Uglies" because of the look on people's faces after they had been there. The humiliation, sadness, anger, resentment, embarrassment, and other emotions combined to actually change their appearance and create a stare those unfortunate ones gave. It was the appearance and stare James' friend, Isaac, had on his face now. An agonizing reality now etched in his soul.

"Isaac. I—I'm sorry."

Without looking at James, he barely replied, "Me, t-t-too."

"What—what happened? I mean uh, I, uh—how did it go? I mean—you know."

"They had us in st-st-stalls. J-J-Jest l-l-like horses, James. They sat th-th-there and—uh, watched. Or jest talked. Watched—and, uh, t-t-talked. Like we wun't e'much th-th-there," Isaac answered while he calmly picked leaves.

James stood there, frozen in time, as he slowly shook his head. He had heard the stories in the shack, but the trip to The Uglies had seemed far away. Now, confronted with the stark realization that it was closer than he wanted to believe, he cleared his throat and asked, "Who was it? Who was she?"

"I don't know. I don't know she n-n-name. I seent her befo'. B-B-But I d-d-don't know her. At, uh, at the readins'. In church and stuff. I d-d-don't know she."

"I don't know what to say, Isaac," James responded as he started picking leaves again.

"Me, neither. It was—uh, I feel—uh, I don't know h-h-how I feel! I'm r-r-runnin'. First chance I gits, I'm r-r-runnin'," his voice beginning to crack and quaver under the weight of his mourning in the late afternoon.

"Shh, not so loud!" James warned as he looked around to see if anyone was in earshot. "You remember what happened to Shadrach, don't you? It ain't been 2 months yet, and—" James whispered a scream as the ringing of a bell interrupted their conversation. "Huh—what's that clanging for?"

"We gotta go to the Big House, James. Th-th-that bell mean that."

"The—Big—House? J-J-Johnson Hall?" James uttered between the lumps in his throat.

A late summer chill came over him as they began walking in that direction. He hadn't been there in more than 2 years and immediately began thinking about Ruth, Carlton, Webster, the forbidden room, and the last time he was there—that episode in the study, when he didn't have any of the answers or any of the questions. A situation that still haunted him as the pounding in his chest thumped harder with each step.

Maybe Carlton's home—or dead. It's been—shoot, uh, it's been what, 2 years? Maybe I'll see Ruth. God, I'd love to see her. Huh, will she even recognize me? . . .

"Somthin' big goin' on now. That bell ain't rung fo' how long? Since Miss PEE-nelope got herself kilt, that's when. . . ." said an overtimer, and others agreed.

Overtimers were people who had been on Penelope Farms for more than 10 years. Usually, between 4 and 7 years was how long Master Johnson kept slaves. Only the ones with some special skill or talent stayed longer. The growing crowd seeped through the forest of slender oaks and continued toward Johnson Hall.

. . . Oh, no! What if Carlton's there? Would I recognize him? What would he say to me? What would I say to him? Hey, you no good, evil, wicked, piece of—yeah, right. I'll say hey, Massah Carlton, suh. After all, I'm still the slave, the chattel, in servitude, not free . . .

James gasped as Johnson Hall came into view. Fresh paint gleamed off the front, and the steps and porch showed signs of recent repair. The pillars stood like toy soldiers protecting Johnson Hall, the headquarters of so much wonder and woe.

He struggled to see a friendly, familiar face on the porch. The only ones he recognized were Master Johnson and Pastor Lee, and his spirit sank.

He looked down upon the familiar ground of his youth, recalling the times he'd chased Carlton and vice versa. The two of them scampering all around Johnson Hall, with Deeohgee tagging along. And he with Ruth in Johnson Hall and out to the orchards. His days of innocence snatched away in one fell *whoosh* of a whip crashing on Jacob's back. And the sickening memory of that last day of naiveté, before the world of bondage was fully realized.

Isaac grabbed ahold of him so he wouldn't walk over others who stopped because the surging crowd had come to a spot where they could go no farther. James looked up to the porch of Johnson Hall at Master Johnson and several other men near him.

Master Johnson stood up, walked to the first step, and proclaimed, "Mr. Stanley is gone. I fired him. I told you people theah was gonna be some changes. Well, meet y'all change—Rogers. Y'all new overseer." Then he sat back down in a chair perched near the oak doors.

Slowly, Rogers walked forward and down the stairs one by one. He paused at the bottom of the stairs as he scanned the crowd with a scornful gaze; then he continued out into the crowd, which parted. Ten armed men were on the porch, and several followed him down and walked several feet behind him. Six of Stanley's men who remained were standing off to the side or sitting on horseback in front of the porch, adding to the toy-soldier scene.

After a spit that landed on a little boy's shoulder, Rogers announced, "I'm a goddamn mean son-of-a-bitch. Y'all gonna' find that out d'rectly. I don't play. I don't take no shit. As long as y'all valuable to Master Johnson here, y'all live—maybe. Break any rule—whuppins' comin'. Look at me wrong—whuppins'. If'n I have a bad day—whuppins'.

"Slow down on work—whuppins'. Massah Johnson 'bacca come out black—whuppins'. Come out green—whuppins'. Best come out nice and brown. And runnin'! Huh—well, you best pray to yo' God that you die 'fo I catch ya'. And some of y'all better pray, too. I whup any slave I wanna when anybody run. As many as I feels like."

He paused his stroll near an elderly lady, looked her up and down, and barked, "What yo' name, gal?"

"Moriah, suh," she sheepishly replied, her worn body hunched over with age and practiced humility.

"Huh. Well, how old you, Mo-rye-yah?"

"I don't rightly know, suh."

"Ah, c'mon. Fitty? Maybe sixty, huh?"

"I reckons, suh."

"You reckon? What the hell you *do* 'round heah, Mo-rye-yah?"

"Much as I can, suh. Cook and clean mostly, suh."

"Yeah, that probably ain't too damn much," Rogers replied.

He reared back and punched her in the face. She took a stumbling step back and then crumpled to the ground. Drawing out his gun, Rogers cocked it, looked around at the crowd, and aimed it at Moriah. Prostrate and motionless, soft moans escaped her lips. A slight grin creased Rogers' evil countenance; then—*Bam, Bam, Bam*—he shot her three times, the echo ringing through the souls of the slaves.

The men who'd come with Rogers snickered. Stanley's former men calmed their steeds and cautiously cast their eyes over at Master Johnson. He remained seated in the chair on his porch, looking out at the scene. The slaves were shocked; a few muffled their sobs, but most stood there in stunned silence.

Oh, my God! He—he—he shot her! For—for nothing! Why?—Why?—Oh, my God! He shot her—why? Why!

The grin grew to a smile now as Rogers continued his walk and uttered, "Hey, hey—that felt good. Like I said, keep yo'self valuable, you live. Ol' Mo-rye-yah here wun't doin' shit. Jest eatin' and sleepin'. Costin' Massah Johnson here money. Breathin' my air, too. I needs my air."

He inhaled deeply as he twirled the still-smoking revolver on his right index finger and released a sinister snicker.

Oh, no! He's coming near me. Don't—don't look, James. Don't look! Calm down. Calm down—don't look! Help me, God. Help me. . . .

Rogers' cronies laughed with him as he exhaled and continued, "I don't care 'bout yo' feelins'. I don't care 'bout yo' babies. I don't care 'bout you. Any of ya'! I jest care 'bout runnin' this here PEE-nelope Farms here fo' Massah Johnson. I hope I makes myself clear."

Stopping in his tracks, he looked at James and asked, "You don't like me, do ya' boy?"

. . . Help me, God. Please don't let him kill me. Please don't let him kill me! Please . . .

Struggling to keep his heart in his chest, James humbly muttered, "I-I'se don't know whatcha' mean, Massah Rogers, suh."

. . . Please, please God. Don't let him kill me. Please . . .

"I said—do—you—like—me—boy?"

"Ya' seems like a—" James began saying when Rogers kicked him in the stomach, which sent him to his knees. Rogers then delivered a blow to James' head with the revolver that knocked him to the ground, and James curled into the fetal position. Rogers kicked him several more times and then walked off and continued, "I know y'all don't like me. Well, good. 'Cause I *hate* all y'all. There ain't no good nigger exceptin' a dead one. Or one that make Massah Johnson here money."

. . . Oh, God, please don't let him kill me. Please don't . . .

Rogers and his group continued laughing as he finished, "I hope I makes myself clear. Yeah, Mel, I'm gonna like it here. Go 'head."

"All right, all y'all git on back to the tree over yonder," Mel yelled as he pointed toward the slender oaks and the whipping tree beyond them. One of Stanley's men who remained, he whistled as they walked back through the forest. James struggled to his feet, Isaac being afraid to help, and followed the crowd along. Approaching the whipping tree, each of Rogers' 10 men grabbed a slave, and strung them up, having added to the number of straps on the tree. The other 6, including Mel, stood by and watched.

"We gonna call this our weekly git together. The furst time evr'y body git three. One fo' the Father. One fo' the Son. One fo' the Ghostly Spirit. How that sound, Pastor?"

"Sounds might righteous to me," Reverend Lee chuckled.

"That's fo' a good week. The badder da week, the mo' y'all gits. Go 'head, boys," Rogers ordered.

The sickening sounds of leather whooshing through the air and crashing on backs filled the air, exceeded only by the shrieks and wails of the men, women, and children who were unfortunately selected.

"*Grunt—whoosh—grunt—pow—whoosh—grunt—arrgh— pow—grunt—whoosh—arrgh—pow—arrgh—whoosh—grunt— arrgh—pow—whoosh—grunt—arrgh—whoosh—pow—arrgh— whoosh—grunt—grunt—pow—arrgh . . .*"

James looked around at the faces, reminding him of Jacob and his first time seeing a whipping, and of his own time being whipped. Luke was one of the ones chosen, the only one James knew by name.

"*Grunt—whoosh—grunt—pow—whoosh—grunt—arrgh— pow—grunt—whoosh—arrgh—pow—arrgh—whoosh—grunt— arrgh—pow—whoosh—grunt—arrgh—whoosh—pow—arrgh— whoosh—grunt—grunt—pow—arrgh . . .*"

As the slaves stood there—their eyes, ears, and souls assaulted— Rogers said with finality, "I hope I makes myself clear!"

"*Arrgh—grunt—whoosh—grunt—pow—whoosh—grunt— arrgh—pow—grunt—whoosh—arrgh—pow—arrgh—whoosh— grunt—arrgh—pow—whoosh—grunt—arrgh—whoosh—pow— arrgh—whoosh—grunt—grunt—pow—arrgh . . .*"

CHAPTER 3

" James. You 'sleep?" Isaac, stooped near James' cot, asked later that night.

. . . You like me, boy? . . . Best I can, suh. . . . God, please don't let him kill me. . . . Bam! Bam! Bam! . . . Best I can, suh. . . . Grunt—whoosh—pow—arrgh! . . . You like me, boy? . . . Gotta stay valuable. . . . Bam! . . . Best I can, suh. . . . Please don't kill me. . . . Bam! . . . Grunt—whoosh—pow—arrgh. . . . Bam! . . . Best I can, suh. . . . You like me, boy? . . . You like me, boy? . . .

"James."

You like me, boy? . . . You like me, boy? . . . Gotta stay valuable . . .

"James?"

"Yassuh," James replied.

"James. It's me, Isaac. James," Isaac said as he gently shook his friend.

With eyes wide open, James could see and hear only the events from earlier in the day.

. . . You like me, boy? . . . Gotta stay valuable. . . . Bam! . . . Best I can, suh. . . . Bam! . . . Please don't kill me. . . . Bam! . . .

"James. James!"

"Huh? Oh, Isaac. How long you been here?"

"A minute. H-H-How yo' belly?"

. . . I reckon, suh. . . . You seem—bam, bam, bam! . . . You like me, boy?

"Yes, suh. I do, suh."

"Huh? James?"

"Huh? Oh, Isaac. What?"

"I say how's yo' belly?"

"It still hurts, but I'll be okay."

"I sorry I didn't h-h-help ya' up."

"That's all right, Isaac."

"That Rogers somthin', huh."

"Yeah—ugh, yeah, he is," James replied as he gently rubbed his ribs. "My head still hurts, too."

"What Miss Netty say?"

"She said I'll be okay. Just a bump."

"Good. That good. Things gonna change, huh?"

"Yeah. It—uh, it will be different," James grunted as he sat up.

"How you doing?"

"Me? Shoot, I-I-I all right. I'm good. Yeah—good. He didn't git me. Luke, though. And Andrew. He—uh, they got it. And Miss Moriah. She was so nice."

"Yeah. She always had that smile when she gave us our dinner," James added; then he began to cry.

"It's okay, James. She in a b-b-better place. Ya 'member—the quickest way to freedom."

"It's not that. I'm sorry for her. But—I—I thought I was next. I believed Rogers was gonna shoot me. I didn't—I ain't ready to die."

"I'm glad he didn't kill you, too. I woulda felt badder than 'b-b-bout Miss Moriah."

"Thanks. Huh. It—I, uh, it seems selfish of me. I wasn't worried about Miss Moriah. Didn't care she got shot. I was only worried—I was only thinking—about me."

"Shoot. Nobody want to d-d-die, James. 'Quickest way to freedom' don't mean we *want* to die. Just that d-d-death is better than being a slave."

"Yeah. I sho' want to live."

"Boy, whole lotta folks got got today, huh? Luke. Andrew. Two ladies—I d-d-didn't know they names."

"Yeah, I know. I saw them get got. How are you doing?"

"Me. I'm good. Didn't get me—this time. But Luke—"

"I was talking about you—and, uh the—you know."

"Oh, that. Shoot, I kinda forgot 'bout that. Kinda—yeah. Hey, that Rogers somethin' else. I'll be okay. Jest gotta stay valuable."

"Oh, yeah. Stay valuable."

"What that mean? 'Valuable'?"

"Uh, well it means giving Massah Johnson something he wants or needs. Especially needs. Like picking his tobacco."

"Or makin' b-b-babies."

"Yeah—or that."

"James, uh, there's s-s-somethin' else I needs to tell ya', J-J-James. Somethin' 'bout The Uglies. I wuz gonna t-t-tell you in the fields today."

James rubbed his head and asked, "Uh, huh—what?" James adjusted his lean, and after some silence, he looked at Isaac and repeated, "What?"

"Uh—uh, th-th-they had us in horse st-st-stalls. When I came in, th-th-there wuz folks in 'em when I passed by."

"Yeah, you told me that already."

"Oh, I did. I tolt you 'b-b-bout they watched us and stuff? Laughin' at us and st-st-stuff?"

"Yeah, you did."

"Okay, th-th-then—nothing. Uh—n-n-nothing," Isaac said as he got up and began to walk away.

James grabbed ahold of his arm, spun him around, and said, "C'mon, Isaac. There's something else? What is it? Huh? What is it?"

Lowering his head, Isaac replied, "Well, uh. In, uh, in the, in th-th-the Uglies, J-J-James. Uh, they—they got girls th-th-there 'round C-C-Chloe's age."

James jumped up from his cot and shouted, "What!? No, they can't do that! Not that young! She's younger than me! They can't—"

"James! J-J-James—sit down. C-C-Calm down! Everybody lookin'."

James looked around at the pairs of eyes trained on him through the dark, and he slowly sat back down.

Oh, my God. Calm down, James. But—they can't do that! They, they . . .

"Sorry, James. I jest thought you should know. 'Bout Chloe and stuff. She wutn't there. But some girls 'round she age was."

After some silence, Isaac continued, "James, that Rogers. You think he crazy? I mean Cephas came from Georgia. And he s-s-say Massah Johnson nice next to some other owners he seent. And Stanley wuz good. Things gonna' ch-ch-change here, now. You right. Yep, that man sho' nuff crazy. Gotta stay valuable. First chance I git, I'm gone. . . ."

James heard very little of the rest of Isaac's conversation. The physical pain from the beating was overwhelmed by the mental pain of his impending mortality—when he believed he was next to die. But that pain, in turn, was insignificant compared to the emotional devastation currently ravaging his spirit. Three words clung to his consciousness—'round Chloe's age.

Dear God. This is James. I ask for help in doing what I can here as a slave. Living like this don't seem right. That preacher man says so—but I don't know. Why can't we have freedom? Freedom—freedom to choose who we want, what we want. I don't understand why we're chattel, not citizens. I don't understand. God—why you allow slavery to be? Why you allow men like this Rogers to live, and, and people like Miss Moriah to be murdered? Why, God? Why You allow girls like Chloe to, to, to be made to do these things Master Johnson wants them to do? Why, God? Why!? . . .

❧

James had worked in the orchards for a week after Dr. Andersen confirmed his bruised ribs but was now back in the fields and carrying bundles of tobacco from the fields to the curing barns. He saw Chloe leaving the curing barn and mumbled to himself, "Now is the time."

He walked up and blurted, "Hi, my name is James," so fast he wasn't sure if she understood him.

Smiling, she giggled, "Hi. I'm Chloe."

"I know."

"Oh, yeah? Well, what else you know 'bout me, James?" she replied as they stopped in their tracks.

"Uh, nothing. I meant I—I just knew your name, that's all." He searched her face and eyes for signs of The Uglies.

None, thank God. Thank God, I don't see none! Thank You, God. Thank You.

"Is that it?" she asked with a grin of anticipation.

"Huh? Uh, I was just kind of, you know, uh, noticing you around, you know."

"Well, I kinda noticed you, too."

"Really! I mean—I didn't know."

"You not supposed to know, James," she replied with a smile that melted his heart.

"Oh, yeah. I kinda noticed you."

"James. You already said that!"

Chuckling, James rubbed his forehead and added, "Oh, yeah. Huh, I forgot what I was going—oh, yeah! How do you know me? You work over in the orchards."

"James! The smart one. . . .

Smart slave, a dead slave, smart slave, a dead slave . . .

. . . Who don't know you? We used to call you 'whigger' 'round here when you was wit Carlton. Wearin' them fancy clothes. And shoes! James—you wore shoes! Some people say you the one comin' up with all these ideas. Everybody know you, James."

. . . smart slave, a dead slave, smart slave, a dead slave . . .

"You heard me, James? Everybody know you."

"Huh, I didn't know that. I am glad *you* know me, though."

"Yeah. Me, too," she replied with that heart-melting smile.

James got lost in it again, as many times before. He finally shook himself out of it and said, "Uh—hmm. Anyway, I'd like for us to, uh, to get together sometimes. Maybe sit together at church service. Or at supper when we can."

"Okay. Yeah, that will be nice."

"When do you go to church, Chloe? I don't think I ever seen you there when I went."

"I really ain't been goin'. I gotta reason fo' goin' now. I'll be there Sunday fo' sho'," she replied as they dove into each other's eyes.

James inched closer and could hear her breaths. He gently grabbed her hand and gave it a slight squeeze. The thumping in his chest became noticeable as a wispy whimper flowed out of her. After what seemed like an eternity to James, he let go of her hand, cleared his throat, and sighed.

"Well, I better be getting—" James muttered before a sharp pain crumpled him to his knees. He looked back and realized the butt of Smitty's rifle had crashed into his back.

"Git yo' ass back in dem fields, boy!" he screamed at James from his horse, the rifle barrel now trained on James' face. Picking himself up, James contained his rage as he glanced, embarrassingly, at Chloe.

"Yassuh, Massah, suh," he replied, the words more painful than the blow. He slowly walked away as his ears were assaulted by the demeaning, racial epithets Smitty spewed at Chloe.

As James reached the door of the curing barn, he glanced over his shoulder and saw Smitty slap Chloe to the ground. He froze for 237 years and clenched his fists as every fiber of his being screamed for justice and revenge. He stared as Smitty stood over Chloe and thrust his finger less than an inch from her face in an animated way, and James imagined the racial epithets Smitty continued to hurl.

Go, James. Go now. Leave. Turn around. Walk away. The Lord is my Shepherd, I shall not want. He maketh me to lie down in the green pastures. He leadeth me beside still waters. He restoreth my soul. He leadeth me in the path of righteousness for His namesake. Yea, though I walk in the valley of the shadow of death, I will fear no evil. For Thou are with me. . . .

❧

Chloe and James' relationship grew despite their situation. The only time they saw each other was at church services and occasionally at supper and back and forth near the storage barns. James always went to church early, but now he made sure to keep a seat for Chloe. They kept their feelings a secret, sure that it would be used against them if anyone knew.

Rogers and his men took over the chapel, so church services were held in the main clearing between the slave quarters and the curing barns. The most crowded Sundays had drawn twenty-five slaves. Many more had found religion since Rogers arrived, however. There was no choir, so the congregation sang all the songs.

"Micah, row your boat ashore. Hallelujah! Micah, row . . ."

". . . I'm an overtimer. I could be sold any day now," James whispered to Chloe as they sat side by side on the grassy earth.

"Don't say that, James. Anyways, they ain't gonna sell you. You got valyah they gonna use."

"Huh? What do you mean?"

She looked away and uttered, "I mean—The Uglies."

"Oh, yeah. The Uglies," James replied, lowering his head.

"Yeah," Chloe replied with a melancholy tone. She turned and looked helplessly at James.

". . . Micah, row your boat ashore. Hallelujah. Micah, row your boat ashore. Hallelujah. Oh, yeah! Iyin the Lord! Hallelujah! . . . Amen! . . . Praise the Lord! . . . Yeah, yeah! . . . Amen! . . . Hallelujah! . . ." the congregation exploded with hoops, hollers, and handclaps.

"Let us all pray. Owah Father . . ." Reverend Lee began as the congregation settled down.

"You know—you're closer to the uh, the age, than me, uh, Chloe," James said while he tenderly clasped her hand.

"Yeah. Yeah, I know. My momma say when I'se become a woman, whatever that mean. She say it won't be so bad," Chloe replied and then paused.

Her chin sunk to her chest, and a sigh escaped as her voice cracked a whimper. "I—I don't know, James. What if I don't like him? What if he—he don't like me? This ain't right, James. Makin' us do this. That—it ain't right!"

James squeezed her hand and resisted his instincts to comfort her in his arms. He cut his eyes toward his weeping lady as he pondered their situation.

Why do we have to live like this, God? Why are we slaves? Why do we lack liberty? Not citizens. Chattel. In servitude. Property. Slaves. Why are we—slaves, God? Why? What did we do? What did our parents do? What could anyone do to deserve this? Why, God? . . .

". . . we ask in Yo' son Jesus' name on His precious blood. A-men. Now, today we gone read from the Fuhrst Book of Peetah, Chaptuh Two, vuhrse 18. 'Slaves, submit yo'selfs to yo' massahs with *all* respect.'

"See that? In yo' Bible, it say *'all respect.' I* ain't sayin' this heah. *God's* sayin' it. Then in vuhrse 21 it say, 'To this you wuz called, 'cause Christ suffered fo' you.' Now, I'll be talkin' 'bout y'alls' callin'. And, and God's plan fo' y'all. And how slav'ry is a part of it. 'Cause y'all made Christ suffah fo' y'all. Amen. Now, it began wit good Abel and bad Cain . . ." spewed Reverend Lee.

. . . Respect—honor—obey. Why can't we have these things, God?

"James, meet me over by the storage barns tonight. 'Round midnight, okay?" whispered Chloe.

"Huh—what? Chloe, are you crazy? If Rogers catch us out there, there's no telling what he'll do. I take that back. I *know* what he'll do!"

"James, please! Hold yo' voice down."

Only then did James realize his labored breathing was secondary to the pounding in his chest. He was amazed at the range of his emotions in such a short period of time. From agonizing heartache to passionate heart lust—and back again.

"James, baby. I don't want my first time to be in The Uglies. Stuff, stuff been happening, uh to me. I don't know, James. Please! I think it gettin' close."

It is, Chloe. It is!

"Chloe. I—I don't know, Chloe. Your first time. My first time! I, uh, I don't know. The Bible says not to be joined together unless we get hitched. And I don't want no child of mine to be born into slavery, either."

"'Hitched'? Look 'round where you at, James. Gittin' hitched? What world you livin' in? You don't have a choice where yo' baby gonna be born, neither. Sooner or later, you gonna go to The Uglies. What you gonna do? Say 'No'? Huh? Huh!?"

"Uh, no—I guess."

"Will it be your first time or not? That's the only choice we got! Will it be your first time or not? And with someone you know. Someone you care for. Someone you like. You do like me, don't you, James?"

James swallowed hard as he cut his eyes toward her. He leapt into the dark-brown portals of her soul that framed her cherubic face.

"Yeah! Yeah, I do. When I see you, Chloe, I just want to grab you and hold you close to me. So—so close to me—yeah, I do."

"Well, come by there tonight. You can hold me all you want, then. As close as you want. Okay? Okay!"

"Huh? Okay," James answered in a husky whisper, his body alive and tingling.

The closeness of sitting next to her and the anticipation of seeing her that night overwhelmed him. He tried to control his breathing, each breath seemingly deeper than the previous one. He cut his eyes over at her again, and the thumping in his chest intensified. He touched her arm, and the warmth sizzled his soul. The sensual stirrings of his flesh became the sermon that day.

<h1 style="text-align:center">CHAPTER 4</h1>

Like every night before, James lay on his cot. This night, however, his heart pounded as never before. Sweating profusely, he thought about her. About his love for her. About his lust for her. About what they were going to do that late summer night.

If Rogers catches us, I may not survive. Shoot, we may not survive. Is it the Christian thing to do? "Thou shall not fornicate."

One of the Bible's absolutes. Maybe during those times. I don't know. During ordinary times, yeah. But these are not ordinary times. "Thou shall not fornicate."

We don't have a choice to have sex or not. They are forcing us to fornicate, so why can't we choose at least who we do it with? At least the first time. "Thou shall not fornicate."

And I promised. If she's caught out at night waiting on me, I'd never live with myself. But what if we're caught? Shoot, I'm going! I don't care if—shoot, I'm going!

Sliding out of his cot before midnight, he tiptoed toward the window.

"J-J-James. Where ya' goin'?" asked Isaac in a hushed tone as James passed his cot.

"Shh, be quiet. I'm going to see Chloe."

"Umm, look at 'cha n-n-now."

"What are you doing up so late?"

"Huh? Uh, J-J-James. I been thinkin'. Th-Th-Thinkin'—'bout runnin'," Isaac replied and slowly turned his head away from James.

James moved closer and sat on the ground near Isaac's cot.

"No, you should wait. Rogers is still too new. It's only been a couple of months. Give him time to settle here first. He'll get careless."

"Can't wait no m-m-mo'. I'm not saying it's tonight. But maybe. I jest up tonight thinkin' 'bout it—that's all. Maybe you right, James. G-G-Give him some time to make a mistake."

"Good. I'll see you later then, okay? Okay? The first one will never make it, okay? You gonna be here, Isaac? Don't go."

"You be c-c-careful out there. Rogers would whup you sumthin' fierce. And wit Chloe, too. Y'all b-b-bein' pure and all."

"You gonna' be here, Isaac? Isaac? Isaac. I—I don't want to leave you, my friend. But, but Chloe may get in trouble waiting on me. Wait. Please—wait. I—I can't leave you like this. Rogers might catch you. He may—he will kill you. You would be the first to try and run."

"I don't care. Don't care no mo'. Quickest w-w-way to freedom, huh. Yeah—freedom."

As he looked past James and into the darkness, his voice trailed off. James slumped his shoulders, lowered his head, and realized he was running out of words—and time. After some moments, Isaac looked back at James and allowed a smile to crack his solemn demeanor.

"J-J-James, you can keep me here tonight. Tomorrow. The next day, the next. But one day, you won't, and I'll be g-g-gone. We all gotta do what we gotta do. You go 'head—be wit Chloe. If'n I'm here when you git b-b-back, then I'm here."

James embraced and said goodbye to his friend. As he slid out the window and headed for the storage barns, he was startled by the way his heart was being ripped apart by this emotional entanglement. A chunk stayed behind with his friend. A chunk came along for the journey to Chloe. And pieces dropped along the way, leaving a trail of sorrow and emotional uncertainty he hemorrhaged—as certain as any footprint—with every step he took.

The half-moon shone enough for him to make his way through the night. The silence and solitude made the area he had walked so many times before seem new. He turned the corner of a building and caught sight of her. The supple curves of her body were enticingly highlighted by the partnership of dancing shadows from the moon and trees.

"Wow! You—you look different. I mean good, Chloe!" James blurted as he approached her. Seeing her immediately reminded his body of the wonderfully, queasy sensations he'd felt earlier.

"Thanks, James. I tried to fix my hair up. Folks always said I was big fo' my age."

"Well, I think you are beautiful for any age."

A flushed Chloe giggled, "Thanks, James."

Finally coming down off the Chloe high, James realized that standing where they were wasn't a good idea. Most of the buildings on Penelope Farms were built up on bricks because of the regular overflowing of nearby riverbanks, so they slid under one of them.

"You nervous, James?" Chloe asked as they lay next to each other, the underside of the floor of the building twenty inches from their faces.

James, for the first time, felt the warmth of her body and the thumping of her heart. After a hard swallow and a forced laugh, he mumbled, "Huh? Uh, yeah. A little. You?"

"A little—huh, a lot," she said with a laugh-like anxiety.

"Yeah—a lot." The tingling now reached his fingers. He looked at his hands and added, "Yeah, uh—a lot."

"Whew!" both simultaneously marveled as James' nervous eyes finally looked into Chloe's, which he had been avoiding all night. Smiling, she looked back as best she could, and then she turned away.

"What's wrong, James?"

"Uh—huh? Oh, nothing. I was just uh, thinking and looking and—ooo, look."

James pointed to a spot beneath another building. What first appeared to be more dancing shadows from the moon and the trees were the sensually rhythmic motions of bodies. Giggling, they looked under other buildings around them and saw several couples doing what they came there to do.

And, so, they did.

♣

An hour had passed since the lovers had introduced themselves to each other, and James gazed upon his lady's beauty. He noticed the fullness of her lips. The way she breathed slowly in and quickly out. The way her eyebrows arched when she was excited. The way her lips curled crookedly when she was thinking. And now, the way her face exuded a calmness of contentment. The rhythm of their heartbeats matched the rhythm of their bodies minutes before. James let out a slow sigh as he held Chloe tightly to his chest and listened to her speak.

". . . My momma and daddy still here. She work wit Miss Netty. My daddy work in the orchards 'cause of his age. What 'bout your family, James?"

"Huh—what? Oh, my family? I don't remember them, exactly, you know? I mean I used to see faces, hear stuff. Talking, singing—stuff like that. No more, though. She, my mama, she used to sing me 'Amazing Grace.' That's all I remember."

"Yeah! That was you when, what was his name? Shadrach! Yeah, he was singin', and you ran up there hollerin'."

"Yeah, that was me."

"I'm sorry for you, James. I don't know what I would do if my momma or daddy—or me—was sold. I would just cr-y-y-y-y."

"It is unusual for Master Johnson to keep y'all together. Folks say he splits up families whenever he can. Y'all must be valuable to—"

"Shh," Chloe warned.

The sound of footfalls got louder as someone approached. James could discern steps, shuffles, whines of reluctance, and grunts of pains. Out of the darkness appeared Mitch, forcibly leading a lady by the arm.

"Her name Martha," Chloe whispered as the couple passed by and then disappeared into the night. "She old—'bout 30, I guess. She work in the orchards. My momma say she done finishin' havin' her babies for Massah Johnson. Momma says you gotta have babies or it bad for you."

James' emotional roller coaster took another dip. He held her closer as his heart ached with remorse and sorrow.

"How—how are we supposed to live like this? Chloe—we shouldn't have to sneak around. We shouldn't have to rush. I can't live like this. We shouldn't live like this!"

"Now, James, don't go doin' nothin' crazy. Gittin' no crazy thoughts in yo' head. Okay? You hear? You ain't thinkin' 'bout runnin', is ya'?"

"What? Uh, naw. Not me."

"Good. I don't want you to git hurt. . . ."

. . . slave . . . nigger . . . chattel . . . property . . . servitude . . . freedom . . . liberty . . . citizen . . . slave . . . nigger . . . chattel . . . property . . . servitude . . . freedom . . . liberty . . . citizen . . . slave . . . nigger . . . chattel . . .

". . . I had a—uh, I had fun. You? James? James!"

. . . nigger . . . chattel . . . property . . . servitude . . . freedom . . . liberty . . . citizen . . . slave . . .

Chloe looked into James' distant eyes and whined, "James!"

"Huh—uh, what's wrong, Chloe?"

"I said I had fun tonight."

"Yeah, me, too," he replied with half a smile as he focused again on her.

Her look begged to ease some of the torment she sensed in James, to relieve a bit of the anger that was building. It was somewhat successful. He lost himself in her gaze, wrapped himself in her embrace, and escaped that strident bondage, if only for a fleeting moment. For him, it was something. Something where nothing was all he had.

"Anyway, we better go, huh, James. James? You hear me?" she asked as his stare became more intense. "James!"

"Yeah, I heard you. But I was just thinking, Chloe. Laying here, with you in my arms. Enjoying these moments. I just don't think our second time should be in The Uglies, either," he said as he pulled her closer.

"I likes the way you think!"

James arrived at his shack an hour before dawn and ruefully discovered Isaac's empty cot. The emotional roller coaster he'd been on all the night took another devastating plunge, forcing him along for the ride.

"Dear God. Please protect my friend Isaac as he seeks his freedom. Keep him safe from harm, and don't let Rogers catch him. Amen," prayed James. He lay down as his soul sang for Chloe and sobbed for Isaac. He was soon awakened by the yelling and greeted by, "G-G-Good morning, James."

"Isaac! You're back!"

"Shh, James. Not so loud. I just went out to the th-th-thicket to see how far it was. And how long it would take. I think I'll wait, like you s-s-say, though. Rogers gits comfortable, then I'm gone. Anyhow, I'll ask ya' 'bout last n-n-night wit Chloe later," Isaac said as they left the shack.

CHAPTER 5

"I can't believe this shit! The nerve of these goddamn Abolitionists! And a nigger—takin' a white man to court! To the white man's U.S. Supreme Court," Master Johnson screamed as he slammed the newspaper onto his desk.

Rogers, continuing his stroll around the study, viewed the extensive collection, rubbed his hand over the intricately designed, leather-bound volumes of literature and muttered, "You sho' gotta lotta books in here."

Master Johnson, still reading his newspaper article, never looked up as he shook his head from side to side. He tapped his right index finger on his desk as he murmured, "Can you believe this shit, heah! Huh—Rogers, you ever heah of any shit like this!"

"Like what, uh—Mr. Johnson, suh?"

"Like this heah—what I been readin' to ya'!"

"'Bout yo' son? You mean that?"

"Nah, nah! I'm past that. That boy can cry all he want—his ass stayin' right wheah he at. I already got the telly ready to send. I'm talkin' 'bout these Abolitionists."

"Nah, suh, uh—Mr. Johnson, suh," Rogers, unsure, replied as his stroll was leading him toward the desk.

"And for freedom, like any slave could ever be free. Hell, they wouldn't know what to do if'n we didn't tell 'em. I swear, what Bible these Nawthurners readin' anyhow?"

Dong! Dong!

"Don't rightly know, suh," Rogers replied as he peered onto the desk and picked up a piece of paper.

. . . Dong! Dong! Dong!

"What?"

"I said I don't rightly know, Mr. Johnson!"

His proximity caused Master Johnson to finally look up, and he saw Rogers holding the piece of paper upside down. He smirked, took the paper from Rogers, and asked, "Anyway, how's everything goin'?"

"Fine, suh. Been fo' months, and exceptin' for Caleb, no one even tried to run. Had to kill a couple, though. Old ones wit no value."

"They got some value. My medical bills keep gittin' higher."

"Well, suh. You beat some. You kill some. The others git a-scared. You have less problems. If I beat 'em less, then mo' will run. You want that?"

"Nah. I guess you right. What you think of James?"

"Who? Which one he?"

"Young buck, 'bout fifteen. The first day you was heah, you kicked the shit outta him after you shot that old wench."

Rogers shrugged and said, "Okay. If'n you say so. I ain't had no dealins' wit him. He jest like all the other niggers here."

Chuckling, Master Johnson continued, "I shoulda' known. Keep yo' eye on him. He's a smart one. And probably sneaky. He sho' got you fooled."

Master Johnson then dove back into his article as Rogers seethed.

❧

"So, honey, how's the school?" Mama Harris asked Bobby, who was looking past her and outside the sitting-room window. Situated to the left of the front door, it offered an expansive view of their Boston neighborhood. The Arnolds' house, with its brown and tan color scheme, sat off to the right. The Marts' house sat directly across Bellens Street, with the white, wooden swing slowly swaying in the gentle summer breeze. And their own manicured lawn and the serpentine walkway that eventually found its way up to their front door framed the scene perfectly.

Two days home from his prep school, several of Bobby's friends were on their way to take him out for some fun, which made him anxious.

"Fine, ma," he replied, barely glancing her way.

"So, tell us about your classes."

"Ma, it's just classes. It's just a school like any other!"

"Boy, don't sass yo' mother like that," Papa Harris warned as he stared at his firstborn from across the room.

"Boy, don't sass yo' mother like that," William repeated in a whisper.

"Yes, sir. Shut up, William! Ma, I gotta go," Bobby implored as his eyes went from his father to his brother to his mother, and then to the window, where he saw his friends turning a corner and heading for the house.

"Ma! Bobby told me to shut up."

"Both of y'all be quiet!" Papa Harris declared with paternal thunder. "Sit down, boy. You don't leave 'til we say you can leave."

"Yes, sir."

"Bobby. Son. There's fellas here, Bobby. Even these here boys coming now and in the South who would love to have the chance you got."

"I know, Dad. I know."

"We spending a lot of money keeping you in that school."

"Yes, sir, I know. I'm doing my best."

"That's all we can ask, baby," Mama Harris added as she looked toward her husband. "Bob, let the boy go."

"That boy need to learn to appreciate what he got. When I was his age . . ." Papa Harris vented as Bobby kissed his mother and rushed off.

❧

Luke had had enough. The twenty-two-year-old had been on the plantation for more than eight years, eight years longer than he wanted to, eight years past his comfort zone—and he was running. Having been moved to the shack nearest to Johnson Hall and away from the younger boys, he slid out a window, raced through the slender oaks, scurried past Johnson Hall, and dashed into the orchards, his bare feet pounding the dirt and grass. By dawn he was miles away—but not far enough.

Leaving the shack that morning, James saw Rogers as he brought bloodhounds out of Luke's shack. For an instant, their eyes met before James turned his head away. Rogers' glare sent a chill through him, though.

There was evil and hate in them. More than usual. What did I do? Why did he look at me like that? Did—did they find out about me and Chloe? . . .

Rogers, three of his men, and four bloodhounds headed northwestward. James stood there watching and wondering about the glare until the crack of a whip across his back snapped him back to the present.

From his horse, Mitch screamed, "Git on goin', boy," as he placed his hand on his revolver at his side.

"Yassuh, massuh," he muttered as he headed off. He continued in the line heading to the fields when Jerry yelled for him. Another of Stanley's men who'd stayed, he was growing accustomed to his new authority and new boss. In the nights Chloe and James spent together, he and Mitch were seen regularly taking women into their company.

"C'mon! Git yo' ass movin'," he ordered as he pushed James in the desired direction.

Oh, no, The Uglies! It's time for the Uglies. It—it—it's time . . .

A sense of dread drained James, and he stumbled. Only Jerry's prodding and pushing kept him moving. Recalling what Isaac had told him, he considered running right there and then. He glanced at the revolver Jerry carried tucked in his side holster. Then he cautiously scanned the area around them.

Take the quickest way to freedom, James. If I can get that gun, I'll be able to get away then. Yeah—to freedom. Or die trying. . . .

As they walked, James slowed down, causing Jerry to move closer to him. He looked up ahead of them again. No one in sight. He stumbled once to get Jerry closer. He thought about Jerry's gun again, looked ahead again, and then swallowed hard. He slowly rubbed his palms together and tried to calm his knotted stomach.

. . . God. Please help me. I'm gonna run now. Please—please keep me safe from harm and danger. Bless me as I—

"Where you takin' that boy, Jerry? To Cupid's Cabin?" asked Tarner, who came up behind them and shocked James out of his thoughts.

"Him? Nah, this 'un ain't ready fo' no Cupid's Cabin. Probably wun't know what to do even if we drew him a map. Nah, Master Johnson takin' this boy on a lil' trip. That's all."

CHAPTER 6

James was shackled and loaded onto a wagon. It reminded him of his arrival at Penelope Farms nine years earlier. Five shackled slaves—two adult males, two adult females, and him—were on this wagon. Mitch and Thompson rode alongside the wagon with Master Johnson and the driver, Mr. Boo.

I remember him. The first slave I met here. The storyteller. God, how I miss those stories. They were so—valuable. Yeah, valuable. Huh, I wonder how valuable Mr. Boo is to Massah Johnson? He's been here a long time. A overtimer. I wonder what his value is?

They left through the freshly painted iron gates with the "BA" initials on it that James hadn't seen since his arrival. The journey was quiet and uneventful. The road turned left and then right, as it meandered through the woods and over several streams.

An hour after leaving Penelope Farms, they approached a small town. A crowd gathered around the dock near a building with the name, "STUART TRADERS," stenciled across the top. Though there was a variety of noises from the crowd, James could make out some of what was being said. A rotund white man in his 50s stood on a platform above a screaming throng of hysteria and rattled off a series of numbers. James remembered the stories he'd heard in the shacks too many times from recent arrivals.

Auction—it's an auction! Oh, my God! I'm being sold! Chattel . . . property . . . slave . . . servitude . . . liberty . . . chattel . . . property . . . chattel . . . property . . . chattel . . . property . . .

Fifteen minutes later, the five slaves—standing on the dock like figurines in a storefront window—were eyed by the throng. They were pulled forward one by one, bared to the waist, and bid on. The auctioneer's voice was the only discernible sound among the noise.

The auctioneer, perched on a stool off to the right of the platform, began reading the first of the papers Master Johnson had handed him.

"This heah a 25-year-old Negro male of good stock. Lookee the muscles on this buck. Likes bein' a slave, too. Answers to the name of 'Saul.' The biddin' gonna start at $2,000. Gimme two-thousand, 21, 21, 21, 21, 22. Gimme 22, 22, 22, 22, gimme 23 . . ."

James sneaked a peek out at the throng of mostly white men, all yelling or gesturing something in what seemed like total disorganization. Being cautious not to be caught looking, he noticed several women and some Negroes, too.

Where am I going? I didn't say goodbye to Isaac! Or Chloe! . . . I haven't seen her all week. . . . Will they ever know? This ain't right. Chattel . . . property . . . chattel . . . property . . . chattel . . . property . . .

The slam of a wooden gavel on the pedestal and the shout of, "*Sold,* for $2,850!" by the auctioneer brought James back. The next two didn't receive high-enough bids for Master Johnson. Then Martha was sold for $1,700. One of the auctioneer's helpers then pushed James forward.

I wish I was at the Uglies. The Uglies got to be better than this. God, I can't believe I'm saying this. Something's worse than The Uglies! . . . Chattel . . . property . . . chattel . . . property . . . chattel . . . property . . .

The auctioneer looked at Master Johnson, seemingly questioning what was on the paper concerning James.

"Everythin's right on theah," Master Johnson insisted, and the auctioneer began.

"Heah we got a 15-year old boy, if'n y'all can believe that. Look at dem feets. He gonna be way over six foot tall 'round 20 years. More than 200 pounds, too. Answers to the name of 'James.' We gonna start at $1,500. Who gonna gimme 15, 15, 16, 16? Gimme 17, 17, 18, uh—gimme two-thousand dollars! Gimme 21, 21, 22. Twenty-three, 23, 24, 24, 25, gimme 25, 26, 26, 27 . . ."

James wobbled slightly as a long-forgotten memory shot through him. It was a place like this—the same sounds, the same feel. He glanced over at a nodding Master Johnson and then at the exuberant crowd, trying to remember.

"... *Three thousand dollars!* Gimme 31, 31, 32. Gimme—" the man barked until interrupted by Master Johnson.

Something about this . . . Oh, my God. I remember! Yeah, I remember. Oh, my God, I remember—

"I changed my mind. He ain't fo' sale right now," Master Johnson declared as he hurriedly walked off the platform, causing an uproar in the crowd. James was led down off the dock and back to the wagon by Mr. Boo.

"That ain't good bitness, Hiram," the auctioneer warned.

Master Johnson strode to the wagon. In his head, he was figuring the money he made and the revelation regarding James.

♣

The group, minus two, plus two, headed back to Penelope Farms, but James' mind remained at Stuart's Traders.

"I remember," James whispered.

"This been a good day, Mr. Boo," Master Johnson said as they rode off, the barks and the catcalls of the disappointed crowd fading in the distance.

"Yassuh, Massah Johnson. I reckon it wuz."

"I made $200 on John, $300 on Martha. Gotta good deal on dem two new ones I got. And I finds out I got a new prized buck, too."

"Guess that why you gots the money, suh," Mr. Boo replied, clenching the reins tighter.

. . . I remember being on a dock like the one I just left. Somebody yelling numbers. Some man yelling numbers. Lots of people yelling. Five hundred—a thousand—two thousand. Yeah! I was there with some people. A man. A woman. A baby. My—my parents? My sister or brother? My family?

I see faces. I can see their faces! My Mama? My Daddy? M-M-My Mama and Daddy! I can see them fighting. I can hear their screams while some white man grabbed me. I remember the look on this lady's—on my mama's—face. The terror. The anguish. The heartbreak! The pain! . . .

"Yeah, Mr. Boo. This heah wheah I makes my money," Master Johnson proclaimed as he put the counted money into a satchel he carried.

"Yassuh," Mr. Boo replied, clenching the reins to pain.

. . . I remember this man—my daddy being knocked down and kicked, and he still struggled to get to me. To his son—to me! His anger. His—his rage! He would have killed to get to me—if he could. I remember screaming "Mama" over and over and over. I remember the trip. Coming to Johnson Hall. I—I remember. I remember. Oh, my God! I remember! . . .

"They loved me. They loved me," James mouthed another whisper as the tears built up in his memory, flowed from his soul, and spilled out through his eyes while the creaking wagon jerked and swayed along the journey.

"My Mama. She loved me. M-M-My daddy. He—he—he fought for me. My daddy did. . . ."

"Let's see. I'll call that tall gal theah Ruth since I ain't got no mo' Ruths theah. The other one, I'll call Rachel. I hate this naming shit. Miss Penelope was so good at this," Master Johnson complained while writing on the bills of sale he'd retrieved from the satchel.

"I 'member, Massah Johnson."

"I really miss her, Mr. Boo."

"We's all do, suh. We all misses her somethin' terrible."

The wagon pulled off onto a side road leading to a small farm. "Hiram! How the hell ya' doin'?" a man yelled as he walked out of a shack in need of repair and painting.

"Jest fine, Andy. You in the market?"

"Whatcha' got? I do need me a strong buck 'round here. How 'bout fifteen hunnerd fo' that one?" he said and pointed at a despondent James.

. . . They were fighting for me. For me—their son. Fight 'em, daddy! Fight 'em hard! Fight—fight 'em, Daddy. . . .

Master Johnson hopped off the wagon and strode toward the back as he said, "Oh, no, no! Ol' James there gone be my prize buck someday when he finish growin'. I jest stopped biddin' on him at $3,000."

He paused for a moment; then he slapped a slave on the back and motioned to Mitch to unshackle him.

"How 'bout Isaiah heah? Good stock, already made three babies, and he like bein' a slave. You can have 'im fo'—$1,700."

"Okay, I reckon that's fair," Andy replied. "Oh, by da way. I seent yo' new man draggin' a dead nigger behind him earlier today."

"Damn! Must be Luke," Master Johnson said in disgust as he kicked at the ground.

Once they were on the way back, Mitch, now riding alongside, asked, "Mr. Johnson. You coulda got mo' fo' Isaiah at the auction. Why didn't you ask fo' mo'?"

"Yeah. Ol' Andy theah is a good, longtime customer. And he a good neighbor. It's good bitness to keep neighbors happy. I'll make up fo' it on other deals."

Mr. Boo clenched the reins to bloody fingers and palms.

. . . My—mama. My—daddy. They—they loved, they loved me! They loved me! They loved me! They loved me. Thank you, Mama and Daddy. Thank you. . . .

❧

That night James tried explaining to Isaac what the auction was like, the hideous humiliation that, incredibly, dwarfed even their existence at Penelope Farms. Having his soul bared to a flock of fools, having a sea of strangers examine his being, and realizing his value as a human being determined by this assembly of antagonists left James woefully searching for the words to convey the moment.

"I never thought I would *want* to go to The Uglies, Isaac. I wanted to cry. I wanted to run. To fight—anything! I just wanted to get away. If I could've killed myself right there, I would have! I understand now! I understand, Isaac. The quickest way to freedom. I—I understand now. If I could have right there, I would have died."

James' head remained lowered as he sat on the ground next to his cot. Isaac squatted next to it and looked past him, toward the other denizen.

"They took me n-n-nowhere. Jest The Uglies. I reckon I good fo' makin' babies. Not fo' sellin'. Jest workin' in the fields and makin' babies. It jest ain't right, J-J-James. The way they treat us. I don't care what th-th-that preacha' man say. It ain't right."

"Yeah, I think you're right. Huh—I *know* you're right! Isaac, uh I, uh—I remembered my parents, too," James said as distant thunder rumbled.

"Huh?"

"I said I remember my parents, Isaac."

"What! What you m-m-mean?!" Isaac exclaimed as he snapped his head toward James.

"Yeah, when we got to the auction, I felt something—something strange. Something, uh—familiar, like I had been there before. But it was new, too. After we left, we went to some town. I remembered hearing some boys talking about an auction, so I knew . . ."

Lying on his cot later as the rain had come and gone and come again, the still of the shack was interrupted by the patter of dripping water and several snorers. James kept going over the day in his mind.

. . . My mama and daddy loved me. I got a brother or sister, or maybe even both by now. Fifteen years old, huh. This is the first time I heard anyone say how old I am. Let's see—

Ka-boom!

. . . Whoa! Uh, I've been here for more than nine years, so that means I came here when I was six. Hmm, Mark and Sarah are about six, maybe a couple of others. They're still babies. Just babies....
Ka-boom!

The tympanic rumblings, getting closer with each lightning strike, rattled the walls of the shack as the wind picked up. The stale air that lived there was pushed out by the refreshing scents that came in on the cooling eddies.

"It's about time. If I'm going, it's now," James mumbled as he got up from his cot.

"You g-g-gonna still go out on a night like this?" Isaac asked as James tried to sneak past him.

"Yeah, I got to. She's going to be waiting on me."

"I think it's mo' than j-j-jest she waitin' on you. You want some, huh? You want some bad."

"You got me on that one," James laughed. "God, it's great being with her."

"You better get goin' then 'fo it starts."

"Yeah, you're—"
Ka-boom—boom—boom!

"Yeah—you're right. See you later," James replied as he headed off for his rendezvous.

"Okay. I—I—"

"What? Isaac, what is it?" James asked as he came back to Isaac's cot. "You ain't running, are you?"

"It would be a g-g-good night to. They couldn't follow my tracks, huh? But, nah. It's jest—I jest wish—I wish I d-d-did it like you and Chloe. You know, yo' f-f-first time not in The Uglies. Wit somebody you know—someone you like—and stuff."

"Yeah."

"I miss out on that, huh? G-G-Go 'head, now. She waitin'."

"Yeah—I'm sorry."

"Thanks. Go 'head—go!"

"Okay, I'm—"

Ka-boom—boom, boom, boom, boom.

"I'm going."

"Stay close to the b-b-buildings. So you don't git hit, huh?"

"C-r-r-r-a-a-c-c-c-k-k-k—KA-BOOM—boom—BOOM—boom, c-r-r-r-a-a-a-c-c-k-k-k—KA-BOOM," nature exploded, shaking everything on Penelope Farms. Gusts and gales buffeted dirt, leaves, and rain over, around, through, and under the buildings. Pairs of bodies shimmering in the shadows glistened from the sweat and mist in a sensually delightful duet as only intimates do. Chloe and James held each other tight while water and sweat squished between their bodies.

". . . I—I, oh—James, baby! . . ." Chloe cooed as she gasped, grasped, and giggled.

". . . uh, huh, uh huh, uh huh—ooo . . ." James replied while he grunted, groaned, and ground.

". . . Oh—oh—oh! Oh, God! . . ."

". . . Oh, God, Chloe! I—I love rainy nights—oh! . . ."

"Oh, baby. I love rainy, oh, yeah—"

KA-BOOM—BOOM—BOOM!

"Oh! Baby, wuz that you? Oh . . ."

". . . You know it, girl! Oh, God, you know it—oh, shit! This—is—so—good! . . ."

". . . ugh, oh, baby, I love—oh, I love bein' wit you, baby. Oh, God, on rainy nights wit you, baby! In the mud. Oh, yeah! . . ."

". . . I love you—oh, God! I love you . . ."

". . . I—I—I—ooo, baby . . ."

C-r-r-a-a-c-c-k-k—KA-BOOM! Boom—boom—KA-BOOM! C-r-r-a-a-c-c-k-k—BOOM! BOOM! BOOM! . . .

Chapter 7

The noon summer sun shone unmercifully on all in the tobacco fields. Isaac was led out of line again that morning. Looking over at an old lady, James wondered why she was out there in that heat and not over in the orchards, where there was some shade. Remembering Moriah, James went over to her and placed some of his leaves in her bag.

"Take it easy for the rest of the day. Don't sit—just make it look like you are work—" James said just as Rogers rode up hard, his steed snorting and clomping in place.

"Git yo' ass back over there, boy," he screamed. "Hey, gal. You okay? Huh?"

"It too hot fo' she, suh," James said as he walked away.

Immediately, he knew it was the wrong thing to say. Saying anything was the wrong thing to say. Rogers whistled twice quickly while he unholstered his gun, and two men rapidly rode up. They strung James up between two plants.

Administering five lashes, Rogers screamed, "You think I'm stupid, huh? You think I'm stupid? Huh? Smart-ass nigger, I'll show yo' ass! . . ." as the 3 men pummeled him with fists and boots to his torso.

James was forced to remain in the field for the rest of the day. He never saw the lady again. Isaac was lying on his cot when James finally got in that night from the hospital shack. He told Isaac what had happened in the fields.

"You okay?" he asked.

"Yeah. I'm glad he didn't tear off my shirt. I got some bruises, that's all. Chloe's mama took care of me," James answered and cautiously lay down.

Isaac followed him and said, "I-I-I was at The Uglies a'gin. Somebody diff'rent, too. This ain't right, J-J-James."

"Yeah, ugh—yeah, I know."

"Do you ever think 'bout havin' a family, James?"

"Whoa! Where did that come from?"

"I wuz jest th-th-thinkin' 'bout bein' free. Bein' in The Uglies, that what Massah want. For us t-t-to make babies. B-B-But no families. Jest babies. Like they want us to think that way. No family. No love. Jest sex. So, I jest been th-th-thinkin'. Not that way. 'Bout bein' free. If you wuz free—then would you want a f-f-family?"

"Nah! Not here!"

"I don't m-m-mean here. I mean someday, when we's free."

Lying on his side now, James contemplated for a moment and then said, "Then—yeah. I guess so. I just want to be free first. I got to be free, first. Then I'll think about a family. I don't want no family here! I don't want no slave baby!"

"Don't g-g-git mad at me, James."

"I'm sorry, Isaac. I'm not mad at you. But aren't you angry? Aren't you mad at this—at our lives? If you can call this a life!"

"J-J-James, I was mad six years befo'. I was angry five years past. What come after angry? Then what come after that? And after th-th-that? And after that? Keep on goin' twenty times. Th-Th-That's what I am now. I tell ya' whenever I gits my chance, I'm gone. I'm sorry if'n you get whupped 'cause of me. But I'm runnin'. I wanna family. A free f-f-family. I—I want a free, a free life. Yeah—a life."

The strength of his friend's conviction forced a smile onto James' face. The risk he was willing to take for freedom, the fact that he trusted him with his plans touched him deeply. He propped himself on an elbow, peered deep into Isaac's eyes and asked, "So. What are you going to do when you get free?"

"You mean besides a family? I don't know," Isaac answered with a shrug. "Huh—I—I don't know. I jest know I wanna be free. That's all."

"Huh? How do you know you want to run?"

"I don't know. I jest started havin' these dreams 'bout r-r-runnin', ya' know. I guess that's it."

"What do you dream of?"

"Lots of stuff. In one, I dream I c-c-can fly, James. That's how I gits away. I flies away like a bird. High in the clouds over everythin'. B-B-But I comes back to drop sumthin' on Massah Johnson head. Then I flies away forever."

"Just be sure you say goodbye before you run—or fly—away."

"Okay," Isaac smiled.

Walking to their meeting spot one night, James wondered how different his and Chloe's life could be if they were free. The conversation with Isaac about families had him wondering about a family with Chloe, and what a fantastic mother and wife he thought she would be. The ribs no longer throbbed, but were still sore. The thought of seeing Chloe was the salve that eased all that ailed him. Turning the corner, he saw her, the sensual curves of her body capturing his heart. Their eyes met, and James saw pain in hers.

Oh no! The Uglies! Not The Uglies—no!

"Chloe, what's wrong?" James reluctantly asked as he approached her.

She grabbed his hand, and they slipped under the shack.

"Jest hold me, please," she replied and began crying.

"Chloe—tell me. What's wrong?"

God, what's wrong with Chloe? What's wrong—I really don't want to know the answer. What if I'm right? God—please let me be wrong. I hope I'm wrong! Is it The Uglies? Why, God? Why do you allow this?

Nearly an hour passed before her cries died down to whines and whimpers. Ten minutes later, James found the nerve to ask the question he was terrified to hear the answer to.

"Uh—Chloe. What's—what's wrong with you? What's—"

"James, that lady—my momma—that lady," she interrupted before bursting into tears again. James held her in his arms and gently rocked her.

Her mama? Oh, my God. Massah Johnson sold her mama? Did Rogers kill her mama? Oh, no, I hope that ain't true. Neither one. What could it be?

"That lady who I been callin' momma. She ain't my momma, James!"

"What? How—how do you know?"

"I was tellin' her 'bout we talking 'bout family and stuff. I ask her if Mr. Reuben really my daddy, but her face looked funny. I asked her what's wrong, but she jest say, 'Don't you fret 'bout that, chile.' But I keeps askin' her and askin' her and askin' her. James, my momma was sold right after I was born!"

"Oh, my God!"

"She had three girls befo', and Massah Johnson wanted her to make some boy babies. When I was born, that was it. Mr. Reuben, he my daddy. But my momma, James, I—I don't know where she be. I got sisters, but they was sold off, too. But he keep me here. My momma was sold 'cause of me, James. If I had been a boy, she still be here. I—I—I don't know what to do, James. I don't know what to feel. I jest know I'm scared, and I—I don't know why I'm scared."

"Chloe. I—I'm sorry. I don't know what to say. Damn slavery!" James exploded as his fist crashed into the ground.

"Shh, James, hush now. We can't get caught here."

"I'm tired of it. The way we get treated, selling our family like we was nothing! It just ain't right. We're people!"

"Shh, James! Shh. Jest hold me, James. Be quiet, and jest hold me."

Property . . . chattel . . . slave . . . property . . . chattel . . . slave . . . property . . . chattel . . . slave . . . property . . . chattel . . . slave . . . property . . .

They lay there through the night, the silence broken only by Chloe's intermittent sobs and sighs. Later, James opened his eyes to darkness, and, as he rose, he realized two things. One, that Chloe was still lying near him and that two, they were still under the shack—as his head crashed into the bottom of the floor.

"Oww! What—what time is it? Chloe, wake up! We got to get back!"

"Huh, what? James, what time is it? How long we been out here?" Chloe responded as she struggled to regain consciousness.

"I don't know. Let's go now!" he whispered. They scampered back and, fortunately, arrived minutes before the wakeup call was sounded. Leaving the shack that morning, James was exhausted. He and Chloe had just slept, but the emotions of the previous night had drained him.

Just when I thought The Uglies was the worst that could happen, the auction comes and changes my perspective. Now, huh—now family bonds are ripped apart. Respect. Dignity. Our history. All these things are taken from us. If you cut us, don't we bleed? If you pain us, don't we cry? If you wound us, don't we hurt? Huh! Don't we! DON'T WE!...

James' mind swirled as he followed the line out toward the fields. Isaac, three boys ahead of James, was led away from the line. He glanced back and made eye contact with James.

... To The Uglies again.

The Cambridge Preparatory School for Boys had 105 students and a faculty of 12 set among 40 acres of immaculately manicured landscape, housed in 4 separate structures. One 1-story building housed the administration and the President's quarters. One 4-story building housed the dormitories. And 2 3-story buildings housed the classrooms, cafeteria, and gymnasium.

Bobby was one of 4 Negroes enrolled there, though none of the other 3 were in his classes. His feeling of isolation began to mute his positive attitude as he became cranky and ill-tempered. And certain classmates exacerbated these feelings. Most of his classmates were ambivalent toward him, but a vocal few, like Nick, let their disdain be known.

". . . I bet you know! Yeah, Boy-bee, you know. One of my cousins in Tennessee owns somebody look just like you. He smarter than you, though, 'cause he know his place," Nick taunted from across the room.

"I'm free," Bobby weakly replied, the shallow words dying amid the snickers.

"You free here, Boy-bee. Go see my cousin, huh. I'll even buy you a train ticket! One way, of course. You'll be just another nigger slave."

"Boy-bee, Boy-bee, Boy-bee," rained taunts from 2 other classmates.

Bobby shot, quicker than lightning, out of his seat and was all over Nick, grabbing him in a headlock before any of the classmates could move. The 2 taunters eventually made it there. One grabbed Bobby's neck while the other tried to break his grip by pummeling him with his fists.

"All right, all right, settle down, boys," Headmaster Willis commanded upon returning to the room. "Everybody back to your seats—now!"

The combatants dispersed and trudged back to their assigned areas. Bobby plopped himself back into his seat, still huffing and puffing from his rage and exertion.

"Okay, I don't know what happened here. But it ends here and now! Mr. Harris? Do you have that problem finished?"

"Yes, sir, I do. The answer is seven."

"Very good, Mr. Harris. Everybody got that?"

"You guessed one right—Boy-bee. Even a broke clock is right twice a day."

❧

It was nearing the end of the growing season, and most of the work shifted to preparing the field for the winter, the wrapping and shipping of the remaining tobacco, and the cleaning of the buildings used in the process. These were also the busiest times for The Uglies. Master Johnson didn't want many babies being born during winter. As Dr. Andersen had recommended, they wanted their first few months to be warm, to give them a chance to grow and thrive—to add value.

. . . I wonder where Chloe is? It's been nearly 3 weeks since I've seen her. God, I hope Massah ain't sold her. A lot of boys been coming and going in the shacks. Maybe he did. I guess he did sell her. He did because he could. God, I miss her. Think of something else, James. Think of anything else. . . .

"*. . . we'll be goin' by and by. By and by, we'll keep goin' by and by. Amen, hallelujah . . . amen . . . praise the Lord . . . amen, . . .*" exalted the crowd. James sat among them, with a small clearing to his right reserved for Chloe. His head continued its swivel back and forth, hoping to see her.

"We gone be readin' from Genesis. Da beginnin', da furst, wheah it all started. . . ." began Reverend Lee.

The thing James missed the most about leaving Johnson Hall wasn't the creature comforts or the less-physical form of slavery. Or Ruth—even though he missed her immensely.

It was the reading. Like a hunger, this desire to read and learn began in his gut and encompassed his being. He craved the poetry, stories, and Webster. Especially Webster. Repeating the words, reciting the poetry, and recalling the stories helped him remember. Reliving those minutes and months in the study within the confines of his mind maintained the memories. And leading the church group and helping them read satiated the desire somewhat.

. . . I love this. Helping people read. I love reading. And those words, especially Webster's words. I wouldn't dare use those words out in public. I can't even tell the stories. I can never let anyone—even Isaac—know just how much I can read. And write. Reverend Lee's preaching. Huh, much of it I question. I'll stick it out, though. Yeah, for the chance to read and teach others to read. That makes it tolerable.

"C'mon, follow with me, everybody. Sarah, honey, you need to be still if you want to sit on my lap, okay?" James said while he tried to balance the squirming seven-year-old on his knee. A group huddled around him and the copy of the Bible he held in his hands.

"Okay," she replied with an innocent grin.

"Everybody, follow my finger. You other ones who got books, follow with your fingers, and everybody else, follow along. *In the beginning, God created heaven and earth . . .*" James whispered the reading to his groups as the Reverend Lee led the lesson.

§

Coming out of one of the buildings being cleaned later that week, James saw Chloe off in the distance. He hadn't seen her since that night they'd fallen asleep together several weeks earlier. His heart leapt at her sight; then his mind questioned why he hadn't seen her. Looking around to spot any of Rogers' men, he headed for her. She and some other girls were carrying laundry baskets.

From the angle he approached her, she didn't see him until he was already upon her.

"Hi, Chloe. How are—" he began until he looked in her eyes. The look he dreaded to see stared back at him. "Uh—how are you doing?"

"I—I'm fine," she replied as she turned her face away from him.

"When can I see you? It's getting colder. So, we can't be outside so late."

"I don't know, James. I—I might be at the church on Sunday, maybe. Maybe then, okay? I don't know. I gotta go."

He reluctantly agreed and went on his way, never turning around to see her. James knew she was right, and as he turned the corner, Rogers came riding through, giving James that look again. He rode his horse so close it knocked James to the ground. He got up, brushed himself off, and wondered why he was feeling anger toward Chloe.

"James, you think we ever gonna be free?" Chloe cooed.

She snuggled in her lover's embrace and gazed upon his noble Nubian features. His thick, curly, jet-black hair with a full hairline. The ragged scar on his forehead, courtesy of the butt of Smitty's rifle. His deep brown, compassionate eyes that were rapidly filling with frustration, impatience, and rage. The crooked path of his broad nose, broken long ago by Rogers' right cross. The small scratch marks on his cheeks from the knobby bark of the whipping tree. The peach fuzz of a moustache barely visible over his mocha-brown skin. The thick, full lips, indicative of people of African descent, that took her to incredible erotic peaks. And the strong, jutting jawline that made her and others swoon.

"I think—I don't know. Everywhere it seems to be slavery. The books I read talked about places in the world far away from here. Maybe if we get there, then we can be free," James replied as he lay on his back and looked up at the floorboards of the curing barn.

"I don't wanna have to go nowhere to be free. Why can't we jest be free right here?"

"Because here—because here we have to do the things we *have* to do, you know. There, we can do the things we *want* to do. And *when* we want to do it. And *how* we want to do it. And especially *who* we want to do it with!"

"Umm, I likes the way you do it here, James," she replied. She made eye contact with him, and he contentedly returned the smile. "I had a dream the other night. We was free, James! And you was our leader. Maybe you can lead us here when we all gits free."

"Nah. I wouldn't lead y'all here. I would lead y'all *away* from here. Like in a story I read in the Big House."

"You see, you so smart. You can read. All them books you told me 'bout! You would have to lead us. And people would follow you, too. But baby, what story you talkin' 'bout?"

"Oh. This Pied Piper, some man who blew a flute or something, and the children all followed him. First, he got rid of some rats, but the town didn't pay him. So, he called the children. Then they paid him. That's what I would do. I would call all y'all out, but nothing could make me give y'all back, though. We would never come back here."

"Where would we go?"

"I don't know. Anywhere but here. North."

"James, I—I'm sorry we gotta live like this. We could be a family."

James smiled at the thought and the lovely lady lying next to him. "You would be a beautiful wife, too. And a great mother. God, yes. You certainly would be. C'mon, it's time to go. It's getting cold."

The shack swayed, whistled, shimmied, and creaked from the winter winds. The north gale, a refreshing breeze on summer evenings, ushered in the bitter winter elements through spaces between the well-worn planks. Rags and pieces of cloth stuffed into them, along with a mud and straw mixture, offered a modicum of relief.

Looking past the fetal-positioned bodies of his shack mates covered in blankets and out through the ragged cracks, a shivering James saw nature's dazzling white blanket complete the wintry scene. He recalled how pretty it appeared years earlier from the second-floor window of Carlton's comfortable bedroom as the fireplace crackled.

The bare oak trees dusted in white. Footprints and wagon-wheel tracks slowly disappearing with each fresh snowfall. The frost that framed the windows of the bedroom and the study. And the slight whistle that pierced the early-morning stillness as Johnson Hall slept all snug and warm.

"It's so c-c-cold!" he shivered and mumbled as those warm thoughts were snatched away with each new breeze. "I'm glad Massah g-g-gave us these long johns. I never n-n-needed long johns in J-J-Johnson Hall—we just stayed inside. C-C-Carlton gave me a blanket, but it wasn't cold. It's so c-c-cold here! So c-c-cold. After all these years, I'll never get used t-t-to this. . . ."

Early in the growing season, most of the fieldwork was pulling weeds and cleaning bugs from the plants. Many of the men went into the forest to harvest timber. A few went into the orchards, but James remained in the fields.

This time of year, the weather was fantastic. The days were cool enough to prevent a full sweat, and warm enough so joints wouldn't stiffen. The vulgarity of bondage remained, however.

"Hey, boy," a voice rang out to him one spring afternoon. As James turned around, he caught a glimpse of Rogers' horse and, being careful not to look up into his face, replied, "Yassuh, Massah Rogers, suh?"

"Master Johnson says fo' me to keep my eye on you. I wonda' why that is, boy," Rogers said as he moved his steed alongside of James.

"I don't rightly know, suh," James got out before Rogers kicked him in the mouth.

"I want ya' to know I'se watchin' ya, boy. You know I likes whuppin' yo' ass. Watcha' self," he added and then rode off.

What did I do? Do they know about me and Chloe? About Webster? About the study? Huh—nah. I would get whipped for that. But what is it? What . . .

♣

"Looks like we'll be getting some rain soon," James said as the distant lightning illuminated the night sky before the darkness reclaimed it in their ongoing duel of dominance. James peeked down at Chloe, her shoulders slowly rising and falling with each silent breath. Her hair, curly with knots, wiggled with each breeze. The flashes of lightning exposed her curves, which he desired more and more.

"Yeah—smell it? *Sniff*—I can smell the rain coming. I love rainy nights. It helps me to sleep—among other things," James added as he gave her a loving squeeze.

The silence returned as it had been for the evening. Chloe, lying on her side with her back to James, looked out into the darkness. James sighed heavily and said, "Yeah, I'm glad it's late spring. That rumble could've meant cold weather."

"I like rainy days," Chloe finally replied as a gust of wind blew through her hair. The first words she had spoken in more than an hour, they startled James.

"So, you are alive over there, huh? Anyway, being out there in the fields when it's raining. Nah, that's not good. The leaves get sticky, you get mud all on your feet. And then, if it stops raining during the day and the sun come back out—nah, that's not good. I don't know how it is in the orchards, but the flies and bugs come, and . . ."

"They hide your tears," she softly whispered.

". . . mess with your face and eyes. And the heat. And—huh? What, baby? You said something?"

"They hide—nobody can see you cryin' at night. In—in the day—the rain. It look like tears. Nobody can tell," she whispered again as James strained to take in every angst-ridden word.

Holding his love ever so tighter, he swallowed hard and tried to understand what he couldn't possibly know.

"Yeah—the darkness does hide a lot, I guess. But, it just hides it. Doesn't cure it. Don't fix it."

"Guess that 'bout all we can—can expect," Chloe replied as her sobs became audible.

James rocked her gently in his arms as raindrops began to pummel the ground, causing dust to fly up and sending streams of water in on them.

"Yeah—no one can see you crying in the rain. You face is all wet. I see what—"

"My—my first time. It rained. In The—The Uglies. The first time. I was glad it rained. I was so glad it rained. I thanked God it rained. 'Cause all I did was cry . . ."

CHAPTER 9

"I m-m-miss the singin', that's what, James" Isaac said.

Late into the night, it became common for them to stay up late and talk, whenever James didn't go to see Chloe. This night they commiserated the loss of the singing and storytelling time and the camaraderie that grew out of it. Many of the boys got together in small groups and talked late into the night in the dark shack, though many stayed to themselves.

"I enjoyed that, too. The songs made me feel good. Actually, they made me forget I was a slave. For a while, anyway. That's the first time I knew the name of "Amazing Grace." Shadrach was singing it, and I ran up there. I remembered the tune, but not all the words or the name. My mama—"

"Yeah, I remember th-th-that night."

"When y'all hummed it to me—my God. I still get emotional just thinking about it."

"I can hum it fo' you now."

"Nah, that's okay. You sound better when you hum with a crowd."

"Wow—really, James?"

"Yeah. My mama used to hum and sing it to me. I learned a lot about myself then, too. You still thinking about running?"

"Y-Y-Yep. That's all I think about."

James let out a pain-filled sigh. He thought for a second about trying to convince him not to run. He understood the likelihood of success was nil at best. He now understood the reasons someone would risk their life on such an attempt. The scores of times he had tried to dissuade him had failed, and James was reluctantly resigning himself to that reality.

"You are going to say goodbye, right?"

"Yeah, J-J-James. I'll say goodbye," answered Isaac with a hint of melancholy in his voice.

"Are you okay?"

"Y-Y-Yeah. Yeah, I'm fine. I'm fine. Huh—no. No, I ain't. I—I gotta git outta here, James! I'm dyin'. I—I'm dyin'."

"Isaac, I—I—just be sure to say goodbye, you hear!"

"Yeah, I hear ya'."

"Yeah, as long as you're okay, I'm okay."

"I'll be fine."

"Well, I'm not. I don't know what's wrong with Chloe. I don't ever see her at church anymore. When I try to talk when we pass, she say she'll talk later. I don't know. You see her. She ever say anything to you?"

"Nah. I hear the mens s-s-say you n-n-never understand women," Isaac replied as he rose to his feet. "I better go. I kinda sleepy."

"No to what? You don't see her, or you don't talk to her?" James asked as he grabbed him by his arm.

"Y-Y-Yeah, sometimes I-I-I see her. But I don't say nuthin'. It's g-g-gettin' late. I-I-I gonna go," Isaac replied as he tried to walk away.

"Nah, Isaac. Something's going on here. What is it? I want to know."

"Whatcha' m-m-mean, uh, J-J-James? I jest t-t-tired."

"Too much stuttering, my friend. I know you well enough to know something is wrong. C'mon. What's going on?"

"James. I, uh, I, uh—"

"C'mon, Isaac!" James exclaimed, and then he realized how loud his voice had become. He grabbed Isaac by the arm and forcibly pulled him back to his cot as he whispered, "Isaac. I'm sorry for yelling. But I want to know. What is it!?"

"James. I s-s-seent her wit—wit some other mens."

"What! Some!"

"Shh! Yeah, some. Even a lot, I don't know."

"Hell, what kind of girl is she? I—I thought I knew her, but she's just a—"

"James! She been in The Uglies what, five—six months. Been wit you mo' than that. She ain't got no baby comin'. 'Member what Rogers s-s-say? You gotta stay valuable. 'Round here, girl who can't have no babies. She lose her v-v-value quick-like! She jest doin' what she gotta do. Don't be mad at she, James."

"I'm not mad. I'm—mad. Damn, I'm just mad."

"Don't be mad at she, James. It bad fo' all us."

"Yeah. Yeah—but, shit!"

"Don't be mad at she!"

It was a month before James finally got a chance to talk to Chloe. He went to church every Sunday with hopes of seeing her. The spot he saved next to him and that special place in his heart reserved for her remained empty. His thoughts ranged from depressed to terrified to horrified and every emotion in between. But this Sunday, he was certainly blessed with his song, his favorite book of the Bible and a source of strength—Job—and the presence of Chloe.

The congregation sang, "*. . . how sweet the sound, that saved a wretch like me. I once was lost, but now I'm found. Was blind, but now I see. . . .*"

"Chloe. I know you're—you are doing what you got to do."

"I'm scared. Really scared. It's been near eight months now. Ain't no babies comin', James. I don't wanna be like my momma. I mean my real momma. Git sold off 'causin' you can't make no boy babies. James—I can't even make no girl ones!"

James continued to hold his head down, his chin pressed into his chest as his mouth barely moved with the song being sung. Chloe, totally distraught, held his limp hand in hers, and she leaned forward to look into his eyes, desperately seeking compassion or comfort. A trickle of a tear out of the corner of James' eye was all she got. She sighed, lowered her head, and continued.

"You 'member Martha, the one we saw wit Mitch that night long time befo'? She was wit Miss Netty five days after that! That's how they treat you! Worsern' a slave."

James looked over at Chloe as she softly whined. He opened his mouth to silence, closed it, and tried again as he uttered, "Maybe—uh, maybe if we keep on trying I, uh—we—"

"James, I don't mind being wit you. Shoot, I like bein' wit you—a lot. A lot! But we been together ten months and—nothin'. I figure maybe I need a different one. So—so I ask. Uh—I gotta ask. I got to, James. Even Isaac, I ask. But he say 'no.' Well, he say 'n-n-no,'" she said, and then giggled through her sobs. James tried to respond with a smile, but it couldn't break through the despair as she continued, "Say somethin', James"

He struggled to get out, "I—I don't know—I don't know what to say."

"J-J-Jest say you not mad at me! James! Say it. Please say it!"

I'm—not—mad—at—you. I'm—not—mad—at—you. I'm—not—mad . . .

"I'm—not—mad—at—you, uh—Chloe."

Yes. My God. I am mad at her.

♣

"Don't be mad at she, J-J-James."

"Isaac, I told you three or four times now, I'm not mad—uh, at her. I'm just mad! Nothing seems right anymore."

James lay on his back, with his hands cupped behind his head, barely looking at Isaac, who paced up and down the side of his cot.

"We all jest survivin' b-b-best we can. You. Me. She. We all jest doin' the best we can!"

"Yeah, I'm sure."

"You jest now gittin' what slav'ry's 'bout, James. I know you a slave all yo' life, jest like me. But it was d-d-diff'rent. You say it don't f-f-feel right anymo'. It ain't *never* felt right to me. You don't got no ch-ch-choice. Or whens ya' got one, it's a bad one, like Chloe's own. I know it d-d-don' feel right. That's 'cause slav'ry ain't right. Chloe, she jest tryin' to save she life. And you mad at she."

James sprang up from his prostrate position and glared intently at Isaac. His chest heaved from the deep breaths he was taking, as the snorts were audible from the air rushing out his nostrils.

"I said I'm not mad at—at—"

He then paused, as the words caught in his throat forced tears from his eyes. He lowered his head and mumbled, "I am mad at her. Shit, I am mad—at her!"

"It's okay, James. It's okay," Isaac replied as he placed a comforting hand on James' shoulder. Several more sobs escaped James' mouth as he shook his head in disgust with his selfishness.

"No, no, Isaac. It—it's not okay. She—she wanted me to tell her. That I wasn't mad at her. She just wanted to hear it. I—I said the words, but—but I didn't mean it. I know she knew I didn't. I just couldn't do it—say those words and mean it. God, I hurt her. Even more than slavery does."

"Well, the first step is t-t-to know it. Then the next t-t-time you see she, you say it, huh. Say it loud. Say it f-f-fast, huh! And mean it! Then say you sorry, okay? As many t-t-times as it take. You hear? No matter what she say, you keep sayin' you was wrong. You sorry. Forgive me. Any others words you think about. And say it over and over, you hear?"

That stopped James' sobbing and brought a slight smile to his face. He looked into his friend's face, the first friendly face he knew in those dark early days in the shack, and thanked God for him.

"Okay, I'll say it loud, fast, over and over—and mean it. And you call *me* the smart one, Isaac."

"Huh, you is. Everybody using yo' ways. You been teachin' as much as anyone us t-t-to read. You never say so, but I reckon you read lotta of books when you wuz in the B-B-Big House."

Leaning closer to his friend, he whispered, "You know, Isaac, you're right. I read hundreds of books. Hundreds! I wasn't supposed to go in Massah Johnson's study, but I did anyway. I read Carlton's books with him, but Massah Johnson's books were harder.

"He got this book—I call it 'Webster.' It's a book with all the words in it, and what they mean. It's called a dictionary. I read it four times and was halfway through again. Ruth told me never to tell anyone I could read like that. She said a smart slave could end up a dead slave. Yeah, I can read. I can write, too. I told Chloe. I'm sorry I didn't tell you. I didn't know who I could tell."

"It's okay, J-J-James. You can write! Shoot, I reckoned some Negroes could read. But write! Shoot, I didn't think that!"

"Yeah, I can write. Not good, but yeah. I never told Chloe that. She knows I can read, but not write."

"You, you think you can teach me some writin' words?"

"Like what? What do you want to write?"

"Isaac. My name. Isaac."

"Yeah, I can do that."

"And 'James'—and, and 'freedom.' Them t-t-too. Yeah, I wanna write 'Isaac' and 'James' and 'freedom.' Oh, and 'friend,' too. Y-Y-Yeah. *Isaac, J-J-James, freedom,* and *friend*—yeah. That's what I wanna write."

"Okay, my friend. I can do that, but don't let anyone know. Maybe we can write stuff to each other—to the slaves."

"Huh? What you mean?"

"When Carlton used to ask me questions, I gave him the wrong answers on purpose—except for this one time. Anyway, when I think of it, the answers sounded like nonsense. It didn't make any sense. We could do that here."

"Yeah, like we c-c-can say let's work harder fo' when the massah's comin'."

"Uh, huh, or that 'blue is green' for 'it's okay to sing.'"

"Yeah! You see! You is the smart one!"

CHAPTER 10

"Well, Mr. Johnson. It's been over a year now. Five runners, all got caught. Kept four of 'em alive. Ya' said you had fifteen the year befo', and eight got away. All ya' crops harvested. Ya' got nigger babies runnin' all 'round. I think we worth that bonus we talked 'bout earlier," Rogers said as he stood opposite Master Johnson with the desk in between.

"Y'all git your bonuses after I take out fo' the extra medical bills y'all caused. You remember that contract you signed? You did read it, didn't ya'?"

"Yeah, I read it!"

"Good. Shootin' the old ones is one thing. Whuppin' them all is okay, too. Y'all been breakin' bones, hurtin' innards, costin' me money. Doc Andersen been here too damn much."

"I tolt ya' how I work! You say okay. You say stop 'em from runnin'."

"I said okay to fear, even to terror. Hell, you can give 'em nightmares fo' all I care! But you gotta stop hurtin' my moneymakers so bad. Shoot the old ones, I don't care. Beat 'em, whup they asses—I don't give a damn! Just don't hurt them so bad I gotta fetch Doc Andersen."

"Yeah, yeah. Hey, what 'bout some mo wenches fo' us? We—me and my mens—tired' of them old ones."

"Now see! Theah you go tryin' to git in my bitness! The young ones fo' makin' nigger babies. That go fo' me, too. I don't touch 'em. Jest the old ones. Nobody want no mixed slaves. Folks want they slaves all nigger!"

"What 'bout that wench, uh—Chloe. She ain't got no baby, and it been near nine months now."

"Who? Well, whoever, we usually give them a yeeah, and then we see."

"She 'bout so tall. Healthy lil' thang. That nigger boy James kinda' sweet on her. 'Member the one you—"

"Yeah, I remember. Hmm."

"Yeah, that'll hurt his ass some if I—if we can git her."

Master Johnson leaned back in his chair and smiled wickedly.

♣

". . . I can git 'em to Miss Netty. Like befo'. She know mo' f-f-folks than me," Isaac said as he stuffed paper into his shirt.

"Yeah—folks," James replied with a distant look on his face.

"James? James!"

"Huh—what? Oh, I'm sorry. The codes—yeah. Uh, yeah, this way in the fields or anywhere we can talk. Even in front of them. And write messages that look like nonsense to other people. Like 'A4114A' for 'let's agree to do or not to do something.'"

"Yeah, you say that's from a book you read."

"Yeah. *The Three Musketeers*. All for one, one for all. Don't ever get caught writing, Isaac. And uh, watch out using these other words. It don't matter who is around—be careful. Look around at all these new faces."

He motioned his head toward all the strangers they now shared the shack with. Nearly two-thirds of the boys there when he arrived were gone, either moved to the adult shack, sold off, or dead.

"Yeah, I'll b-b-be careful, James."

"I want you to enjoy longevity, my friend. That's long duration of individual life. I want you to live a long life, Isaac."

"Me, too. I want you to live a long life, t-t-too. What's on yo' mind? Chloe?"

"Yeah. I mean, when I can't see her, I know it. But, when she say she's coming, she's there—always. I just wonder what happened."

"I guess somethin' c-c-came up."

"Isaac—you don't know something, do you?"

"No, I don't, James. This time I really d-d-don't. Anyway, you wuz jest so lookin' forward to bein' wit her, that's all."

"Yeah, you're right. I was looking forward to it. I always do."

"D-D-Did you tell she that you wutn't mad at she? That you wuz sorry?"

"Nah, I haven't had the chance to tell her. I was going to tell her tonight, but she didn't come."

An hour before the wakeup call, before nature's first sounds of the dawn, the alternating sharp and throbbing jolts of pain awoke Rogers. Grunting, he looked over at the lady in his bed and smiled between groans.

"You gotta lil' spunk there, gal. I kinda like that for the first time. And even sometimes. But no mo' of this shit unless I tells ya," Rogers said as he began to rise from his bed. "Ugh, ow, shit! Gal, I ain't puttin' up wit this here shit no mo'! You, ugh, you hear me? Git yo' ass up, and fix me some food. Hey, gal. Git on—git yo' ass up! I tolt ya' not to fight me."

Rogers staggered through the pre-dawn and made it to the washbasin, where he threw two hands full of water on his face.

"Ow! Shit!" he screamed as the water touched the scratch marks and welts. "Shit, gal! I ain't puttin' up wit no mo' of this, you hear! You mine now. Git used to it."

He lit a candle and brought light to his cabin. Then he saw his mangled ear and the scratches for the first time in his mirror. His face wrinkled up, and his jaw clenched into a mass of rage as he screamed, "I gonna sho' whup yo' ass fo' this here, you goddamn nigger wench! Shit! Hey, gal? Hey! Git yo' ass up!"

He jerked around and saw the source of his ire lying halfway off the bed and stormed over to her. Forcibly, he grabbed her by the arm and shouted, "Hey, *hey*! Git yo' ass up, I say! Hey!"

He tugged on her arm until her limp body slid off the bed and onto the floor with a thud. The covers, pulled partially off, exposed the massive amount of blood on the mattress and a sorrowful trail leading to the lady sprawled on the floor.

"Oh, uh-oh, shit! Oh, shit!" he exclaimed as he rushed out of his cabin with a staggered stride, returning five minutes later with Netty.

Groggy when she first entered, Netty's eyes stretched wide as she caught sight of the horrific scene before her. "Oh, my Lord Jesus! Please, Lord—protect this child," she exclaimed with a shrill cry while she fell to her knees beside the lady. She feebly dabbed at the blood flow with a rag that was nearby, as a torrent flowed from her eyes and demanded, "I needs to git her to the hospital shack, Massah Rogers! I need to git her there right now! You hear me! I needs to—"

Rogers bare left foot landed in the middle of Netty's face, sending her sprawling on the wood floor. The incredulous Rogers declared, "Who the hell you think you talkin' to?"

Without a pause, she jumped back up and huddled over the victim. "Oh, my God—no!" she cried as drops of blood from her nose splattered on the girl's face. Netty touched her own face and only then realized the magnitude of Rogers' strike.

Don't matter 'bout me. I gotta help this child, she thought.

"Uh, Massah Rogers, suh. Suh, I sorry, suh. But—but she hurt somethin' awful, suh. She need help, suh. And, and—"

"Shaddup! She ain't goin' nowhere. Fix her up, here," he demanded between grunts and moans as he sat down in his chair less than 10 feet away.

Netty looked down at the lady and noticed her mouth moving. "Shh, baby girl, shh," she whispered as she leaned closer to her. "Don't try to say nothin'. Just lay there still."

"You better fix her, you hear. Or I'll whup yo' ass!"

"Yassuh, Massah Rogers, suh! Yassuh, I will," she replied to him; then she leaned in closer to the victim, listened for a moment, and then whispered, "Shh. Jest be quiet, baby girl. Jest lay there. Don't say nothin'. . . ."

♧

"Good morning, Isaac," James said as they headed for the door.

"'Morning, James. Another d-d-day, huh."

"Yeah," he replied as they continued through the line until Isaac was pulled out ahead of him.

Off to The Uglies again. Servitude . . . freedom . . . slavery . . . property . . . liberty . . . chattel . . . freedom . . . servitude . . .

Running to the Future

CHAPTER 1

James struggled against the maelstrom. First, shuffling one step to maintain his balance and then trudging forward with the next step, he tried to get to the top of the hill. His sweat, combined with the torrents, left him soaked as the wind blew the rain into him with a stinging force. Crackling lightning bolts illuminated the countryside; the inevitable thunder boomed and shook everything near and far.

Finally reaching the top, he proclaimed, "I'm free."

His feet, spread shoulder-width apart, kept his balance as he raised his shackled hands and shouted, "I'm free! Thank You, God! I'm free!"

Suddenly, a lightning bolt struck the chain connecting his shackles, shattering them into a thousand fragments. The impact sent sparks flying and knocked James 10 feet backwards and on his back. When he tried to get up, the pain in his wrists caused him to crumple back to the ground. The lightning crackled again, and he could see the shackles—they appeared to be melted, his clothes were singed by fire, and he coughed from the suffocating smoke.

Oh—oh, my God! What—what happened? Where am I? Where am—am I?

His mind cleared, blue skies replaced the ominous clouds, and the wind calmed. He stood up and took several measured steps. Looking around, he realized the shackles and chains were gone. The birds were singing again, and a smile appeared.

"So—this is freedom," he giggled and marveled at the serene scene.

"I am free," he repeated—and then awoke in the dark, dank shack.

"I—am—not—free."

The clanging of the cowbell and someone yelling, "Git yo' asses up," along with the bustling of the shack, brought his reality into complete focus.

Another day in captivity. Another day as a slave. In bondage. In servitude. As chattel. As property. Man, that was a crazy dream. Not my first dream about being free, either. Maybe not my last. Maybe, it's time. Yeah, Isaac. Maybe it's time.

He sighed and marched toward, through, and out of the door of the shack, and on to the fields.

"Yeah, yeah. Y'all be doin' real good. Heah's y'all bonus," Master Johnson said as he begrudgingly handed an envelope stuffed with legal tender to Rogers.

"Thank ya', Mr. Johnson, suh. We sho' like this here," Rogers said as he excitedly emptied the envelope and counted the bills.

"Listen, heah. That James—you know the one. He my prized buck now. I stopped biddin' on him last week at $6,000! Hot damn! Six thousand bucks fo' a young buck. And he ain't even made no babies yet. I can git ten, fifteen thousand dollahs for him one day. Not bad for a $30 investment twelve yeeahs ago, huh?"

". . . thirty-fo', thirty-five—nah, suh. I guess that's why you gots all the money, suh. Uh—thirty-fo', thirty-five, thirty-six, thirty-seven . . ."

"Yep—you got that one right. I don't want him whupped no mo', unless he be runnin'. And nobody beat him neither, you heah? No mo' beatins'."

". . . forty, uh—yes, suh. No mo' beatins'. Forty, forty-one . . ."

"I mean it, goddammit! Nobody mess wit him or yo' asses in the fi-yuh fo' sho'," he exclaimed.

Master Johnson slammed his fist on the desk, and, as Rogers looked up, he dropped several of the bills. Master Johnson grinned slightly as Rogers hurriedly gathered the currency.

"You can count that money all you want, you heah! That ain't shit compared to what that boy is worth! He gots value, a hellava lot mo' than yo' ass! Don't touch him no mo', you heah!"

Rogers returned Master Johnson's glare as he seethed, "Yes—suh—Mr.—Johnson—suh." He resumed counting the bills and mumbled, "Ten, twenty—that boy give me any trouble—he dead. Thirty, thirty-one, thirty-two . . ."

❧

It had been one of those hot, humid summer days where the flies buzz about just to stay cool. Leaving the field at dusk, James kept his mind focused on what it had been on for weeks—running, running to the future. Running north, anywhere in the North—and always away from the South. To Philadelphia, maybe even to New York City, or so he considered on many late nights.

James, nearly 6 feet tall, had broad shoulders and muscular arms from his work in the fields. The most productive worker on the plantation, he was a leader and constant target for a relentless Rogers.

That night, eating dinner, he hadn't heard much of the conversation. The muted talk and subdued laughter seemed distant to him as he swam in his personal sea of thoughts, scenarios, and plans.

"Hey, James! What's on yo' mind, boy?" Paul, the boy sitting directly across from him, asked. "Or is it—*who?*"

"Nothin'. Just takin' it all in," he replied as he feigned interest and then returned to his thoughts.

. . . Who? What? When? Where? Why? How? The "who" is obvious. The "what" and "why" crystal clear! The "where"—anywhere away from here. The "when"—soon. Very soon. The "how"—huh, I don't know that—yet.

"He got no knowledge 'bout this here stuff," Ezra replied.

"I know y'all crazy for girls wit big booties. Huh, that much I know."

"Oh, so you have been listenin'," added Paul.

"For me—it's okay. I don't mind, you know."

"Oh, yeah."

"Shoot, I can't even tell you if the girl I was wit had a big butt or not."

"Oh, you can tell! If you don't notice, she don't got no butt," chimed Daniel.

"Yep, no booty. None. You go down to grab it, and you at her thigh before you know it," added Ezra.

Tossing in his cot that night, James got up, walked to the window, and viewed the starry night sky and its grinning moon. He took a deep breath and pondered his past and future.

I'll sneak out of the shack just before dawn. Make a dash through the fields to the thicket. Once the sun rises, I'll strike out north, running, running to the future. To my future. Several days before a new moon. Several more days. . . .

James knew the risks and the consequences. The 14 who'd tried to escape since Rogers' arrival were all caught. Luke and Lot died. The others were beat, whipped, and, in several cases, sold. He hadn't gotten close to a friendship with anyone since Isaac disappeared. Philip and Peter were on either side of him in the shack, and they were nice, but not like Isaac. No one knew of his plan. Since Rogers would beat others, James felt this was the best idea.

. . . I understand, Isaac. I understand now. I can't breathe here either. Being a slave is—suffocating. It's like having a sack over your head, a rope securing it around your neck, and a hand over the sack and your mouth, but not your nose. A wicked master giving you just enough air to maintain the existence he wants for you. An agonizing existence. A not-having-control-of-your-body-or-your-life type of existence.

I can't breathe here. Surviving with each swing of the pendulum. Wasting away tick by tock of the clock. Minute by minute, hour by hour, day by day, season by season, year by year. And witnessing those who look like me suffer the same fate.

I can't breathe here. This knowledge I have—these books I've read are all conspiring against me now. Perhaps if I was ignorant to the possibilities, to what was beyond this plantation, in the North, in Europe, and everywhere else, it wouldn't be so bad. Well, as bad. But I do know, and it drives me! It keeps me awake at night. It's a major part of my torment

It's the reason I can't breathe here. . . .

He turned around and took in the scene before him. Way too many men, cramped in a way too small an area, in a way too terrible situation. He sadly shook his head in silence as his mind continued to scream.

. . . Slavery attempts to dishearten a person's spirit—but not my spirit. Squelch their desire—but never mine! Eliminate their dreams—but I'll dream forever. Make them give up hope—but I'll never give up hope. I know—I know there's more out there. Much more! True, it has been more than three years since I read in the study, but I remember. My mind won't let me forget.

Carlton's books. Webster. The magazines and newspapers. I should have looked at them more—especially the maps—instead of reading all those stories! Maybe I would've known the "how" by now! But the books spoke of places and ideas beyond here. And the stories do fuel my dreams. There's a future to be had, and I'm going to run to it. I got to run to it.

I could get lost over there, and they would never find me. I could be free. Chloe asked me what I was going to do. Say no? No, I'm going to run. I'm getting out of here before summer ends. God, I miss her. Why did Massah have to sell her? Why does God allow this?

"Huh, I guess 'cause he can," he mumbled as he walked back to his cot with a memory of Ruth tagging along.

I can't breathe here either, Issac.

♣

One by one, the boys in the shack escaped to slumber in the moonless, pitch-black night—a perfect night for his plan. Trying to control his breathing, James' heart pounded as he strained to see his surroundings. Slowly, he rose, looked left and then right, and then straight ahead. The lone window was the only discernible feature.

I know—I'll shut my eyes for a minute. Then everything will be clearer.

"Git yo' ass up!" screamed the morning announcer as the shack reluctantly came to life.

James dolefully got up and followed the line. That day passed leaf by picked leaf. Glancing up at the dusky sky as they made it back to the shack that night, James thought about his next chance.

I got to stay awake. I can't go to sleep tonight. The moon's coming back. I got to get out of here. By the next time, it could be too cold.

♣

Slowly, James rose from his cot and looked around the dark, still shack. The snores and whistles of the sleepers were the only proof the shack was inhabited. Feeling his time was now, he swallowed hard and prepared to leave his cot when footsteps pushed him back down on it. He lay back down just as another slave scurried past him and out the window.

Maybe I should go with him. Huh, I don't even know him! I'm running out of time!

Coming back from the fields that evening, James saw Silas, last night's runner, bound, gagged, and being dragged by Rogers.

I could've made it. I can make it. I got to make it. I will make it!

As the line snaked around toward the cafeteria, James saw Silas being shackled to the whipping tree. He imagined those sounds from his distant viewpoint along with those poor, unfortunate souls who happened to be nearby.

Grunt—whoosh—pow—"Arrgh!"

CHAPTER 2

The calls of the wild seeped into the slumbering shack as a sliver of the returning moon barely illuminated the room. James, worried his labored breathing and pounding heart would give him away, headed for the window. He looked back at the young bucks sleeping, thinking this must have been what Shadrach, Luke, and the others saw. Then he crawled out.

He scampered from building to building, pausing only to make sure the coast was clear. He reached and ran through the field, stopped at the knee-high thicket, and waited until just before dawn. As the sky transformed from deep indigo to a dawning shade of orange, James headed north.

Galloping through the forest of oak, maple, and pine, along with assorted underbrush, the early-morning mist filled James' lungs, and cardinals provided a musical backdrop. His husky breathing and the crash of his bare feet on freshly fallen leaves completed the dawning sounds.

Foxes and deer peeked out from their hiding places as he raced past them. He was careful to stay off the roads, so every step and scene was new for him. The sky was clear, so his bearings remained true. He ran as fast as his legs allowed, but it was a snail's pace compared to the speed at which his mind galloped.

Ruth—God, I miss her! I miss her so much. She reminded me of my mama. Isaac never had a chance to run. Sold off like, like property! Chloe sold, too. Maybe even being treated worse than a slave by now. God, after two years, I still miss her!

This isn't working so well. Think positive. Let's see—yeah, freedom. Yeah! What will I do when I'm free? How is it to be free? What do

*you do when you're free? Being a citizen. Having liberty! Yeah, no
more servitude . . .*

☙

"Rogers! Rogers!" Mitch yelled as he approached Rogers' cabin.
"Rogers! Somebody's runnin'! And guess, Rogers! Go on, guess
who it is! Huh, go on!"

"Tell me it's James. Tell me—please, tell me it's him. Pu-leeze—"

"You been sayin' that fo' a year now—but guess what? It's
James, Rogers. It's him!"

"Hot damn! I wuz hopin' it wuz him. Send Smit fo' the dogs,"
Rogers ordered as he jumped out of his bed, knocking the woman
there with him onto the floor with a thud.

"Already done that. He gonna meet us at the thicket."

"Ol' man Johnson still gone, ain't he?"

"Yep."

"Saddle up the boys. Let's go git 'im," he replied as he pulled on
one boot and grabbed the other one. He glanced at the woman and
barked, "Clean up this here place fo' I gits back. Won't be long."

"Yassuh, Massah Rogers, suh."

☙

"But Mr. Campbell, I—I don't understand. My grades are
good. I got letters of recommendation. I go to Cambridge Prep.
Four of my classmates come here. My daddy is a businessman. He
owns a hardware store. Why can't I join the Key Club?" Bobby
asked as he sat across the neat desk in the immaculately organized
office of Mr. Wesley Campbell, Esq., Chief Administrator of the
local Key Club.

"Mr. Harris—Bobby. Can I call you Bobby?" Mr. Campbell
replied as he leaned on his desk, sparsely covered with a quill pen
and blotter, a small lamp, and Bobby's application. He looked at
Bobby with a condescending smile.

"Y'all people are good peoples. And you all can do most anything that you set your minds to. I believe that. I really do. I know some of you all do some good things, Bobby. But there's limits. You got to know your limits.

"This Key Club, it's just for White folks, Bobby. White men. We do stuff here you all, well, that you all just can't do! You got to know your limits. If I had known you was a Negro, I could've saved you the time."

He picked up Bobby's application with his thumb and index finger. While maintaining that condescending smile, he slowly tore it in half with the other hand.

"So—so, that's it, huh?" Bobby finally said as tears welled up in his eyes. "S-S-So, that's all, huh?"

"Well, I don't know, son. Is there anything else I can do for you?"

From lessons learned in the months of discrimination he'd faced alone, Bobby controlled his rage with measured inhales and halted exhales. He focused his stare on the object of his ire, this bespectacled, rotund representative of the system that oppressed him and those like him.

"Yassuh. There is one more thing you can do. Could ya' kindly make me White? Huh, can ya', Massah? . . ." Bobby replied in the manner that prevented his temper from exploding. He grabbed the man's nameplate, read it, and then added, ". . . uh, Massah Campbell, suh! Can ya' kindly make me White?" Then he shuffled out of the office and headlong into his sorrow.

♣

. . . slavery . . . either you're sold, or you're beaten, or you're violated. Made to do—do—stuff! . . . servitude . . . It ain't right, it ain't right. None of it is right. . . . chattel . . . Isaac knew. He knew it was never right! I had to learn what he already knew—and he called me the smart one. . . .

James was lost in his thoughts when he heard the foreboding sounds of bloodhounds in the distance. His head went back, forth, up, and down as he scanned the forest for assistance. Twenty strides later, James tore off his shirt, waved it around in the air, on the ground and on nearby bushes and trees, then threw it high up in a tree. Then he backtracked across the field to a river he passed, jumped in the ankle-deep water, and headed downstream.

♣

"Damn, we lost him," Smitty said as their dogs yelped and circled each other.

"Nah. Ol' man Johnson said he wuz a smart nigger. He probably backtracked in yonder river we passed back. C'mon," Rogers replied, his head jerking right to left as he strained to see through the forest.

♣

. . . freedom . . . When I'm free, I will make my own choice of who I live with. Who I sleep with. What and when I eat. What clothes to wear. I'll be free. I'll be a citizen—huh, have liberty! . . .

Taking a breather, he realized he'd been gone for half the day. He looked around him and then up toward the sky. Following the meandering river had disrupted his bearings, and the high-noon time offered no assistance. While most of the riverbank had been a gradual grassy slope, this portion was rocky, with chest-high shrubs down to the waterline. James snuggled up to a stand of brush with ankle-deep water to wait for the sun to leave its zenith.

. . . What the hell am I doing? My God—I must be crazy! I'm lost. I'm hungry. I got to make it. I got to. I can't get caught. I can't go back. Not alive anyway. Quickest way to freedom, if necessary. I got to. What am I doing? I got to—I-I-I'm running to my future. Running for freedom. Yeah, yeah, that's it. Freedom, liberty, citizen, . . .

An hour passed before James regained his bearings. Not having heard the dogs during the hour, he took off running due north, his waterlogged clothes straining against him.

. . . when I'm free, I'll live where I want. Yeah—New York City. The city so nice, they named it twice. New York, New York. Yeah. What time will I get up? When I feel like it. And—oh, no! Chains and dogs! . . .

James went from a gallop to a full sprint as he searched the horizon for a lake, river, stream, puddle—anything that would help him elude his pursuers. He ran through and huffed and jumped over and puffed his way through the dense forest for 30 minutes. The sound of the clomping horses' hoofs, dangling dog chains, and incensed intonations drew closer.

James, a hundred strides past exhaustion, thought, at first, and then, he imagined, and then, with sheer elation, realized he heard the bubbling rumble of a rushing stream. Fifty yards later, he was high-stepping in the calf-high currents and feeling somewhat relieved, though he still looked back every 5 steps.

Eventually, the sounds of his pursuers overwhelmed the stream. As James continued to follow a serpentine section, he spied a tree that had fallen across it. He slid underneath it, hoping to hide. The leaves were changing with the season, and the tree was getting bare. But it was his only option. James stooped far enough down to get chin-deep in the water, with the leaves and branches partially hiding him.

Now, he saw Rogers' group. The first 2 men approached—and passed him—but the dogs picked up his scent. Soon he was face to face with a beautifully ugly bloodhound who gave him a full-face lick.

Quickest way to freedom.

James jumped out of the water, up the bank, and ran as fast as his legs would allow him. Rogers' men threw nets over James; then they beat and kicked him until Rogers screamed for them to stop.

Oh, my God—why? Why? I failed. Why, God, why? Why did You let them catch me! . . .

"Y'all go back to PEE-nelope Farms and get dem niggers ready for the show that's comin'. Git 'em all ready. I got they leader."

Rogers led his captive back at a leisurely pace, a 3-inch-thick twine tether between his saddle and James' bound wrists. A soiled kerchief that smelled of tobacco, whiskey, and bad breath filled James' mouth as he resisted and staggered.

The oak tree-lined road they traveled, the main road in those parts, was busy that day. Several wagons passed, and James could hear the questions and comments.

Children asking parents, "Why was that slave tied up like that?"

And parents who replied, "He's a runaway, honey. That's how they're treated when they're bad. You know how we treat King."

Rogers casually tipped his cap at the travelers and smugly chuckled.

"Hey, James, James, James. You in a heap o' trouble now, boy! I gonna whup you somethin' fierce, boy. You one of dem leaders, huh, boy. Huh! Answer me, boy! I gonna break you. When I get finished, you ain't gonna wanna run no mo'."

Rogers looked back and laughed at the dejected James. He yanked on the rope, causing James to stagger toward him. Rogers stopped his horse, dismounted, and strode toward James.

"What the hell wuz you thinkin, boy? Niggers ain't never smart enough to git aways from me. I been huntin' niggers all my life, boy! I always catch 'em, or they die. And—and—"

James lunged, swung, and landed a blow on Rogers' cheek, knocking him on his back. James then jumped on top of Rogers and began swinging wildly, his bound hands hitting more ground than Rogers until James lost his balance and fell over. Rogers quickly jumped to his feet, pulled out his revolver, cocked back the hammer, and glared at James lying on the ground, the trembling gun barrel aimed at James' face.

The quickest way to freedom. Yeah, here we go. The quickest way. God, forgive me, for I have sinned. I have hate in my heart for White people, for slave owners. Help my people, Lord. . . .

"Oh, no. I ain't gone kill ya' here. You goin' back to PEE-nelope Farms," Rogers huffed as he fought to catch his breath. He wiped his mouth and face with a dingy kerchief from his pants pocket. A sinister grin creased his mouth as he remounted his horse. He dragged James behind him until he made it to his feet, all the while continuing his tirade.

"Oh, hell yeah. You ain't gonna die here! Gonna git whupped in front o' all yo' peoples. Yeah, that's what I gonna do. Whup yo' ass good! Make a 'zample out yo' ass! Everybody gonna 'member this day! I caught the great James *fo' supper. . . .*"

James lamented about this failure with each step. The pain in his body was excruciating. The anguish in his heart was overwhelming. But it was the embarrassment of not dying that devastated him. The tears that flowed on the inside did nothing to wash away the emotional hurt.

. . . Not only did I not escape, but I got caught—alive. I'm alive. I'm not free. Death is more noble. The quickest way to freedom. I was too slow. I'm a leader. If the leader can't escape, what hope does anyone else have? I've failed my people. I've failed, I've failed . . .

". . . Yeah, I figured you'd run sooner or later. Yeah. I wuz jest waitin'. Not that smart now, huh, boy? Yeah, James. I got James and—hey, yeah! Wait a minute. Yeah, you wuz the one. Yeah, you wuz," Rogers tormented as he stopped his steed, turned, and gazed at his captive.

His face, dirty and bloody from several scratch marks and a right eye that was swelling, had an evil joy etched on it. He laughed out loud and nearly fell off before he regained his balance and rubbed the sore spot near his eye.

"Yeah—you. That wuz you. You wuz sweet on that gal. What wuz her name?"

. . . No one else is gonna try to run now. All because of me. Because I couldn't get away. I—I failed my people. I failed . . .

"You know, don'tcha? That purty lil' thang you wuz sweet on. I had fun wit her jest that once fo' she make me hurt her. Damn,

I wish she wuz still heah. But no, that wench had to fight, so I kilt that wench. Shit! . . ."

. . . my people. I failed. I failed me. I failed my people. I—what? "Sweet on"? He mean—he mean Chloe? Chloe? He—he—killed— Chloe? He killed Chloe! Oh, my God—no! . . .

". . . I wanted some mo' of that. Huh, I see why you liked that. Did she squirm fo' you like she did fo' me? Anyhow, when I'm through wit you, I git my new wench when I git back, and we gonna have some fun. . ."

. . . Oh, my God—no! HE KILLED CHLOE! HE KILLED CHLOE! I . . . I can't—let—him—know. I—can't—let—him—know. He—killed—Chloe! I—got—to—keep—walking. Keep—walking—James. Just—keep—walking. Can't—let—him—know. He— killed—Chloe. My God, why? Why You let him kill Chloe, God? . . .

James trudged on behind Rogers, his grief knee-deep and rising. His strength, slowly draining from his body. His jelly-legs striding through sheer will. His heart beating by instinct. His tears, over-flowing his soul into a bitter sea of despair.

The world around him began spinning, the greens and blues and reds and browns and yellows and violets and oranges all combining into a kaleidoscopic hue of heartache. His legs grew weary with each step, until he collapsed a mile later.

". . . I gonna have her kiss me all over. And I gonna make her know—" Rogers continued until he noticed the sound of dragging on the gravel and dirt road. He turned around, and without stopping said, "You tired, boy? Too damn bad. I ain't stoppin'. I gonna drag yo' ass 'til you git up. Yeah, me and my wench sho' gonna . . ."

. . . he killed Chloe. He killed Chloe. Oh, my God! He killed her . . .

Chapter 3

Signaling their proximity to Penelope Farms, a subtle north breeze carried the pungent aroma of tobacco to James. Staggering and resisting, his wrists bloody raw from the twine bindings, James heard the squeak of the iron gates as his mind agonized.

. . . He—he killed Chloe. He killed her! He—he . . . You let him kill Chloe, God. You did, God. You let him kill Chloe! . . .

Rogers triumphantly passed the thicket of branches and shrubs that formed the perimeter of Penelope Farms and through the gates.

"We back, James. We at PEE-nelope Farms. In front of yo' peoples. All the folk ya' supposed to lead."

Arriving 40 minutes earlier, Mitch and Smitty had the slaves lining both sides of the meandering trail. Those who didn't remain silent let muffled sobs and heart-wrenching wails escape. Rogers untied the rope from his saddle and gave it to Mitch, who headed for the whipping tree. James—beaten, bloodied, and broken—staggered 15 feet behind the grinning Mitch in his solitary lament.

. . . You let him kill Chloe. You let me get caught alive! You should've let me die, too. Why, God? Why?! WHY!? . . .

James, his eyes shut tight, felt the looks of the slaves as he passed. Their gasps, shrieks, screams, and cries pierced his soul. Faces, colors, scenes, sounds, and smells—all were a blur as he was pulled toward a vulgar spectacle.

. . . You are destroying my people's spirit, God. You are crushing us, God. Why are You doing this? Why are You allowing this, God? Why? . . .

Rogers arrived 10 minutes later and smugly eyed James. His hands shackled to a rope overlapping a limb, James' toes touched the ground just enough to support his weight as he slowly swayed and spun. Rogers strode through the disheartened group and then looked at James.

He let out a sinister laugh and sarcastically bellowed, "Aw, James. You sho' don't look so good. Had a bad day, did ya'? Hey, y'all. Guess who I caught fo' supper? Y'all leader. Ol' James here!"

. . . My God. You are destroying my people. He murdered Chloe. He caught me. Why You let this happen? Answer me, God! Answer me . . .

"Mitch, po' water all over his ass! Git 'em good and wet so this here whip sticks good. Oh, yeah, James. You gonna git it now, boy! In front of yo' peoples. Ol' man Johnson ain't here to save yo' ass! Oh, yeah!"

. . . Didn't I pray long enough? Didn't I run fast enough? Didn't I hide good enough? Didn't I try hard enough? Didn't I believe in You deep enough? What was it God? What did I do wrong? Where did I go wrong? Why are You letting this happen? . . .

"Here go y'all hero! Look at 'im. All beat up. All tied up. Gonna be all whupped up! I beat his ass all the way here. And I gonna beat his ass some mo' now! Can't none of y'all git away from me. Ain't a nigger alive that can git away from me. Y'all hear. Ya' hear! Y'all was born a slave. And y'all gonna die a slave."

. . . God! Why? You let him kill Chloe. Why You let him? You let him catch me—and whip me. Why, God, why? Answer me! Answer me, please. Why?—Why? If You won't answer me, then please, God, please give me strength. Amen. God, give me strength. Amen. . . .

Rogers, with a wicked snicker, walked toward him, a 15-foot-long, braided-leather whip wrapped around and coiled up in his hand. He moved closer, stared for a moment, and then struck James in the face with his fist and the coiled rope, opening a gash on his cheek.

"James, James, James. What the hell wuz you thinkin', boy? Huh? Huh! Gittin' me up outta my bed early this goddamn mornin'! Gonna whup yo' ass fo' that, too."

. . . God, please give me strength. Amen. God, please give me strength. Amen. God, please. Give me strength. Amen. . . .

Striking him again, this time drawing blood from his mouth, Rogers looked around at the growing crowd and ordered, "C'mon, c'mon—git y'all asses up here. Closer. Closer! I want y'all to see this. I want y'all to hear this. I want y'all to *feel* this!

"Hey, James, look at ya' folks. Look at 'em! Look at yo' peoples. They gone see ya' git ya' ass whupped. Whupped good!"

God, please give me strength. Amen. . . .

Rogers turned, walked back behind James, and slowly uncoiled the whip. "All y'all here. I want y'all to count—count loud on every whup! You hear!"

"Yassuh," came a murmur from the crowd.

"Louder, goddammit!"

"Yassuh!"

"Yeah, that's it. And if'n y'all git too low, I gonna start over. Y'all that can count best tell them that can't. You hear!"

"Yassuh!"

"Yeah—I got James. Look atcha', caught, huh—I caught yo' ass fo' supper. Tied up—beat up—and now fittn' to be whupped up—*grunt* . . ."

. . . God, please give . . .

". . . Look at y'all boy! . . ."

". . . whoosh . . ."

. . . me strength . . .

". . . pow! . . ."

"One!"

. . . Amen. . . .

". . . uh, huh. I gonna whup—*grunt* . . ."

. . . God, please give . . .

". . . whup his ass good! . . ."

". . . whoosh . . ."

. . . me strength . . .

"...*pow!*..."
"*Two!*"
"...uh, huh. Look at 'im..."
...*Amen.*...
"...hey, hey, hey—*grunt*..."
...*God, please*...
"...*whoosh*..."
...*give me*...
"...*pow!*..."
"*Three!*"
"...Oh, so you ain't gonna holler, huh? *grunt*..."
...*the strength*...
"...We gonna see..."
"...*whoosh*..."
...*Amen.*...
"...*pow!*..."
"*Four!*"
"...'bout that, hey, hey, hey. *grunt*..."
...*God—please*...
"...oh, yeah..."
"...*whoosh*..."
...*g-give me*...
"...*pow!*..."
"*Five!*"
...*the strength. Amen.*...
"...hey, I sho' gonna—*grunt*..."
...*God*...
"...whup this here..."
"...*whoosh*..."
...*please*...
"...*pow!*..."
"*Six!*"
"...nigger boy! *grunt*,..."

. . . give me . . .
". . . hey, hey, . . ."
". . . *whoosh* . . ."
". . . *pow!* . . ."
. . . strength . . .
"Seven!"
". . . *grunt* . . ."
. . . Amen. . . .
". . . *whoosh* . . ."
. . . God . . .
". . . *pow!* . . ."
. . . please . . .
"Eight!"
". . . *grunt* . . ."
. . . give . . .
". . . *whoosh* . . ."
. . . me . . .
". . . *pow!* . . ."
"Nine!"
. . . strength . . .
"Hee, hee, hee—how ya'—*grunt* . . ."
. . . Amen. . . .
". . . feelin', boy? . . ."
". . . *whoosh* . . ."
. . . God . . .
". . . *pow!* . . ."
"Ten!"
. . . please . . .
". . . Yeah, y'all leader—*grunt* . . ."
. . . give . . .
". . . gittin' his ass . . ."
". . . *whoosh* . . ."
. . . me . . .

"... whupped ..."

"... *pow!* ..."

"*Eleven!*"

... strength ...

"... somethin' good. *grunt* ..."

... Amen. ...

"*... whoosh—pow!* ..."

... God ...

"*Twelve!*"

"... Hey, hey. James, James—*grunt* ..."

... give ...

"*... whoosh—pow!* ..."

"*Thirteen!*"

... me ...

"... yo' ass is mine, boy! ..."

"*... grunt* ..."

"*... whoosh* ..."

... strength ...

"*... pow!* ..."

"*Fourteen!*"

"... Yeah. Big, bad James—*grunt* ..."

... A-Amen. ...

"*... whoosh—pow!* ..."

"*Fifteen!*"

"... Ain't so bad now—is ya? Ain't so smart now—is ya'? *grunt* ..."

... G-G-God ...

"*... whoosh—pow!* ..."

"*Sixteen!*"

"... hey, hey, hey, hey—*grunt*"

"*—whoosh—pow!* ..."

... please ...

"*Seventeen!*"

"... hee, hee. I got James—*grunt* ..."
... g-g-give ...
"... *whoosh—pow!* ..."
"Eighteen!"
... me ...
"... *grunt—whoosh—pow!* ..."
"Nineteen!"
"... *grunt* ..."
"whoosh—pow! ..."
... strength ...
"Twenty!"
"... *grunt* ..."
"whoosh—pow! ..."
"Twenty-one!"
"... *grunt* ..."
"whoosh—pow! ..."
"Twenty-two!"
"... *grunt* ..."
... A—amen. ...
"... *whoosh—pow!* ..."
"Twenty-three!"
"... *grunt* ...
"whoosh—pow! ..."
"Twenty-four!"
"... *grunt* ..."
"—*whoosh—pow!* ..."
"Twenty-five!"
"... *grunt* ..."
"whoosh—pow! ..."
"Twenty-six!"
"... *grunt* ..."
"whoosh—pow! ..."
"Twenty-seven!"

"...grunt..."
"whoosh—pow!..."
"Twenty-eight!"
"...grunt..."
"whoosh—pow!..."
"Twenty-nine!"
"...grunt..."
"whoosh—pow!..."
"Thirty!"
"...grunt..."
"whoosh—pow!..."

CHAPTER 4

Ten lashes had been standard punishment for running under Stanley's regime. Rogers increased that to fifteen, with Master Johnson's consent. Twenty for a second attempt, which no one had ever tried. But thirty-eight lashes later, Caleb had to first grab the whip and then Rogers to stop him. Smitty unshackled James, and four slaves carried his limp body toward the Hospital Shack and into the care of Netty.

She heaped mounds of salve on his shredded back, carefully wrapped bandages on his mangled wrists, prayed for his shattered soul, and cried aloud and silently against this travesty of humanity.

"This boy may die. Keep puttin' this heah on his back every three hours. Cool him down as much as ya' can. Nature—and God—will take care of the rest," instructed Dr. Andersen. He casually checked her work and added, "Not bad. Not bad at all. You gettin' good at this, Netty."

"It's all 'cause of the Lord. I trust the Lord—Dr. Andersen, suh. He guide me. It's His will now," Netty whispered, as she gently stroked James' forehead. Her bloodshot eyes testified of her pain, anguish, and exhaustion from the 40 consecutive hours she had nursed him.

♣

The gentle, melodic humming was the first thing James sensed, three days after the whipping. As his head cleared, he realized he was in a room, lying face down, and that various conversations were going on around him—and about him.

"Yeah, he sho' nuff gotta fever. We know by mornin'," he heard someone say.

Another replied, "Don't know how he made it this far."

A third sternly answered, "Don't be talkin' like that in here! We don't *need* that kinda talkin' here! Take that outside witcha'! *Go on—git out! Now!*"

Forcing his eyes open, James found himself lying on a bed, the first time he'd been on a bed since his days at Johnson Hall. He tried to move, but the searing pain of a thousand red-hot pokers raced through his body. Although his mind screamed, a barely audible moan was all that came out of his mouth.

Netty rushed to his side and whispered, "James. James, don't try to move, baby. It's me. Miss Netty. Just be still, okay? You in the Hospital Shack. We gonna take care of you. Just lay there. I'll bring you some water."

Netty continued her humming, part of her nursing technique. Along with applying the medicine Dr. Andersen left, singing soothing songs, doling out love and compassion, and fervently praying. She had been on Penelope Farms since she was bought by Master Johnson as a young lady. Master Johnson's wife took a liking to her immediately and named her after a doll she once owned, one of the few slaves whose name didn't come from the Bible.

Unless needed at the Hospital Shack, she worked in the orchards in the morning and helped cook for the slaves in the evening. Netty and three other ladies lived in the Hospital Shack, taking care of the sick, injured, and the pregnant. The slaves' nursery was in an adjacent building within earshot. The experience of pain and despair in her 40-something years had left indelible scars in her mind and spirit.

"What am I doing here? My parents spend too much money for me to mess this up. But, but I'm tired of this shit," Bobby whispered to himself.

Crouched behind shrubbery bordering Cambridge Prep's meticulously manicured lawns, Bobby held a 5-foot long, 2-inch diameter elm branch in his tight clench. Having been there for an hour, he waited for the source of his ire to approach.

As the only Negro in his classes, he expected isolation. Callous remarks weren't surprising. But the heartless evil that spewed daily from Nick Hawthorne's soul had filled Bobby with criminal intent.

"I just can't get caught. I can't—I can't get caught. Nicky Boy usually comes this way by himself. One good swing on his shin. A second one on his back. Then get outta here. Fast. I don't want to kill him. I wouldn't be sad if he died. But if I wanted him dead, I'd use a rifle. I just want to see him limping and slumping for a while and *know* I did it. Whatever happens, I can't get caught. I can't get—ooo, here he comes . . ."

Netty and James spent hours and days together as he slowly recuperated. She read to him from the Bible and talked about the Word. James appreciated being taught for a change as he gained a new perspective on the Bible. And a genuine appreciation of Netty.

She has an elegance, an air of grace about her. She doesn't walk—it's more of a glide. She should be somebody's queen. Definitely nobody's slave.

James smiled as he viewed her working her special brand of magic, moving from bed to bed and depositing joy, laughter, and comfort at each stop. The shack now contained several men who were injured, victims of Rogers or his men, and of accidents, as well as six pregnant women. She continued her rounds and caught a glimpse of James' gaze and returned his smile.

This was the first time James had spent any time with Netty. He had eaten her cooking, especially that sweet-potato pie, and had spoken to her in passing in the dinner line. He remembered seeing her when he and Ruth ventured out into the orchard and the time he was beat in the fields. That was the extent of their interaction until now. Her nursing skill helped heal his body. Her soothing voice and warm, maternal care helped heal his spirit.

"Hey, James," she said as she arrived at his bed and rubbed her hand over his hair. "How you doin'?"

"Okay, Miss Netty. I'm tired of being here. I want to get out," he replied, his spirits lifted by her attention.

"I think in a coupla' days, you be ready to start walkin'. Anyway, what else is on your mind?"

"Huh?"

"Oh, I can tell the way you lookin'," she answered as she began checking his bandaged wrists. "Oh, yeah. I think you always be thinkin'."

"Tell me some more about the Bible and slavery."

"You mean the true meaning of the Word, not that—that—"

"That asinine interpretation?"

She leaned close to him and whispered, "Uh, yeah, I guess. That whatever that Massah Johnson and the Reverend say. We supposed to be free, James. Especially the Christians 'cause we ain't pagans. It says so in Philemon and other places. Let me go get the Bible."

She walked across the room to a table filled with bottles, gauze, bandages, and a solitary book as James answered, "See—*ugh*—see, I always thought that way. But the Reverend, Massah Johnson, and Carlton all say the same thing. Ruth say—*ugh*—she didn't understand."

"It is hard to understand with our minds, baby. We gotta understand with our spirit. Are you okay? Still in pain?" she asked as she walked back with a thick leather-bound book under her arm.

"Uh, yeah. A—*ugh*—dull kind of pain."

"Yeah, I think you been up long enough. And you talkin' 'bout walkin'. C'mon, lay back down, baby," she insisted as she helped him back down onto his stomach after she'd placed the book on her chair.

"Thank you, Netty. I—*ugh*—I noticed when you pray—uh, I don't know. It's the same, but then again, it's not the same. It's hard to describe."

"I don't know, James," she shrugged. "First, I confess my sins. 'Cause we always sin. Especially slaves 'cause we sin in our thoughts, huh?"

"Amen to that."

"Then I humbles myself. Next, I acknowledge His greatness. Then I ask for what I want or need."

She sat in the chair, opened the Bible, and began thumbing through the pages.

"Yeah, that's it. That's what I mean. You only change what you ask for. Everything else is the same."

"Well, it works. And I do this every day, morning and night. Anytime I need Him. And not jest when I *think* I need Him, 'cause we *always* needs Him. And—oops, gotta go," she said as a very pregnant woman staggered in moaning and sweating, escorted by two other ladies. Not being able to see, James lay there and allowed the sounds to complete the scene.

Feet shuffling and scurrying; tables and chairs being moved; water being poured and splashed; authoritative voices giving commands; anxious voices following orders; the mother-to-be's screams and provocative language; all building up to a crescendo of silence—followed by the joyful noise of the newborn's wail. Then another one. James smiled into sleep.

ＣHAPTER 5

Ｓunrises and sunsets came and went as James' strength slowly returned. Going from sitting up for seconds to standing for minutes to now taking his first tenuous steps in nearly a month, James' progress was steady. He looked into Netty's caring eyes and wondered how something as terrible as being nearly killed by Rogers could turn into something as wonderful as getting to know her.

". . . Thank you for taking care of me, Miss Netty."

Maintaining a firm grip on his elbow to steady him as she walked by his side, Netty replied, "You're welcome, James,"

"You ever ask God why he made slaves, Miss Netty? I mean made us slaves. I know I do."

"You know, James, Proverbs 3, verses 5 and 6 has been one of my favorite verses. That and Psalms 19, verse 14. The proverb tells us to not depend on our understanding, but to depend on Him. I don't know why slavery is, James. But I ain't God. We gotta have faith and trust that His plan for us is good. I believe it is. God is a just God. A righteous God. We will be free someday, James, 'cause we supposed to be. Be careful, baby. . . ."

So, wanting to run is not against God's plan.

". . . You did great today. We went around the room 3 times, so let's sit."

"One more, Netty—please!" he pleaded as he took another step.

"No, James. We already went around one time more than I planned. Tomorrow, maybe."

"But," he began but soon conceded. "Yes, ma'am."

"We can probably finish Hebrews tonight, okay?" she replied as she led him back to the bed.

"Okay," James replied as he continued through his fourth and by far most meaningful journey through the Bible as he recovered from his sixth and by far most severe whipping.

♣

James' eyes squinted in the sun's glare. His first day out of the Hospital Shack since being captured, the foliage was well into its annual morphing from greens to reds, yellows, and browns. Netty was at his side, a brisk breeze was in his face, fresh air filled his lungs, and hope sprang eternal.

"Okay, now, James. We gonna take this slow, okay?" Netty warned as they took the steps down from the shack one by one.

"Okay, okay," James replied, unable to contain his anxiousness to step down to the ground and feel Mother Earth beneath his feet again. He looked over to Netty only when she'd stopped moving, her left eyebrow slightly raised and a smirk across her face.

"We gonna go over to yonder tree. Rest a spell. Then come back, okay?" she stated while nodding.

"Yes, ma'am. I promise—no more tricks. I already lost a week from the last one."

"Well, I'm sorry you got hurt but glad you learned yo' lesson," Netty replied.

They continued down the steps and on toward their destination, 50 feet away.

As they walked with measured steps, James caught a glimpse, off in the distance, of Rogers riding his horse, his blond mane flowing in the breeze. James' rage started to rise.

James inhaled deeply, slowly exhaled through quivering lips, and uttered, "Miss Netty. I know God say only He takes revenge. Not us. But—I wanna kill someone. That damn Rogers! I-I-I want revenge on Rogers."

"I understand why you wanna. He whupped and beat lots of young bucks like you. But wanting revenge ain't Christian-like. C'mon, keep walkin'."

"Okay. *Ugh*—uh, it ain't just the whippings, Miss Netty. He— he said he killed Chloe. I just found out he killed Chloe. He told me himself! When he was bringing me back here. He kept saying he killed Chloe, he—"

"You—you that *Jay* she was talkin' 'bout?" Netty asked. She looked up into James' searching eyes, filled with questions.

"Huh? What? She—she's dead? She really is dead? You saw her? Before she died?"

Netty nodded. As a sigh escaped her lips, she recounted, "Rogers, he come runnin' up, well, staggerin' up, yellin' fo' me to get over to his place. Early fo' dawn one mornin'. I got there—and, and I saw her. She was lying half on the bed, half on the flo', in—in her blood. She fought him. She fought him good, James. Them scratches he got, that piece of ear missin'. I reckon she bit it off. She hurt him in his man place, too."

She paused and looked away as tears trickled down her cheeks, and a low whimper escaped her trembling lips. Looking off into the distance, she shook her head slowly and continued.

"He—He was yellin' fo' me to save her or he was gonna whup me. I tried James, but she was hurt too bad. I tried. I swear. I held her, and she kept sayin' 'Jay.' That's all she said, over and over. I guess that was all she could get out. I didn't know she mean you. I didn't know no 'Jay.' I thought it was a name. I didn't know she was tryin' to say *James*."

"He did—he killed Chloe. He killed—Chloe. I guess I was hoping he said it to get me mad. That, uh—that he really didn't do it, you know. He killed—" James replied until his crying choked off his words. For 10 minutes they stood there, 42 feet from this day's goal, crying.

James finally muttered, "Uh, Miss Netty. You mind if we don't walk today? I—I don't feel like walking today—uh, anymore."

"Okay, baby. Let's turn around and go back inside."

"Thank you for what you did for her. She died calling for me, huh . . . She died with me on her mind. Uh, what else can you tell me about Chloe. Tell me everything you can about her, please."

♣

"Son, I—I'm sorry, son," Papa Harris said as he stared at Bobby, who was sitting on the edge of his bed, with his head bowed in shame.

"It's okay, Dad. I'll get over it."

"No! No—it's not okay! Nobody should have to go through that."

"Yeah, I'm glad I didn't attack Nick. But I wanted to. And it wasn't that I chose not to do it. It was the people who was walking behind him that stopped me. All I could think about was how I would've made y'all feel. I *knew* better, but I was gonna do it anyway."

"I'm glad God intervened. But—that's not what I mean. I mean I didn't tell you. I didn't warn you enough. I—I didn't say it hard enough. I didn't say it often enough."

Papa Harris stood up and walked over to the window overlooking their backyard. He now understood his firstborn's attitude—and reluctance—about going back to Cambridge Prep. Confused at first, he accepted his role in creating this situation. And he was determined do something about it.

"Son—I, uh, I told you 'bout them slave catchers. You already know 'bout Southerners and how they think. But I didn't tell you 'bout people, son. People *here* in Boston. I know how people can be. How they can smile with their faces and have hate for you in their hearts. And they're still teachin' that garbage to their children! I prayed it would be over when y'all were born. Or by the time y'all grew up."

228

He turned away from the window and hesitated speaking as he looked into his little boy's brown eyes and youthful face—the innocence long gone. Bobby returned the stare, searching his father's face for answers, for the truth, for comfort. Papa Harris slowly walked over to his son, still sitting on the bottom bunk, grabbed him up in his arms, and hugged him tightly.

"I thought I was protectin' you by not tellin' you the whole truth. By lying to you. My Lord, I lied to my own son. And for what? Bobby, I—I can't vote. No Negro man can. As much as people here in Boston support the Abolitionists, they don't support Negro men having the right to vote. Makes you wonder why they want us free. I was wrong, son. For lying. For not tellin' you the truth, the entire truth. Folks can be plain hurtful, and—" Papa Harris cried until they were interrupted by William, who burst into the room.

"Oops, I'm sorry, Daddy. I didn't know y'all in here. Ooo, Bobby in trouble, Bobby in trouble, Bobby in trouble . . ." William teased as he backed out.

"No, son, stay here. *Eve, Martha! Get up here now!* I'm not gonna make this mistake again, Bobby. They all gonna know." Papa Harris walked past William and leaned out of the bedroom and screamed again, *"Martha! Eve! Get up here right now!"*

The girls, along with their mother, arrived. Papa Harris looked around the room at his family without uttering a word for a full minute.

Finally, he smiled a sorrowful smile and softly said, "I want all of you to listen to Bobby tell y'all what's been happening at that school—then I'm gonna talk. Go ahead, son. Don't be scared. Don't worry. It's okay. Tell them the whole story. All of it."

A week after Netty's revelation of Chloe's final moments, James was getting strong enough not to be the focus of her attention. It remained that way, though. She doted over him in a maternal way obvious to everyone except those who chose not to see it. And James anxiously looked forward to the attention.

". . . and this would mean three. So, the signs we did today are to set up meetings. And the one last week, the A4114A code is for us to watch out for each other."

"I understand, Nimba," Netty replied.

James quizzically looked around the empty room.

Huh? Nimba? Who is she talking to? Who is she talking about?

"James, you heard me?"

"Uh, yeah. And when you add in the three types, you have nine—uh, codes."

"I see. And the marks tell which codes. I get it, James, baby. Gettin' whupped is never a good thing. Never! But me bein' able to work with you like this—it's wonderful! It's a blessin'. That's what it is."

"Right. I thought about that several weeks ago. Almost getting killed by Rogers made it so we could spend this time together. They say God works in mysterious ways, huh?"

"Yes, they do. And yes, He does. I always got bits and pieces, and nobody knew who it was."

"Yeah. My friend Isaac said he could get them to you."

"You see, that's why I didn't know who you were, James. I thought it was Isaac, and he wouldn't tell," Netty pointed out as she reached over and gently hugged James.

James chuckled and said, "Yeah, he told me he wasn't going to tell anyone. You know what happened to him? To Isaac?"

"Yeah. He was sold near three years ago. Yeah, 'bout three years."

Huh, around the last time I saw him. That's why he didn't say goodbye. Never had a chance to run. He was sold before he could run to his future.

"Thanks for telling me. Uh, Miss Netty—uh, who, who is 'Nimba'?"

"What! Who you been talkin' to, James?" Netty shrilled.

She pulled back, glared through his eyes and into his soul, and repeated, "Who—you—been—talkin'—to—James?"

Never having seen this side of her, James was startled to fear. He blinked twice, swallowed once, and looked away from her.

"Uh—uh, nobody, uh, ma'am. You've called me Nimba several times now. Twice today. At first, I didn't know you was talkin' to me. I was just wonder—"

Then he heard her sobs. He turned back and saw tears welling up in her eyes. She turned her glare away from him and sat motionless. He leaned over, embraced her, and rocked her gently as her sobs became cries.

"M-M-Miss Netty—uh, I—I'm sorry. I—I am sorry—"

"Nimba. Oh, my baby, Nimba," she whined and then sighed deeply, trying to inhale her cries.

She walked away from his embrace, crossed the room, and plopped down in a chair as a chorus of sighs accompanied her. She buried her oval face in her hands, her cries echoing in the empty room.

"It's okay, Miss Netty. It—it, uh, it's okay."

James gingerly rose up from his bed, limped over to her, and placed a compassionate hand on her shoulder as she wept. He peered out the window at the comings and goings of the slaves. His back began to ache, but he stayed there in hope he could return the comfort she had so graciously given him over the months.

Searching for anything to say, he added, "You know, Miss Netty. These codes of ours. They can work but, but I'm scared somebody will—"

"Nimba—Nimba was—no! No. Nimba *is* my son!" Netty interrupted in a wispy, whiny voice as her hands slightly trembled.

She looked up at James with her face contorted in anguish, as standing became more difficult for him. She held in her cries, although several sighs seeped out. She slowly shook her head while she lowered it.

"He—uh, he be 'bout your age now. Uh, Nimba is. I guess bein' 'round you so much—I don't know. To—today his birthday. August 31st was when he was born. Fo' noon. He was sold when he was two years, five months, and 21 days old. I looked it up. And I keep countin' and rememberin'."

"You remind me of my mama. The way you sing and stuff. At least that's all I can remember 'bout her. I figured I was about six when I came here," James replied, but his words sounded as helpless as he felt. James stood there in pain, realizing saying nothing else was the best thing to say.

"God, I know she missed—she *misses* you. Lord know I miss my Nimba every day. I can remember the way Nimba cried when he was hungry. When he was tired."

She sniffed the air, and a smile creased her face.

"I remember how he smelled. I remember the way he cried when he was wet. How he sounded when he tried to talk.

"I remember the first kick, the last push, and all the joy in between. All of it! I could look into his face, at those big brown eyes, and know he was my son. Know it! My firstborn. Whew, Lord! It's been long ago. Best forgotten. Lots of things best forgotten."

Netty rose from her chair and walked aimlessly around the room, tidying up things that were already neat.

"I don't know, Miss Netty. Maybe we should never forget. You remind me of my mama, and I remind you of your son. I'll be your son if you'll be my mama. Okay?"

Netty froze her stroll, and then slowly turned to face James. His eyes searched hers for a clue. Finally, her smile cracked the mystery, followed by a full-blown grin.

"Okay, James. But only if you call me 'Netty.' But first, sit back down. You gotta be in pain." She helped him to his bed, kissed him on the head, and uttered, "Now give me some more of those codes you came up with—son."

"Okay, mama."

CHAPTER 6

The first cold front of the season whipped through Penelope Farms as Master Johnson, Dr. Andersen, Rogers, Mitch, and Smitty huddled in the study and discussed the running of the plantation during the winter months.

". . . and gettin' as many babies started as ya' can betwixt now and thaw is jest as good a idea as it's been all the while," said Dr. Andersen.

"Ya' needs to keep the young bucks busy, too," Rogers added as he stood near the table with the magazines and newspapers, all the while pretending to read them.

"Yeah, that always a good idea, Doc. Me and Mitch heah, uh, we gone git a list together 'bout which young buck gone go when," Master Johnson replied as Mitch nodded.

"I'm jest glad these heah brutes of yours stopped damaging the others. Hell, I wuz missin' bitness in town comin' out heah so much," Dr. Andersen replied as he glared over at Rogers.

Rogers, standing with his back to the group, noticed the room's silence, and he turned to see Smitty and Mitch looking at him, while Master Johnson and Dr. Andersen were not.

"He called us 'brutes,' Rogers," Smitty whispered loud enough for all to hear.

Not quite sure of what it meant, Rogers replied, "Oh, yeah?"

"Hell, yeah! Brutes, beasts, heathens—"

"Beasts!" Rogers screamed as he latched on to a word he recognized.

"Hell, yeah. Beatin' up them folks fo' the fun of it," Dr. Andersen replied as they took strides toward each other.

"All right, all right!" Master Johnson proclaimed as he sprang from his chair, his lanky frame dominating the room. "Everybody calm down, now. We got all that fixed, Doc. Me and Rogers come to a understandin' a while back, huh, Rogers?"

Walking back to the table, Rogers mumbled, "Yes, sir, Mr. Johnson. I ain't no goddamn beast or, or brute. I'm a man. . . ."

"Anyway," Master Johnson continued, "I want all them boys who ready to have one chance or mo' and—hey, wutn't that James I saw walkin' the other day?"

"Yeah. Today, too. He jest getting' on his feet a'gin," smirked Rogers.

"Shit! I don't wanna hafta' sell that boy. He a real moneymaker. Smitty, go git him. Bring him heah."

"I'll go git him, sir," Rogers replied.

"Oh, hell naw, you won't! Sit yo' ass down. Smitty. Git."

"Yes, sir, Mr. Johnson. Be right back."

Coming back from their daily walk to the orchards, Netty and James saw Mr. Boo headed their way. Even though he was still at a distance when they first spotted him, his unique gait gave him away. As he approached, the background scenery of reds, browns, yellows, and oranges gave way to the most revered slave at Penelope Farms.

". . . and this is my favorite time of the year. All the colors!" Netty exclaimed while walking arm in arm with James and looking all around.

"Yeah, it's gonna get cold soon."

"How ya' feelin', boy?" Mr. Boo asked as he came up on them.

"Good, Mr. Boo. Getting stronger and stronger every day," James replied as he glanced at him and then looked away.

"Not *too* strong, huh," Mr. Boo replied with raised eyebrows.

"Huh—what?" asked Netty, who was still admiring nature's mosaic hues but picked up on Mr. Boo's tone. She turned to James and repeated, "What?"

"You can't get too strong, Mr. Boo."

"Ya' can git too strong fo' yo' own good."

"Nah. James, you ain't thinkin'—'bout runnin', is ya'? Rogers loves beatin' young bucks like you. Especially you," Netty replied as her voice cracked under the tension.

"Next time, you may not survive, boy! He gonna shackle ya' up at night. Might sell ya'! I heard some even cut your foot off! Uh, huh—you can still do what they want you to do with one foot."

"Well, I need two feet to do what *I* want to do, so I just won't get caught again."

"Some of the other bucks mad, too. Ol' Rogers didn't whup 'em this time, but maybe next."

"Well, that's why I ain't told nobody. I'm sorry if they get whipped. But I ain't staying. Mr. Boo, Netty, I can't breathe here. I can't stay here. The Uglies coming! They're coming. Slavery—shoot, Mr. Boo, it ain't right. Netty—it ain't right! I got to run—run to my future. My future is freedom—or death. Nothing in between. No other option. Freedom—or death."

"James, baby. Please don't—" Netty said.

"Hey, boy," Smitty called out as he came up on them. "Master Johnson wants to see ya' now. Let's git!"

James' heart pounded as he walked up the steps to Johnson Hall. Entering through the double doors for the first time in 4 years, his mind rushed to the past.

Johnson Hall seems different—I'm not sure. Smaller, maybe. Huh, the picture is still here. Carlton at 5 years old.

Memories of his days running up and down the stairs, reading with Carlton in the bedroom, helping Ruth polish the silver, sleeping on the floor, sneaking in and out of the study all flooded his mind as he climbed the spiral staircase. His head remained still and straight, but his eyes darted all around, soaking in every bit of scenery he could. When they reached the landing, he turned left, Smitty a step and a half behind him with his hand on his holstered revolver.

They walked past the seven-foot tall, ornately decorated time-piece in its familiar position. The gold-plated pendulum glistened and swung as they passed.

Ah, yes, my partner in crime. God, I hope it dongs before I leave.

They kept walking, coming closer and closer to the study, as James gave a subtle, silent sniff.

Huh, there's no—no smell. I guess after the years in the shack, no smell is a smell.

They turned the corner into the study. Master Johnson was seated at his desk, Rogers at the table, with the newspapers to James' left and his hand on his revolver. Dr. Andersen and Mitch were sitting in chairs to James' right, and Smitty stood behind James.

"Hey, James. How's the back, boy?" Rogers laughed.

Go to hell!

James' eyes surreptitiously scanned the room he had spent so many hours in, eventually eyeing Webster in the corner, on its stand. Seeing it there, he imagined all the "l" words exposed for all those years, including "longevity," and it brought a smile to his heart.

There were times I didn't think I'd see "longevity." Here I am, though. Still here. So are you, my friend. Aardvark to Zanzibar. Slave—nigger—servitude—chattel, huh. Also, honor—respect—trust—freedom—liberty—friend. Yeah, a book filled with beauty and ugliness, with hope and heartache...

"James, I didn't mean for you to get whupped like that. You're my prize buck!" Master Johnson began. "But dammit, you shouldn't have run. You try, you run again, and I swear, I'll sell your ass off! I tolt Rogers heah not to . . ."

. . . I can sense the words in this room. I can smell the stories. I can taste the times. "Longevity—Long duration of individual life." Can't forget that one! Escape—citizen—future . . .

". . . beat yo' ass like that no mo'. Lessen you runnin'! Hell, I can sell yo' ass off anytime I want. You seen how people act when I take you to auctions. Some of them are mean and will do worse things to you than I would ever do!"

. . . David Copperfield—I will be the hero of my own life. Shakespeare—to be or not to be. The Three Musketeers—all for one, one for all. . . .

". . . If you want to stay on this plantation, don't you try to run again, you heah! I'll put you in charge of the boys in the shack— how 'bout that, huh? I'll, I'll . . ."

. . . New York City. Paris. Brazil. Katmandu. A place that sounds like fun. . . .

". . . I'll take you out of the tobacco fields and let you work in the orchards. I might let you have a family someday if you're good. Okay?"

. . . You got to be out of your mind! Nothing you can say will keep me here. First chance I get, I'm gone.

"Oh, so you ain't gone talk, huh? You jest 'member what I said, 'bout folks worse than me. Git his ass outta heah!"

I'm not scared of you anymore.

James imagined looking directly into Master Johnson's eyes and telling him exactly what he thought about his offer. Twelve years of anger and rage that festered into hate would spew out in torrents, flooding this room and washing everyone and everything away with the tidal currents, leaving only memories of what is and what never was. But, alas, the pain would still remain, the dignity would still be denied, and the respect would still be refused. And James would still be half a step above an animal—a slave.

Huh, that would scare the shit out of him, though!

James and Smitty arrived at the double doors of Johnson Hall and prepared to leave when his secret partner cooperated.

Dong! Dong! Dong! Dong!

Huh, Carlton will be home soon.

♣

Fully recovered, James was back in the shack and working in the tobacco fields. Netty, fearful her time to convince James had run out, begged Mr. Boo to say something to get James to stay. The most respected slaves on the plantation, Netty prayed that fact would help.

Every time she got a chance to bend Mr. Boo's ear, she did. When their paths crossed walking to and fro. During supper, after all were fed. On Sundays during church and reading. And during days when work was slow, no one was hurt, and he hadn't left with Master Johnson.

". . . Mr. Boo, please. Go talk to him. Please! Rogers gonna kill that boy if he run again. Please stop him. Talk him out of it. Please. Rogers gonna kill that boy!"

"Shoot, Netty! If'n I was a young buck, I'd run, too. This ain't no way for nobody to live! We men! You women! Human beings with feelings, uh huh! What right we got to tell him not to do something we would do if'n we was young enough?"

Mr. Boo, sitting on the porch of his cabin in a wooden rocker, paused for a couple of drags off his pipe. He looked at a sobbing Netty, nodded, gave her a wry smile and a wink, and added, "Don't worry none, Netty. I gotta idea. Lemme tell ya' a story 'bout a brave—"

"Mr. Boo. I don't wanna hear no story! No disrespect, but help James. Help him, Mr. Boo! Tell *him* yo' story if you needs to. Just help him. Please!"

Mr. Boo had hair like snow and a heart of gold. He was past 50 and the father figure for all the slaves. This had been Master

Johnson's reason for not selling him. Once, Stanley was going to whip him, and five young male slaves took the beating for him.

Mr. Boo had been on the plantation for more than 25 years, longer than any other slave. He even garnered enough respect from Master Johnson to get to pick his own name. Initially named "Jeremiah," he never told anyone how or why he chose the name "Mr. Boo." He was also, the only slave who lived in a cabin by himself, a fact he appreciated.

He traveled with Master Johnson to towns, auctions, and other plantations. Mr. Boo had chances to talk with other slaves and the few free Negroes that were around. He witnessed many slaves come and go and all the trials that happened in between. He'd seen James come in as a little boy and grow into a young buck. From a scared, confused child to a strong, soul-searching Negro man.

And he had a plan for James to get his freedom. However, James was going to need to prove to Mr. Boo his desire to run, run to the future. Mr. Boo wanted to make sure James wasn't a Judas. He didn't want to risk telling his plan to the wrong person. After okaying it during a trip with Master Johnson earlier in the week, Mr. Boo sent a message for James to come and see him.

Seeing James approach his cabin, Mr. Boo silently considered, *that boy jest got whupped something fierce. Went up to the Big House to talk wit Johnson. Coulda' sold us out, uh huh. I heard stuff. I gots to be careful. Sho' do, uh huh.*

"Hey, Mr. Boo. Ezra said you wanted to see me."

"I got Massah Johnson to let you help me and the other boys out some. You gonna do most of the work. Miss Helen boys ain't gonna work so hard no mo'. I kinda sweet on Miss Helen. You gone bring me fresh-cut tobbacky ev'ry night. Not so Rogers suspects anythin'. Oh, yeah, and gimme that 'tater pie Netty fixes up!"

"I gotta give you my potato pie? How long I got to do this, Mr. Boo?" James asked, still unsure about the circumstances.

"Until I tell ya' it's done!"

"But why? Why I got to do this?"

"Shh, boy! I gots a plan fo' ya'—maybe. Miss Netty tolt me you been talkin'. 'Bout runnin'. If you ain't, then go. If you is, then jest hush, and do what I say," he screamed a whisper as he alternated looking at James and past him, out toward the surroundings, for listeners.

"A plan? A plan for what? For running? How? When?" James began before Mr. Boo motioned for silence with a finger pressed against his lips.

"Jest hush! And do what I say."

James' day began like all the others. Getting up before dawn, he reported to Mr. Boo in the morning and then to the orchards or special duties Mr. Boo gave him in the afternoons. This day was day number three of painting Mr. Boo's cabin.

". . . and jest as the princess thought all was lost, the Big Beautiful Savin' Bird came a-swoopin' down so purty-like, uh, huh. He covered her with his wings. Beautiful wings filled wit feathers of blue and red and brown and orange and purple and green and yellow and—crow-black. But no white ones. Nope, not one white feather, uh, huh, . . ." Mr. Boo narrated from his chair on the porch.

What once had been center stage on those nights of singing and storytelling now was a porch too big for this man and his tales left untold.

". . . The arrows and rocks those fellas was throwin' at her just bounced off like. After they run out, he stretched out his wings, reared back his head, and let out a scream that scared everythin'. Even the trees and stuff. That's why this time of year the leaves change color, uh, huh."

"Oh, Mr. Boo! It's because it gets cold," James argued as he continued painting the front of Mr. Boo's cabin near the porch. Miss Helen's boys, who came outside from helping their mother, were nestled at Mr. Boo's feet, staring up with eyes wide and minds open. Mr. Boo completed a drag off his pipe, while slowly shaking his head, and then continued.

"The cold jest remind the trees of that scream, boy! It just so happen it was this time of the year when the Big Beautiful Savin' Bird was here. Anyways, like I was sayin', uh—oh, yeah, it makes the leaves change colors when he screamed, uh, huh. Used to be a big ol' yellow and orange and pink and purple bird, wit black and gray stripes and green dots 'round here, too. But no mo'. Ain't been back since, uh, huh. . . ."

Continuing his painting, James smiled at Mr. Boo's remarkable tale, remembering other yarns he'd spun when James was first sent to the shacks. He realized he missed that almost as much as the study and found comfort in hearing them—and him—again. He went about his job of painting, listening to Mr. Boo, and thinking.

I should be glad he got me out of the fields. I think I've been fooled, though. It's been two weeks. Mr. Boo has got me doing his work—and his girlfriend's sons' work. And I miss Netty's sweet potato pie. I'm beginning to think Mr. Boo and Netty's plan is to keep me here forever, and that ain't gonna happen. They want me to give up. Forget about running. That ain't gonna happen! I can't breathe here. I got to run. I'm gonna run, run to the future. Whatever that may be. Freedom—or death.

The following night, James snuck out of the shack and confronted Mr. Boo on his porch. He stayed in the shadows, crouched low, and whispered, "Mr. Boo, I'm tired of this—"

"Boy!" Mr. Boo exclaimed as he jumped in his chair and landed hard. "Ow! You scared the shit outta me! And made me hurt my ass! What you doin' out 'chere? Git yo'self back to yo' shack, now!"

"Nah, I ain't going nowhere. I'm tired of all this extra work! I'm tired of working for your lady friend. I'm tired of being on this plantation! Mr. Boo—I'm tired! You told me you had an idea. Huh, said you had a plan. But I think your idea was to keep me here! Your plan is to make me give up and stay here until it gets too cold to go! I'd rather freeze to death out there; I'd rather die out there than stay here!"

"Boy—James. Boy, I—I don't wantcha' to die. We—Netty and me, we don't wantcha' to die, boy."

"I'm dying now, Mr. Boo. I'm dying a slow death. I can't stay here. I can't breathe. I can't—*arrgh!* I can't do it anymore. I got to run—run to my future. Mr. Boo, I—I got to. I got to get out of here! I'm getting freedom, or I'm going to die trying. Will you help me? Please, Mr. Boo! Help me."

Deeply inhaling and then slowly exhaling, Mr. Boo leaned back in his chair. Taking another long drag off his corncob pipe, he looked out into the distance and pondered. *I reckon it's 'bout time. I gotta trust somebody sometime. I guess it's gonna be this boy here.*

He cleared his throat and recounted, "You know. I'se been 'round these here parts purt near thirty years. Goin' wit Massah all over. Gots to talk to lots of folks. Ol' man Selmon in town. Derrick over at Shyler Plantation. Meets lots of peoples all 'round these parts. Hear tell 'bout all kinds of stories. Let me tell ya' a special one, 'bout Moses. . . ."

I know about Moses. I know the Bible. I read the Bible. He led the Jews out of Egypt. I already know that! He know I know that!

". . . They calls her Moses 'cause she leads folks from slavery. Just like Moses in the Bible. She don't ask like Moses in the Bible did. Nah, she jest come and *gits 'em*, uh huh. She got purt near a hunnerd slaves free, I hear. Once she . . ."

A woman, huh. Not many stories have women as the hero. Uh— Joan of Arc. That's the only one I can remember. This should be good—but hurry up, Mr. Boo. Hurry up! Get to the point.

". . . led 20 folks to they freedom. Mens, womens, chillins. All kinds. Moses, uh, huh, yeah. A giant of a woman. But not in size, 'ceptin' fo' the size of her heart, uh, huh. Big in bravery, too. . . ."

James struggled to focus on the story. He squirmed in his crouch and tried to remain patient.

Reminds me of some of the stories I read in the study. But Mr. Boo, please get done so you can tell me the plan. Or get to the point.

". . . I heard tell one time a fella was chasin' her. And she took *his* horse. Hee, hee! Folks shot at her, but she keep on comin' back, uh, huh. A man had his gun pulled out on her like. She ended up wit it. Don't know how. But she left him his bullets. Hee, hee. That lady somethin' else. I think the word is brave. . . ."

Huh, I think the word is fiction—or fable. C'mon, get to the point!

"... Yeah, that Guardian Angel she got is good—real good. She travels at night. By the stars and the moon! She came back to get her family. Then she keep on comin' back and back, uh huh. ..."

Oh, so I'm supposed to travel at night? That's the plan? How am I supposed to find my way? Mr. Boo, please hurry up!

"... plenty folks try, but nobody can catch her. She say angels look out fo' her. And they watch over—"

"Mr. Boo, I'm sorry. But how is this going to help me get out of here? I think—" James blurted out as he stood up.

"Hush, boy! " Mr. Boo implored. "Git back down!"

He glanced around to see if anyone could've seen him. "Shoot, you made me lose my place. Hush—and listen. If ya' can't do that, then go."

"I—I can do that. I'll be quiet."

"Good. Now where wuz I at? Yeah, the Guardian Angel wit her, yeah—she say angels look out fo' her. Her Guardian Angel, uh, huh. Must be good, too. 'Cause she keep comin' back fo' mo'. Lots mo' uh, huh. ..."

Patience and respect, James. Patience and respect. If he don't tell soon, just leave. Do it on your own. ...

"... Mr. Lewis in Frederick County says he seent a poster fo' her fo' $20,000. I seent one at Stuart's Traders. I guess the massahs want her bad, huh? ..."

... Just run faster this time. Stay in the river longer. Just—huh? What? The massahs? Mr. Lewis—Frederick County—seen posters for her? St-Stuart's Traders? That's where the auction was. I-I-I been there! He—he's whoa. He's talking about this lady like—like she's—like she's real.

"... they say she go all over. Way past Dotelli's Plantation. Over two weeks away. They seent her at the armory. And she come by here, too," added Mr. Boo.

He reached into his pocket for tobacco and filled his pipe. He got up and strolled around the corner, past James, and into the darkness.

James followed Mr. Boo by spinning in his crouch, his eyes stretched to the limit as he, at first, blurted out, and then whispered, *"What!? She—She's real? M-M-Mr. Boo. She's—real?"*

"You gotta light, boy?" Mr. Boo asked as he reached in his pocket.

"Huh? What? Nah, they don't let us carry anything."

"Dangit! These here too damp to light. Gonna have to go inside to find some dry one fo' I git a light—"

"Wait a minute, Mr. Boo. Give them to me."

James frantically lit a match on the sixth try.

Mr. Boo took a long drag off his pipe, exhaled a cloud of smoke, and stared down at James. He searched for an answer, for a clue, for an insight into this young man behind the face illuminated by the flame of the lit match. He considered his next words as he thought, *Gotta trust somebody, I reckon.*

"Mr. Boo. *Is—she—real?"* whispered an incredulous James, his stretched eyes now threatening to break skin.

"Yeah. She real. Come by here, too. I'm too old to go."

"How—how will I know she's here? I mean, how will I know when?"

"Yep, she come by here. I'm too old to go. Maybe you—maybe—"

"Uh, yeah, Mr. Boo, I'm young. I can make it. How will I know when uh, she's here?"

"Yeah, maybe you can. You may have a chance," Mr. Boo said, all the while looking over and past James and into the dark. Taking another full drag off his pipe, he exhaled the smoke and proclaimed, "Umm, this here some good tobbacky."

Stay calm, James. And patient. He'll tell you. He will. Stay calm, James. Nah—

"Okay, Mr. Boo. *Please* give me that chance."

"Boy, you get Moses caught—I swear, I'll kill you myself."

"Huh? I—I won't get her caught. I'll be quiet. I won't say nothing."

"You didn't sell us out, did ya'? I hear tell Massah say you could have a family. You gonna have it good here, huh?"

"*Mister Boo—I'm not*—I'm not a sellout! I love my people. I don't want a family in a—a—a cage. He would use it against me. I'm running with or without your help. I'm gonna run to freedom or die. Yeah, the quickest way to freedom. I understand now. If I die, then I die. But please, help me live, Mr. Boo. Please! I got to run to my future—I can't breathe here. Please, I'm dying now. *Where* I die is the only question. Do I die free? Or do I die trying to be free? Help me—please, Mr. Boo. Please!"

Mr. Boo walked back onto the porch and returned to his chair. After a few seconds of contemplation—and a spit that barely missed James' head—Mr. Boo slowly, and, at first, softly sang, *"Swing low, sweet chariot. Coming forth to carry me home . . ."*

James squatted there for a while, his eyes still stretched, and finally said, "What? Is that it? Is that some type of code? Huh, Mr. Boo? Is it? Is it? Huh, is—"

"Yeah. Yeah, boy. Not much dif'rent from yoursown. And late, late at night, listen for them sweet sounds of 'Swing Low, Sweet Chariot.' When ya' hears it, run to the sound as fast and as quiet as ya' can. Say 'friend of a friend.' Then *shaddup* and do what Moses tells ya' to do."

"Thank you, Mr. Boo. Thank you," James said repeatedly with subdued glee as he backed into the darkness, his hands clasped in a prayerful pose. He hesitated his anti-stride for a moment, his full-face grin covering the entire front half of his head as he alternated between nodding his head and profusely thanking Mr. Boo over and over, and then disappeared into the night.

Mr. Boo never looked at him. Instead, he puffed his pipe and mumbled between clenched teeth, "Don't thank me 'til ya' makes it."

CHAPTER 8

James was rising off his cot again. Out through the window of the shack and upward, toward the stars. Viewing Penelope Farms from this panoramic perspective, he thought how peculiarly serene it appeared. The farm, foliage, and forest masked the travesty of humanity that existed mere feet beneath the treetops.

He trained his eyes up and toward the direction of a melodic beacon. A gasp filled his chest as he gazed upon an ebony siren, dressed in a sheer-white, flowing gown who was singing his name. Moving ever so closer together, their hands joined, and a sense of joy washed over him. He floated along with her as they glided over the countryside, toward the North and to his future.

"Thank you, Mr. Boo," James murmured as he woke up to the morning screams. "Is this my last day at Penelope Farms?"

"Here's yo' money," Master Johnson said as he offered a handful of bills to his overseer.

"Thanks, Mr. Johnson. Uh—you still mad 'bout that nigger, James?" Rogers asked as he began counting the money.

"If he had died, yo' ass would've been workin' heah fo' free. But he didn't, and nobody even tried since. You might o' broken theah spirit. And you didn't hurt him as a man. I can still send him over to Cupid's next month. Really start makin' some money. So, you okay."

"... twenty-fo', twenty-five, twenty-six—uh, yes, suh, uh, Mr. Johnson—uh, twenty-seven, twenty-eight, ..."

Between the excitement of Mr. Boo's revelation and the dreams, restful slumber for James was elusive. He worked with Mr. Boo during the day, but he still slept in the shack. Each morning when their eyes met, nothing needed to be verbalized. Mr. Boo hadn't spoken about it since that night, and James hadn't asked any more questions. All that was left was for it to happen.

Each night, James would lie down to a myriad of sounds—the rustling of the windblown leaves, the animals moving about near and far, the breeze whistling through the cracks in the shack, the triumphant and tragic calls of the wild—as he strained to listen for those sweet sounds. When he finally dozed off, the dreams would come, and he would wake up in the morning disappointed.

I hope I haven't slept through it. It's been a couple of weeks since Mr. Boo's story, and nothing! God, Lord Jesus! I hope I haven't missed it. The trees are getting bare. First frost is coming soon. God, I hope I haven't missed her!

"Father God, forgive me, for I have sinned. Please don't let me sleep through and—" he prayed that night until he heard something. Closing his eyes, he held his breath, and focused his hearing.

"Swing Low, Sweet Chariot" wafted hushed and gently on a melodic current through the shack.

He sat up. He listened. Some birds had sounded like this before. But yes, this was it! James' pulse quickened, his heart raced, and sweat began beading on his face in the sub 50-degree weather.

"Heavenly Father, forgive this sinner, I hate my master, my overseer, other human beings. You are my Savior, please bless this journey I'm about to go on, Amen," he prayed as he headed to the window. He looked back, as before, and then slid out of the window and ran toward the sounds.

His thoughts went to Mr. Boo and Netty, his heart heavy at the thought of leaving them. He wanted to say goodbye to them. To thank them, to cry with them, to pray with and for them, but the sounds were calling—his song was being sung, and he kept running, running to the future.

"God. Bless Netty and Mr. Boo, and Isaac, and Ruth. And bless everybody here. . . ." he mumbled between strides and gasps. When he got to the thicket, he saw her, stooping in a crouch.

This—this is Moses? How is she going to get me to my freedom? Certainly not the woman of my dreams. . . .

"F-F-Friend of a friend," he whispered as his mind raced.

. . . God, I hope she knows what she's doing! Mr. Boo says I can trust her. He says to be quiet, no—to shaddup—and follow her. Please, Lord Jesus, help us! . . .

Moses replied, "Friend of a friend," and then motioned him to follow her. They stopped a hundred yards later, and she let out a "barn owl hoot." A group of men, women, and children emerged from the forest. The crunching of the multicolored leaves underfoot was the only sound as they traveled through the frosty night, their clouds of breaths dissipating with each step. Moses gave hand signals that the others knew, and James followed suit.

. . . I have no idea where we're traveling to. No sun. No hills. No buildings or any other landmark. The local road. Nothing! I'm totally lost. Mr. Boo says I can trust her. That she knows what she's doing. God, please bless this journey, and bless Miss Moses. And bless us! Guide her so she can guide us. Lord Jesus, I sure hope she knows what she's doing! . . .

They traveled through the night, knee-deep in marshes and streams. As the crack of dawn approached, a farm nestled near a glistening lake came into view. Moses motioned for them to stop.

"I'm going up there. When I waves my hand three times, y'all come a-runnin'. If'n I don't, y'all run fast that-a-way. To the North."

Stealthily, she zigzagged in the shadows of trees and buildings, until she made it near a window with a flickering candle. Knocking on the door, it barely cracked open. After a few tense moments, she turned and waved three times. They were taken to the barn, where they stayed that day. The owners of the farm swept away their tracks leading to the farm and spread onion mixture around the home.

The runaways huddled around the lone fireplace and slurped down warm broth. James was glad to peel off the wet clothes and dry out. He observed their benefactors. A White man and woman with brown hair and slim builds.

I would have never come here. Even if I saw these people, I would've run right past this house. How, how did she know they would help her? Help us? Is it You, God?

I had the right idea about running in the river, though. I just didn't do it soon enough, or long enough. I know now, maybe I should go on my own. I'm smart, and, and—okay, Mr. Boo. I'll be quiet—I'll shaddup—and do what Moses tells me. As long as it makes sense. . . .

"Y'all needs to eat—and sleep. So do that," barked Moses, as she sat down in a corner, wearing a pair of long johns and a stern disposition.

. . . Thank you, Mr. Boo. Thank you, Netty. Thank You, God.

"He's on the run a'gin, Mister Johnson, suh! I whupped 'im sum'um' fierce, too. He jest a runner. You need to sell him South. He too close to the North, here," Rogers reported, an hour after James was reported missing.

"Bring him back alive! And in one piece. I can't sell no damaged property, you heah!" Master Johnson yelled from the front porch of Johnson Hall as Rogers and three of his men galloped down the main trail leading out of Penelope Farms.

"Yes—suh—Mi—ster—John—son—suh," Rogers sarcastically replied. He thought, *That boy give me any trouble, he dead.*

"Bobby! William! Bobby! William!" Mama Harris yelled up the stairs for the third time that morning. "Get up! Time to go to the station!"

Bobby rose from his bed and pulled his brother, William, out of the top bunk. He hit the floor and bounced, which brought laughter to Bobby. Always the jokester, he loved picking on his younger brother. William was getting bigger than Bobby, though, and reminded him of it.

"Hey, lil' brother. What's your problem?" William asked as he rose from the hardwood floor.

"Lil' brother, huh."

He ran into his brother and knocked him back down. They wrestled, the thumps and groans echoing throughout the house. Soon, another set of thumps predominated, as Mama Harris came upstairs, full of attitude.

"I said-duh. It's time to get ready to go!"

"Yes, ma'am," the boys chimed in unison.

"See. You got me in trouble."

"No, I didn't."

♣

James awoke thinking about his decision. Scanning the room, most of the travelers were asleep. All looked like him—people of African descent. Each with their own story. Each having their own history. But all with the same purpose—running to their future. Eventually his thoughts went back to Penelope Farms.

. . . I wonder what the slaves are saying. "Oh—that James running again. If he get hisself caught, Rogers gonna sho' nuff kill 'im.' Huh, he probably would kill me. Shoot, going back there would kill me. Anything other than freedom would kill me. No matter what happens, I can't get caught. I can't go back. At least, not alive. I'm gonna die free or die trying to be free. Taking the quickest way, huh, Isaac? Yeah. The quickest way . . .

♣

The Harris family waited in Boston's North Station for Bobby's 2:15 p.m. train back to Cambridge. During a week of sometimes intense conversations, Bobby shared with his family and Pastor Beard everything he had to endure. The Key Club incident. The harassment he endured at Cambridge from many of his classmates, some teachers, and especially, Nick. He also confessed his plot to hurt Nick—a plot he didn't complete that time but remained on his mind. And the rage that was building in him. A rage that scared him. Despite it all, Bobby decided to return and complete his school year.

"You got everything?" Mama Harris asked her firstborn.

"Yes, mama, I do."

He studied his mother's face, and he saw the concern she desperately tried to hide. Turning toward his father, the strength he shared daily with the family continued. His siblings turned their heads away and avoided eye contact, although William made a funny face first.

"I want to thank all of you for being here. For listening to me. For hearing me. For being there for me. It means a lot. It means everything to me. You mean everything to me. I—I want all of you to know I'm okay.

"You all are the reason I can go back to Cambridge. Without each of you, I would not be going back. I felt so alone. I was alone. And not telling anybody about what was happening at school made my loneliness worse."

"I'm sorry, son, for—"

"No, dad. It's okay. Really, it's okay. You and mama gave me so much, put so much good inside of me. I—even in the middle of my rage at Nick, y'all put enough good in me to not do anything bad. Though I wanted to, I still want to—bad. The only reason I didn't do it, the only reason I've lasted as long as I have is because you—both of you. All the support and love you put in me. Somewhere in the Bible, it says to raise your children in the way they should go, and they won't leave it. That's what happened to me. You taught me what I *should* do, and when the time came, I did what you taught me, not what I wanted.

"It's the only reason I lasted as long as I did. And when I did tell you, y'all said all the right things, did the right things—just like you always do."

"Thank you, baby."

"It's funny—the thing is that, now, I don't feel I'm getting on this train alone. I'm not going back by myself. This time, each of you are going with me. I won't say anything, except that each of you shared things with me that was for me from you. Each of you gave me something that I will carry with me forever. I don't know—it's almost like telling you all how I feel, what I was going through, makes it feel lighter somehow."

"I'm glad. Thanks for telling us, Bobby. Write me, telegraph me about anything you want."

"Thanks, Martha. I will. I look forward to writing all of you with your own letters. Even you, William."

"Th-Thanks.."

"You okay, Eve? You're mighty quiet back there."

"Uh, huh. I don't want you to get hurt. Or—or, I don't want you to hurt nobody else."

"I'll be careful, and I won't hurt anyone. Don't worry about me doing something that will bring embarrassment to our family. All of you helped me to not hurt anyone. Like I said, I'm going back on the train by myself, but I'm not going back alone. Not only—"

"2:15 TRAIN TO CAMBRIDGE BOARDING AT GATE C. 2:15 TRAIN TO CAMBRIDGE BOARDING AT GATE C."

"Not only that, but I'm returning there a different person. Mama, Daddy, y'all taught us the importance of education. It's too important to me to let somebody run me away. I got the ability. You gave me the opportunity. And I will do something with it. I got these few months. I'll get the education. I'll graduate. Then I'll leave and won't have anything to do with Cambridge Preparatory School again.

"Thanks for everything, everybody. I love all y'all. Yes, including you, William."

"I—I love you, too. Can I carry your bag?"

"Sure, you can."

The family walked in silence to the loading platform. There, Bobby looked each one in the eyes again and shared hugs and tears.

"LAST CALL. ALL ABOARD TO CAMBRIDGE, MASSACHUSETTS. ALL ABOARD TO CAMBRIDGE, MASSACHUSETTS."

"I—I gotta go."

"Don't say 'gotta', say—never mind. You can say 'gotta,' baby."

Bobby slowly stepped up the stairs to the locomotive car as he resisted the urge to look back. The train jerked and swayed as it began moving north. Bobby reached the door of the car, glancing back in time to see his family waving. He smiled, waved back, and entered the car.

⚘

Daytime morphed into dusk, and Moses got the group ready to head out. James, nervous about staying in a house all day, was relieved to finally be moving again.

"I'm not being taken back, alive. I got farther with her than without her. I guess she knows what she's doing, huh," James commented to one of his traveling companions as they left in the dusk.

"Shh!" Moses warned as she cut a peek at him. "It's my Guardian Angel, boy. It always protects me. Now, say no mo' 'til morning!"

And they left the barn, 10 silhouettes plastered against an ever-darkening sky, led by a woman called Moses.

Chapter 9

Rogers and his men made camp for the night, less than 20 yards from a glistening lake. They sat around the flickering campfire with the lake as a backdrop. The tied-up horses several yards away stomped and neighed every time a kindling crackled or popped.

"Ya' suppose he somewheres dead, or somethin', Rogers?" Mitch asked as he poked at the fire and stared at the floating embers, cautious to not look at Rogers like the other men.

"Don't know. He got smarter. We already caught him last time. We gonna git 'im. Don't worry. We gonna git 'im. You can count on that!" he animatedly answered, quickly got to his feet, and strode over to the pot of simmering stew.

"Yeah. One ain't got from us yet. Right, Rogers? 'Member ol' Luke? 'Member when we—"

"Shh. Be quiet. Somebody's comin'," Rogers commanded as he stopped in his tracks, un-holstered his gun and pulled back the hammer. The others brandished their weapons, and all looked out toward the sound as Rogers asked, "Who out there?"

"Jest some bounty hunters lookin' fo' some niggers," replied a voice in the dark as the footsteps got louder.

"Ham? Ham, that you?" Rogers asked the familiar voice as a grin broke his frown.

"Yeah. Who that?" the voice responded.

He walked into the light and exclaimed, "Rogers! You ol' son-of-a-bitch. How ya' doin'?"

Rogers uncocked and re-holstered his gun, and then embraced his friend. Ham's disheveled band of 6 slave hunters emerged from the darkness.

"Okay, okay. Y'all sit a spell. We trackin' a runaway we got. What the hell ya' doin' 'round these heah parts?"

"The same thang we wuz doin' back when. Trackin' that nigger wench!"

"Moses? Shit. She 'round heah?"

"We reckon. Almost had her a coupla times, but dem damn Abolitionists help her some. Whatcha' got in that pot?" Hamilton asked as he sniffed the aroma.

He and his men strode toward the simmering stew.

"Y'all been chasin' that wench fo' what—goin' on five years now. And y'all ain't got her yet?" Rogers added and laughed heartily.

A frown grew on Hamilton's face as he filled his bowl. His men, relishing the break from jerky and hardtack, quickly filled their dingy metal bowls with stew and just as quickly filled their mouths.

Rogers' men joined in his laughter until Hamilton said, "Y'all laugh all y'all want. But most likely she got yo' boy, too."

"Oh, shit!" Rogers exclaimed as Hamilton snickered and then filled his mouth.

Moses motioned for the group to stop and gather in a heavily wooded area. The thick canopy and the darkness of the night made seeing more than 2 feet in front of them impossible.

"Y'all stay here. And be quiet. Listen fo' the barn owl 'hoot, hoot'," she whispered.

She left as they huddled around a tree. James' thoughts went back to Penelope Farms as he looked around at the shadowy figures of his traveling companions.

I've been gone for a whole day now. Word must have gotten around the plantation by now. I hope Mr. Boo ain't whipped because of me. He knows if this works, if I get away, then others can, too. I got to make it. I can't fail this time. I can't get caught! Look at the 10 souls here. Look at us! We all are taking a life-or-death risk. I'm totally lost.

I don't even know if we are going North or not. Deep in these forests, knee deep in streams and lakes. I just pray that she knows what she's doing. I know, I know. Be quiet—no, shut up—no, shaddup, and do what Moses tells ya' to do.

James smiled as he mumbled, "Okay, Mr. Boo."

Five minutes later, Moses returned with two young men running, running to the future, and they continued traversing the forest. Dawn approached before Moses said anything else. Most huffed and puffed from the weight of the journey and the magnitude of their decision to flee slavery. All intently focused on Moses and awaited her next instruction.

"We gonna settle here, today. Y'all gonna sleep outside, so git comfortable."

Everyone sat down and began eating what Moses returned with. James, sitting off to himself, listened to the conversations that were going on. The two latest ones obviously knew each other. A family of 4 talked. And the 5 single male runners who were there before James joined had formed friendships.

"Hey, boy," Moses said and motioned for James to come near her. "What yo' name, boy?"

Huh? What—why she asking me? I—uh, say something, James.

Swallowing hard he replied, "James. My name is—I mean, my name James, Miss Moses, ma'am."

"You got some book learnin', ain'tcha' James?"

Oh, no! A smart slave. A dead slave. I don't know nothing!

"I don't know nothin', ma'am. My massah, he allow—he let us read the Bible and stuff. You mean them kinda books, ma'am? That's all," James lied as his gaze remained toward the ground.

A sarcastic laugh accompanied a smile from Moses, but both dissipated quicker than they appeared. She stared at James for a moment and then whispered, "I tells ya'. Ol' Moses been back and forth through these here parts. Plenty times. Live a long life, too. And some folks still thank she stupid. That be you, huh, James?"

Oh, Lord! I'm dead. A smart slave. A dead slave. They gonna kill me!

"Ma'am, I don't think—"

"Don't you *ma'am* me, boy! I ask ya' a question. And you lie!"

"Yes, ma'am," James replied, his tears forming a sorrowful puddle at his feet.

Moses glanced over at the group, who were now staring at them.

"Don't y'all worry none. He jest a tad scared. He all right."

She leaned closer to James and asked, "Why you lie to ol' Moses?"

"I—I'm sorry, Miss Moses, ma'am. I—I didn't know if I should. I let two people know back at Penelope Farms. Both were sold. Nobody else knew how much reading I was doing. Not even my master, or he would've killed me!"

Moses nodded with understanding and replied, "Uh, huh. It okay. You safe here. Go on."

"When I first got to Penelope Farms, I—I stayed in the Big House. He sent me to the fields later, and I been there ever since. But I did read a lot of his son's books. And his books. I'm sorry I lied to you, ma'am. I was told not to tell anyone."

She slapped her knee and exclaimed, "I knew it. I knew it! I heard you use words Negro folk don't use. Pro'bly write, too. You right, though. Don't let jest anyone know 'round here. In the South, a smart slave usually a dead one. We keep this to ourself, okay?"

"Yes, ma'am. Thank you, Miss Moses. Ruth, the lady I told, she said the same thing. About a smart slave."

"Yeah! Huh—I gotta smart one. A book-learned one. Ol' Fred be happy 'bout this here!"

⁂

One by one, each person dozed off, except for James. The dawning sounds of the awakening countryside, the flickering of sun rays breaking through the canopy, and he excitement of the escape all conspired against him and slumber. He looked over at Moses, sleeping near him, and marveled at her bravery. He stretched out on the grass and wondered about Penelope Farms.

Netty is nursing the sick. Mr. Boo going around taking puffs off that pipe and telling stories to anyone who'll listen. Most would be out in the fields by now, picking that tobacco. Or in the orchards—or that other place. And Rogers is still out there somewhere looking for me.

The noon sun glistened brightly in the high azure sky. Through the chilly autumn air, the joined hunting groups devised and coordinated their plans over lunch. Rogers' group of 4 men huddled together as their anxiety rose with each passing moment without James, though none dared verbalize it. Each tick of Mitch's pocket watch screamed of the tension rising and indicated the time spent away from Penelope Farms was increasing, none of which bode well for anyone near Rogers. They looked at each other and then over at Hamilton's men, who were huddled several feet away. Then they looked off in the distance at Hamilton and Rogers, who alternated between arguing and pleading on the next step in the quest for their common quarry.

"Okay, then. I gone take some dawgs, and me, Boone, and Tom Boy gone go west, followin' the crick heah. My other boys gone go north through the forest and head fo' Dawson Corners. Rogers, y'all go east. We'll meet up at Dawson Corners d'rectly. Okay, Rogers?" Hamilton suggested as Rogers, downing the rest of his coffee, nodded in agreement.

With a face etched with disgust, he ordered, "You and yo' boys jest 'member that nigger boy James is mine! I want 'im bought to me—alive!"

"Okay, Rogers. We know his massah want 'im back and—"

"I don't give a shit 'bout ol' man Johnson! This here's fo' me! I want his ass alive!" Rogers exploded as he stormed off toward his men while his tossed coffee cup reached the ground with a metallic *clang*.

"Uh—g-g-give a three-shot salute if'n y'all catch 'em."

"Yeah, yeah. Saddle up!" Rogers yelled at his men as he mounted his steed.

Chapter 10

"Y'all see it. The Promised Land!" Moses venerated as she stretched out her arms, showing her followers a picturesque valley several yards away from their forested viewpoint. All dozen pairs of eyes, wet with emotion, peered through the final stand of trees, out beyond the hill they were perched on, and onto the serene landscape. A multitude of people, many of them Negroes, and animals of all sorts, co-mingled together in Edenic peace and harmony.

James, with a grin as wide as the panoramic view, stepped apprehensively forward from the crowd to get a better view. His pounding heart eased by the natural beauty before him, he saw couples and families sitting in pairs and groups laughing, singing, and enjoying the moments. Suddenly, his eyes trained on someone familiar. She turned her head and peered into James' memory.

"Chloe!" James marveled.

He gasped and rapidly blinked, hoping to clear the fantasy from his view. His perplexity turned into incredulity as her companion turned, and James was looking into his own eyes. James shook his head until he was awakened by someone shaking him.

"I gonna go git some food, now. Y'all can talk quiet-like. If'n I ain't back by sundown, there be a river some miles that way. Be careful. The marsh gits deep in these parts. They dogs can't follow 'cause it's over they heads. Jest look for dry trees. But don't walk on dry ground. Keep in the marsh. When you git to the river, follow it north," Moses softly said.

"Uh—yes, ma'am," James replied.

"You okay, baby? Look like you seent a ghost!"

"Huh—I guess you can say that. I'm okay, ma'am," he replied as he watched Moses walk off through the forest.

Well into the afternoon, most of the runaways were up already. The sunlight pierced the thick canopy, but it appeared to be dusk instead of mid-afternoon. This was the first good day of rest James had had since he left; he shook off the slumber and walked around the site. He approached the ridge of a hill and spotted the family huddled in prayer. Not wanting to interfere, he stopped, but the crackling of the dry foliage gave him away. The father motioned for him to come over; the family finished praying and began talking with James.

". . . Yeah. Massah Phillips had 'bout 20 of us—families mostly," said Mr. Eddy as he cuddled his small son in his lap.

"Master Johnson had more than 200 of us most times. And he sold families apart on purpose. He bought me—he took me away from my family—when I was young. From my mama and daddy. He did that to lots of families. How old is he?" James asked as he pointed at Mr. Eddy's son.

"He be seven, come November."

"I was about his age. I don't even know my birthday. My Mama. My Daddy. Nothing! I—" James tried, but the emotions choked the sounds from his mouth.

"We sho' sorry fo' ya', James," Mr. Eddy finally said as his wife sadly nodded.

"Thank you, sir. Let's go back to the group and wait for Miss Moses," James replied as he turned and walked away.

Amazing grace, how sweet the sound that saved a wretch like me! I once was lost, but now I'm found. Was blind, but now I see. . . .

"Rogers. You think we gone catch that Moses? I mean, shit, Ham and them been lookin' fo' her fo' 5—shit, 6 years! And they ain't got her yet," questioned Clem.

Riding in 2-horse columns in the rapidly approaching dusk, that question was on all their minds. Clem, however, was the unfortunate one to speak it.

Rogers' face wrinkled into a frown as he subtly moved closer to Clem. Slowly sliding his rifle out of its holster, he asked, "What you sayin', Clem?"

"Shit! It been 2 whole days! Maybe we ain't gonna catch—" Clem began, but was interrupted by the butt of Rogers' rifle crashing against his jaw, which viciously knocked him off his horse. Clem landed on his shoulder with a sickening thud and cracking sound. The other riders stopped their movements, and all but one resisted looking in Rogers' direction.

"Rogers! Don't," screamed Mitch as Rogers trained his gun on the moaning Clem.

Rogers cocked the hammer of his rifle and deliberately uttered, "We gonna catch that nigger wench. And we gonna get that James. And he a dead man. I don't care what ol' man Johnson say. I don't care if'n he fire me. James is a dead man when I git 'im."

Moving his horse several steps away, Mitch hesitantly asked, "I—I thought you said Master Johnson want him back alive!"

"I don't care no mo'. I don't give a goddamn no mo'! You ready to quit, Clem?"

"No. I wutn't ready, *ugh*, to quit. I wuz jest, *ugh*, oh shit, jest asking a question, that's all," he replied as he stood up, holding his injured shoulder as blood oozed from his mouth.

"You got anymo' goddamn questions?"

"Naw, Rogers."

"You, Mitch?"

"Nope."

"How 'bout you, Shell?"

"Naw," the third of Rogers' men replied.

Mitch helped Clem back on his horse, and they continued their travels in silence except for one.

". . . No goddamn nigger ever got away from me. Ain't gonna start now. And when I sees that nigger son-of-a-bitch, I gonna beat 'im to death this time, and . . ."

♣

Moses had been gone for nearly 2 hours; the sun was setting, and an already-dark forest was turning black. The runaways, huddled against a large oak, whispered among themselves. All stopped when they heard a strange sound coming their way. A metallic sound grew louder and closer as nearby bushes rustled. The runaways gathered closer together as a few whimpers escaped.

"Shh, be quiet. Miss Moses told me what to do if she don't come back. Don't be afraid. Mr. Eddy, me and you, uh, we gonna go and see. Rest of y'all stay here—and be quiet! If—uh, if y'all hear two whistles, run that way."

"No!" Mrs. Eddy whispered a scream as she ran to her husband.

"Now go on, honey. Do what he say."

"It'll be all right, ma'am," assured James.

Cautiously, James and Mr. Eddy moved toward the sounds until the metal scraping was upon them, separated by a 3-foot hedge.

"*Hoot, hoot.* Friend of a friend. *Hoot, hoot,*" cracked the intense silence, as Moses emerged with food, blankets, and another young male running, running to the future. The shackles that he tried to silence were making a metallic sound. They got back to the anxious group just before dusk. Jones, one of the other runners, took a rock and broke the chains that tethered the shackles on Michael's legs, reminding James of one of his dreams.

"Y'all hurry up and eat now. We goin' when we done," Moses declared as she passed out food.

"How much longer we got, Miss Moses?" someone asked.

"As long as it takes! That's how long. James, here, read this," she said as she handed James some papers with her free hand.

Scanning the papers, James looked around at the group and then back at her, and whispered, "Should I try to read them? Is it safe, you know?"

Her mouth, filled with food, allowed only a muffled, "Go 'head."

James took a closer look, cleared his throat, and said, "These are wanted posters, ma'am. One says—'Wanted, Quenton, a 22-year-old Negro male from Virginia. $1,000.'" He paused to look around at the 12, but no one said anything.

"This one says—'Wanted, Anthony, a 30-year-old Negro male. $2,000.'"

"That be me," Anthony said as he nodded to James.

James shuffled to the next sheet, paused for a moment, and looked at Moses. His face contorted into a distressed gaze as he stammered, "This—this one is for you, uh, ma'am."

"Well, go 'head. Read it. Read it!"

Clearing his throat, James continued, "Uh—okay. This one, this one say, uh, it says—'Wanted, the slave Harriet Tubman, also known as 'Moses.'" James paused and then continued, "'Wanted—uh, wanted d-d-dead or alive. $25,000.'" He lowered his head as the others gasped.

"Hoo wee! Make ya' wanna turn yo' ownself in, huh. Alive, of course," Moses joked.

James wasn't sure if his companions' gasps were from the amount of money being offered for her or the fact that her master didn't care if she was brought back dead or alive, which is what troubled him so.

That don't bother her? Don't she understand? How can she laugh? Don't she understand?

"Uh—Miss Moses, ma'am," James began in a shaky tone. "Uh—how, how—ain't you scared?"

"Baby, folks been chasin' me fo' years now. I learnt long time back jest trust in the Lord. Follow Jesus. My Guardian Angel. That's what I calls it. Everythin' that supposed to happen, happens."

"So, the Guardian Angel, he . . . it talks to you? You hear it giving you directions?" asked Anthony.

"Hear it? Well, not wit my ears. Wit my heart. Wit my Spirit, I suppose. I jest know."

"Wow. Netty said something similar. About hearing with our spirit," marveled James.

"And it's jest not when I travel. He speaks through other folks. They teach me from Him. Like that stuff on that tree there help me."

They looked at the oak she'd pointed at, and James said, "You mean the moss?"

"Huh, moss?"

"Yeah, the gray stuff."

"Moss. That's what you call it. Never knew the name. Heard tell from somebody that—moss—it grows on the north side of trees round these parts. So, when I can't see the North Star, I jest feel for it, uh for the moss. And you see, James. He jest let you give me the name of the stuff. Moss."

James shook his head in wonder as he shuffled to the next page. He froze.

"Hmm," he mumbled and then continued, "This one says— 'Wanted. James, a 18-year-old Negro male. $5,000.' I guess that's me. But I can't laugh like you, Miss Moses. I'm scared."

She casually shrugged as she worked on a chicken bone. James slowly shook his head again as he shuffled the sheets and continued, "'Wanted—a Negro family. A man, woman, and child. $7,000.'" James continued, looking at the Eddys. "Uh, okay. The next one says . . ."

Chapter 11

They finished eating and headed out, with Moses, as usual, leading the way north, toward a river. Thunderstorms, which had broken out hours earlier, gave way to gentle showers that continued to soak the runaways through the night as the now-distant lightning intermittently illuminated their path. Moses motioned for them to stop as they approached a clearing. Off in the distance, James could see several rickety and worn buildings, one with a flickering light in one of its windows.

"We be okay. Light in yonder window mean friend of a friend," she whispered over her shoulder while she peered through some bushes that bordered the property. "C'mon. Follow me," she ordered, and led them away from the building.

Am I the only one who is wondering what she's doing? Why are we not going to the house? She says it's okay! It's dangerous being out here. Shaddup and do what Moses tells ya' to do, boy!

James and the others continued to follow her until she stopped and knelt. After brushing away dirt and leaves, she pulled on a handle that opened a trap door. It led to a secret tunnel under one of the buildings. Reverend Ebeneezer Wilson and his wife, Marsha, ran this church and welcomed the runaways.

Food was brought in, and Michael got his shackles removed. Most sat in the basement in flickering candlelight, eating and talking with their hosts. Those few that could—slept.

". . . the lady tolt us 'bout some train—or railroad—or something," Mr. Eddy said as his wife and son sat next to him. "She used to come by Massah Tom's sometimes. Don't even know her name."

"Yeah, the Underground Railroad. Many church folks—and regular folks, for that matter—help set up and maintain routes of escape for runaways. We call it the Underground Railroad because it's secret, and we do sometimes use tunnels," Reverend Wilson answered as the buzz of conversations filled the room. James, who had been talking with some of the young boys, turned his attention to what Reverend Wilson was saying.

"Your mystery lady, Mr. Eddy, was an infiltrator, like Miss Moses here. Some come down here once or twice. A rare one-in-a-hundred come down repeatedly. You have been here what—30, 40 times now?" he asked Moses, who was sitting comfortably in a rocking chair, taking in the surroundings.

She casually shrugged and said, "Humph. Don't rightly know. You know I can't count good, Rev. I jest keep comin' back. That's all."

With a chuckle, Rev. Wilson replied, "Yeah, yeah, Miss Moses. You jest come back again and again—and again. And we pray for you again and again—and again. And all those like you. Many ordinary folks who just allow a slave to sleep in a barn for a night. Who give them something to eat. Who don't tell anyone they saw a slave. They all are participants in this special transportation system. Jest doin' the Lord's work. Doin' our part."

"How do slaves know to come to you?" James asked. "If I was running by myself, I would've never come here. Huh, *everywhere* we stopped at. If I had been by myself, I would not have stopped."

"I can't answer that one, son. They just come, led by the Spirit, I suppose. We put out the light. Other than Miss Moses here, we get 'tween 2 and 5 runners a month comin' through here," Mrs. Wilson said.

"Miss Moses," Michael asked. "How did you know to come here? Your Guardian Angel?"

"I'se follow God first, then the North Star. Nights like last night, I'se follow the Guardian Angel that be wit me. And God give us rain, to cover our tracks. And pray. I always prayin'. You see how it work?"

"I—I think so, ma'am," Michael replied.

"She's our best person 'round these parts. What is it now, more than a hundred she's rescued?" Mrs. Wilson asked.

"Mrs. Wilson. Where—what is the name of this place?" James asked.

"Well, this here is Claremont Baptist Church of Frederick County. Folks 'round here call this area Dawson Corners. . . ."

♣

The conversations went on all day, as some runners fell asleep and woke up again. The early morning was chased away by the late afternoon, as they waited for the friendly cover of night to make their departure.

"Y'all young bucks gits the runnin' in ya' quick-like. Most times it's like this here," Moses replied to a group enthralled in her tales.

"My friend Isaac said when you start dreaming about being free, then it's time," James added, and the other young men nodded in agreement.

"I always dreamed 'bout bein' free. My momma was a-scared fo' me. I went back and got them, when I got free. I wuz so glad. I thanked God so much. He jest keep sendin' me back. So I go," Moses replied as Reverend Wilson re-entered the room.

"Reverend Wilson, we had a preacher man who came to Penelope Farms and told us we was *supposed* to be slaves. That we shouldn't want to be free. That God meant for us to be slaves and—"

Moses bellowed out a laugh, as the Reverend chuckled and then said, "Well, James. Yeah, there are many of them around. I know, though, that Jesus Christ talked about us being brothers in peace. How can I be at peace with someone—my brother, no less—and own him as a slave? Or agree that they should be slaves? It goes counter to the God of my Bible. And God is not a God of confusion or contradiction. Slavery was never meant to be. It's in the Bible as the way *not* to be. As an example of how it used to be before we became enlightened, became Christians. Yes, Negroes have every right to expect to be free and treated as equals. Many church folk up North and here in the South are fighting for—"

Reverend Wilson stopped in mid-sentence as faint trembles grew into the thundering sounds of horse hoofs. They approached, rattling dishes, and shockingly awakening those who were asleep. Moses got them all back into the tunnel, ready to run, as Reverend Wilson went up the stairs and outside to greet the visitors, all the while praying feverishly for calm for his knotted nerves. Mrs. Wilson secured the tunnel door and, amazingly, moved a large dresser back in front of it.

Though the sounds were muffled, it was apparent they were slave catchers looking for Moses and the slaves. And one of the voices sounded familiar to James as he strained to hear. It was Rogers. James shut his eyes, fell to his knees with a thud on the dirt floor of the tunnel, and began to pray, as Netty had taught him.

"Lord, You are great. I am nothing. Lord, I need You now. We need You now. We need You now. We need You now. . . ."

"Can I help you gentlemen?" Reverend Wilson asked the group, the familiar knot twisting ever so tighter in his stomach. At least twice a month, would-be slave catchers would ride by, many times while there were runaways in hiding 10 feet from them. They all remained slave seekers as they rode off but gave him good practice at masking his anxiety.

"Hell, yeah. We lookin' fo' some niggers. You seent any today?" Rogers asked as he and his men jerked their heads, looking around for clues.

"I don't recall seeing any today," he replied. With a steady hand, he reached up and adjusted the round, gold-rimmed glasses on his face.

"Oh, hell naw! You said that mighty quick-like. You ain't hidin' any niggers, is ya'? You ain't one of them goddamn Abolitionists, is ya'?" Rogers retorted as he leaned forward in his saddle and glared at Reverend Wilson.

"Y'all free to look around, if'n y'all like."

"Hell, we gonna do that anyhow!" Rogers exclaimed as he dismounted. "Mitch—you and Shell go check yonder barn. Clem—you stay here. Me and the good Reverend here gonna check his lil' ol' church. How 'bout that?"

"That's fine with me, sir. Like I said, I haven't seen any of those people you refer to."

"Yeah, yeah. We gonna see. We goin' through all yo'—" Rogers proclaimed before he was interrupted by three gunshots ringing in the distance. They quickly hopped back on their steeds and rode off in its direction. Arriving 10 minutes later, they saw one slave had been caught, and he wasn't James.

"Shit!" Rogers cursed as he glared at his and then Hamilton's men, hoping one would give him a reason to shoot. Finally, Rogers' group reluctantly rode off in the direction of Penelope Farms, having run out of ideas, as Hamilton and his men continued their 5-plus years' quest of Moses.

♣

". . . Shit! What I gonna tell Mr. Johnson? . . ." Rogers angrily questioned as he and his men trudged back dejectedly along the gravel trail. None of his men dared make eye contact or answer him, afraid of the ramifications. He continued to stew; he finally looked at Mitch and asked, "Mitch. Whatcha' think? What I gonna tell ol' man Johnson, huh?"

Mitch swallowed, let out a barely audible whimper, and replied, "Uh—I don't rightly know, Rogers. Shit, that boy could be dead."

"Yeah—huh, yeah," Rogers said as his angry face released a bit of its rage.

"Uh, yeah," Clem cautiously responded while he kept an eye on a quick escape route. "Tell 'im he dead. We'll back ya', Rogers."

Rogers looked over at Clem, who had not been asked a question. With his right arm in the sling and his left hand nervously gripping the reins, he stared in the opposite direction. Shell, already 2 horse lengths ahead, added another for good measure. Rogers' gaze slowly went from man to man; then he looked back down, toward his saddle, as he said, "Yeah. That boy pro'bly dead fo' sho'. Hell, ain't no goddamn nigger ever got away from me!"

"Yeah, yeah, Rogers," Mitch chided in. "His ass floatin' somewheres up the crick over yonder. Uh, huh, we'll back ya', Rogers."

"Huh—yeah," Rogers mumbled a response that he hoped would convince himself as the group continued their journey back. "Yeah, we—uh, jest ain't seent him. That's all—and, and—aw, hell! Hi-yah!" he screamed and struck his horse into a gallop, his men following his dusty trail.

An hour after the slave catchers were gone, Moses and the Wilsons signaled for the runners to come back. "Whew!" sighed Reverend Wilson as the runners filed back into the basement. His insides were trembling a hundred times faster than his wringing hands; his practiced smile hid his uneasiness.

"Excitin', huh, Rev.?" Moses asked as she found her rocking chair.

"Oh, yeah. I know the Lord's with us, but—whew! It always gets me going!" he replied as he looked out at the terrified faces staring back at him. "Y'all can relax now—and breathe again."

Slowly, jocular conversations eased the tension. Moses asked James to go with her to the main church building to bring back some food. Walking down a corridor, James stopped in his tracks. Taking two steps back and turning to his right, he stared at the reflection of a stranger in a mirror.

His slim build at 14 had been replaced by broad shoulders and ripped biceps. His powerful forearms tapered down to hands strengthened through the years of harvesting tobacco plants. He stepped closer and looked at his face—recognizable *and* foreign. His eyes, hair, and lips hadn't changed. His skin tone, jawline, and neck were different. He peered even closer and viewed the past 4 years of his history. His nose—broken once by Luke and once by Rogers. The scratches from the knobby bark of the whipping tree—and Rogers. The scars from the butt of Mitch's revolver and Rogers' rifle. The cuts from the floor of the curing barns—and Rogers' assaults.

"Wow! Who—who is this—this *man*?" James stammered in amazement.

"That you, baby. How long since you seent yo' self?"

"I don't know, Miss Moses, ma'am. Four—5 years, maybe. Not since I left Johnson Hall, uh, the Big House and uh, Carlton's room. The last time . . . yeah. Mas—Mr. Johnson was calling me to come to his study. I tripped on the rug, and when I looked up, I saw my reflection—at age 14. Now, I'm 18 and—wow!"

"Been a pretty big fo' years, huh?"

"Yeah! It sure is!" he exclaimed through a laugh as they started toward the kitchen. James went back for another peek, flexed his biceps, and then caught up with her.

After a meal and a worship service, the group left, traveling through the starry night without a break. Dawn was an hour old, and Moses still hadn't given the rest signal as she trudged along steadily.

When is she gonna stop? These people are tired. I'm tired! Maybe I should remind her. Shaddup and do what Moses tells ya' to do. Yeah, Mr. Boo. I remember. I'll be quiet—I'll shaddup and do what she says.

The forest, thick with red maples, gave no clue as to what was on the other side. Suddenly, a house, with enough land cleared for it and a vegetable garden, appeared. The house had been made from the native timber, and smoke was curling out of its lone chimney, suggesting occupancy. Moses, in a crouch, gave 2 hoots, paused, and then growled out 3 grunts. Silence returned for several moments as the group waited for what was next.

It's not good to be outside in the daylight like this. She should at least take us back into the forest and wait—

"Hoot-hoot. Hoot. Hoo—*hoo, hoo,*" rang out, and a side door creaked open.

Moses led the group right up to the door and went in. The owners, Henry and Jo Ann Smith, living off the land there, matched their surroundings perfectly. His hair, reddish-brown in color, was long and his beard so full and scraggly that it was hard to tell where his mouth was. Rotund and animated, he moved around the house with surprising agility for a man his size. His eyes, steely blue and intense, darted back and forth constantly, taking in everything and everyone.

Mrs. Smith had the same glazed, wild mannerisms about her, although hers were somewhat subdued. Her jet-black hair was stringy and unkempt. Their clothes, like the house, had the look and feel of originating from the surroundings. Their courtesy and kindness, however, were very civilized and identical to the Wilsons'. They, too, opened their home and their hearts to a band of strangers on the run, running to their future.

"So, Moses, this is yo' latest group, huh," Mrs. Smith added. Turning to the group she asked, "So, how does it feel to be in the North?"

"*North! The North!?*" they all shouted in sheer disbelief.

"Miss Moses. Why didn't you tell us?" asked Mr. Eddy.

"It don't matter no mo' anyhow. We been in the North fo' 3–4 hours now. It don't matter no mo'. This train here goes to Canada. We's gots to git to Canada."

"Huh? Canada? Why we got to go to Canada?" James asked.

Mr. Smith answered, "There's this thing called the Fugitive Slave Law. It means they can take you back—back to slavery—if they catch ya'. It don't matter if you're in the North or not. Slave catchers can still come and git ya'."

"What!?" James exploded. "You—you mean I ain't free? We—we ain't free?"

"Well, kinda. You can move 'round mo' easier. You ain't no slave. We gonna give y'all papers that say you free," Mr. Smith replied as he continued his scurrying and darting about.

"The mo' North ya' go, the mo' safer you is. But them slave catchers can still gitcha', 'ceptin' you be in Canada. I leaves this evening. Them that's comin', leave wit me," Moses said with finality.

I'm not free. I'm—I'm a criminal. No more a slave. Still chattel. And now, I'm a—a criminal. And, and still hunted! Damn. I'm not free!

CHAPTER 11

After lunch, James took a walk in the woods near the Smith's cabin. The recent lessons were harsh and hurtful. The Fugitive Slave Law shattered his dreams of freedom. He had traveled three days and nights but wasn't any closer to the ideals of liberty and citizenship. He walked for an hour as he pondered on and prayed for his future.

". . . Heavenly Father. All Mighty. All Powerful. All Knowing. Thank You for saving a wretched soul like me. Thank You for Your blessings, mercy, and grace. Thank You for Moses. Thank You for my escape and for my life . . ."

". . . When will I, when will we be free? I believed I'd be free once I got to the North. But, I'm not a free man. I'm a runaway. I'm a fugitive. I'm a criminal. I'm still hunted! Give me guidance. Heavenly Father, please give me guidance . . ."

Emerging from the forest, the cabin came into view. He paused, inhaled deeply, then entered.

☙

James silently lamented amid the bustle of the cabin's activity, as his traveling companions prepared to leave. Some checked their food supplies for the long journey. Others went through their clothing for the cold climate of Canada. The Eddys, praying together in familial splendor, caused James' mind to wonder. What if he and Chloe had had the chance? Would their love have produced a family by now? This scene exacerbated James' already melancholy mood.

And his attempts to avoid looking at their benefactor failed. She was everywhere. He stared at the ceiling, and realized the blessing of her leadership and guidance that came from God. He looked down at the floor, and remembered his earthly savior that led him and the others on a journey through rivers, marshes, forests, hills, and dirt—like the dirt floor he now stared at. He looked at the activity of the groups. She was the reason they made it out of the South. She was the fountain of hope that sprung from all of them. This champion of Christianity. This woman of God. Harriet Tubman. Moses to those she saved. Or would save.

His heart ached. His mind swirled. His eyes teared—again.

What am I doing? What should I do? Am I doing the right thing? Should I go with them?

As the curtains of evening were pulled over the late afternoon sky, James' traveling companions finished their goodbyes. The Smiths—depositing their love, support, and instructions to this bands of travelers—continued their special brand of sacrifice.

James, knowing this portion of his journey was over, accepted what he was going to do. Where he decided to go. He never imagined how difficult it would be, though. All the goodbyes were emotional. The final one was excruciating.

". . . Miss, Miss Moses, ma'am. I-I-I don't know what . . . I, uh I don't know how to, to say what, uh what I feel," James attempted to explain.

"Baby. You got to do what's inside you. Go the way God leads you. Go yo' own direction."

"My own direction, huh. New York was the first city I read about in Mas- in Mr. Johnson study. I think my future is there. In New York City. I feel that's where I'm supposed to go."

"Well then, go. Go! Follow God. He will sho' nuff bless you."

"He—He has already. With you, ma'am. Before you, death was my future. I-I was ready to die. I didn't *want* to die. But, I would be dead by now if it hadn't been for you. You, you saved my life."

"Well, you take care of that life then, you hear?"

"Yes, ma'am, I will. I pray He keeps on blessing you. Thank you for everything. Thank you for my life. Thank you for just—*so much*," he uttered as he embraced her mightily.

"You're welcome, honey. You're welcome."

"Miss- Miss Moses. H-H-How can you pay—how can I repay you for giving me a—a chance at life? How? . . ."

"I suppose just help others, baby. That's all you can do. Just help other people. When ever you can. Any way you can."

"Yes, ma'am. Yes," he replied as a smile creased his pain. "I won't ever forget you. You will be here—in my heart forever."

"Thank you, baby. That's nice to know."

"James, son. It's time for them to go," Mrs. Smith interrupted as she tapped him on his shoulders.

James stole one last hug, released her and watched the group leave. With halted breaths, the tears streaming down his cheeks glistened from the fireplace light. The echo of the closing door smothered him in silence. He plopped down in a chair as the strength in his legs drained. He looked around the cabin, the bustle now but a memory. Still wondering if he was doing the right thing, he sat there staring at the door as the cabin blurred through the flow of his tears.

Bye, Miss Moses. Thank you.

♣

The following afternoon, Rogers rode hard into Penelope Farms. He trampled the tobacco fields. He nearly ran over several slaves. He rushed past the hospital shack. He zigzagged through the slender oaks. Approaching Johnson Hall, Rogers jumped off his horse that had barely stopped. He hopped up the entrance stairs in one leap. He burst through the front doors, ran up the curved staircase, and after a bang on the door, barged into the study.

Master Johnson looked up into Roger's puffy cheeks and flared nostrils. "Well? You got him? He alive? He dead? What?"

Rogers inhaled deeply and said, "Mr. Johnson. We gotta problem. We got a big goddamn problem."

❧

"Looks like a man who didn't find what he was looking fo'," Mr. Boo said to Netty as they continued walking, once Rogers' dusty trail had settled.

Both laughed as Mr. Boo began humming while Netty sang, "*Swing low. Sweet chariot. Coming for to carry me home. Swing low. Sweet chariot.*"

"You know, Mr. Boo. I think I'd like to hear that story now. The one you told James. What kind of story did you tell him anyway?"

"Jest told him a story, that's all."

"Must have been some special story."

"The story—nah. The woman—now, she special. It's a story about a brave woman named Moses. Woman who heart is bigger than anybody I ever knew."

"Oh. A woman is a hero in this story, huh? Don't recall you telling a story before where the woman is a hero."

"Uh huh. She helped him like you did. Different. But the same, though. She not as big as you neither. Exceptin' fo' the size of her heart. Both of y'all got good hearts. Uh, huh."

"Hmm. So, you're saying this lady is like me?"

"Don't rightly know. I'll let you tell me, uh, huh."

Transitions

CHAPTER 1

Having left the Smiths' place with the cover of darkness under the false bottom of a wagon with crates of vegetables and planks of lumber above him, James could not tell if it was day or night. Choosing to lay face-up, he now wondered if that was the best choice. It reminded him of the nights he and Chloe stole away under the shacks, but without the pleasant benefits. With his face less than a foot from the bottom of the false bottom, he realized how confining the space was.

The sways and creaks of the wagon, the bumps of the road, and the anxiety of his journey kept him awake. James' mind continued to race through the hopes of his dreams and the revelations of the past 48 hours, which constantly forced their way into his thoughts. He closed his eyes and tried imagining his impending, but tenuous freedom.

Yeah, I'll wake up when I want to . . . go to bed when I feel like it . . . never say "Yas, suh" and "No, suh" again in my life . . . unless the person has earned my respect . . . and then it will be "Yes, sir" and "No, sir." I can like who I choose . . . I can love who I like . . . I can—well, who I want to . . .

. . . fugitive slave law . . . criminal . . . hunted . . . on the run . . . not safe . . . not human . . . not free . . . this train goes to Canada . . .

fugitive slave law . . . sort of free . . . criminal . . . not human . . . would Rogers stop at the Pennsylvania border . . . on the run . . .

"James. James, we're here," said Joey, the driver of the wagon.

. . . freedom . . . chattel . . . liberty . . . property . . . fugitive slave law . . . citizen . . . hunted . . . New York City . . . yas, suh . . . criminal . . . liberty . . . captured . . . go where I want . . . servitude . . . no more no, suh . . . not free . . . criminal . . . property . . . get up when I want . . . fugitive . . . citizen . . . hunted . . . sort of free . . . love who I want . . . captured . . . would Rogers stop at the Pennsylvania border . . . captured . . . freedom . . . captured . . . I can like who I choose . . . captured . . . hunted . . .

"James. James? You okay in there?"

"Huh, what? Oh, yeah. I'm good. I—I'm good. What about you, uh, Mr. Joey?"

"Me? I'm good. I'll get you out in a minute."

Only then did James realize that the wagon had stopped and the cargo was being unloaded. Joey grabbed him by his ankles and pulled him out from his hiding place. James' eyes squinted as he went from darkness to bright sunlight in seconds.

Although they were one hundred yards away from the train depot, the crowd of people startled James. The only times he'd seen a crowd of Whites were at the auctions Master Johnson took him to. This crowd was larger and their movement more haphazard.

What am I doing here? What was I thinking? I should've stayed with Miss Moses. I'm a fugitive. I'm a criminal. I'm scared . . .

"So, here's yo' papers, James. . . ."

. . . There's probably slave catchers in the crowd. Just waiting for someone like me. A fugitive. Chattel. Criminal. Hunted. Captive. Bondage. Slave. . . .

". . . and let's straighten out your clothes. Okay, James?"

. . . A fugitive. Chattel. Criminal. Hunted. Captive. Bondage. Slave. . . .

"James? James. James!"

"Huh, oh yeah. We're here," James finally responded with eyes opened as wide as the gap between where he had been and where he was going.

"What? James, are you listening to me?"

"Yeah, I—I, no I'm not. I—I'm sorry, Mr. Joey. I didn't hear what you said."

"James. Breathe in and out slowly. Come on, try with me. Breathe in—hold it. Good. Now, let it out slowly. Good. Keep on going—breathe in, breathe out, slowly."

James, trying to concentrate on Joey, couldn't ignore the bustle of the scene. The crowd of mostly White males and females were going every which way, and all directions in between. Trying to subdue the rantings in his mind, he focused on his breathing.

"How am I doing, Mr. Joey? Am I breathing good?"

Joey stared at James for a moment, as James continued breathing as directed. Then he released a sorrowful smile.

"James. Uh, James—yeah, you're breathing good. Yeah, James, but . . . but you got to do better. You got to. James, I'm probably 5 years older than you—if that much. I'm 'Joey' to you, not 'Mr. Joey.' You, you got to do better than you're doing. You can't go in the station like this."

"I'm sorry, Mist—uh, Joey. It—just, I don't know. It's—just it's so many White people. No offense."

"None taken, James. If you're gonna make it to New York, you gotta pull yourself together. You got to walk to that station by yourself. I can't—I won't walk there with you. You must walk there like you belong there—because you do."

"Okay, Joey."

"I'm gonna be straight with you. There are probably slave catchers there, at the train station. Looking for Negroes *acting* just like you are."

"Really?" James whined.

"Yeah. But that don't matter. That—does—not—matter. They're slave catchers. James, you are no longer a slave, huh. You're a free man, you are . . ."

Free . . . fugitive . . . hunted . . . criminal . . . runaway . . . freed . . . slave catchers looking . . . fugitive . . . hunted . . . all the people . . . criminal . . . slave catchers . . . runaway . . . freed . . . hunted . . . freedom . . . chattel . . . liberty . . . property . . . fugitive slave law . . . citizen . . . hunted . . . captive . . . captive . . . captive . . .

". . . they leave empty-handed. They go back by themselves. How that sound, James?"

James blinked—and realized he'd missed much of what Joey had said—again. Joey lowered his head and then slowly looked back up at James.

"Come on. Get back in the wagon."

"What . . . no, Joey. I, I want to go to New York."

"James, I want you to make it. But, you're just not ready."

"Joey, please! I want to. Give me another chance—please!"

"But you got to listen—really listen. You got to understand. You got to do what I say."

"I will, Joey. I will. Give me another chance. Please."

"Okay. Listen. Like I said, there's probably slave catchers in the station. This is the closest major train station to the South. They'll be looking for young Negro males, but not any that are dressed like you. . . ."

James remembered the clothes from the Smiths that he was now wearing. A brown suit, a white, buttoned shirt. A pair of black shoes—the first shoes he'd worn since being banished from Johnson Hall. He thought how unnatural it felt having something covering his feet. And a hat that he knew where to put it but was unsure how he should put it on.

". . . You need to act free. Carry yourself like you belong there, like anyone else. Act like you're supposed to be there. Because you have the right to be there."

"Okay, Joey."

fugitive . . . hunted . . . criminal . . . runaway . . .

"You can do this. But you got to walk to that train station by yourself. Whatever you got to do, sing, pray, hum, think . . . whatever gets you there, do it. . . ."

. . . fugitive . . . hunt—yeah. Amazing Grace, how sweet the sounds. That saved a wretch like me. Thank you, mama. I once was lost but now I'm found. Was blind, but now I see . . .

"You carry yourself like you're free, James, and those slave catchers will be just slave hunters, goin' back home empty-handed, huh?"

"Slave *hunters*, not slave catchers. I like that."

Our Father Who art in heaven. Hallowed be Thy name. Thank you, Netty. Thy kingdom come, Thy will be done . . .

"And remember, it don't matter to you if they're slave catchers or slave hunters—because you are not a slave! You're free."

. . . Thy kingdom come. Thy will be done. On Earth as it is in heaven. Thank you, Netty.

"I'm free. Not a slave. Thanks for everything. I'm ready to try, Joey."

"No! Don't *try*. *Do it*, James. You got to do it."

"Yes. I'm ready to do this, Joey. I will do it."

"Good. I'll stay here until your train leaves. In about an hour. Good luck."

An hour! Help me, Lord. The Lord is my shepherd, I shall not want. He maketh me to lie down in green pastures. He leadeth me beside still waters. He restoreth my soul . . .

"Thanks, Joey, for everything."

One 8-minute trek later, James sat in the middle of the train station—*hiding in the open*, as the Smiths referred to it. Being in the midst of the multitude of White people—and in the daytime, no less—began to overwhelm James' mind again. He resisted the urge to cower off to the side or near the back of the station. Instead, he sat there as this new existence bustled around him.

. . . hunted . . . criminal . . .fugitive . . . captured . . . NO!

I can do all things through Christ Who strengthens me. . . . runaway . . . fugitive . . . Amazing Grace, how sweet the sounds that saved a wretch like me. . . . free . . . slave . . . liberty . . .

He looked down at the satchel the Smiths had given him and took a mental inventory. The two sets of clothes. Several sandwiches. The train ticket from Philadelphia to Trenton, and then on to Newark, New Jersey. The ferry ticket to New York City. And a name—Marie Howard—and her address: 1020 W. 57th Street. Also in the satchel was his document of freedom that identified him: James Smith, his birthdate: July 4, 1841, and his birthplace: Riley, Ohio. As he pondered the contents, he recalled the lessons from the Smiths.

My name is James Smith. I'm from Cincinatti—no, Cincinatta—in Ohio. My folks are dead. Lived with my aunt and uncle for a while. Going to New York to visit another aunt. Don't know nobody else there. Gonna stay for a month, maybe more. You are a free man, James. Act like you're free. Speak clearly, look people in the eyes when you talk to them, stand upright, walk with a purpose—

"8:45 TRAIN TO HARRISBURG BOARDING AT GATE B. 8:45 TRAIN TO HARRISBURG BOARDING AT GATE B," bellowed the station announcer, which interrupted James' thoughts. Two people who had been sitting near him left, and another sat down near him.

All these people . . . any of them could be a slave catcher looking for me . . . criminal . . . runaway . . . fugitive . . . hunted . . . NO!

Let the words of my mouth, and the meditation of my heart, be acceptable in Your sight. Oh Lord, my strength, my redeemer. I'm James Smith. I hope my name is common enough not to stand out. Don't want to draw attention because of an unusual name. From Cincinatta. Born July 4, 1841—huh, that day sounds familiar. Marie Howard. I wonder what Miss Howard looks like. . . .

He glanced around the station as the bustle continued. It seemed everyone there was moving except him. He bent down, opened the satchel, and saw several other items he had forgotten about. The five $1 bills and a new, leather-bound Bible. He took the Bible out and noticed a familiar name embossed on it—Webster. He opened it and realized the author was the author of his tutor.

This Bible is my new Webster. All things work together for good for them that love God, that are called according to His purpose. God, I pray it's my purpose to go to New York. What's that Bible verse about God knowing the plan He has for us? I got to start taking notes. . . . Fugitive. Runaway. Hunted. NO!

Amazing Grace, how sweet the sounds. That saved a wretch like me. I once was lost but now I'm found. Was blind, but now I see. . . . Huh, 1020 W. 57th Street. I wonder what the building looks like?. . . Sit in the middle of the station. Don't be afraid to make eye contact. Don't stare, though. . . . Oh, yeah—Swing low, sweet chariot, coming forth to carry me home . . . freedom, liberty, citizen, fugitive, hunted, criminal—

"9:10 TRAIN TO DOVER, DELAWARE, BOARDING AT GATE D. 9:10 TRAIN TO DOVER, DELAWARE, BOARDING AT GATE D."

. . . My God, more people are coming. I wonder if Joey has left, yet. No, James. Stay here. Act free. Think free. Be free. Free. Freed. Fugitive. Runaway. NO!

The Lord is my shepherd; I shall not want. He maketh me to lie down in green pastures: he leadeth me beside the still waters. He restoreth my soul: he leadeth me in the paths of righteousness for his name's sake. Yea, though I walk through the valley of the shadow of death, I will fear no evil: for thou art with me; thy rod and thy staff they comfort me. Thou preparest a table before me in the presence of mine enemies: thou anointest my head with oil; my cup runneth over. Surely goodness and mercy shall follow me all the days of my life: and I will dwell in the house of the Lord forever. . . . New York City. The city so nice, they named it twice. New York, New York. . . . No more getting up to screams . . . No more whippings—unless I'm caught. Fugitive. Criminal. Hunted. Captured. NO!

Amazing grace, how sweet the sounds, that saved a wretch like me. I once was lost but now I'm found. Was blind, but now I see . . . Yes, I can see myself being free. Walking like I'm free. Talking like I'm free. Freedom is—huh, what is freedom? Is it like—

"9:30 TRAIN TO TRENTON, NEW JERSEY, BOARDING AT GATE A. 9:30 TRAIN TO TRENTON, NEW JERSEY, BOARDING AT GATE A."

Okay, James—this is it. Our Father Who art in heaven. Hallowed be Thy name. Thy kingdom come. Thy will be done. On Earth as it is in heaven. God. Thank You for my journey so far from the South to here. Thank You for Ruth, Isaac, Netty, Mr. Boo, Moses. For the Smiths, for Joey. Please bless slaves everywhere. Please calm my nerves as I continue to New York. Please keep me safe. Amen.

Leaving the station, the train lurched forward, jerked back and forth, and then slowly swayed side to side. The chug-a-lug of the steam engine slowly gave way to the ever-increasing clickety-clack of wheels against the rails as the locomotive gained speed. James settled into a seat as the scenery passed faster and faster. He noticed a newspaper in the adjoining seat but was reluctant to pick it up. He looked straight ahead, to the right, and to the left as he masked his trembling nerves and knotted emotions.

. . . I'm from Cincinatta. Goin' to see my uncle. My name, uh, it's James. Yeah, James Smith. My folks dead, they—

"Anybody sittin' here?" boomed a fully bearded, salt-and-pepper haired giant of a man.

A startled James replied, "No, uh, sir."

Sitting down, the man asked, "This yo' paper, son?"

"No, sir. I—uh, it ain't mine," he answered with the apprehension of a lost child.

Calm down, James. Calm down. Act natural—huh, whatever that is. Uh—uh I-I-I'm from uh—Cincinnati. No, no! Cincinatta! I'm going

288

to visit—to see my uncle. No, my aunt. Yeah, visit my aunt. My uncle died. Amazing grace, how sweet the sound, that saved a wretch like me.

Leaning closer to James, the man whispered, "Listen, son. You jest run away, ain'tcha?"

"Huh?! Naw! I, uh, I just ain't supposed to talk to strangers. That's all. I don't know you."

"Uh, huh. Well, I think I know you. I been around here for a while. Look, son. Ya' gotsta carry yo'self likes you free. Ya' sho' gotsta do bettr'n ya' doin' now. Grab that paper, and act like you can read it."

"I *can* read, sir," James replied, as his trembling hand grasped the newspaper.

"Good. Read it. And act like ya' free!"

"I am free, sir," James doubted.

. . . Act like I'm free? Act like I'm free? . . . What does he mean? What does that mean? Act—act like I'm free. How can he tell? How can anyone tell? Can everybody tell? . . .

"Since you can read, read it out loud to me. So other folks on the train know you can read, too."

"Yes, sir."

James scanned the paper, which had multiple articles on the front page. He then noticed the heading.

"Uh, what is a African Methodist Episcopal Church?"

"Why you ask?"

"This paper, it's says, *The Christian Recorder.* Published by the African Methodist Episcopal Church."

"It's a Negro church. The African Methodist Episcopal Church began with the Methodists, but broke away—I don't know, 30 or 40 years ago."

"I thought—the Bible says the church Jesus started was the only one. Didn't He say, 'Upon this rock I'll build *My* church'? There are more than one?"

The man chuckled and then added, "Oh, if it was only that simple. There are so many now, I can't keep up. They all consider themselves Christian churches. They're called denominations. They believe in God, Jesus, and the Holy Ghost. They believe Jesus died on the cross for our sins. They believe that He rose in three days. And that He is in heaven now, interceding for us. Aside from that, there are differences."

"How, how many are there?"

"I'm a Quaker. There's Catholics. Baptists. Methodists. Protestants. Episcopalians. And more, many more. What your name?"

"James. James Smith."

"Well, James Smith, you always ask such thoughtful questions?"

"I don't know. My Aunt Ruth said I asked a lot of questions. Sometimes too many."

"I don't know, son. You stop asking questions, you stop learning. Anyway, go on and read aloud. People would never think a runaway could read. Or have such good thoughts as you do."

James leaned nearer to him and asked, "How—how did you know? About me being a runaway?"

"I, we—the Quakers—help runaways throughout Pennsylvania. Sometimes, I escort them. Sometimes I hide them. Other times, I look out for them and help them move on. I go to train stations; sometimes I ride trains."

"You're with the Underground Railroad?"

"I guess you can say that."

"What's your name?"

"My name is—James. I take the name of whoever I meet on my journey. Now, go ahead and read."

James cleared his throat and began.

"'*Confused but Hopeful,*' *by Rev. Shawn Ernest Cleveland.*

"*I'm confused, readers. We live in the great city of Philadelphia, Pennsylvania. The most important city in the state, founded and named by the most important Pennsylvanian ever—the prominent William Penn—some 150 years ago. He set a noble goal for future residents of this city to aspire. Combining two Christian/Greek words,*

Phileo (love) and Adelphos (brother), he established our nickname at the inception—the city of 'brotherly love.'

"This city, nestled between the Delaware and Schuylkill rivers, hosted the birth of our nation with the First Continental Congress in 1774. It hosted the signing of the Declaration of Independence in 1776. And most recently, it hosted the first Republican National Convention in 1856.

"Truly, our great city has been on the forefront of liberty and justice for all. It has been a righteous spear that pierced injustice, impaled intolerance, and stabbed at the inhumane treatment of all people. So, I ask today, tomorrow and forever, how can a city so named, how can a city with such a rich legacy of right allow the wrong of racial animosity to flourish within its limits?

"These attacks on Negroes and recent immigrants are a stain and plague on this great city. The city authorities seem uncaring, the politicians seem unwilling to address it. It makes a joke of our nickname, and it begs the question—just how many people of good conscience live in Philadelphia? Our history tells me there used to be many of these citizens here. Are you still out there—people of good conscience?

"If so, I implore you to stand up, to speak out and to renounce this boorish behavior as un-American, un-Godly, and contrary to what the city of Philadelphia was founded on and still stands for. Brotherly Love. No matter the brother—or the mother of the brother. I believe you are out there. That—is why I am hopeful. Rev. S. E. Cleveland."

James blinked his eyes twice and slowly shook his head. An incredulous chuckle escaped as he enjoyed the thrill of an emotional chill traverse his spine.

Wow, this—this is, is great! I wonder how much more is like this? And how many more write like this man, Shawn Ernest Cleveland! Mr. Johnson would've never had this in his study. I look forward to reading more articles from the North.

James looked at the man to ask a question, but his eyes, welling up with tears, were already trained on him. That's when James noticed the 24 pairs of eyes in the car trained on him as well. Then applause erupted. After a minute, it died down, and a woman approached James.

"Will you read this for me, please?"

James glanced at his travel companion, who gave him a smile and a nod.

"Yes, ma'am. *'The Philadelphia Society of Arts and Culture hosted a grand celebration on Saturday, September 10th. It was fabulously hosted by Mrs. Mary Lois Jackson and Mrs. Martha Eunice Phillips—'*"

"That's me, Mary. Martha is my twin sister. Go on."

"Yes ma'am. *'The event helped raise $5,000 to fund the newest wing to the Philadelphia Museum of Fine Arts. The high society of Philadelphia was well represented, beginning with the mayor of Philadelphia, the Honorable Alexander Henry. . . .'*"

♣

Late afternoon in New York City, like in Philadelphia, overwhelmed James. The sheer number and variety of people made him reluctant to leave the ferry station. After studying the map of the city, he began a 20-minute walk along the crowded streets.

. . . I'm from Cincinatta . . . Act like I'm free . . . I got my papers . . . I'm going to see my aunt . . . Act like I'm free . . . Walk with a purpose . . . free . . . citizen . . . fugitive . . . Trust in the Lord with all your heart, and lean not on your own understanding . . .

As James calmed his nerves with scripture, he imagined what Mrs. Howard would look like. Mrs. Smith and Wilson came to mind, as did the few White women he had barely glanced at during the auctions. The painting of Miss Penelope. And the 3 women on the train completed the images of the only White women he had ever seen.

Act like I'm free . . . walk with a purpose . . . stand straight up . . . I belong here . . . fugitive . . . freed . . . think like I'm free . . . freedom . . . criminal . . . inhale deeply, exhale slowly . . . believe that I am free . . .

James made it to the address on the paper but walked past it initially. He arrived at the corner, turned, and looked at it for several minutes. At the end of a row of 2- to 6-story buildings, the 6-story, appropriately nondescript stone-and-mortar building was similar to others in the area. People and wagons traversed up and down 57th Street, coming from and going to places. After three trips up and down the block, James went up the flight of stairs and knocked once. After several minutes, he knocked again—this time with three knocks and much harder. The door cracked open.

"May I help you?" asked a lady.

"I'm James. My name James Smith," he replied. Then he handed her the papers the Smiths had given him.

She glanced at them, looked quickly up and down the block, and then ushered him inside.

"I am Marie Howard. Welcome to my home. Now to be your home, hmm."

In contrast to Moses, Mrs. Howard was an imposing woman. Nearly 200 pounds on a 5-foot-10-inch frame, she had fair skin, deep blue eyes, and dark hair streaked with gray. She led James up three flights of stairs and into a room.

"You sleep here, James. Your bed. This room, you share with Alfred, hmm."

"Thank you, Miss Howard, ma'am."

"You had quite a trip? And with Miss Moses, herself."

"Yes, ma'am."

"So, tell me about her, hmm," she said as they left the room and continued the tour.

"She was great. Brave. I—I never knew someone could be so brave. And . . ." James began as they walked down the five flights of stairs to the ground floor.

The building manager's apartment, vacant for more than a year was located there, as was the kitchen and dining area. Floors 2 to 5 had 6 apartments each, and Mrs. Howard's apartment and office took up the top floor, which was two-thirds the size of the other floors.

". . . I met her once, oh, 2 years ago, perhaps. Well—me and 200 other people. Everybody, this is James. He just got here," Mrs. Howard announced to the 15 other young men seated at the dinner table. All said, "Hello," and Alfred, who was to be James' roommate, called for him to sit near him. Mrs. Howard said the blessing, and all began the meal.

Calm down, James. Calm down. Freedom. Criminal. Fugitive. Hunted. Property. . . .

❧

James and Alfred were in their room later that evening. Gaining comfort with each passing moment, James casually looked around his new home. Two beds and a dresser. The bare-wood floor that creaked with each step, stone block walls, a pair of six-paned windows. And a second door. James took it all in as his roommate rambled.

". . . it's been so long since somebody was here wit me. I'm sho glad Mrs. H. say you can stay wit me. We gonna have us some fun fo' sho'. . . ."

About the same size as Carlton's room. More furniture. Huh, a bed for me. Have some fun, huh. Sounds familiar—but not really. Something else—something is different. . . .

". . . Here's the closet here. When you get some mo' clothes, I mean. You can have the two bottom dresser drawers, too. I been using this bed here, but if you want it—it's all right. Huh, I guess you don't . . ." Alfred continued as he opened the doors while clearing his throat.

. . . yeah, maybe the freedom. The bed. My bed. So, this is freedom, huh.

"If you don't like—"

"Nah, nah. That one is fine," James answered as he came out of his inner ramblings.

Alfred continued, "Good. Good! I'm glad you . . ." as he hopped up on his bed, his face filled with grins.

Slowly walking around the room, James continued taking in his new surroundings, eventually ending up near the windows with their third-floor view. Even three stories up, the bustle of New York's byways was audible as the masses scampered about below, hurrying every which way. Even smoke and various scents reached James, all which began to overwhelm him again.

My God! What am I doing here? Why did I come here? To—to New York! All the people! I—I didn't realize there would be so many people. This isn't even Union Square. This is just a regular street, at night, and it's still packed with people. All kinds of people. I should've gone North with Miss Moses to Canada. What was I thinking? All these people. All these different people . . .

". . . Yeah, I'm from here. New York City. My mama and daddy went to Canada, but I stayed here. I like it here, don't you? I mean, I know you jest got here and all—"

"Yeah, I like it here, Alfred. Nice view."

"Good. Good!"

James turned, walked toward his bed, and asked," You want me to blow out the lantern?"

"Nah, that's okay. I'm the closest."

"Okay—but I do have lots of experience blowing out lanterns," James chuckled.

"Huh? What's so funny 'bout that?"

"I'll tell you about that some other time."

"So—you wuz a slave. I mean, you is a runaway, huh?"

"Yeah."

"Shoot, I ain't never had one stay wit me befo'. Some come. But leave quick-like. You ain't gonna leave, is ya'?"

I should've never come. I should've stayed with Miss Moses. All these people—any of them could be a slave catcher. How, how can you tell? How can I tell?

"Nah, I—I'm not going anywhere, Alfred."

"Good. Good. We gonna have fun. . . ."

♣

Mr. Bill, a clean-shaven mystery man, came around weekly, dispensing a variety of information. A member of the Abolitionist movement, Mrs. Howard was one of his many contacts and a close, personal friend. Dressed in business attire, complete with fancy black-and-white shoes, he blended into the melting pot called New York City.

He walked deliberately around the dining room table of pine as the click of the taps on his shoes pierced the silence. The 12 men there this night, ranging in age from 16 to the early 40s, intently followed Mr. Bill's every move and hung on each utterance as he strolled and spoke.

"Marie's caring nature for you men, you runaways, treating you like you are her sons, is exemplified by her actions. She risks everything for you. You all need to understand that. She's been an Abolitionist for years. Helping recent runaways acclimate themselves to the North. Helping you get used to freedom. Believe me—for most of you, it will be quite a transition. Freedom dreamed for and freedom as a reality are often very different things, men."

That's for sure!

"She helps you with food and shelter. She finds employment and medical help for you. She helps you realize the dangers aren't over—not by a long shot. And most important, she stresses the importance of carrying yourselves as freemen. This is part of my job, too. Helping you and bringing her information. Always remember this—*think free*! Think! Free!" he implored as he poked at his temples with his index fingers.

"Agents. Bounty hunters. Slave catchers. They are everywhere. Everywhere! They're constantly trying to find runaways. They are looking for you. To take you back to slavery. The Fugitive Slave

Law makes slave catching a lucrative business. That means people make lots of money on it. Lots . . ."

I'm here now. No use thinking about what I should've done. Just commit to what I did do. Go to New York City. Freedom . . . citizen . . . servitude . . . hunted . . . fugitive . . . criminal . . .

". . . police, politicians, judges. Even Negroes—yes, I said 'Negroes.' They all cooperate because of the money. The police will arrest you! They will turn you in. Free men or runaway, it doesn't matter.

I hope all of you are paying attention. They'll hold you until the slave catchers come. The drawings on the posters are poor quality, so if any of you look like the drawing, or fit the general description and don't have your papers, then, yeah. You could be arrested and held. And if anybody comes from the South to claim a runaway, it doesn't matter if they know you aren't the person they want. They will take you anyway, for money, of course. They don't care about you, so you need to care about you—and your freedom. It starts here, and it starts now."

James helped set the table for breakfast as Mrs. Howard prepared the morning meal. On his tenth day in New York City, James was still waking before dawn. Always engaging her in conversation, he learned a lot about her, the city, and his situation. She made it a point to keep a low profile—attempting to be as nondescript as the building she owned. She was known in Abolitionist circles, but to the majority of the people in New York, she was an immigrant in a rapidly growing city of immigrants. She went about her daily life in relative obscurity, like many Abolitionists did. She purposefully avoided bringing attention to her building or her tenants.

". . . The Abolitionist movement spreads, James. Frederick Douglass is—well, he is Frederick Douglass! The most elegant and eloquent voice for our cause, hmm. A true tribute to what all can become. William Lloyd Garrison founded the first Abolitionist newspaper, *The Liberator*, in 1831. Levi Coffin helped organized the Underground Railroad."

"Yeah—Reverend Wilson spoke about that. The Underground Railroad," James interjected as Mrs. Howard came in from the kitchen. She stood there for a moment, admiring the job James had completed.

"You do this so well, hmm."

"What? Huh," James muttered as his focus was on his comment. He looked at her, and then, following her gaze, he replied, "Oh, thank you. I guess it's just natural now. I grew up in the Big House, called Johnson Hall. I always helped this lady named Ruth clean and set the table. She taught me."

"Hmm, she taught well, I see."

"Thank you. She also said I ask too many questions. If I do, I'm sorry."

"No, James. No. I do not get to speak of these things very much. I enjoy."

"Okay, then tell me some more, please."

"*Oui, oui*. Henry Beecher, a preacher, has helped the movement for years. His sister, Harriet Beecher Stowe, wrote a novel, *Uncle Tom's Cabin*, in 1851, I believe. A book about slavery. It has sold more than 100,000 copies! It has encouraged many Northerners to action. And it has helped the growth of the Abolitionist movement. I do not suppose ol' Massah Johnson would have a copy of *that* in his library, hmm?"

"Nah, I don't think so. You might have found it in his fireplace," he replied, and they both shared a hearty laugh.

"*Oui, oui*. In a way, *Uncle Tom's Cabin* is bringing the issue of civil rights and civil treatment for people like you, people of African descent, into the living rooms, dining rooms, and bedrooms of America. Many people I know and have met talk about it and slavery now. It made it real without folks like you being there. It has given our cause power! It has given it a face, and, and uh—humanity, hmm. *Oui*, humanity."

James slowly shook his head as he gazed upon Mrs. Howard. Closing his eyes, he allowed her words to flow over his tattered soul. He opened his mouth—and then closed it as his mind searched for a response. He finally opened his eyes and uttered, "Wow. That—that's beautiful. Uh—I don't know—uh, special. And you say the North don't do much."

"Well, James. It is true. We do not usually go South. Only special ones like Moses, hmm. Once you cross that Mason-Dixon line, though. Then, *oui*. But you all must first get here."

"You have a point, there. Uh, listen—if you want me to go with you sometimes, to add a body with that face."

"Hmm, that is interesting. Maybe—maybe. A body and a soul, hmm."

"Yeah—and a soul. So, tell me your opinion of church and slavery as it relates to God's will."

"I do not know much on such things. This I will say, though. God does not want anyone to be slaves. This I know. This I feel. Why it is in the Bible? You need to ask someone who knows a lot more than me, hmm."

CHAPTER 3

The street lanterns illuminated both ends of the dark alley of the city. A brisk breeze blew through and scattered the assorted trash. The group of men, numbering 5, huddled in the darkest part of the alley, under a fire escape of a 6-story building.

One White man, scruffily attired, sat on the buckboard of a 2-horse wagon, puffing a cigarette. Another White man, immaculately dressed from head to toe, slowly unfurled a wad of bills and started counting in front of 2 other men.

One was an officer of the law, a New York constable, all decked out in his black uniform, adorned with buttons of silver, which glistened when the light hit them just right, and topped off by his official cap. The other man, a husky Negro in ordinary clothing, stood next to the police officer, grinning as each bill was peeled off and counted.

And lying face down in the back of the wagon was the unfortunate one. A young Negro man. His arms were pulled behind his back and bound at the wrists with rusty iron shackles. A 2-inch thick rope connected it to a like pair of shackles binding his ankles. He squirmed and struggled against his bindings as muffled grunts and groans escaped through a filthy cloth gag.

"So, Officer Palmer," the well-dressed man said, "Here's the money for you and your associates."

"Thank ya' kindly," he replied as he grabbed the money and counted it aloud.

"Twenty, forty, sixty, eighty, a hundred for my main man, Harold Winters, Jr.—"

"Hey!" shouted the Negro man as his head jerked toward either end of the alley. "Don't be usin' my name! It Winnie! Call me Winnie!"

"Okay, okay. Kinda touchy, huh? Well, here you are—Winnie. $100. Thank you for your services."

"Yeah," he replied as a grin flipped the frown.

"When are you going to have some more?" the dapper man asked both Winnie and Officer Palmer.

"When you gonna be back?" Winnie asked.

"We're taking off for New Jersey right now. My associates will be back most likely in a month or so. I'll be around next week."

"Okay, then. Get in touch with Palmer—he'll git wit me. That is, if we ain't already got one locked up." All three men agreed with nods and went their separate ways.

♣

"But, Bobby. There's plenty of colleges around here you can go to," Mama Harris parented with her husband.

"Mama, I wanna go to New York University. I wanna be an Engineer. They got a good school for that," Bobby replied as he squirmed in the grass. The 3 were in their backyard, a spacious garden-like environment bounded on 3 sides by an 8-foot-high hedge, and on the 4th by the house.

"That's a big city, son. A wild city, too. All kinds of folks livin' there, now. Lotta slave catchers," Papa Harris warned as he held his wife in his arms.

"Aw, Daddy! I ain't no slave. Or no runaway. I'm free."

God, how do I make him understand? Papa Harris thought as he shook his head. He glanced over at his wife, her concern evident, and then stared back at their son.

"Son—it—it don't matter. You're a young Negro man. If they get the chance, they will take you. The police. The slave catchers. They will!"

"I'll be careful, Daddy. I'll always carry my papers. I'll watch where I go. Who I talk to. I'll, I'll—"

"Harvard is a fine school, baby. Try it there for just one year. Then you can decide," Mama Harris implored.

"Nah, Ma! I wanna go to New York—uh, University."

❧

"*. . . Who shall separate us from the love of Christ? Shall tribulation, or distress, or persecution, or famine, or nakedness, or peril, or sword? As it is written, For thy sake we are killed all the day long; we are accounted as sheep for the slaughter. But in all these things we are more than conquerors, through him that loved us,*" James read out loud to his wide-eyed roommate.

"Boy! You sho' read good, James!" Alfred marveled as they sat in their room.

"Thanks. The first time I read out loud like this was on the train coming here. I love reading out loud. It feels good."

"Yeah, I can read some. But, but you *good*. Boy, you good!"

"Thanks, Alfred."

"Really, James. You good. Will you—uh, will you teach me, huh?"

"Sure, Alfred. I don't mind. I've helped lots of people."

"Thanks. Go on—read some mo'."

"Okay. Here we go . . .

"*For I am persuaded, that neither death, nor life, nor angels, nor principalities, nor powers, nor things present, nor things to come, nor height, nor depth, nor any other creature, will be able to separate us from the love of God which is in Christ Jesus our Lord.*

"Boy, I'm becoming persuaded!"

"Amen, James. Amen. Read on!"

"*I say the truth in Christ, I lie not, my conscience also bearing me testimony in the Holy Spirit. . . .*"

CHAPTER 4

"What do you want?" screamed James as he scuttled in a field of wet, waist-high grass. Running hard. Moving slow. Breathing heavily. Looking back. He couldn't tell who or what was chasing him. Echoing footfalls was the only answer.

Who wants me? Who's chasing me? Rogers? Oh, my Lord—is it Rogers?

"Who are you? What do you want?" he screamed again, which shook him out of the nightmare. He rose, soaked with sweat and mentally drained. He blinked and tried to orient himself to the surroundings.

Yeah—New York. I—I'm still in New York. Just before dawn—again. Huh, will I ever get used to sleeping through dawn? I don't have to get up anymore. It's been, what? Weeks. And the dreams—man, these dreams!

As he walked to the wash basin, he looked over at his slumbering roommate. "Who was that?...." he mumbled as he listened to Alfred's throaty solo. ". . . Yeah—Cyrus. That boy sure could snore. But Alfred might give him some competition."

He laughed softly as he finished washing. He then knelt and prayed, "Heavenly Father, thank You for my life. Bless Mr. Boo and Netty. Lord, please bless them. Please don't let them get beat because of me. Everybody at Penelope Farms, too. Give me the strength to make it. To do Your will. Amen."

He rose from his knees and went downstairs, careful not to wake Alfred.

"*Bonjour,* James. First one again, hmm?"

"I guess I'm still on plantation time," he replied, plopping himself down in a chair. Mrs. Howard's movements in the kitchen reminded him of Ruth, which meshed into his already melancholy mood.

"Sleep well?"

"So-so."

"Still having those dreams, hmm?"

"Yes, ma'am. They're not so, uh—so bad anymore. The one of Mr. Boo and Netty getting—well, I just pray I never have those again."

"I pray this as well."

⚜

Mrs. Howard set James up with a job in a local factory that made machine parts, working 10-hour days, 6 days a week. The North was industrialized, as opposed to the agricultural economy of the South. Most of the emerging jobs in the North were in the factories of the northeast and shipbuilding farther north in New England.

"Okay, uh—James. Here's where you'll be working. All ya' gotta do is pick out the bad ones that come by—like this one," the Plant Manager, Mr. Cornell Maxwell, said as he grabbed a defective part. A 50-something White man, Mr. Maxwell was introducing James to his surroundings, and, after a half-hour, they were at James' work area.

"Yes, sir, Mr. Maxwell, sir," James replied. He took the part and studied it closer as Mr. Maxwell continued.

"No, James. 'Maxie.' Everybody calls me 'Maxie.' You not gonna change that, is ya'?" he asked with a disarming smile.

"No—uh, Maxie."

"The bad ones, throw in the can over yonder. The parts come by about 6 a minute."

"Yes, sir—uh, Maxie. Uh, how about this one?" James asked as he grabbed a part off the conveyor belt.

"Good. Yeah, you might have a good eye for this. A good eye for detail."

"Uh, yeah, Maxie. I developed a good eye for detail. Everything had to be in order—uh, back home in Cincinatta. I learned that early in life."

"That's good. Marie has sent me—what? Four now, wit you. The others worked out good. I think you will, too. Anyway, this is yo' area, and—" he added until interrupted by a commotion across the warehouse. A group of men barreling over in laughter filled the warehouse with jocularity.

"What's going on over there, Maxie?"

Looking across the expansive room, Maxie replied, "Jest Big Man holdin' court. Anyways—ya' need to be here by 7 a.m. Ya' git a 30-minute lunch and leave before 6 p.m."

"Yes, sir—uh, Maxie. Thank you very much."

". . . Shoot. Can't wait to git outta here. Gonna see Rebe tonight. . . . They sho' workin' the shit outta us, today. . . . You right. And a 30-minute lunch break ain't enough. . . .Uh, huh. And I don't like...." went conversations all around James as he focused on his job.

He ended up grabbing every third part that came by for closer inspection, and throwing out a fourth of those, which earned him accolades from Mr. Maxwell and his superiors.

What are they complaining about! The number of hours they have to work? The working conditions? On Penelope Farms, out in the fields from dawn to dusk. Where your only payment is to not be whipped. Huh—this ain't nothing! And I'm getting paid. They paying me! Working side by side with White men, now that's definitely different. Never considered that as a part of freedom. Keep it all to yourself, James. Listen, but keep quiet—keep quiet. But really, I never even considered getting paid as a part of freedom. And, uh, oh—a bad part!

". . . Hell, yeah. Mr. Man work us too goddamn hard! . . . What's up with Jack? He's been gone three, fo' days. . . . Yeah, I ain't seent him since Sat'day night. . . . I'm goin' back there to see Lulu a'gin fo' sho'! . . ."

In the months James had been there, Mrs. Howard began to realize the depth of his capabilities and the breadth of his knowledge. Once, he rearranged items in her kitchen in such a way that it cut 15 minutes off of her meal-preparation time. She was upset at first but quickly learned to appreciate the benefits of its efficiency. And their conversations revealed to her his ability and love of reading.

"So, James, tell me. You speak well, and you read. Can you write?" Mrs. Howard asked.

"Write? Not great, but yes," he answered, while he scanned the collection of books Mrs. Howard had brought back from the library.

"Have you ever heard of Dumas?"

"Uh—no, ma'am. That name isn't familiar to me. I haven't read this one," James replied as he eyed an unknown-to-him Shakespeare book. He eagerly began thumbing through the pages.

Seeing the book he'd picked up, Mrs. Howard said, "So you have heard of Shakespeare, hmm?"

"Yeah! Mas—Mr. Johnson had a lot of books by him. I remember one night I was with Chloe. She had just found out her mama was sold when she was a baby. The lady she thought all those years was her mama, wasn't. She was crying, and I was trying to find the words to say. I said, 'If you cut us, do we not bleed; hurt us, do we not cry.' I was trying to say that we are people—human beings, too. That we have feelings like other people. That we hurt and hope like other people. That was the first time it was more than a book to me. It was the first time it brought meaning to my life."

James continued to scan the other books. He noticed a Dickens novel he hadn't seen in Johnson's study. He opened it and read the first page. He turned to Mrs. Howard to ask a question and saw her face an emotional crimson, and wet with tears.

"Mrs. Howard! What—what's wrong?" he asked as he put down the books and took several steps toward her.

Clearing her throat, she said, "I am so sorry, James. Forgive me. *C'est triste.* So sad, *oui.* You—uh, you think after hearing stories like—like that—over and over, I would get used to it. *Mon Dieu*. But *oui*—you understood what Shakespeare was saying. Uh—*mon Dieu*—uh, what is 8 times 6?"

"Forty-eight."

"What is 25 divided by 5?"

"Five. I like arithmetic."

"What is the capital of France?"

"Paris," James replied as he continued surveying the books.

"Have you ever taken a schoolbook test?"

"Just in Carlton's books. Mr. Johnson's books were kind of hard. I read Webster 4 times and was halfway through a 5th time. I looked up lots of words, too. Like—uh, respect, and uh, servitude, chattel, freedom, honor—"

"Have you ever thought about going to college?"

"Yeah. I'm gonna be President, too. And go to the moon," he laughed out loud. His laughter ceased when he saw the seriousness on her face.

She's got to be joking. She is joking, right?

"Mrs. Howard, stop teasing me like that."

"What is so funny, James? I do not tease here, hmm."

James' mind struggled to contemplate her words.

College? Me? I—I mean, she has to be joking. But she looks so—so serious.

"Mrs. Howard, how can you ask me that question? One hundred days—not even one hundred days ago, I was a slave. Working from sunup to sundown in tobacco fields for a mean master and an evil overseer. Having no control over my life. At least none of the parts that mattered. Like life, liberty, and the pursuit of happiness.

"Now, I'm free—well, sort of free, and able to make my own decisions. Well, some decisions. I'm working, getting paid for it. I'm learning about freedom. I have a future. But college? You think college is in my future!? James, in college? *Me? Me in college?* Mrs.

Howard, you can't be serious. I—I—I'm a criminal. A fugitive. I'm hunted. My future is to not get caught and sent back to bondage."

"But *oui*, I am. Serious, yes, I am. I know what I say. I know what I hear. I know what I see."

"What—uh, what do you see?"

"I see a man who is smart. I see a man who is educated already. Who is ready for more education. Who wants more education, hmm. So many runaways I meet are smart, *oui*. I believe 'intelligent' is the word, hmm. But not *educated*. Never taught to read. To write. To do Arithmetic. But you have. You are ready."

"But what would I do in uh, in college, Mrs. Howard?"

"James! I cannot believe you are asking me this question."

Up until now, James' adjustment to his newfound freedom was marginal. His transition was slow in progressing, and she understood the dangers associated with that. He still sought Mrs. Howard's permission to go anywhere or do anything. Last week, James stayed home when most of the other tenants went to the shore. He didn't have the chance to ask Mrs. Howard, and she wasn't home when they left. She tried to help him in this transition constantly as her warnings echoed in his head, similar to the Smiths'.

"*. . . Stop acting like a slave. Look people in the eye when shaking their hand. Do not hang your head down to avoid eye contact. Walk straight and upright, not slumping. Speak with an authoritative tone, not apologetic. Walk with meaningful strides, not shuffling. Stop acting like a slave . . .*"

Mrs. Howard warned him and the others constantly, getting particularly frustrated at having to admonish James repeatedly.

"Stop acting like a slave, James! You are a man! *Oui*, you are. You are free, *libre de faire*, uh, free to do, free to be—whatever. The way you act will bring attention to you, perhaps get you caught. Taken back to the horrible South, hmm. Maybe you need to go to Canada. At least you will be safe there, hmm."

"No, Mrs. Howard! I—I want to stay here. Please! I do," he begged.

"Then your way of thinking must change, hmm. What would you do? What would you do in college? James, you would gradu-ate—that is what!"

Taking a deep breath, she continued, "James, you need to—to discard this slave mentality, hmm. This is a tough transition for you, I know. I have seen plenty of men and some women come here. Runaways and free. You are smarter than all of them. You may be prepared for college, too. Some of the things you do around here amaze me. The changes in the kitchen, very good—*tres mag-nifique*, hmm. As long as you ask first, all is okay," she said with her reassuring smile, which James returned.

"You are capable of being successful in college. You may need to go to a Prep school first to get ready for college. I think not. We will see. You can do it. I know you can. But you must believe in yourself. You must want to do it for yourself. Not me. Not anyone else. I will help you pay for the classes and the books. I will reduce your rent so you will not have to work so long. I will speak to Maxie. But none of this matters if you do not believe. It must start with you. It must start here—in your heart. And here—in your mind. Well? What do you say?"

Me—James, in college? Me!

"Uh—Mrs. Howard. I—I, uh, don't know what to say. Th-Thanks for your confidence in me. Y-Yes, I'll—I will try. I will go to college. I will. I—uh, will," replied James as he tried to convince himself of the possibilities.

In college—me? James, the Slave of Carlton. In college? Me! James Smith—in college?

"This is amazing, Mrs. Howard. I never considered this as part of my future. Working and getting paid for it. Working side by side with White men. And now, college. Going to college. This is overwhelming."

"But not impossible, hmm."

James laughed as he replied, "No. Not impossible. Definitely possible. This new Dickens book you brought me has me thinking.

I've only read one sentence—one long sentence—and it has me thinking."

"You have read other Dickens?"

"Yeah. *Oliver Twist. A Christmas Carol.* Uh, *David Copperfield.* I'm looking forward to reading this one, *A Tale of Two Cities.*"

"What do you think about it?"

"Well, first, this is a long first sentence. It takes up a whole page. But most importantly for me, this sentence begins with 'the best of times, the worst of times.' That's my life now. The best of times—being sort of free, not a slave anymore. Being encouraged by you to go to college. Working—and getting paid for it.

"It's also the worst of times—every corner I take brings me fear. And a big part of my heart is still on Penelope Farms. My mind has dreams about slavery and all the bad things that happen to those good people."

"This is what I mean about you being prepared for college. You understand—you apply what you read to your life. *Tres magnifique*, hmm."

"Thank you. I always thought Dickens was writing about me. The people he wrote about were poor, treated terribly, just like slaves."

"Hmm, Dickens, Shakespeare, but not Dumas, hmm? That Johnson man is certainly a heathen. *The Three Musketeers* is a fine story and—"

"*The Three Musketeers*! Yes, I read that. All for one, one for all. And uh, *The Count of Monte Cristo.* They were by Dumas."

"No, no James. Pronounced not Dumas. Doo-mah. Doo-mah!"

"Oh! Doo-mah. This French language. I got to learn more. . . ."

♣

Mrs. Howard set up an appointment for him to take a test at a Prep school, on which he scored 100%. Then the college entrance exam, where he scored 90%. James entered New York

University that spring semester, but a new education had begun long before that.

". . . and this is *chaise* because it is a wood chair. This one is *fauteuil* because it is fancy," Mrs. Howard instructed as they walked through the lobby. The single door with a slender window opened up to a room with three chairs and a settee. The doors on either side led to the stairs and other rooms.

"Shazz. Fa-tee-el, huh. What about—'foot'?" asked James as he pointed at his shoe.

"*Le pied.*"

"Luh pea-ay. Clock?" he asked as he pointed at a small clock hanging over the fireplace mantle.

"Big ones—*horloge*. Little ones—*pendule*."

"Or-loge. Pon-jule. I love your language, Mrs. Howard. It sounds different, almost with a melody or rhythm."

"*Oui, oui*. It is one of a kind, for sure. I am glad you are trying to learn."

"It's in my blood. Learning is. Always will be. Mrs. Howard, uh, why didn't you get married again? I mean after your husband died. If you don't mind me asking."

"No, James. It is okay," she sighed and looked wistfully at a portrait on a wall near the door. "Oh, James. I had my love. My one true love. *Mon seul amour*. He was 30. I was 16. We had the best 25 years anyone could ever expect or dream of. He was the best, *oui*."

"You really loved him, huh?"

"*Oui, oui*. Very much so."

"But 'Howard.' That's not French."

"*Oui*, James. He was an Englishman. Yes, Frank was English by birth. But I will tell you this, James—he was a Frenchman in his soul," she replied as she cupped her hands over her heart.

"Yeah, me and Chloe. She was my—how did you say it? Mohn soo-el ah-more."

"Truly, you think. I hope not. It would be very sad if it happened so soon. And ended so tragically. I do not think so, James. Your love of a lifetime, your *mon seul amour* is still to come, hmm."

"Yeah, maybe. But it won't be like her. It'll never be like her."

"Perhaps. Perhaps. Come, let us go start dinner," she said, as they walked toward the door leading to the kitchen.

"Okay. What about 'freedom'?"

"Huh—oh, *liberte.*"

"Lee-ber-tay. 'Friend'?"

"*Ami.*"

"Ah-mee. Runaway?"

"*Le fugitif.*"

"Luh foo-gee-teef. 'Praise the Lord'?"

"*Louez le Seigneur.*"

"Loo-ay luh Seeg-nee-ur. 'My Lord.'"

"*Mon Dieu.*"

"Mahn Do. Uh, 'Africa'?"

"*Le Afrique . . .*"

CHAPTER 5

"So, James. Where you from?"

Jeremy, one of his classmates in several classes at NYU, was the first to approach him. Although they sat next to each other in this class, James sensed a chasm between them.

"Ohio. Cincinnatta, Ohio," he replied as the Smiths and Mrs. Howard suggested.

Other than New York City, Cincinnati had the largest population of Negroes in the North at that time. Many Underground Railroad routes crossing the "River Jordan," as the Ohio River was known to Negroes, at points like Cincinnati and Riley, Ohio, made them common destinations.

"You pretty good. I seen your grades. What prep school you go to?"

"I didn't go to a prep school. I did a lot of reading, though. We had lots of books."

"Oh, yeah. I got a 88 on the entrance exam here. What you'd get?"

"'Bout the same."

"Humph," he said and turned away, giving James a chill and confirming his suspicions. That was the last time Jeremy spoke to him, but not about him. Because Jeremy reminded him of Carlton, James made it a point to watch out for him.

Who else will watch out for me? I got to be careful. I never know . . .

"Okay, class. We'll be on page 116, dealing with polynomials . . ." Prof. Brown announced as he turned pages at the lectern.

❧

Mrs. Howard's inspirational support buoyed James' emotional and psychological—as well as his academic—well-being. She continued checking out library books for him. She purchased a journal for him to document his academic journey. James especially reveled in the journal.

The catharsis of the written word gave him peace and allowed him to fully investigate the concept of freedom, something he'd learned to appreciate. That day James boldly wrote in the journal things he would never say in the public arena of NYU—things he'd never let out of the privacy of his consciousness until now.

"This first semester has been fantastic. Some of Carlton's books are similar to these, so I've had little trouble understanding my classes. My days with Webster have proved invaluable. It allowed me to develop an extensive vocabulary, which is blessing me with comments like 'good thought' and 'well put' on my work. 'Work on handwriting' also appears a lot. I blame Carlton because I mimicked his handwriting all those years.

"Amazingly enough, things are going so well that I've been offered a full scholarship! I can't believe it. Me—a scholarship! James, the Slave of Carlton—that's who they want to give a full scholarship to. To me! Of course, I've graciously accepted it. I still can't believe it, though. A full scholarship. For me, James—the Slave of Carlton. The runaway. The fugitive. The hunted. The criminal. Me!—James!—got a full scholarship. This time last year, I was in the fields picking tobacco. Happy not to get whipped. Now I'm getting A's in college—me, James! Thank You, Lord Jesus!

"No doubt my confidence in myself and my abilities has increased with my successes. I realize now I'm capable of achieving anything I'm willing to work at. I find it hard to believe I questioned my ability. Me. James. I have the right to expect my dreams to be fulfilled, even the recent ones of college graduation. Especially these. Coming from my earlier existence no longer matters. I am a Negro. I am a successful college student. I am my own person. I am not a slave. I am a man. Not brave, at least not yet. Not nearly as brave as Miss Moses—or Frederick Douglass. Not even close! Where does one get that type of bravery?—James Scott, 1859."

He enrolled at school as James Smith, knowing he would change it once he decided what his last name was to be. Often runaways kept their "slave name" and took their former owner's last name. James decided early on he would not take Mr. Johnson's surname. His first name, however, was an honorable one, even if it came from dishonor. His Christianity made him aware of the significance of it, and he decided to keep it.

As for the last name—Scott—James chose it because of one of the first assignments he completed earlier in the school year. Entitled "The Most Significant Event in the Last Decade," he researched past newspaper and magazine articles and found out about Dred Scott, who, in 1857, sued the United States government for his freedom.

James scribed in the assignment, among other things, ". . . Mr. Scott was taken into free territory repeatedly by his owner, mostly in Illinois and Minnesota, and claimed his freedom based on that and the Missouri Compromise of 1850. The U.S. Supreme Court, in a unanimous decision, sided with the slave owner, though. The decision went far beyond just deciding a case and returning a slave.

"Led by Chief Justice Roger Taney, they made statements so inflammatory, it may have set this country on a path to war. They held that no Negro could ever be a citizen and, therefore, could not bring suit, 'in the White man's courts,' as they wrote. The laws of the land didn't apply to Negroes, no more than it would apply to a horse. In their judgment, slaves were three-fifths men and two-fifths property. That they, that *we*, are not human beings. More along the lines of talking horses.

"They expanded the power of the slaveholders, strengthened the Fugitive Slave Law, and threw out as unconstitutional the Missouri Compromise of 1850, the basis of Mr. Scott's argument. The court returned Dred Scott to his master and increased tension and dissension between the North and the South. I pray it hasn't begotten a prelude to war—a United States Civil War. . . ."

James felt taking Mr. Scott's surname as his own showed demonstrable support for him and the cause. He understood the significance of this Supreme Court decision—that it kept men like Mr. Johnson in power and made men like himself a criminal. James didn't officially change his name at school, though. And he didn't hand in that version of his assignment. That would have to wait, but his transition was progressing.

♣

"It's amazing—the power of words and how you can use them. For instance, listen to this—uh, yeah, here it is. You listening?" James asked Mrs. Howard from the dining-room table.

Most evenings, James arrived home from work or school after everyone else had finished their meal. He would go to the kitchen, fix a plate, and eat alone, or with Mrs. Howard, who sometimes waited.

"*Oui*! I am!" she yelled from the kitchen as James heard the clatter and clanging of pots meeting each other in movement.

"This is from an assignment I have in my Political Science class. They gave us this book to read and answer some questions. I want to show you this," James shouted until she walked into the room with his dinner. "Thank you, Mrs. Howard."

"You are welcome, James. Now, what has you so excited, hmm?"

"This here—uh, let's see—yeah. Listen to this part . . .

"*. . . than those who framed the Government. Washington did not believe, nor did his compatriots, that the local laws and domestic institutions that were well adapted to the Green Mountains of Vermont were suited to the rice plantations of South Carolina. They did not believe at that day in a Republic so broad and expanded as this, containing such a variety of climate, soil, and interest, that uniformity in the local laws and domestic institutions was either desirable or possible.*

"*They believed then as our experience has proved to us now, that each locality, having different interests, a different climate, and different surroundings, required different laws, local policies, and local insti-tutions, adapted to the wants of that locality. Thus, our Government was formed on the principle of diversity in the local institutions and laws, and not on uniformity."*

"Sounds reasonable, huh?"

"*Oui*, James, I think. Well—I am not sure."

"I know. It's a lot of words. The article is saying that the law in New York City must be different than the law in—uh—uh—in the Indiana Territory somewhere. This is a city, and out there are farms. Here people can build buildings as tall as they can because they have to. Here, there are so many people. In the Territories, there are not as many people, so the buildings are not built so high. Makes sense, huh?"

"*Oui.*"

"Out west, you have animals roaming all around on farms and in the woods. In New York City, animals must be more controlled. But it's not until you realize it's Stephen Douglas speaking, and what his intentions are, that the true meaning comes to light."

"Which is?"

"He wants states like Alabama and Virginia to have slavery because the economy of agriculture—farms and things like that—work best with slave labor. And that the people there want it. And in states like New York and Pennsylvania, with their industrial economy that doesn't depend on slave labor, they can choose not to have it if they so desire."

"*Oui, oui.* The language of politics!"

"Yeah, the power of words."

"What is that you are reading?"

"Stephen Douglas ran against Abraham Lincoln for a Senate seat from Illinois in 1858. They had a series of debates that have been put into a book—this book. I guess it's because they're running against each other now for President."

"Oh, I see."

"And he makes other points, too. Like uh, he—Douglas—talks about when the country was founded, 12 of the 13 states had slavery. Lincoln says since most of the states are free now, all should be free. Douglas answers by saying that if that had been the case when this country was founded, all would be slave now. But no, the founding fathers decided to leave it up to each individual state to decide, and that we are just approaching a natural balance based on local needs and geography. Slavery is evil, and what he says is vile, but he's good. Scary good!"

"That is the language of politics, James. They say what they wish to get what they wish, and then they do what they wish, hmm. Eat your supper before it gets cold. This book will still be here."

"Yes, ma'am."

CHAPTER 6

"Dear Mom and Dad. All is going fine. Getting good grades. See you soon. Say hello to everybody. Love, Bobby," dictated Bobby. "That's the end, sir. So, you gonna send that today, mister?"

"Yeah, son," the telegraph operator replied. "That'll be a bit for the telly. Ten cents more for the five letters."

"Thank you, sir."

He paid the man and walked away while reading his letters from home. The usual worries from his mother. His father reminding him to be careful. His brother and sisters being, well, brother and sisters. His parents' warnings made him question everyone he met. *Maybe that's the point*, Bobby considered.

His classmates, all White and mostly cold toward him, worried him with questions of where he lived, with whom, and where he was from. Staying vague and unresponsive in time became second nature to him, honed from lessons learned at Cambridge Prep.

All the strangers peering through the pairs of blue, green, hazel, and brown eyes he passed on his daily 20-minute walk to school kept him suspicious of their gawks, glares, and even grins.

Even the ones he had gotten to know on a limited basis, like a couple of professors at college, Mr. Peterson—the bakery owner, and Mr. Toretilli—the fruit man, seemed friendly enough. As did the few Negroes he encountered in his daily travels. He remained leery of them all, though, and kept his distance.

♣

"Heavenly Father. You are everything, I am nothing. Your grace and mercy overwhelm me. Thank You for blessing me and my people with Mrs. Howard and others like her. Thank You for helping me in New York City. Thank You for blessing me with the ability to go to college. Thank You for helping me get used to being free. Please keep me safe. Amen."

James' days began with prayer, then a 5-minute walk, 20-minute train ride, and another 5-minute walk and he's arrived at New York University. Four classes and 6 hours later, he was at work until 6 p.m. Most days, he went to the library after work, stayed until it closed, and then came home to eat late and study long. This day was different.

"Ah, yeah. Home, sweet home," James mumbled as the apartment building came into view. It had been months since he made it home in daylight.

"Hey—look! I don't believe it. Nah—nah! It can't be James," Alfred sarcastically said at the concept of seeing his roommate during the week.

"Very funny. Look out. I'm hungry!"

"Oh, yeah. It's James," said Ominira and slid over to make room.

"You are here early, James."

"They're re-tooling some machinery, so I got off early. All my schoolwork is caught up. I thought I would share dinner with you all—but if I'm not wanted...."

"Bye," joked Junee, and others mimicked him.

"Bye . . . see ya' later . . . gimme his food then . . ."

"Okay, everyone have a seat, hmm."

Along with 8 Free Negroes, 6 runaways currently lived in Mrs. Howard's building. Many runaways moved to other places in New York, but kept a low profile. Others moved on to Boston, Philadelphia, or Canada. The ones currently there came in their own unique ways. Tales of adventure and heartache were told by most. James was the only one currently there whom Moses had rescued, though all had heard of her. He'd shared his story, including his first attempt, as well as the incident in the church basement during the year he'd been there.

". . . I hope to see her again. And the Eddys. I was shocked when she—Miss Moses herself!—picked me to lead if she didn't come back! Not at the time, but later, when I realized what had happened, I was—wow"

"Over the past years I had *cinq* runaways that Moses helped. And 20 more came through other Underground Railroad routes. Most go to Canada now."

"Yeah, that's where she went. I didn't want to go, though."

Boxer, one of the oldest tenants, shipped himself to freedom from Virginia. Surviving in a wooden crate for three days was quite a challenge, and worth the risk. He jumped in a crate marked "Philadelphia" with a canteen of water before the shippers nailed it shut.

". . . I couldn't read then. But anywhere had to be better. Somebody say it was goin' North, so I jumped in." He gave the shippers in Philadelphia quite a shock when they opened the box. He made it to New York within a month."

James added, "Oh, yeah—*anywhere* else is better than slavery. Hey, what's the quickest way to freedom for a slave?" Most shrugged their shoulders as James chuckled, "Death."

Only the runaways laughed.

Boxer had an additional tale of many years past, when he was a boy of nine. His first master and family were killed when Nat Turner went on his rampage. Boxer never saw his family after that. They were all sold to different people.

"*Oui*, that Nat Turner. John Brown. They got both of them. Hung them dead, hmm. Frederick Douglass had to go to Europe. Lived in my hometown for a while."

Junee had traveled on foot for 3 weeks from Alabama to Ohio, where he lived for a while; then he went on, to New York. Receiving no help, his journey was the most isolated of all the runaways'. Eating not only fruits and grains, but bugs and grass, sleeping in trees because of wild animals, and trying to find cover during bad weather were a few of the challenges he'd faced.

". . . This old lady tolt me how to git to the North. I just did it. When I seent the Rivah Jerd'n, I reckon I wuz close. Followed another runaway I met on a barge across. Took 'bout a munt', I suppose."

Ominira stowed away on a ship leaving South Carolina for Boston and jumped off when it docked in New York. He was part of a group of 10 slaves who were unloading their Master's winter crop in Charleston. The free Negro workers on the ship made sure he ate and had water.

". . . I heard New York was the place to go. So, I jumped off the boat. Didn't know how to swim. Didn't care. Quickest way to freedom, huh, James?"

"Yep."

"I had to live my name."

"What that mean?" asked Boxer.

"My name—*Ominira*. It means 'freedom' in the Yoruba language."

After splashing and paddling for a time, he reached the dock. Five days later, he was at Mrs. Howard's building.

"This is two examples of regular folks helping, hmm. If you ask them if they are the Underground Railroad, they would say no. They just help out. But they are. That is that. It is what we are all about. Folks helping folks. Feed them. House them. Show them the way. Do not tell you saw them. That is the Underground Railroad. We in the North. We help once you get here. Down South, we cannot do much. You are on your own. And you still get here, hmm."

John was from Tennessee. He escaped on foot initially for several days. While he was staying in a barn because of a severe storm, a circus troupe stopped at the farm for the night. One of the clowns saw him and gave him a sign to be quiet. Later the clown, Edward, returned and told John he'd help him escape to the North. John wasn't sure if the other troupe members knew this or not. He helped him hide all the way to Pennsylvania underneath the tiger wagon.

". . . I gots me a cat, when I'se got free. I lived in Riley, Ohio fo' a spell. They talk 'bout the slave law. So I'se come here to blend in. I guess they was the Underground Railroad, too."

"So that's your cat I see around," James remarked.

"Yeah. Bet' not mess wit my cat. I gotta thing fo' my cat."

Then there was Beau, who was over 6 feet tall and approaching 200 pounds. ". . . I kilt a man. Maybe 3 or 4," announced Beau. "Masser Miller was gonna whup me agin. I was jest tired of it!"

Beau's master had a small farm and 4 slaves, quite typical of most farms in the antebellum South. He always complained about most of his father's plantation being stolen by crooked bankers and deceitful politicians as he struggled to make a living. He beat his slaves to release his frustration, and, this day, he'd come in upset.

Beau was cowering in the corner of the barn as Master Miller struck him again and again with a leather strap. Beau saw a rock near him, and, after a strike, he grabbed the strap, pulled Master Miller toward him, and hit him with the rock and the force of his hand in the face.

Master Miller crumpled to the ground and lay there motionless. Beau turned him over and, seeing his face was a bloody mess, ran. Originally from Louisiana, he got to the Mississippi River and stowed away on a barge headed north. The only one of the 6 who didn't plan his escape, it was winter when he ran.

Days later, he was found by 3 of the crew. Fighting his way out, he hit one in the head with a 2x4 board, threw another through a glass door, and then dove into the frigid Mississippi. It was the middle of the night, and he barely made it to shore. Cold and shivering that following morning, he came upon a White man camping in the woods.

"All I wanted was his horse. I was jest tired. And cold. Real cold. He pulled his gun on me. I wuz a-scared. A rabbit jumped out da' bushes. So he looked at it. Then we fought fo' the gun. I was jest holdin' him. I swear, jest holdin' him, so, so he don't shoot me. He stopped movin' after a while. I guess I choke him dead. I stayed until I was dry. I took his horse and left. I took his coat, too, 'cause, 'cause he wuz dead."

Beau made it to Illinois in a week, and after a month he was in New York City. These were some of the tales these men had lived while running, and they riveted the other men.

"You know, Mrs. Howard. It must be—what?—20, 50, maybe even 100 runaways out there right now. Out there down South, running to here. To the North. Running to their future," James reasoned as he paused his bites and chomps, and a few followed suit.

"Yeah, in the woods. In the dark just like we was. In the water. A-scared and hungry. In a open field. Jest runnin'," agreed John, as all now stopped what they were doing or saying.

"*Oui. Oui.* Many will not make it. Many will not—let us join hands and pray for all them out there tonight, hmm."

"Yeah, and pray for God's guidance for them. Heavenly Father. Most High, Most Holy. Please hear our plea. We ask You to lead these runaways to safety, O Lord, and watch over people like Miss Moses . . ."

"God. We ask Yo' help fo' dem slaves. The ones who's runnin'. Keep 'em safe and let them get here. . . ."

"*Mon Dieu. Écoutez mes prières. Protégez les braves hommes et femmes qui courent vers le Nord en ce moment. Aidez-les à trouver leur chemin. Protégez ceux qui les aident, Seigneur, . . .*"

"Our Father who is in heaven. Hallow is Yo' name. Yo' kingdom come. Yo' will be done. . . ."

"Swing low, sweet chariot. Coming for to carry me home. Swing low, sweet chariot. Coming for to carry me home . . ."

"Please, Lawdy. Help them fellas runnin' tonight. We's askin' that You lead 'em right. And that You help 'em . . ."

"*Baba orun. Jọwọ tọju awọn asare lalẹ. Ran wọn lọwọ lati de ibi. Gege bi o ti ran awon okunrin won lowo nibi, . . .*"

"Jesus. I ask Ya' help fo' da runners. Jest like You did fo' me. Do fo' them, Lord. . . ."

"Help 'em, Lawd. Help 'em, Lawd. Help 'em, Lawd. Help 'em, Lawd. Help 'em, Lawd. . . ."

"*Chè Seyè. Ede esklav yo ki kouri isit la kounye a. Sove yo, Bondye ak . . .*"

". . . I looked over Jordan and what did I see. Coming for to carry me home. A band of angels coming after me. Coming for to carry me home. . . ."

CHAPTER 7

" . . . New York has more than one million residents. The next two largest cities in the country, Boston and Philadelphia, barely have 200,000 people each. . . ." Professor Garrett lectured during history class, which included an attentively distant James.

That's the reason I stay here. To disappear in this sea of humanity. Kind of like what John said. Or the Smiths—hide in plain sight. This is my second-favorite class—after arithmetic. Here, I don't need a partner, or ending up getting whoever is left over for a partner.

". . . The completion of the Erie Canal in the 1840s catapulted New York ahead of Philadelphia and Boston as the nation's most important city after Washington, DC. Why do you suppose that is? Come on—somebody? I know somebody knows . . ." Prof. Garrett asked as he scanned the 23 pairs of eyes, most of them purposefully looking other places. Silence was the only response as he continued to scan the room, and finally saw a pair of eyes that didn't dart away—and the accompanying right hand slowly raised.

"Finally! Yes, Mr. Smith?"

"Economics, sir. Money! The natural resources prevalent in western New York State and along the uh, the St. Lawrence River is the main reason. All the animals, timber, furs, minerals, gems, stuff like that. Also, it's a direct route to Canada. The Great Lakes. And the Midwest territories that weren't there before."

"Very good, Mr. Smith! Everybody got that? Believe me, you will see it again. New York City's population includes many immigrants—that's with an "i"—people from other countries that come here. Most of them come from Europe. But we also have an influx of emigrants—that's with an "e"—people who come here from other parts of the United States.

"These include a new type of emigrant—runaway slaves. I suppose they come to New York to blend into this melting pot. I'm sure the Fugitive Slave Law is always near the forefront of their consciousness, though. These are some of the reasons why the diversity of New York is growing. Indeed, New York's diversity is becoming its signature. . . ."

"Ain't no way a slave that smart," whispered Jeremy to his neighbor, but loud enough for James to hear.

Stay calm, James. Stay calm. I'm from Cincinatta. I'm here to see my aunt and uncle. My Ma and Pa died . . .

". . . your assignment. How will the immigrant and emigrant conflux impact New York City over the next decade? Will it be positive or negative? And always—why do you think that? Five hundred words, due next Friday."

"Yeah, boy. When I'se gits outta here today, we goin' over to Miss Molly's. You wanna come, James?" Big Man asked in his sonorous tone. He and James worked across from each other now, since James had been promoted to die caster.

"Nah, I gotta go home," James replied. He continued to focus on his duties and ignored the jocular taunts from his co-workers.

". . . Gotta go home. Gotta go home. Gotta go home. Gotta go home . . ." the men teased.

Big Man is okay. The things they do ain't for me, though. If what the men are saying is true. If it's true, they are doing freely what Mr. Johnson forced his slaves do. Would've forced me to do. And the women are doing—doing what Chloe was—uh, was forced to uh—uh, she was forced . . .

". . . Gotta go home. Gotta go home. Gotta go home. Gotta go home . . ."

"Y'all gone and leave ol' James here alone. If it ain't his thing, it's okay wit me. That mean mo' fo' me," Big Man bellowed, and a hearty laugh followed. Then he leaned over to his workmate and whispered, "Uh, James. You uh, you do like girls, don'tcha'?"

"Yeah!"

I ain't forgot about that! I'll never forget about it! It—it just won't be the same—ever!

James recalled his thoughts the first time he met Big Man, as he looked across at his workmate and friend. Although he was about the same physical size as Beau, his personality filled 2 rooms. The most popular worker, both White and Negro liked him. And he took James under his wing by showing him the nuances of the worksite and the area's restaurants, stores, and businesses. James appreciated it, but his situation made it difficult. No one knew he was a runaway, a secret he intended to keep. No matter how friendly anyone acted.

"Oh, yeah, Big Man! I love women. Just got to go home. Just got to go home!" James answered with a smile.

"Okay, lil' man. Jest had to ask, you know."

". . . and in closing, it's an honor to be president of New York University. I'm sure all your experiences will be good, as mine have been, and hopefully continue to be for . . ." President Ferris discoursed, 20 minutes into the second hour of his one-hour speech. The assemblies were required attendance 3 times a semester, and James always dreaded them.

"Yeah, yeah. Get on with it," James mumbled as he peered upon the sea of Europeanicity from his back-of-the-auditorium perch. The black, blond, brown, auburn, and fire-red hues of hair in his field of vision indicated their ethnicity and served to exacerbate his feeling of isolation. "I don't want to be here any longer than I have to."

"C'mon. I got a train to catch, Mr. President," Bobby mumbled as he thought about spending the weekend with family and friends. "How can he talk so long and say nothing? I wonder if he gets paid by the word?"

❧

". . . and that ends my presentation."

"Finally," James mumbled as he exited with the throngs. Out of the corner of his eye, he saw another Negro, exiting another door, something he rarely saw. Another runner, perhaps. Maybe not. Who knows? He disappeared into the ruddy sea of faces as quickly as he had appeared.

❧

Succeeding during his first year at New York University, James' comfort level increased. He journeyed around the culturally diverse city with an increasing sense of independence and freedom. When he wasn't in school or working, James enjoyed himself, especially liking the ocean. However, he did no swimming or any other activity for which he had to take off his shirt.

Riding more than an hour on a packed ferry to reach the Atlantic shore, James would deeply inhale the salt air, allow it to circulate throughout his soul—and then spill out into his second journal, the first one was filled 2 months earlier. Spending hours there, James peered out toward the ebbing horizon and contemplated the endless possibilities of his life and the journey of his life to this point.

"The experience of the beach. The palatable salt air. The refreshing sea spray. The unique variety of life on the ground beneath me, in the water before me, in the air that surrounds me, and in the skies above me depend on each other for survival. And the myriad of sounds completes the experience, making it a place like no other on the planet.

"The possibilities, my possibilities in this life. Are they as numerous as the grains of sand on this beach under me? As limitless as the sky above me? As vast as this Atlantic Ocean before me? Possibly, possibly. But that, too, may be a trap. A trick as dastardly as the one of freedom for runaways. As always, prayers for the Africans who died crossing this vast ocean.—James Scott, 1860.”

♣

Mrs. Howard viewed James coming home from her 6th-floor perch. He was a loner, a fact that worried her. Many runaways were loners at first, but James was hanging on to it, she thought.

“James, *si'l vous plaît*! Tell me why to be alone you like, hmm?” she asked as she met him at his door.

“I don't, Mrs. Howard. I think maybe—well, maybe because I was in the Big House when I was young. Did all that reading and stuff. I'm just used to being by myself. Plus, because I could read and write, I couldn't tell anyone. So, I kept it to myself. And I kept *to* myself.

“I mean, I did tell Ruth and Chloe. And Isaac—and Netty. But it was hard telling them. Even Miss Moses—she said a smart slave is a dead slave if they weren't careful. Just like Ruth did,” he replied and then opened his door. “Come on in. Alfred's staying with somebody tonight.”

“I know what you mean. I understand, *oui*. But what about now, hmm? You are no longer a slave. You have *liberté*. You have freedom. What are you going to do with it, hmm?”

“I have friends here. Al, Nira—we do stuff.”

“Do you have a best friend, though?”

“Yeah, but—no, not really. But most of my time is spent in school or working—or studying. When I'm here, I'm working, studying, or reading. I go to work. I go to school. I read. I guess my best friend would need to do those things, too—especially school. No one here goes to college with me. The men at work don't. All my classmates are White—not that that's bad. But being uh, *le fugitif*, huh? I don't want to risk myself. Or you. Or anyone else here.”

"*Oui*, James, you have a point."

"I'm caught between these worlds, true enough. Remember, the best of times, the worst of times. But Mrs. Howard, don't worry. Don't worry. I'm happy. I have a newfound freedom. I can read what and when I want to. I'm in college! Look, tonight I'm going to finish *Uncle Tom's Cabin*. Boy, it sure brings back memories. But thank God I'm not a slave. I'm happy, Mrs. Howard. Thank you for worrying. *Merci beaucoup.*"

He walked to his window and peered out.

"You are welcome. I will always worry about you. You do not even say you are free anymore, hmm?"

"Huh—no," replied James as he turned around. Half smiling and slowly shaking his head, he added, "No, ma'am. I'm not free. *Le fugitif,* remember?"

"*Oui, oui.*"

"'Tree'?" he asked as he threw his thumb back over his shoulder, toward the window.

"What tree?" she asked as she shrugged.

"*Francais, si'l vous plaît.* 'Tree'?"

"Oh! *Arbre.*"

"Ah-bray. 'Ocean'?"

"*Ocean.*"

"O-say-un. 'Mountain'?"

"*Montagne.*"

"Mon-tan-ya. I love this language."

"You like changing the subject, I think."

"Uh, 'snow'?"

"*Neige.*"

"Nej. Uh, . . ."

"Yeah, I been here 'bout ten years now. Come from Pennsylvania. Got hitched once—couldn't behave, though. She and the kids finally left my ass. Been on my own since. Just workin, havin' fun. How 'bout you?" Big Man asked as he and James shared a lunch table.

"Oh, I'm from Cincinatta. Like I told you. Never been married. Been in love once, though."

"Uh, oh."

"'Uh, oh'? What 'uh, oh'?" James replied as he finished his meal and looked up into a broad grin.

"That love thang. Boy, mens ain't meant for that love thang," Big Man answered with that hearty laugh that turned heads in the dining area.

Smiling, James shook his head in mild disagreement and said, "I—I don't know about that, Big Man. Loving her got me through a lot."

"Yeah, yeah. But lovin' her and bein' in love wit her two dif'rent thangs."

"Huh—I'm not sure of that, either. Maybe, with Chloe and me, it was the same thing, you know. We had something special," James replied, which caused Big Man to barrel over in laughter again.

"Okay, James. You okay. C'mon, let's git on back fo' they try and dock us. Gotcha' own mind. I like that. Who you know here?" he asked as they left the area.

"Several people at school. Some where I live. Why?"

"I jest tryin' to figure out why nobody ain't set you straight yet," he replied and bellowed again, causing James to join him in laughter.

"Nothing to set straight. Anyway, tell me—what was your wife like? What kind of woman would want you?"

"You mean what type?"

"'Type'?"

"Yeah! Boy, James. You sho' gotta lot to learn. There's womens that make ya' wanna take a bath and get a shave. There's womens that make ya' wanna go pick some flowers and give 'em to her. There's womens that make ya' wanna eat a full-course meal 'fo ya' gits with 'em. Then there's womens like Shelly—make ya' wanna slap anyone who git in yo' way of bein' wit her. I mean yo' mama, yo' daddy, yo' bossman, yo' friend—anybody!"

Laughing hard, James replied, "Yeah. It seems like Chloe was a little bit of all of them. Yeah, all those types."

"You lucky then."

CHAPTER 8

"*. . . A**nd so now as the White House goes to this new political party—the Republican Party, the future of our country is tenuously undecided. No doubt, the President-elect is anti-slavery, but how far he will go with this is unknown. Join me in praying for guidance and wisdom for our new leader—and this new party in power, the Republicans and their candidate, Abraham Lincoln, the 16th president of this great nation. T. Boone Price, editor-in-chief, Brooklyn New York Gazette. November 20, 1860,*" James shared as he read aloud the daily paper one Saturday morning.

Many of the tenants crammed into Mrs. Howard's 6th-floor office weekly to hear James read the news. And he relished in it, being taken back to one of the few joys of life at Penelope Farms and his revelation on that Philadelphia-to-Newark train.

"Do you think anything is going to change, Mrs. H.?" Alfred asked.

"I do not know. I pray and hope. These Republicans, they believe in our cause. At least, they did to get elected. We will see after their stomachs get filled with power, hmm."

"*Oui, oui.* Uh—me-oo vo uh, ah-jeer uh—ah-jeer uh, kay par-lay," James attempted to say as the others giggled.

"*Oui, oui,* James. Good try. Actions do speak louder than words. Much louder."

"Okay, okay. I tried," James said to the men there as he joined in their laughter. "How do you say it, Mrs. Howard?"

"*Mieux vout agir que parler.*"

"Mee-oo vo ah-jeer kay par-lay."

"*Oui, oui.* Much better. I have been to several of their rallies. They seem sincere. Here, let me show you something," she said as she reached into one of her desk drawers. The cluttered room she called her office was next to her room. It was filled with a desk, three chairs, a table, and shelves of books and paper. James was reminded of Johnson's study at first, though it was only a fourth of the size.

"See here. This is their party platform for this year—for 1860. You know what 'a platform' means?"

"Yeah—uh, it what they plan to do, or stand for—for the year," James answered.

"*Oui, oui*—listen. Uh—I will read only seven through ten, hmm. Most interesting, I think, to you men.

"*Number seven. That the new dogma that the Constitution, of its own force, carries slavery into any or all of the territories of the United States, is a dangerous political heresy, at variance with explicit provisions of that instrument itself, with con-tem-po-ran-eous exposition, and with legislative and judicial precedent, is revolutionary in its tendency, and subversive of the peace and harmony of the country.*

"That is what is happening in Kansas and Nebraska now—settlers fighting each other. Trying to choose between slave or free. Many are dying, hmm."

"So, this means the Republicans are saying that people who think slavery is right and supported by the Constitution are wrong?"

"That is how I understand it, James."

"Huh—this kind of thought could lead to war."

"It already has. In Kansas and Nebraska Territories. People are dying because of it."

"Wutn't John Brown from there? Kansas, I mean?" Boxer asked.

"Yeah! I 'member you tolt us that, Mrs. H.," Junee added.

"*Oui, oui.*"

"So, the belief that the Constitution supports slavery—the Republicans are against that?" James asked as all eyes went back to Mrs. Howard.

"*Oui*, James. This platform uses *beaucoup* legal words. But that is what I understand. Okay, uh—number eight.

"*That the normal condition of all the territory of the United States is that of freedom: That, as our Republican fathers, when they abolished slavery in all our national territory, ordained that 'no person shall be deprived of life, liberty or property without due process of law,' it becomes our duty, by legislation, whenever such legislation is necessary, to maintain this provision of the Constitution against all who attempt to violate it; and we deny the authority of Congress, or a territorial legislature, or any individual, to give legal existence to slavery in any territory of the United States.*"

"Whoa! A major political party said that?" James exclaimed. "Th-They're against slavery anywhere in the United States?"

"Well, James. They say. There are, uh—four now. Four political parties. The Democrats split into North and South. The Whigs are still around. I do not know about the Federalists. Then there are the Republicans."

"Stephen Douglas called them the Black Republicans," James added.

"*Oui*, I have heard that."

"I don't like it. It sets us up for conflict."

"How so?" Ominira asked as the men's heads snapped toward James.

"White and black—the most extreme shades of colors; diametrically opposed hues of the color spectrum. Black and white. It sets up conflict."

"Dia-whatically, James?"

"Sorry. Total opposites."

"Thank you."

"That is interesting, James."

"To me, Mrs. Howard, the name 'Black Republicans' implies something negative, sort of—segregated, I guess. Like you must choose. Black—or White. There is no middle ground. Nothing in between. I don't know."

"No, no, James. You are making sense, hmm."

"Sho' is. Keep goin'."

"What I fear is one day they will begin calling us—calling Negroes—'Blacks.' That will really set up conflict. Like, in nature, as day goes fighting into night. In literature, the forces of good and evil—dark and light, huh. In science, where white is light, and darkness is the absence of light. Then you will have White people and Black people. I'm afraid we will begin to believe it—that we have nothing in common. Just as the colors black and white have nothing in common. A natural conflict."

"*Mon Dieu*, James!" Mrs. Howard exclaimed as she slapped her hands to her face. "I never have that thought."

"I think we should be called uh—'Brown.' Yeah, the Various Shades of Brown People. And y'all, uh—'Pink.' Yeah, the Various Shades of Pink People. Yeah, Vashabs and Vashaps. Nice names, huh?"

"*Oui*, they are. Vashab and Vashap, hmm."

"Vashabs . . . Vashaps . . ." the men murmured.

"You see. Vashabs, Vashaps. No conflict, no clash. Two neutral, agreeable, non-threatening colors and names. Actually, somewhat related, just as we are—Negroes and European-Americans. Pink and brown both have yellow, I guess, and both our blood is red. The power of words, huh?"

"*Oui, oui*, James."

"Boy, you sum'um else," Alfred marveled at his roommate.

"Okay, okay. Anyway, I'm done preaching, now. I'll read, uh—let's see, number nine," James replied as he grabbed the pages from Mrs. Howard and she settled back in her chair.

"That we brand the recent reopening of the African slave trade, under the cover of our national flag, aided by perversions of judicial power, as a crime against humanity, and a burning shame to our country and age; and we call upon Congress to take prompt action and efficient measures for the total and final suppression of that execrable traffic."

"Huh—is somebody allowing slaves to be brought in again?"

"It would seem so. Or maybe still some want to make it law again, hmm."

"Number ten. That in the recent vetoes, by their Federal Governors, the acts of the legislatures of Kansas and Nebraska, prohibiting slavery in those territories, we find a practical illustration of the boasted Democratic principle of Non-Intervention and Popular Sovereignty, embodied in the Kansas-Nebraska Bill, and a demonstration of the deception and fraud involved.

"So, this says that the people in Kansas and Nebraska voted against slavery, but the Federal Governors there trumped up a case against the votes?"

"*Oui*, James. I am not sure of all the details. Both sides say the other cheat. Who knows? But the Republicans are speaking out against it, hmm."

"Huh—yeah. I think the Republicans would have, uh—10 votes if we could vote, huh?" James asked and looked around the room.

"*Oui*, James—*oui!*"

"Oh, hell yeah!"

"Fo' sho'!"

"You doggone right!"

"So, Lincoln won by getting forty percent of the vote, huh. Not a majority—but only forty percent of the White, land-owning men vote. In this country, only that many think we should be free," James mused as he scanned the newspaper for the next article.

"*Oui*. I fear that until Negroes and women are allowed to vote, you men will remain in danger, hmm."

"Here's one I'm interested in. The East River Commercial Freight Company Seeks to Halt the Roebling Bridge Design. Yeah, this is an engineering story. Civil Engineering. This is what I might end up going for in college. Building buildings, roads, and bridges.

"The East River Commercial Freight Company petitioned the War Department to halt development of a bridge spanning the East River.

Calling it, "Roebling's Ruse," they claim it will never succeed. That it will cost the citizens of New York hundreds of thousands of dollars—perhaps millions—and leave us with nothing but dissipated hopes. It will, however, leave Mr. Roebling rich on our money.

"Others claim the East River Commercial Freight Company—and other ferry providers—are worried their monopoly on travel to and from New York City is in peril. Once the first bridge is successfully built, many more will follow. This will lessen the need for their ferries and . . ."

CHAPTER 9

A beautiful spring afternoon, and James was on his way home from school. Another test. Another "A." Picking up groceries for Mrs. Howard, he strolled along the bustling sidewalk, thinking about the next couple of days. He was looking forward to a weekend of rest and relaxation.

The crowded metropolis' hum was, as usual, prevalent. The myriad of smells and languages was indicative of the diverse nature of New York's populace. The variety of conversations in German, Italian, Spanish, Swedish, Russian, and the increasingly recognizable French, interspersed with varying levels of broken English always entertained James on his travels to and fro. Even the good English offered James some delight, except when it was laced with a Southern twang.

As he walked, James marveled at the variety of not only the people, but the buildings and the businesses housed in them. He passed tailors and gunsmiths and bakers and lawyers and doctors and manufacturers. He wondered how a country so diverse would ever come together as one—and if his freedom, this tenuous and deceptive allowance of personal decision, would ever come to be fully realized.

". . . I don't think I'll study at all this weekend. Just lay around and go to the beach. Leisure time is definitely something new for me. Even being able to plan days in advance—I got to get used to this. Oh, yeah—" James mumbled while he strolled. His idle rambling screeched to a halt as a sight chilled his soul to a scream.

Oh, my God—No! Please, God—No!

The midday sidewalk, crammed with people, allowed James to blend in as time seemed to slow. He dropped the groceries, turned, and walked in the opposite direction as fast as the crowd moved, hoping to not raise attention. His heart raced; he prayed and resisted the urge to dash to a corner 20 seconds away.

It seemed he could discern each individual voice, every sound around him, as he strained not to hear a familiar one. The fruit man who yelled, "Two for a dollar." Two ladies who talked about a weekend social. Several men who argued passionately about nothing. A wagon that rolled by, its rusty wheels creaking at each rotation. A nearby American flag, its 34 stars and 13 stripes that flapped and waved proudly. Several birds as they flew by. And a dog that barked to protect its territory.

"James," he thought he heard someone say through the din of the crowd, as his racing pulse increased.

No, this can't be. This—can't—be! No, God! This can't be! Please, God—no!

James reached the corner and took the first step in a gallop before he was grabbed and spun around. James looked away from his future and into his past—the bane of his beginning.

"James!" Carlton said, through the evil grin of years past.

"No!"

He shoved Carlton, who fell first into the crowd and then onto the pavement. Turning the opposite way, James ran as fast as his legs would move, knocking down several people, two food carts, and a small tree. Thirty minutes later, he took a breather in a park.

I'm glad—I'm glad I didn't have—have my books! Does he go to NYU? My God, I bet he does! He'd be a senior—uh, now! I got to avoid upper-level areas! Damn, I saw Carlton! I, uh, I won't go anywhere near where I saw him today! Wait a minute. Where was I when he saw me?

What if he sees me—in, uh, in school? I better start coming out only when I absolutely have—have to! Shit, I saw Carlton! And he—and he saw me! He saw me. Oh, my God! What if he finds out where I live? Oh, my God! Carlton saw me! . . .

♣

In the middle of the largest park in the city, in the middle of the most populated city in the country, two men were making plans to continue the greatest injustice in the history of mankind.

"Dammit! I been here four days, Winnie. Whatcha' waiting on?"

"Nothin', Bradley. I still workin' on a couple. One don't go nowhere wit me. Another I can't git alone. Gimme a coupla mo' days, huh?" Winnie requested as he looked around nervously at the people passing by in the approaching sunset.

"You ain't gone soft on me, is ya' boy?" Bradley asked. He took out his kerchief, wiped his leather boots, and polished the silver tips.

"Soft! Shit, naw! *Broke* mo' like it. Believe me, when I gits one—you'll have 'im!"

"Good. Three folks I know already got theirs and gone back South. And I'm still here."

"Don't worry. Meet me back at this spot in three days. Ya' hear?"

"Okay, okay."

"Oh, yeah. Check wit Palmer every day, too. Jest in case I gits one befo'."

"That'll be good, Winnie."

". . . and Mrs. Howard, I was so scared! Look. See, I'm still shaking," James recounted as he extended his trembling hand. An hour after he'd made it home, and two hours after dusk, James was assuaging his anxiety with words and gestures.

"When uh, when he grabbed me, that last time I saw him shot through me. He had that look, a smirk or something. Like the one he had when he got me whupped—I mean 'whipped.'"

"I am so sorry, James. *C'est triste, oui*," Mrs. Howard answered with a strained face.

James, caught up in his own calamity, failed to notice the distant wistfulness of her stare until now.

"What's wrong, Mrs. Howard?"

"Hmm?"

"What's wrong? I mean, I know my news is bad, but you seem—"

Mrs. Howard sighed heavily, allowed several whimpers to escape, and then uttered, "I am sorry—I am sorry to have to tell you this. So soon after your day. Slave catchers caught Ominira earlier today."

"What!? Oh, no!"

"*Oui*, I had Mr. Bill go down there. *Oui, c'est triste*. He is there. In the jail. He will be on his way back to the Carolinas soon."

Oh, my Lord! It—it can happen! It really can happen. Please, Lord help me. I don't want to go back! I can't go back. Kill me first, God! Please, snatch the breath out of my body! Just don't let them catch me alive....

"... Carry yourself in a way that tells people you are free, James. *Libré, si'l vous plaît*, hmm. Once you are in jail, I cannot help you. I—I will not help you. I cannot! James, too many others depend on me. I will hire you as the building manager, reading teacher. Whatever else we may need, hmm. So you won't have to go out so much."

... Please, Lord. Help me, help us. Help all of us! Please, Lord God our Father! ...

"James? James. *James!* Do you hear me?"

"Huh? Oh, yes, ma'am. Uh, thank you so much, Mrs. Howard."

"Thank me for what?"

"Huh, uh . . . I'm 'sorry.' I didn't hear you. I—I was praying."

"Do not say sorry. Praying is always good."

"Yes, it is."

"I said I will hire you as building manager."

"Thank you, very much. You are so kind."

"No, James. I should have done this a long time ago. You have been doing things around here since you got here. Come—let us go to the manager's room, hmm."

"I didn't know you had a room for a manager." He helped her up, and they headed down the five flights of stairs.

"*Oui*, but I have not had one for so long. A manager."

"Mrs. Howard, don't you get tired going up and down these stairs? I think your apartment should be on the first floor."

"No, no James! I love my view! But alas, this is not one of those fancy, newfangled uptown buildings with those uh, el-e-va-tors. *Oui*, elevators, hmm."

"No, ma'am. I guess it isn't."

. . . Man! 'Nira caught. Carlton saw me. I—what—help me, Lord! Help me, help us! Please, Lord. Help us. . . .

They arrived on the ground floor; they continued down and went through a door James hadn't been through. It opened to a dark, dank, sparsely furnished room. James, once his eyes adjusted, looked around, noticing the bed and dresser first.

Mrs. Howard promised, "I bring in more furniture soon. Some pictures, hmm?"

"No, Mrs. Howard. This is fine for me," James replied as he scanned the room. Unpainted walls and large pipes over his head and under the high ceiling led to a large mechanical contraption, which caught his attention. "This is all I need. Except for a rug— and a lamp. And maybe a table to write on."

"Well, a little paint will not hurt. And you have more closet space, see? You have been buying clothes, *oui*?"

"Mrs. Howard. I have all I need."

"James. James. This is part of your transition. People cannot see you wearing the same thing day after day. That is what a slave does, hmm."

"Okay, Mrs. Howard," James replied as he looked around his new room, pointed to a corner, and asked, "What's that?"

"That is the furnace. It should not make much noise. We will see. The last man—Luther—he never complained."

"What happened to him?"

"He got the fever—gold fever. Out west somewhere. You can use this portion of the room here, and we can hang blankets over the pipes if it is too loud."

"There is much more room here, that's for sure. Let's hold off on the blankets. I like the space. I doubt if the furnace makes more noise than uh, Alfred's early morning singing," James replied as he walked to the window and looked out to a knee-high view of New York's humanity.

"Ha, ha. I am going to tell Alfred you make fun of him. . . ."

⚜

Winnie and Officer Palmer pummeled and stomped a hapless boy, no more than 16, to unconsciousness. Dragging him up a flight of stairs minutes later, they entered the dimly lit police station.

"Gotta another runaway here," Officer Palmer proclaimed between huffs and puffs.

"Which one?" the officer behind the desk sneered. He grinned first at Winnie and then at the bloody and battered one.

"Nah! He my helper. Put 'im up fo' a spell. Got somebody comin' fo' his ass d'rectly."

Winnie, understanding the implications, stewed inside as he muttered, "He be here on Tuesday."

Not looking at or acknowledging Winnie, the officer asked, "Where my cut?"

"Oh, yeah," Officer Palmer replied as they dragged the boy toward the jail cell, followed by the officer. "You'll get 20 once we lock this boy up."

"Sounds good by me."

CHAPTER 10

James quickly recognized the benefits of having a room to himself. Gaining a greater sense of comfort, his sleeping moments included dreams instead of nightmares, while his waking moments included more peace, less apprehension. Alas, he became more of a recluse as well. He studied more in his room because of the limited distractions, instead of staying late at the school library and traversing the dark and dangerous streets of the city.

James awoke to a beautiful morning. A familiar *cock-a-doodle-doo* greeted him. Remembering it was Sunday, he stretched out in his bed for extra snooze time. Not one to lie in bed awake for long, though, he got up and washed. Standing in front of the mirror, he examined this person, this reflection of the man, Mr. James Scott. Freed man. His own man—with limits.

"I make decisions in my life. Me and only me. And God, of course. It's my choice. You want me to work. You gotta pay me. You want me to do something. You gotta say *please*!" he exclaimed as he pranced in front of the looking glass. A pirouette reminded him of his horrible history.

"These whip marks will never go away," he whispered and rubbed the back of his hand over the ridges.

"Yes, just a minute," he answered a knock on his door as he rushed to put on his shirt.

"Yeah, Miss H. say breakfast is ready," Alfred yelled.

"Thanks, I'll be there in a minute."

Slave. Servitude. Property. Nevermore—and forever.

$\clubsuit$

". . . and even though the election is over, we will continue to monitor and evaluate it because the country may be facing its greatest challenge since—since, well, since its inception," Prof. Montgomery emphatically lectured during James' US History Today class. His mind wandered, though.

Man, how did I get Alfred to talk me into this? Well, I'll go through with it—but man! How did I get trapped into this? I—I don't want to do this . . .

". . . You all will need to stop by my office to get your copy of the article I am about to read. I will read only an excerpt—I expect you to read all of it. It's from the *Atlantic Monthly*, uh, October of this year. A Mr. James Russell writes . . .

"'*We are persuaded that the election of Mr. Lincoln will do more than anything else to appease the excitement of the country. He has proved both his ability and his integrity; he has had experience enough in public affairs to make him a statesman, and not enough to make him a politician.*'

"In your essays, the ideas I want you to consider are the following. One, is Mr. Russell pro- or anti-Lincoln? Two, is he pro- or anti-politics? Three, is he pro- or anti-United States? Four, do you agree or disagree with Mr. Russell's assessment of the President-elect? And five, what are your hopes of the new president? Five hundred words written *neatly*—to those of you who know I mean you! Due in two weeks. Have a good day, gentlemen."

"Checkmate!" the 30-something man declared; then he moved 2 steps down to the next player in a line of players. He pondered for a moment, and, after a quick move, announced, "Check!" and moved on, leaving that opponent pondering his response. Several yards away stood Bobby, enthralled but subdued at the scene. Most days, the park across from his apartment building teemed with chess players who tested their abilities. And a few, like this gentleman, who most held in the highest esteem, show-cased their talents.

Sounds of "Check—check—checkmate—checkmate—check, . . ." filled the air as he completed one side of a series of 10 tables that each housed 3 players and moved up the other side.

"Boy—he's amazing!" Bobby mumbled to no one in particular. Shaking his head slowly, he marveled at how this man could keep so many games in his head at one time when Bobby struggled focusing on one game at a time.

"I just love watching him. He's so—" Bobby mumbled until a hand forcibly grabbed his arm and spun him around.

"What you doin' 'round here, boy?" interrupted one of New York's finest.

"I—I jest—uh, I jest watchin' them play—uh, chess. That's all, sir," Bobby stammered as his parents' warnings fueled his fear.

"Got yo' papers?"

"Uh—yes, sir. Yes, I do," he replied as he hurriedly went into his jacket pocket and produced the document.

Dressed in a black uniform, matching hat, and an imposing shiny black nightstick dangling from his waist, the officer intently scanned Bobby's papers. He looked at Bobby, back at the documents, back again at Bobby, out at the crowd, and back again at Bobby; then he grudgingly gave the documents back to him.

"They look okay. Don't be startin' no trouble 'round here," he said, his blond mane sticking out from beneath his matching hat.

"Uh, huh. Yes, sir. No—no, I won't, sir."

"Come 'round here a lot, do ya'?"

"Uh—yes, sir. I mean, sometimes, sir."

"Uh, huh. Where yo' family? . . ."

"You've been paid. You can go now," James mumbled as he faced the furnace in his room and away from his guest.

"Okay. Uh, you were great, mister. I—I'm sorry you didn't enjoy it," Madge said as she held her head down.

"It's not that. I—I uh, I did enjoy it, uh—Madge, right?"

"Yeah, Madge. My name is Madge. I'm glad. I'm glad you liked it," she replied with a grin. She walked over and kissed James on the cheek. He never responded or looked her way. Walking toward the door, she looked in the mirror, and straightened her clothes. Getting halfway out, she turned, only to see James still staring away from her.

"She musta been some special kind of woman."

"Huh? Who—what are you talking about?"

"'Chloe.' You called me 'Chloe.' Twice."

James didn't respond.

"Ask for me again—please. Okay?"

Yes, she was special. Why did I do this? How—how can I do this? I—I won't ever do this again.

"This isn't how I thought freedom would be. I'm not free here. No Negroes are free in this country. We're just in a bigger cage. It makes me think I'm free, but one wrong move and *bam!* I crash into the boundary. Down South, it's free forced labor. Up North, it's cheap labor. Neither is respected. Any of us, based solely on our heritage, on our race, can become slaves," James articulately scribed as he contemplated a class assignment.

"Why do Americans have to go to Canada to be free? That's not our country. This is where we, where I was born. In America. The United States of America. But I'm not free here. I'm not even freed. Not in any of the 34 states of the union. I'm running in a bigger cage. But still in a cage and forever running—running to nowhere. I can spread my wings but never take off and soar.

"I'm given choices here, just enough to make me think I'm free. The minute I exceed my bounds, the bounds established by this democratic society, founded on liberty and freedom—*liberté*, as the French say—I'm susceptible to arrest, being shackled, and sent back to slavery. If I was to hand in this paper, my freedom paper, it would be like writing my own ticket back to physical bondage and the degradation that is associated with it. Free? Huh—not even close for me or anyone who looks like me!"

This was the kind of paper I desire to hand in. But reality and Mrs. Howard's warnings dissuade me. Maybe one day. Maybe one day. Maybe—I'll be as brave as Miss Moses or Mr. Douglass. . . .

James rose from the dining-room table and stretched as the door swung open and Mrs. Howard entered the room.

"Maybe one day I'll be able to hand in assignments like this. I'm tired of these double assignments, Mrs. Howard."

"Deux?" she questioned as she placed plates on the table.

"Yeah. I write one that says what I *can* say. Then I write one saying how I really feel, like this one. We are supposed to write a paper on what freedom means to us. But I can't write what I feel. Well, I can't hand it in."

"Oui, James. But maybe one day. One day, hmm."

"Yeah, huh. One damn day!" he exclaimed, slamming down his pen on the table.

"James!"

"I'm sorry, Mrs. Howard."

"What is wrong, hmm?"

"Mr. Douglass. Miss Moses. They don't let their fear stop them from writing or doing what they do. How does one get courage like them? I guess I'm not as brave as them. Never will be."

"James, people like them. Their bravery, their courage—rare. Very rare—and special, *oui*. You are right for that. But do not be hard on yourself, hmm. You did write what you feel, *oui*?"

"Yeah—yeah, I did."

"And your plan. To get a college degree. Handing it in will prevent that, *oui*?"

Letting out half a laugh, James replied, "Yes, ma'am."

"You show your courage by traveling alone in this big city, going to an all-white university, going to work 5 days each week—and all this as *le fugitif,* hmm. And you do well. You excel in all, *oui,* you do."

"Thank you, Mrs. Howard," he replied as he embraced her.

"We all need reminding from time to time, James."

"How much time do we have before dinner?"

"A few minutes."

"'Kitchen'?"

"*Cuisine.*"

"Kwee-zeen. 'Pan'?"

"*Poele.*"

"Po-well. 'Knife'?"

"*Couteau.*"

"Coo-taw. 'Fork'?"

"*Fourchette.*"

"For-shet. Uh, 'spoon'? . . ." James asked as he followed her into the kitchen.

With the turning of the monthly calendars, James evolved as a leader of the 20 runaways that came to Mrs. Howard's apartment during that time. While leading reading lessons, James recognized in their faces what he had been—fearful, unsure, confused, and with a rage seething just below the surface. Looking out over the crowd of 4 new arrivals, all anxiously hanging on his every utterance, he knew he'd had the same wide-eyed wonderment he was now observing. He did his best to brief them with transition analogies and comforting assurances.

This, being able to read and teach others to read out in the open, this is freedom for me. I love this! Making a difference, showing someone the way. Perhaps I'll become a teacher in college. Yes, Miss Moses. I will keep my promise to you. I will keep my promise. I will help others in every way I can—and forever!

". . . That look on y'all faces. I had it, too. You're gonna be all right. I know y'all scared. I see it in your eyes—*boo!*" he taught and faked a charge, which startled a wide-eyed runaway. "Just remember this—you can't afford to show your fear. That's the first thing we will work on. Getting rid of those big eyes—*boo!* Yes, this transition will take time. Even I'm still adjusting. I think I always will be. But I have lost the big eyes—*boo!*"

When not helping at home, or teaching, or being taught, James spent most of the time in the library at school, when he wasn't holed up in his room. Mrs. Howard checked out many books for him from a local library and admired his insatiable appetite for reading, too. But she continued to worry about him.

". . . James, reading is fine. *Tres magnifique!* What about friends? Girls? *La femme*, hmm?"

"I have friends, Mrs. Howard. We've been through this more than once. Girls? Huh, I don't want no family like it is now."

"James. James. There are more things to do with a girl than sex. Walking. Talking. Just having fun. Friendships. Laughs."

"I have fun—fun with my books. They're my friends. Books, newspapers, people like Mr. Douglass. They're my friends. At least for now. Maybe when I'm free, then yeah. Huh—when I'm free."

"There is no need to wait to be free to make friends, hmm."

"Do you believe you can have a girl as a friend?"

"I don't know. I never thought about that."

"If you like, I know people. Perhaps I can help you to meet—"

"Mrs. Howard, no. Thank you—but no. Please. It's okay."

"Very well. *C'est triste.* Such a nice young man. All alone, and so many young girls who maybe would like to meet. That is all I am saying, hmm. . . ."

". . . I'm proud of you, son. You're growing up. Doing well in school. Living on your own," Papa Harris remarked with pride during the Harrises' Sunday afternoon tradition. Its significance had increased since Bobby began going away to school—first to Cambridge and now to New York City.

"Thanks, dad."

"I still worry. It's dangerous in that big ol' city. Baby, there's good schools here," Mama Harris added. The dried tear stains that streaked down her cheeks served as a testament to her angst.

"Aw, c'mon, ma," Bobby replied and grabbed another piece of chicken.

"Baby, I just want you safe."

"I know, ma. Can't nobody bother me. I keep my papers with me. Always!"

"What about friends, son? You got any?" Papa Harris asked as his eyes darted from his son to his wife and back.

"I know some guys who live around me."

"What about at school?"

"Nah. I seen a couple, but none in my classes."

"A couple?"

"Yeah. Some Negroes."

"Be careful, Bobby. Some Negroes will help the slave catchers and will turn you in. Knowing you live there alone and all," Papa Harris warned.

"I will, dad."

"Be careful, baby."

"I will, ma. I will. Ma, I miss this."

He looked around the dinner table at the faces of his life. His parents, brother, sisters. Jaws, linen, arms, china, crystal, hands, and silver in constant motion. The full-course meal being devoured. He inhaled the scents of his home to comfort him. He allowed the warmth of his home to envelop him. It all whispered "family."

"Thank you, Bobby," Mama Harris replied with the first smile she had that day.

"Oh, yeah. You would miss the food," said William between chomps. "But it's good to have you home."

"Yeah, it's good to see you, too."

"Bobby. What's it like in New York City?" asked Martha, with wonderment, which caused her parents to glare at her.

⚜

". . . and the sine over the cosine is the tangent—I think. Man, I hope that's what I put on that test. And those proofs—shoot! I'm never sure until I get the tests back," James mumbled to himself as he walked through the night.

This day was one of James' longer ones, ending late at the library. After helping Mrs. Fleischbaum blow in the darkness and lock up, he walked the evening streets on his way home. These were the times his fear would engulf him. Every stranger he passed, every noise he heard, every corner he turned was potentially a step closer to bondage. Even completely avoiding the area where he'd seen Carlton offered little relief. Way past 10 o'clock, he saw Mrs. Howard's light on as the building came into view.

Huh, she's usually asleep about this time. What is she doing up?

James continued his monologue as he started up the steps, passing the first-floor windows, the top half being visible from the streets. "Let's see—a test on Thursday, the science project due on Monday. A test next week, too—I think. I'll check my board when I get in. Boy, that Ken is pretty smart. He'll know, and he'll tell me, if I ask him when no one else is around. . . ."

James arrived at his room and checked the section of his wall where he kept upcoming assignments and due dates. ". . . Uh, huh, next Friday—a test. I thought so. Oh, yeah—Mrs. Howard," he mumbled, recalling the light in her window.

He headed quietly up the stairs.

I'll just listen at the door—just in case she's busy. I think Mr. Bill gives her more than just information.

He stopped at her door, listened, and heard crying. He softly tapped, waited for an answer, then tapped again. This time, the sobs ceased.

Hesitantly, he uttered, "Uh—Mrs. Howard? It—it's me—James."

"C-C-Come in," she said, and the sobs resumed.

He opened the door and saw her sitting at her desk. Her tear-stained face stood out in the dimly lit room. She struggled to her feet, and they embraced. Several minutes passed before she let go of him.

"What's wrong, Mrs. Howard?"

Sighing, she replied, "James—*mon Dieu*. I have just been here crying. Crying for—for you. For me. For us. For this country. Just crying. I do not know who to believe. Who to trust? *Mon Dieu!*"

"Why? I mean I know this country isn't great, but—why?" he asked, searching her face for answers.

"James. Mr. Bill," she sighed. She walked back to her chair and plopped down; then she continued, "Mr. Bill went to the inauguration for President Lincoln. He told me of his speech and brought back a copy of it. James—Lincoln, he has decided—he said that he will do nothing! Nothing to stop slavery. Or to get rid of it in the country!"

"Huh? Wait! Didn't that uh—platform say they were against it? That they would end it?"

"*Oui.* The language of politics, James. I keep saying—the dirty, nasty language of politics, hmm. They—they say what they wish, to get what they wish, and then they do what they wish. See here—read it for yourself. I put lines under what pained me so," she replied, handed him a piece of paper, and dejectedly leaned back in her chair.

"Okay, I'll read the underlined stuff now and then the whole thing later, okay?"

"*Oui, oui.* That will be fine. Just read, *si'l vous plaît,*" she despondently replied between sighs.

"Okay—uh, let's see . . .

"Apprehension seems to exist among the people of the Southern States that, by the accession of a Republican Administration, their property, and their peace and personal security are to be endangered. There has never been any reasonable cause for such apprehension. Indeed, the most ample evidence to the contrary has all the while existed and been open to their inspection. It is found in nearly all the published speeches of him who now addresses you. I do but quote from one of those speeches when I declare that—I have no purpose, directly or indirectly, to interfere with the institution of slavery in the States where it exists. I believe I have no lawful right to do so and have no inclination to do so.

"What! But I thought—uh, they were for us! The Republicans were for Negroes—and, and against slavery!" James exploded as he looked up at her angst-filled stare.

"*Oui, oui.* He also will continue to support the Fugitive Slave Law."

"What!"

"The language of politics, hmm. They say what they wish, to get what they wish, and then they do what they wish. *Mon Dieu.*"

"*Oui*, Mrs. Howard. The language of politics. But I'm not sure what. I mean, nowhere in the platform did they *really* say they were going to fight it. But it seemed like they were going to do something," James remarked as he began re-reading that portion of the speech.

"What worries me most is where it came. At the beginning. The first thing he talked about. The first, hmm."

"Huh—oh, yeah. In speeches, you usually make your strongest points first."

"*Oui, oui. Mon Dieu*, James. Where—where is this country going?"

"I don't know. I don't know, Mrs. Howard," James replied as he carefully re-read the section he had just re-read, hoping he'd misunderstood Lincoln's position. He looked back at her agonizingly sorrowful gaze, which begged so many questions.

"And—and he called us—property. The President of the United States said we—are—property. Mrs. Howard, can you believe that President Lincoln, the Republican president, called us, Negroes, "property." Not persons. Not people. Not humans. Not citizens. Beings that can be bought and sold. President Lincoln called us property! The property of people in the South. He believes we can be owned by someone. And—what's that you're drinking?"

Mrs. Howard answered him with a sigh. She rested her forehead in the palm of her left hand, with her elbow propped up on the desk. Her right hand grasped a cup of liquid which sat on the desk. Guttural sounds, broken French-English snippets, and sighs were her only audible answers.

James, with a raised eyebrow, wondered if she understood his question. "I—I don't understand what you're saying, Mrs. Howard. What's in your cup?"

A smile curled her lips. She looked at the cup. Then at James. Then back at the cup. Then she giggled and replied, "You mean this cup?"

James, at a loss for what to say uttered, "Uh—yeah. That cup."

"Oh—just a little bit of the grape. Want some?"

"Yeah."

Her smile dissolved as she pulled a quarter-filled bottle from a desk drawer and grabbed a cup from a shelf behind her. A moment of indecision hit as she looked at the cup in her left hand and then at the bottle in her right. With limited coordination, she roughly placed the cup on the desk in front of James. She grabbed and pulled out the loose-fitting cork with her teeth, sloppily poured the wine into his cup and on the desk, and set the bottle on the desk with a thud.

She spit out the cork onto the table and stammered, "To—to—to . . ."

"To the truth! May it always survive," James said as he raised his moist cup.

"To the truth!"

"Mrs. Howard, I know—hey, this is good, Mrs. Howard!"

"I feel betrayed, James. Lied to—to get our support. Our men—the ones who voted. Lied to—to get their votes. This politics—it—it—James, promise me, *si'l vous plaît*! Promise me you will never become a politician. *Si'l vous plaît!*"

"*Oui, oui*, Mrs. Howard. I promise. Let's leave this vulgar language—this political language. Let's go to a more beautiful language, hmm? 'School'?"

"Huh? Oh—okay. Uh—*ecole*. A bunch of liars."

"Ek-col. 'Book'?"

"*Livre.*"

"Lee-ver-ray. 'Teacher'?"

"*Oui, oui.* They teach us well, hmm? Do not believe them, these politicians!"

"Yeah, you're right. Uh—'teacher'?"

"*Instituter.*"

"In-stee-too-chur. Beautiful, just beautiful. 'Laboratory'?"

"*Laboratoire.*"

"La-bore-ra-tor-ree. Uh—"

"James, James. *Si'l vous plaît.* I do not wish no more to do this, hmm. No more tonight. My heart, my soul is sad, hmm. I want to sit and drink only, hmm."

"Yes, ma'am. Let me do one final toast. Here's to the *joke* that's on me—and everyone that *looks* like me. Life, liberty, and the pursuit of happiness. Things we will never achieve in this land of the free and home of the brave."

He refilled the cups and listened to her sobs and sighs throughout the night.

CHAPTER 11

James arrived at his Life Theory class and found his preferred seat on the right and near the door available. The classes at NYU, filled at the start, usually lost 30% of the students by midterm, and another 20% as finals approached. This class was no different. But James not only persevered but excelled in all his courses during his two years in college, despite the stresses in his life.

His fugitivity—and the accompanying criminality. His fragile freedom—and the tenuous nature of his liberty. The specter of Carlton in New York City—and the realization that each step could be his last step of freedom. His living in multiple worlds—majority Negro at home, predominantly White at his workplace, virtually all-White at school, and a hodgepodge of humanity along the highways of New York City, which he willingly faced daily.

Despite this, his mind stayed focused on his goal of a college education. James was determined to get as much knowledge as possible. He was going to use this school to ensure his future. Nothing that had happened, or was happening, or could happen in his life would prevent that. Ruth's charge to him to learn so long ago was a beacon, a heartbeat in his soul, instinctive, like a moth to a flame. It spurred him on minute-by-minute, hour-by-hour, day-by-day, class-by-class, semester-by-semester, toward his goal. His life's travails and tribulations would not deter him, and he was undaunted as his transition from fugitive slave to college graduate progressed.

Professor Randolph Franklin entered the class, strode to the podium, and began speaking as the class quieted.

"Good afternoon. Your next assignment is a reflection piece—worth 30% of your grade. You will not pass this class unless you do well on it. College is designed to take you from childhood into adulthood—academically, mentally, and socially. One goal is to force you to consider, to truly think about what your life has been and what's to become of it after you graduate from this university.

"I want you to reconsider all that you know and think—and question *everything*. All of it. From the meaning of life to the meaning of death, and everything in between. I know next year you will be taking classes that will prepare you for your chosen profession. I know many of you will leave New York University as doctors, lawyers, engineers, artists, writers, teachers, musicians, and so on and so forth. You are to be commended for that accomplishment.

"But, more importantly, consider this—who will you be as a person? What type of human being, sharing this planet with more than 1 billion other human beings, will you be? You see, I like to think of this class, Life Theory, as a gateway to the rest of your life. All the assignments given, all the lectures taught have been designed to help you discover you—your voice, your perception, your deep-rooted beliefs. My goal as your instructor was to introduce you to you.

"I don't want you to leave here thinking the same way you did when you arrived. I don't want you to think the way your father or mother or favorite writer or knowledgeable teacher did just because that's what they think. If you truly agree with them, that's fine. Just be sure the decision comes from you. It-must-come-from-you. Otherwise, this country, this world will not grow. Instead of creating a new past, it will repeat the old past.

"This culminating assignment will help you with that new past—with your future. It will clarify the plan for you to achieve the goals you—not anyone else—desire. I don't want you to leave here as a doctor when your desire is to be an artist. I don't want you to leave here as a writer when you want to be an engineer. This, this assignment may be the most important assignment you will ever have. My hope is that it serves as a guide for your career and personal success. . . ."

For the most part, I know me. I am getting to know me. Smart. Serious. Sensitive. Secretive. Huh, a lot of "s" words. All the days in the study, those hurtful and insightful words gleaned from Webster, my companion in knowledge, reality, and wisdom, feed my passions. The stories in the study took me on journeys far beyond any physical boundary; they aided my insight.

The days of innocence in Johnson Hall. The moment of horror under the whipping tree. The nights of revelations in the shacks. The nights of passion and ecstasy under the shacks. Hey, Chloe. The incredible bravery of Moses and all those who help her. The magnificent model of masculinity in the person of Frederick Douglass. The compassion and sacrifice of Mrs. Howard and those like her. And now, the dynamic potential of my life as it unfurls before me. . . .

". . . in a country as diverse as this one is becoming, it's incumbent on its intellectuals to lead the way, to reveal the truth, and to lift every voice . . ."

. . . I realize that, even though it appears I'm alone, there's a multitude taking this journey with me. My parents, my brother, Ruth, Netty, Mr. Boo, Moses, everybody on the Underground Railroad, Mrs. Howard, the Abolitionists, the tenants at 1020 W. 57th Street, the millions of slaves down South, the thousands of runaways up North, the millions of free Negroes here and in Canada. Thanks for the company.

But what I want, though, I want to know and understand this country, this United States of America. And its "citizens," these European-Americans. If I'm not allowed to be a citizen, I want to know what makes them so special. I want to read every book in this library. Surely, the answers are in them. The reasons why they do what they do, and think what they think, and feel how they feel.

If it is written, I want to read it. If it exists, I want to know about it. I'm going to draw every drop of knowledge I can out of this institution. No, I'm going to squeeze it out. No, I want to wring it out, drop by drop until my hands are raw. I'm going to use New York University like my people are being used.

Proverbs tells me that knowledge and wisdom are the two things to be sought. I will seek them. I remember a time in my life when knowledge was painful. But now, knowledge is a joy to be acquired, something I desire. A desire to learn is righteous; learning is necessary for growth; learning is—learning is what I need to, what I have to do, what I must do. Thank you, Ruth, for the spark you provided. New York University will serve as a banquet table, offering me a virtual smorgasbord of knowledge and wisdom of the world for my consumption. And I will fill my belly of it. I intend to gorge myself until it pours out of my ears.

". . . and I want detailed information. You are in college now and about to complete your second year. I want quality writing from you. All of you! Again, you will not pass this course without passing this assignment. One thousand words. Include articles and artifacts with your assignment. It's due in three weeks," declared Prof. Franklin.

James decided to make a mosaic with magazine and newspaper articles, along with books, poems, and other literature. He also planned to include some of his assignments and writings.

Two weeks later, James was completing his safe assignment, but was unsatisfied. "I'm not throwing these away," he mumbled as he gazed at the rapidly filling box of past assignments. Then he looked over at the already-filled box of duplicate assignments. He looked around at the freshly painted walls of his room, the leaf-green color offering a semblance of nature, and the idea rushed through him like a sudden chill.

"Yeah! That's what I'll do!"

Over the following weeks, he pasted past articles from magazines and newspapers, as well as his completed assignments—both those handed in and those duplicates on the walls of his room. He also wrote headings, musings, and other thoughts over, under, and between the pasted information.

". . . All the academics and the assignments—Arithmetic, Geometry, Science, Philosophy, World History, United States

History, English, Grammar, Writing, and others I read with vigor to pass and to learn. . . . The history of the world has been built on the backs of many people—tragically bloodstained . . .

". . . All the authors of European descent—Shakespeare, Hawthorne, Whitman, Dumas, Twain, Thoreau, Poe, Dickens, Longfellow, Stowe, Emerson—many never assigned—I read because they bring the world to life in words. . . . *To be or not to be*. When it comes to being a slave—definitely not to be. It's not even a question worth considering. . . . The Best of Times, the Worst of Times . . . the best—our possible future, the worst—our present . . .

". . . All the great American leaders—Washington, Adams, Jefferson, Franklin, Madison, Henry, and President Abraham Lincoln—I read about because they are Americans like me. . . . Can a leader lead against the majority's will? The majority says slavery is wrong, but it still exists, and its leader refuses to stop it. . . .

". . . All the Kingdoms, Queendoms, and Principalities of Europe I read about to understand the Europeans, the Americans, and the world. . . . There seems to be a superiority complex at work here. But why? Where is the superiority? Not in my classes! Equality—yes, competent—sure, superiority—absolutely *not*! . . .

". . . All the newspapers, magazines, pamphlets, and articles I read for current events, and to satiate my thirst for knowledge and wisdom. . . . Can we avoid the conflicts of so many other young countries—civil strife and upheaval? Or are we doomed to repeat the history of other countries? . . .

". . . All the Empires—the Prussian, the Russian, the Ottoman, and the Austrian—I read about because another seems to be getting built here in this 'New World'. . . . The American Empire is rising, a modern-day Babylon. Perhaps destined to crash down upon itself. . . .

". . . All the Abolitionists—Garrison, Beecher, Tappan, Pinkerton, Anthony, and Wilberforce—I read about, for they are helping my people. . . . Thank you to all of you. And you who know who you are, thank you very much. . . .

". . . All the Native Americans—Cherokee, Cheyenne, Creek, Chickasaw, Seminole, and others—I read about because I feel a kinship. . . . Not much known about them, except for some names. At least, I couldn't find much on them. I hope to learn more. . . .

". . . All the scientists and great thinkers—Newton, Galileo, Da Vinci, Plato, Aristotle, Socrates, Darwin, Descartes—I read because I want to be one of them. . . . Scientific thinking based on just the facts can be a multi-edged sword—cutting from so many angles. Can truth be both a goal and an obstacle of science? . . .

". . . All the notable Negro Americans, when I could find them—Truth, Turner, Beckwourth, Wheatley, Douglass, Russwurm, Hammon, Banneker, Tubman, Attucks, Purvis, Ruggles—I read and read about because they are Negroes like me. . . . My people have accomplished so much, despite despicable deeds and over-whelming odds against us. Mr. Frederick Douglass. Miss Harriet Tubman. God, I wish I could be like them. I wish I had a pinch of his courage and a dash of her bravery—what an inspiring recipe for leadership! . . .

". . . All the Confederates and the like—Hiram Johnson, Stephen Douglas, Chief Justice Roger Taney, and others I read about to *know thine enemy.* . . . A mission impossible? Maybe the only option is to fight. . . .

". . . All the journeys to all the places on planet Earth—China, and Egypt, and France, and yes, Mother Africa, in addition to London, and Shanghai, and Rio de Janeiro, and so many more I read about because I live on planet Earth, too. . . . Paris. That's where I'd like to go. And, of course, a city that sounds like fun—Kathmandu. . . .

". . . All the great musicians—Mozart, Bach, Beethoven, Chopin—I read, listened to, and study, for they bring the world to life in music and verse. . . . To hear love. . . .

"... All the great artists—Audubon, Michelangelo, Donatello, Rubens—I read about and viewed, for they bring the world to life in pictures. . . . To see love. . . ."

James' "Wall of American Knowledge," as he called the documents, papers, prints, and writings scribbled, posted, and plastered on the walls in his room spread like ivy, as he continually added to it. He earned an "A" on the 8-page assignment he handed in.

CHAPTER 12

The junior year was when students selected their major at NYU. James asked Mrs. Howard for her opinion. First, she reiterated her disdain for politics and politicians. She even went so far as to imply he could not stay in her building if he chose that path. Then she noted her observations of him during the 2+ years she had known him.

"Your love of *Dieu*, your desire to teach. It seems a good start for a preacher or pastor. The Bible the Smiths gave you is now filled with your notes and folded corners, hmm."

James thought about the Bible, how worn it had become during his years of limited freedom. His "Holy Webster" helped him through the tough times while leading him to the better times. His new favorite scripture, Jeremiah 29:11, gave him hope that he, and all Negroes, have the future God promises in that scripture.

"Yeah, sharing God's Word would be purposeful. I don't know about it being a job, though."

"You explain yourself well. And you love to teach others, hmm. What about being a teacher, or perhaps a professor?"

"Interesting thought, one I have had as well. That's one way I can honor Miss Moses' request to help others whenever I can."

"You are also very good at seeing things that have not yet been done or built. You love Arithmetic and Science—I think maybe your favorite subjects. And again, your ability to share your ideas with others who cannot see it. Sounds like an engineer to me, hmm."

"You are definitely right about Arithmetic being my favorite subject."

"*Oui*, James. I will say this and then say no more. You could be a lawyer—but please, not a politician. You could be a writer, but please, not a politician. The lessons you have shared with me—*tres magnifique, oui.* Your mind, your education, your life, has prepared you for so many things. It is nice to have so many choices, hmm? You have choices not many have. Choose the one for you, not for anyone else. I know you will succeed."

"Thank you, Mrs. Howard. I will sleep and pray on it."

♣

". . . These classes will be tougher than the ones before. Much more arithmetic, including The Calculus. Huh—I heard about that. Folks say Geometry and Trigonometry ain't nothing! That's why they call it—The Calculus. Showing it respect! It's going to be tough, but I'm confident. I'm ready. The teachers and many of the students will change. The area I go to class will change as well. Please, God, don't let me run into Carlton," James mumbled as he walked to a building to get his books for the semester. Looking around for the building, he realized something that had been hiding in plain sight.

"On the plantation at Penelope Farms, even though Whites owned everything, there were more Negroes than Whites living there. Well, existing there. I was actually part of a majority on Penelope Farms. It never felt that way because the Whites had all the power—and weapons. I guess that's what Nat Turner realized as well.

"And I'm part of a majority at Mrs. Howard's building. Kind of like and nothing like the shacks at Penelope Farms. There are more Whites at work, but I'm definitely a minority here at the University. A minor minority" he mumbled to himself as he entered the bookstore.

Eyeing a sign, he mumbled, "Uh—yes. Textbooks that way, so I guess I'll go that way."

He continued walking, observing his surroundings, while he mused, "But the thing is, I never realized White people came in so many different—different colors. And shades. I thought they would all be—uh, White! There are dark ones with light hair. Light ones with dark hair. In-between ones with in-between hair! And vice versa and versa vice! And various eye colors. This is part of my ongoing transition."

Anytime James saw a Negro on campus, he took notice. He met one in the library. Jeff from Philadelphia. Maybe like I'm from Ohio, James had supposed. They never went beyond hellos, though.

To his surprise, a Negro man was in another line slightly ahead of him. Their eyes met, and both nodded. They arrived at the counter at the same time, handing their lists of books to the workers.

Could be a runner. I'm not asking. Won't even look that way—

"Hey. Bobby—from Boston. Bobby Harris," the man said as he turned toward James.

"Hey. James. My name is James—from Ohio."

An uncomfortable silence erupted between them amid the bustle of the book store. Their minds raced with warnings from their families until the workers came back with identical stacks of books.

"Looks like we'll be seeing a lot of each other, huh, James?"

"Yeah, it seems. You're an engineer?"

"Not yet. But soon to be. Where you live?"

"In the city. You?"

"Same. Give me your address. I'll come by."

"Nah, I'm gonna be moving soon. I'll give you my new address then. We can just meet here on campus. In the library—and, of course, in class, okay?"

"All right," Bobby replied as they walked away. "So, what kind of Engineer you want to be?"

"I don't know. The kind that builds stuff. Buildings, bridges, roads. Things like that."

"Yeah? Me, too."

"James, James be careful, *si'l vous plaît*. That is all I can say."

"You said I should get a friend, a best friend."

"Will you tell him you are a runner? *Le fugitif,* hmm?"

"No. No, not yet. I don't know—"

"James, wait. Listen, hmm. Uh, some people may not—"

"I know, Mrs. Howard. He could be helping slave catchers. I won't ever forget that."

"*Oui,* that could be. But I—"

"Mrs. Howard. You were right. I need a friend. Honestly, I always realized it. I just needed to admit it to myself. I do—I need a friend. I'm lonely. Amazing, huh? In a city of one million people, I'm—I'm lonely. I want a friend. This is my best chance. It may be my only chance. Someone who does the things I do, goes to the places I go, shares the dreams I have."

"*Oui,* James. I do understand. But what I am saying—if you allow me—is that uh, some people may not wish to be your friend. Be friends with *le fugitif,* hmm. It is a big decision for them also. A chance for danger for them. That is what I am saying. You be careful. Do not go so fast. Listen carefully to what he says and does not say, hmm."

"I—huh! I didn't—I never thought about that."

"I am not saying he feels that way. But you need to know this. It is dangerous for you, *oui.* It is dangerous for him, also. For any Negro man in this country to be your friend."

"Huh, now *that* I understand."

"And James, *oui,* sometimes they work with slave catchers, too. All I am saying is be careful, *si'l vous plaît!*"

"*Oui, oui,* Mrs. Howard. I remember you and Mr. Bill saying that. I'll be careful. I'll get to know him first. How do you say—uh, *mieux vout agir que parler.*"

"Hmm, not bad James, and *oui, oui.* Actions do—they always do speak louder than words. Take time. Look closely. Listen carefully. Hear with your heart, with your spirit, *si'l vous plaît!*"

"See-voo-play, see-voo-play! Don't worry. How do you say 'Don't worry' in French?"

"Alas, James. When it comes to you, 'Do not worry' is not in my vocabulary, hmm."

♣

The chess games were going strong as two men stood off to themselves. Winnie, his back pressed against a wide tree trunk, continually scanned all around and past Officer Palmer, who was animated in his tone.

"... that goddamn sonuvabitch got away! My goddamn money jest ran off!"

"Our money. Shit!" exclaimed Winnie as he pointed to the throng in general and to several Negroes in particular.

He spewed, "Shit, we oughtta jest grab one of these boys right here!"

"Yeah. I been talkin' to a couple. One don't know nobody 'round here. He come fo' the chess. Let's try later tonight."

"Good. Bosch gonna be here tommora'. Shit! How the hell that boy got out?"

"Don't know, Winnie."

"Shit! That boy saw me. Knows my face!"

"Hell, he most likely long gone by now. In Canada. Might've run past Canada," Officer Palmer replied and then chuckled at his attempted humor.

"Yeah—Canada."

♣

James struggled for oxygen. The combination of the thick rope wrapped around his neck and the soiled rag stuffed in his mouth made getting anything more than a whisper of a gasp of air impossible. He was lying face down on the floor of the wagon, bound at the ankles and wrists. The creak of the wagon wheels took him back 14 years to his initial journey to Penelope Farms. A strident, tormenting monologue served as a companion for him on this journey back to the past.

Oh, my Lord! He got me. Carlton caught me!

"Hey, hey, hey. Finally caught yo' ass, huh, James. My daddy gone be so glad. He gone let me stay 'cause I got yo' ass! He gone whup you somethin' good, too," Carlton crowed with glee as he rode on the buckboard alongside a white-haired driver. "I can't wait to see that!"

My Lord! I—I didn't—I couldn't run fast enough! How—why did You let him catch me, Lord? Why? I knew I should've gone the other way. Why . . .

"Yeah, he gone be so happy. He gone let me stay, hee, hee. I ain't gonna hafta' go back to New Yawk City no mo'. All these heah goddamn Nawtherners make me sick. And I gits to see ya' git yo' ass whupped—ag'in!"

Hee, hee. Git yo' ass whupped! Hee, hee. Git yo' ass whupped! Oh, my Lord! Carlton got me! He—he got me! Hee, hee. Git yo' ass whupped! He—he got me! . . .

James rolled over, his face soaked from tears and his body dripping with perspiration. He got out of bed, steadied himself on his trembling legs, and tried to settle his queasy stomach.

"My Lord, Jesus. I—I can't—I just can't keep on living like this. I can't—" he muttered between halted breaths. "I can't live like this. May—maybe I should go—to Canada. Maybe I should. How, how can I do so well one day, and then the next day be like this? I got to do better. I got to—or go to Canada."

♣

James and Bobby ended up being the only Negroes in their classes, which cemented their bond. They had their first choice of partners now when the situations arose instead of being forcibly paired with whoever was left. Even after both had proven their academic acumen, classmates resisted their partnerships.

"Calculus is a bitch," Bobby whispered to James during Prof. Martin's lecture.

"I'm not sure, but I think I get it. If his answer is 15—"

". . . so, when you take the first derivative, you multiply the exponent by the coefficient, and then subtract one from the exponent," Prof. Martin elucidated as the sound of chalk scraping slate filled the room. He completed his writing on the chalkboard and calmly commented, "And your answer is 15. Just that simple. Are there any questions?"

"Simple? Huh, for who? Him? And you, Mr. Brain. Yeah, James, the Brain."

"I just got it right this time."

Leaving school, they talked about weekend plans. "Yeah, I'm going to see Frederick Douglass over at the Faraway Club in Brooklyn," Bobby said as James' eyes went back and forth, scanning the area and people ahead of them.

"Frederick Douglass!" James exclaimed as he stopped in his tracks.

"Yeah. Do you like him?"

Calm down, James, calm down. Hoo!

"Yeah, I uh, really like him. When is it? And where is the Faraway Club? I'll meet you there."

I got to keep calm.

"Just come by my place on Saturday. We can hang out and go there later in the evening. Ever heard of the Luca Family Singers?"

"Nah."

"They're gospel singers. They gonna be there, too."

"C'mon. It's right up here," Bobby said as he and James approached his apartment building. James followed him onto the elevator, and they went up to the 8th floor. Entering Bobby's spacious apartment, he was immediately impressed with its size.

"You got your own bathroom?" James exclaimed as he walked around.

"Yeah."

"We got two on each floor. Uh, that's one reason why I'm moving soon," he replied as he bounced up and down in a cushiony chair. "This is a nice place, Bobby. Nice chair, too."

"Thanks."

"What do you do around here?" James asked. He bounced up and strode to the window.

"Hang out mostly. Go over to the park."

"That park down there?" James asked as he pointed out of the window.

"Huh—yeah," Bobby answered as he looked up from his digging through a desk drawer. "It'll be full soon. Uh, do you play chess?"

"Uh, no. I've read about it, but I've never played."

"I'll show it to ya'," Bobby said as he stood up with a box in his arms. "They play over at the park I go to. They got this man—uh, over there. He plays 20 or 30 people at one time!"

"You can do that?"

"Yeah—if you're good enough! You got to be real good."

"Oh."

"What do you know about chess?"

"I know the piece names. Uh, the pawn, rook, bishop, uh, king, queen. Oh, and the knight. Some of the moves."

"Good. We got some time before the ferry leaves. You set it up like this. The queen always goes on her color, and . . ."

♣

James was apprehensive about bringing Bobby to Mrs. Howard's building. He fully realized the threat to his freedom, but that was not his primary concern. He feared exposing Mrs. Howard and her intrepid generosity. Or revealing to the wrong person the mysteries of the secretive Mr. Bill and his network of contacts. Or the 7 runaways currently living there. Or the scores of potential runaways that may come to live there in the future. Or any free Negroes who may be there.

Too much of a risk. I can't risk it. Or them. But what risk? Bobby's okay, isn't he? Yeah—but I don't know. I mean, sooner or later, I will have to. But when? I don't know. His actions—his words. They seem okay.

Mrs. Howard was torn also with her own reasoning.

"If you do not, he may become suspicious, hmm?" she said as she paced about his room.

"Yes, but we must pick a good time. A good time. Yeah."

"*Oui,* one weekend day would be good."

"We may want to have Mr. Bill here—and you leave."

"I do not understand why, James," she replied with surprise. "We will think on that, hmm."

"No, Mrs. Howard. I don't want to risk you. I respect you too much. 'Respect'?"

"*Respect.*"

"Res-pet. I love our friendship. 'Friendship'?"

"*Amitié.*"

"Ah-me-tee. My desire for Bobby's friendship doesn't mean I'm willing to risk your cause. "Desire'?"

"Uh, James. Why you choose these words, hmm?"

"Oh, no reason. Just asking questions. Making statements. Learning French."

"Okay. Uh, *souhait.*"

"Soo-way. I want you to be safe."

"I, too, wish for you to be safe. You need to use Alfred's room as your own."

"Huh—why?"

"James! Your writings. Your assignments you cannot turn in, hmm."

"Oh, yeah! Well, I could take some of them down—"

"Which one, hmm? This will be better. Alfred will be gone, and you will be safe."

"We will be safe."

"And I will be here, hmm."

❧

". . . I live near the Blue Ridge Building," James replied as he and his main workmate shared lunchtime conversations. James was honored that Empire Metal Works' most popular worker had befriended him. All the Negroes and many of the Whites wanted a friendship with Big Man.

As he dug into a bowl that had James' interest, he asked, "That's uptown, right?"

"Yeah, uptown. What is that you're eating?"

"This?" he asked, and then bellowed out that laughter. "This here is *real* food. Some rice. Tomaters. Lil' bit of okree. Some poke and chicken. Good eatin'."

Laughing, James replied, "Yeah. Makes this here chicken—and, and whatever Mrs. Howard put in here seem uh—ordinary."

"Huh. Mrs. Howard—where she from?"

"Uh, France, I think."

"Dang. You from Cincinatta. She from France. How the hell you end up there?"

Boy! Who do I trust? Who can I trust? How can I tell—who can I tell? Who can I risk everything on? Huh—nobody. Nobody! . . . What they're thinking. What kind of person they are. People—people can say anything. Just like politicians. They can act any way. . . . His actions—his words. They seem okay.

"James!"

"Huh—oh, uh, what you say?"

Big Man's grin eased James' worry as he added, "Who-wee. Boy, where yo' mind at? I said how you end up with this Howard lady?"

"My uncle knows her. Thought she could help me get in college."

❧

Who can I trust? Who can I risk my secret to? Whose safety can I risk? Big Man? Bobby? Both? Neither? Big Man is friendly. Bobby and me spend lots of time together. Who can I trust? Who should I risk?

James scrutinized Bobby's face as he studied the chessboard. His chocolate-brown skin with his youthful texture. His round eyes with the pupils that matched his complexion. The way his forehead scrunched up when he was thinking. The look he got just before he sprang one of his jokes.

God, I hope I didn't make a mistake. How—how can you tell how someone is? Just to fool you. If Mrs. Howard is—God, I hope I didn't make a mistake. She said it was okay to do it, but I still didn't have to do it.

After months of classes, after weeks of discussions, after moments of vacillation, Bobby was at Mrs. Howard's building in Alfred's 3rd-floor apartment. Mrs. Howard made sure all the tenants were gone and wouldn't be back until after Bobby left.

Mrs. Howard entered the room with sandwiches and lemonade and asked, "How are things going, hmm?"

Looking up from the chessboard, sweat beading on his forehead on the cool afternoon, James said, "Okay, Mrs. Howard. I think I got him going."

"Huh, got me going? Pretty soon it'll be over. I'm givin' him a whippin', Mrs. Howard," Bobby gleefully replied. "C'mon, c'mon! It's your move, boy."

"How about that?" James replied as he made a move and glanced up at Mrs. Howard. "I think you taught me the game too well, Bobby."

"Oh, yeah, I gotcha' on the run now," Bobby said and quickly moved again.

"Well, I will leave you two to your game. Have fun and play nice, hmm."

. . . God. Please! Did I do the right thing? Is the risk worth it? Bobby or Big Man—who to trust? I've known Big Man longer, but Bobby and I have more in common. My God! Help me, Lord. Our Father Who art in heaven, hallowed be Thy Name . . .

❖

James' days in school were more tolerable with Bobby in his classes. They usually ate breakfast together and then spent the day learning. Many afternoons and some evenings, they were in the library studying or researching, like this evening. No matter the time or place, they were partners, supporters, and friends.

". . . So, you decided if you're comin'?" Bobby whispered.

"With all this work and studying, I don't know if I'm coming or going," replied James as he rubbed his forehead in contemplation of the assignment.

"Ha, ha. Very funny. You know what I mean. 'Bout comin' home, to meet my parents. My family."

"Should I write it with a cause-and-effect structure? Or perhaps, compare-and-contrast?"

"I'm not gonna stop asking you."

Never looking up, James whispered, "Tell me how this sounds, Bobby. Uh—in the belief that the proper scientific process demands that we determine the causal reasons for—"

Bobby reached over, snatched the paper out of James' hands, and glared at him.

"Huh—what? Bobby, what are you doing?"

"James! My family! Coming to Boston to meet my family!"

Are you crazy? I can't go there! What if they find out? My God, what if you find out? See my whip marks. Catch me in a lie. Many lies. Lose my school partner. Lose your trust. Lose your family's trust before they meet the real me. . . .

"I don't know, Bobby. Do you think it's all right? Do they even wanna meet me?"

"What! Do they want to meet you? The first Negro in my classes! My best friend? My only friend! Oh, yeah, they sho' want to meet you."

"I'll let you know tomorrow."

⚘

Walking straight home that night, James' mind raced over to under to around and around and back again. All the remarkable possibilities and disastrous ramifications of the upcoming decisions weighed on him. If he did go, complicated questions were sure to be posed to him. If he didn't go, possibly tougher questions would be asked. The persona he had created and lived over the past 2 years would soon become the role of his life. Boston would become the stage, with the Harris family becoming both audience and critics. And his nerves, taut with the inner tensions his secret brought, would be tested to no end. That night, he and Mrs. Howard talked into the dawn, after he awoke her with his pacing up and down the stairwell.

"I know it is just the weekend. Be very careful, *si'l vous plaît*. Do not let them see your back. I guess that is the main thing. And just stay calm, hmm. Because they will ask you questions. *Beaucoup* questions, hmm."

"So many things to remember. Wasn't it Shakespeare who wrote, 'The world's a stage?'"

"*Oui*, I believe so."

"I got to get my act together then. I'm James from Ohio. Cincinnati—no, no! Cincinatta. My folks are dead. Killed by Injuns. My aunt and uncle, they went west. I'm here, in New York, to go to school. I may go to meet them when I'm finished. My aunt and uncle, I mean. Don't know anyone back there. We moved a lot as a child. My favorite color is green. I like cats more than dogs. Steak over chicken. Coffee over tea—sweet. Arithmetic is my favorite subject. I broke my nose when I fell out of a tree—an apple tree. My favorite scripture is Jeremiah 29:11. . . ."

CHAPTER 13

As the train slowed, Boston came into view, but James' mind continued its relentless pace.

. . . This is my second time on a train. And going to a new city. But this feeling is so different. So much different. I had no idea what to expect when I headed from Philadelphia to Newark, and then to New York. I got an idea now, but then again, not really. What will they think? Can they tell I'm a runaway? Carry yourself like you're free. . . . Amazing Grace, how sweet the sound, that saved a wretch like me . . . Carry yourself like you're free. . . . The Lord is my Shepherd, I shall not want . . .Carry yourself like you're free. . . . For God so loved the world . . . I'm James Smith, from Cincinatta, my folks are dead . . . I know the plans I have for you . . .

". . . Yeah, I think we'll be able to get some hunting in. Show you what it's like," Bobby eagerly anticipated.

"Sounds good, Bobby."

"We'll be there in less than 20 minutes. I didn't tell them you were coming, so we gonna play a trick on my sister, okay? She always runs to answer the door."

"Bobby? What do you want me to do?"

He turned toward a mischievously smiling Bobby and shoulder-shrugged his question. Bobby responded with an impish smile and a shoulder-shrug of his own.

"Bobby?"

"Don't worry. You'll see."

"I'll see what? Bobby—what?"

♣

Arriving at the Harris home at dusk, they avoided the serpentine sidewalk that led directly to the front door. Instead, Bobby led James along the side of the hedge, and they snuck up to the front door. Bobby rapped on it with a rhythmic *rap-rap, rap-rap-rap*, and then stooped behind James. Soon, the door flung open, with a little girl making a squinty-eyed, tongue-poking face at him. Once she opened her eyes, she embarrassingly said, "Uh—yes. Can I help you?"

James stood there, not knowing what to say, hoping Bobby would soon relieve him of this uncomfortable situation.

Bobby stood up and finally answered, "Uh—no!" which brought a smile to her face.

"Bobby!"

"This is my little sister, Eve. This is James," he said as he strode in past her. "Daddy home?"

"Uh—uh, no. He—he ain't here yet," Eve stammered as she kept her eye on James, who entered cautiously.

♣

The first few hours were spent with James' mouth pushing words past his lips, while his mind raced and his heart pounded. They told him stories about Bobby, especially William. His sisters, Martha and Eve, went from eyeing James to giggling between themselves. Papa and Mama Harris did most of the talking initially.

They all seem nice. Nice family. But I wonder how nice they would be to a runaway. Huh, a runaway who is putting their son, their brother in danger. I wonder?

He seems nice, Mama Harris thought. *He'll be good for my baby.*

"James, do you want some more chicken?" Eve asked.

"No—no, thank you. This has been a great dinner, Mrs. Harris."

"Thank you, James. So, you want to be an engineer, huh?"

"Yes, ma'am. I want to build things. Roads, buildings, bridges. Things like that. I want to build, or help build, the first bridge from New York to Brooklyn!"

"Me and him, ma."

"You boys need to study hard then," Papa Harris said as he eyed the two college students. Then he turned his stare toward his youngest son. "All you boys do."

"We do, sir," Bobby and James replied in unison.

I'm glad Bobby is taking this seriously, Papa Harris thought.

So, this is what a family is supposed to be like. This is what I've missed out on. It's nice.

❧

"Thank you, Charlie. See you next week," Papa Harris said. "That's the last customer. What say we head out to the docks? Get some fishing in before it gets too late?"

"Yeah," the brothers screamed.

"Boy, your daddy sure knows a lot of people, huh?" James asked as he and Bobby took out the trash.

"Yeah, I guess. It's busier during the week."

"Yeah—a lot more!" exclaimed William, who tagged along.

"Really! Man, this is—this is nice."

"Thanks. Up here. We dump up here," Bobby said as they approached a large container in the back of the store. "You ever been fishing?"

"Uh—once, long time ago. Forgot it—how to do it—though," James replied as they dumped the trash and headed back.

"Man! Never been huntin'. Never been fishin'!"

"I have been fishing—once."

"That don't count, James. Yeah, you're different. That's for sure," Bobby added.

"Yeah, I guess with my folks dying, I missed out on a lot of stuff," James replied as the battle with his nerves continued.

"Hey! You boys gonna talk all day? Or are we gonna do some fishin'?" Papa Harris screamed from the back door of the store.

"Yeah!" all three boys replied as they picked up their gait.

Stay calm, James. Stay calm. But—this—is—nice. Real nice.

❧

They attended church early the next morning and introduced James to everyone there. After the service, Pastor and First Lady Beard came to their home for Sunday dinner.

". . . So, after he asked my father's permission, begged my mother to agree, and made a fool of himself on our front lawn, I couldn't do anything else except say 'Yes, I'll marry you'," recounted First Lady Beard.

"Scripture says a man who finds a wife finds a good thing. But it don't say how foolish you may need to get to convince her of that." Paster Beard added. "Every day I thank God for that, and for her."

"Wow, y'all been married for 32 years! Mr. & Mrs. Harris—for 24 years! I know my parents would've been married for a long time, too. I hope I find someone I can act a fool for, Pastor."

"Watch out there. You can find a lot of women you *may want* to act a fool for, son. Just be sure it's God's will and that she's worthy of your foolishness."

"Amen. And keep your hand in God's hand . . ." began Mama Harris.

Thank You, Lord, for this incredible blessing. Opening my eyes to a reality I could've never imagined. I never considered this. Isn't it in Ephesians—I think it is, where God will give us more than we could ask for or imagine. That's what You're doing here for me.

Negroes living like—like humans! Not property. Not chattel. A family. Friends. A lovely home. Owning a business. Not being owned. Have I died and this is heaven? If I'm still alive, this is heaven for me. Thank You, God, for allowing me to see this.

". . . sure she is beautiful inside. But more importantly, you got to get yourself right for her. Right, Bob?"

"Oh, yeah. Took a lot of scrubbing and praying and scrubbing some more before I was good enough for this woman."

"I don't know about all that."

"I do. And James, Bobby—there's nothing sadder than a messed-up man wanting a complete woman—and can't have her. Right, Pastor?"

"Wooo, I've counseled my share of men to know that's the sad truth."

"Yes, it is. I think the food is ready. Martha, Eve—let's go get it."

"Let me help, Marie."

"So, what do you think, James?" Bobby asked.

James looked at the four pairs of eyes there and was at a loss for words. "I—I don't know where to start. How do you speak about a reality you struggle to believe is real? It—uh, y'all, uh—it's all nice. Real nice. I mean, I wish, uh . . ." was all he could utter before his emotions took over.

The men surrounded him as Pastor Beard whispered a prayer in James' ear. Minutes passed before the ladies returned with dinner. Platters of fried chicken, mashed potatoes, cabbage, and cornbread—all succulently aromatic—filled the dining room.

This reminds me a little of Penelope Farms. Well, before Rogers came. Some days we ate good—like this. No families, though. They—Mr. Johnson wanted to destroy this feeling. And—

"Are you okay, James?" Eve asked.

"Yeah. Uh, yeah. I'm good. Just so much food."

"You good. I'm good. We all good. Good. Let's eat," chimed William.

"You better not put your grubby little hands anywhere near this food until we pray, boy," declared Mama Harris. "Pastor, if you please, before I have to hurt my second son."

"Unless I get my hands on him first."

"Let us join hands—quick. Heavenly Father—"

"Uh, Pastor Beard. Mrs.—Mr. Harris. Can I bless the food, please?"

The din of the room went to silence.

"I just want to do this—I need to do this. I never had any-thing like this before. Never even considered anything like this. I couldn't because—well, just because my mom and dad died when I was young. This weekend has shown me what I've missed. And the possibilities of my life—what I *could* become. What I could have—someday. I learned about family. Having parents, sister, brothers. While I'll never have that, I now have these feelings."

"You do have that, baby. From now on, you are part of our family, you hear?"

"Amen to that."

"Thank you, Mrs. Harris. All the stories, the laughter, the insight, the joy—it all screams 'family.' I never thought someone you love could irritate you as well."

"He's talking about you, William."

"Be quiet."

"See what I mean. Y'all make me miss my family—my birth parents—but that's a good thing. Because you gave me this feeling, I will keep it in my heart forever. I've learned that the Thanksgiving Day meal is to thank God for all His blessings. But I'm thankful for all of you as well. Let us pray."

"Finally."

"Bobby."

"Sorry, ma."

"I'm glad Deacon Roberts ain't here."

"Bob!"

"I got to say 'amen' to that, Marie. Food lose its taste when Deacon Roberts starts to pray."

"And don't let him start with the God of Abraham, Isaac, and Jacob!"

"Yep, the greens get cold, and the fried chicken get up and walk out the door."

"But he sure can line a hymn!"

"Now, on that, you're right, Bob!"

"James, baby. Go a—"

"A char . . . ar . . . ar . . . ar . . . ge toooooooooooo keeeeeeeeeeep. I . . . I . . . I . . . I . . . I . . . I . . . I have, a God-duh . . ."

"Oh, glory, glory, glory . . ."

"tooooooooooo glorrrrrrr-i-fiiiiiiiii""

"Go ahead and pray, James. Quick. Before I have to hurt my husband."

"Not before I hurt mine first."

James looked around at his new family, smiled, and began as the men hummed, "Our Father which art in heaven. Hallowed be Thy name. Thy kingdom come, Thy will be done on Earth as it is in heaven. Thank You this day for this meal we are about to enjoy. Thank You for the blessings of food, family, and fun. Thank You for our lives that give us breath and the lives we live. Thank You for all You do for us. Amen."

Thank You, God, for giving me the words to say without saying the words I shouldn't say. Help me to keep calm and enjoy this moment. Watch over my mouth so I don't say anything that will let them know I'm a runaway, a fugitive, a criminal. . . .

"We gotta go huntin' the next time you come," William said.

"Remember, James. You got a place here. With me, my wife, and my family, you hear."

"Yes, sir, Mr. Harris, sir. Okay, William."

"Yes, sir, Mr. Harris, sir," Bobby mocked in a whisper while he kneed James under the table.

☘

On the train that evening, the knot in James' stomach slowly unwound as Boston faded in the distance. Going over the weekend in his mind, he recalled the discovery of a world he had never considered.

It was great to see Negroes owning houses! And, and businesses. Actually, living like real people! Having a family. Friends. All out in the open. And they liked me! But—but I wonder, though. They are nice, but I wonder—how nice would they be to a runaway? How nice would they be to me if they knew I was a runaway? Putting their little boy—their big brother—in danger. Huh, I wonder? . . .

"Whatcha' thinkin' about?" Bobby asked as he stared into James' blank stare.

"Your family. They're real nice."

"Yeah, they like you, too. But that's not what you're thinking."

James cracked a smile and lied, "Yeah. You know me too well, I think. I was thinking about Prof. Edwards' test coming up, and . . ."

Stay calm, James. Stay calm.

⚜

. . . C'mon! Get on with it. I got things to do. . . .

". . . Charles Adams!" the payroll clerk at Empire Metal Works called out. Most times he passed the weekly wages to each individual man during work time. Rare Fridays like these, however, it was well after closing, and all were anxious.

"Shit! I suppose to be wit my gal by now," Big Man complained as he and James stood next to each other, waiting for their names to be called.

"I got homework—from school and home. I'm supposed to meet Bobby in less than an hour!"

"What kind of work you do at home?"

"Huh—oh, I teach people to read, and write."

". . . Billy Ray Baringer! . . ."

"Oh, yeah. What 'bout teachin' ol' Big Man here some writin' words, huh? So I can write notes to my womens."

"Uh—okay. That'll be fine. When—"

"... uh, Richard Pine! ..." the paymaster yelled, and Mr. Pine jostled between James and Big Man, and then through the crowd.

"... when is a good time?"

"Any time after work good fo' me. You give me a time."

"Yeah, whenever me and Bobby—"

"Boy, you and that Bobby guy. Y'all sho' spend a lotta time together."

"... Everett Holston! ..."

"Yeah. But we're in school together, in the same classes. It just works out that way."

"Uh, huh. He gits to come by yo' place, but—"

"... Ken Ashley! ..."

"... but you leave ol' Big Man out, huh."

"Nah, it's not like that."

"I tell ya' what. Since both of y'all college folks, ya' both can teach me, huh?"

"Uh—yeah. I guess so. But I'll have to ask him first and—"

"... James Smith! ..."

"... uh—and see what he says. If not, it'll just be you and me. Gotta go."

"Yeah, yeah. I know. Gotta go, gotta—"

"... Harold Winters, Jr.! ..."

"... gotta go. Oh, yeah—that be me. I'll go up there witcha', James. Hey! The name is 'Big Man'!"

♣

James and Bobby's friendship blossomed during the spring thaw. They spent so much time together, people began calling them "Jabob" in school, out of school, and at the library.

"Good night, Mr. Jabob," said Mrs. Fleischbaum, the librarian at NYU. "And it's good to see you in here, Mr. Harris. And on a Saturday, no less."

"Yes, ma'am. And a good day to you, too, ma'am."

On the way across the campus and to the train, they talked about the family, as usual.

"Got a telegram from home. Everybody says 'Hi.' Especially Eve," Bobby said, with his impish grin.

"Tell everybody I say hello when you write back," James replied without breaking stride or looking at Bobby.

"You heard me?"

"Huh, what?"

"I said *Eve especially* says 'Hi.' I think she likes you."

"Oh, yeah. I heard you. I'm just ignoring you, that's all. How old is Eve, anyway?"

"Fourteen."

That put a quiver in James' knees, a knot in his stomach, an ache in his heart, and a lump in his throat, as a memory of Chloe forced its way into his mind.

God, I miss her. Will this pain—the sense of loss—ever go away? Lord Jesus, please make it go away! Calm down, James. Calm down. God, I still miss her!

"How about that latest Douglass article, huh," James said and then cleared his throat.

As they walked, they came upon a crowd pressing around the bulletin board located in Gallatin Square, which piqued their interest. Newspapers and notifications were regularly placed there to be read by the public, but the crowds were never this large. Jabob began a 3-minute, 100-yard plod toward the literary destination. The people in front of them limited their progress, as the surge of people behind them kept them moving forward.

They were now close enough to see that the people who read it did so quietly, but many screamed, and all took off running in a myriad of directions. When they finally got to the bulletin board, the full-page, bold typeset made them both shudder.

They turned their gaze toward each other and then back to the stunning headline:

"CONFEDERATE TROOPS ATTACK FORT SUMTER, SOUTH CAROLINA! CIVIL WAR DECLARED"

ABOUT THE AUTHOR

AJ Sam, born and raised in St. Petersburg, Florida, is a public-school teacher in Volusia County, Florida. A 4-year U.S. Air Force veteran (1975–1980), he graduated from St. Petersburg Jr. College and worked in the Engineering and Computer fields through the '80s into the 90s. In 1997, he accepted a calling from God, returned to college, and earned an Education degree (Special Education) from University of South Florida. This began his 20+ year educational career in the school districts of Pinellas, Hillsborough, and Volusia counties (Florida).

In 2003, he again accepted God's call—this time to the ministry—and was ordained in 2007. A sports fan—Tampa Bay Bucs, Rays & Lightning—he enjoys watching and attending games. He's married and lives in Daytona Beach, Florida. He has a daughter, son-in-law, and granddaughter.

An avid history buff, his writing attests to this fact with his attention to the details of the historical events, facts, and characters he weaves throughout his fiction. As an author of historical fiction, AJ Sam believes in the necessity of studying the past—but not repeating the past—instead learning from the past to ensure a brighter future for humanity.

www.ingramcontent.com/pod-product-compliance
Lightning Source LLC
Chambersburg PA
CBHW021335310726
48971CB00001B/143